THE INEVITABLE MAN

LARRY CUNNINGHAM

A LOVE STORY

Cover Design – Jaycee DeLorenzo
Publishing Coordinator – Sharon Kizziah-Holmes

Paperback-Press
an imprint of A & S Publishing
A & S Holmes, Inc.

ISBN -13: 978-1-945669-98-9

Here in this peaceful place
The din of battle rages.
Comfort, solace, silence
Succumb to the turmoil.
Hopes and dreams once dear
Lie at my feet and coil

***Author

Chapter One

THE SUMMONS

TERRORIST BOMB KILLS 326 IN ROME CRASH

That headline swept across the world three years ago on May 25. The day began innocently enough, a church bell ringing mournfully, soon joined by others in a concert of different tones and urgencies. The ensuing symphony resonated in glorious pealing harmony spreading the news: "Eight o'clock! Eight o'clock!" The metallic melody lasted one minute, ebbing as it began one bell at a time until the final chime echoed across the rustic Italian countryside to be smothered in rising currents of early morning human industry.

Nothing about the morning generated a foreboding presence. Nothing ominous ushered in a sense of impending disaster. The swelling din of local daily activities swept away the calm of night, replaced in turn by the escalating background noises of low-flying commercial jets. Huge airliners overhead played follow-the-leader through the brisk morning air, wheels and flaps down, engine power reduced on final approach to Rome's International airport.

Flight 8109, a glistening silver 747 from Los Angeles, positioned near the front of the traffic procession, lumbered innocently toward a rendezvous with history. 8109 had refueled at London's Heathrow airport during the night before continuing on to Rome with a crew and passengers of three-hundred-and-twenty-six people, mostly American. As the great aircraft descended

1

through one-thousand feet five miles from touchdown and just as the last church bell tolled, a powerful bomb detonated ripping a gaping hole in the right side of the fuselage above the main wing. Local residents long immune to jet engine noise stopped chores and looked up, alarmed by the thumping explosion and crackling echoes as the huge craft disintegrated overhead. 8109's starboard wing folded upward and separated from the fuselage at the wing root. One engine on the detached wing remained in place as the other fell away along with metal pieces of all sizes, adding to the surreal panorama of plummeting parts. The spectacle reminded one witness of fluttering leaves in an autumn wind, but the splintered pieces simply provided a side show to the big event. Nothing distracted horrified onlookers from the mind-numbing spectacle of the doomed airliner. After surrendering the wing, the 747 pitched violently nose down, rolled inverted and plunged straight into an ancient courtyard. All 326 aboard died instantly.

After the accident, investigators speculated that terrorists had placed the bomb on the aircraft at Heathrow. Their report also theorized that the bombers botched the settings on the bomb's altimeter triggering mechanism, probably intending to fix detonation at a much higher altitude over the Mediterranean Sea. The bomb exploded too late and the 747 crashed over land permitting experts to identify the terrorist organization responsible after analyzing and comparing explosive residue of previous bombings.

*****

The bombing, unknown at the time to Washington newspaper columnist, Denny Blakemore, initiated events destined to change his life forever. The fated change waited until late one afternoon nearly two years after the crash. Edith, his stout middle-aged secretary, started everything by materializing at his office door, coat on and prepared to fend off any unwelcome request he might have to delay her departure. Edith held a permanent stool at The Oracle Bar and Grill out by the stadium and never hung around after work hours for any reason.

"I'm finished for the day," she announced. Edith never asked permission to leave. She usually just walked out. "Oh, and Miss-

Mystery-Caller is on line two." She winked. "Wouldn't give her name. You keeping secrets from me, Dennis?" She smiled sarcastically and snorted, a clear indictment of his non-existent love life.

"Blakemore here!" He always answered the phone shouting.

"Are you Denny Blakemore, the newspaper columnist?"

His eyebrows lifted. *Hmmmm! Nice voice. Certainly no girl.* "That's what I said," he growled. "Who wants to know?" His surly charm usually unsettled callers with ambivalent notions about their reason for calling.

"I'd rather not say just yet," she countered.

Here we go. Get rid of her. "Well, Miss whoever, then maybe I'd rather not talk to you just yet. How's that?" He tapped out a cigarette.

"We are wasting time, Mister Blakemore. I have something of vital importance to discuss with you; something devastating to our government. When can we meet?"

Denny's eyebrows raised again. *Okay, she's got me.* "Look, Miss, if I took time off to meet everyone who thought they had something important, I wouldn't get any damned work done. Now, suppose you cut the flak and tell me what you want?"

"I need to meet with you in person. What I have is devastating for our country."

"Really? Wow! What makes you think so?" His eyes rolled. *Wasting time here.*

"I worked for a senator once, Mister Blakemore."

He snorted. "Yeah, well, big deal, in this town, who hasn't." He only pretended indifference. Now she had him. Senators ranked at the top of his preferred target list. "What senator? What did you do for him?" He scattered papers on the desk looking for a lighter.

"I'm not ready to give his name yet. I'm sure you will know who I am if told you, and that might ruin everything. I will tell you, but only after we meet."

He froze, brow wrinkled. *I know her? That's interesting.* He settled in for the duration, leaned back, placed his feet on the desk and lit the cigarette. "Okay, so why is it so important to keep your name secret?"

"My life is in danger."

He closed his eyes and moaned. "Well of course it is. But, what the hell, I'll bite. Can you at least tell me who's trying to kill you?"

"Two parties are involved–two different countries. I cannot go beyond that until we meet."

Two? This is too much, Blakemore. He usually slammed the phone down when things got ridiculous. She really did have a great voice, though. "Sorry, Miss, but I can't take any more of this." He hung up.

She rang right back.

He snatched the phone and yelled, "What?"

"I have never been more serious, Mister Blakemore. I have information that.... No, I have absolute proof of crimes that will destroy the present administration."

"Well golly gee whiz. Isn't that something? The damned government is falling apart and poor little me doesn't have a clue. Look, what makes you think I don't already know the story?"

A long silence followed. He listened as street noises in the telephone background receded and returned. *Ah, she's not alone. No other reason to cover the phone.*

"Are you still there Mister Blakemore?"

"It's your nickel."

She cleared her throat. "I know for a fact that the American government directed the assassination of Abdel Hafez. I can and will provide conclusive proof if you care to listen. Irrefutable proof."

Denny's thoughts raced. *Abdel who? Hafez?* He couldn't quite place the name at first. *Abdel Hafez? Oh, yeah. That guy.* "Abdel Hafez, you say? Well, evidence would be good."

"I know the assassin and I have absolute proof. Absolute, Mister Blakemore. I can and will provide names, times, places–everything."

He nodded while fanning smoke from his eyes. *Oh, this is definitely interesting.* His feet slipped off the desk and slammed onto the floor. *Okay, I'm in. She certainly seems composed for someone in mortal danger, though.*

"Mister Blakemore?"

"Oh, sorry. Yeah, I'm still here. Bear with me a moment, will you?" He grabbed a pen, stubbed out the wasted cigarette and prepared to write. "Okay, Miss, let's say, just for the hell of it, that what you have said so far is true. Why me?"

"Because we trust you and we need help. They are trying to kill us."

We? Us? "Okay, it's time to cut the crap. Who, exactly, wants to kill you? C'mon, either we ditch all the mystery or I'm outta here."

Another pause. The phone background noise receded again and returned before she said, "The American and Libyan governments."

Denny fell back in the chair groaning. *Ahhh, damn! Why did I suck into this?* "Oh, really? Well why, pray tell."

"I won't say over the phone, but I can provide conclusive proof. This is no joke, Mister Blakemore."

"Okay, Miss, maybe we should talk." Of course he had known from the time she mentioned a senator and after he recognized Hafez that they were definitely going to talk. If nothing else, Denny Blakemore had a nose for news. His syndicated column ranged across the free world.

"Thank you," she said. "Thank you so much. I will call soon." The phone clicked off.

Denny shrugged, thought about it for a moment, lit another cigarette and lost himself in the next day's column.

She called the office twice before he arrived the next morning, refusing to give Edith a callback number. Edith's voice crackled over the intercom the moment Denny sat down: "It's the mystery woman again, boss. On two."

He punched the button, rocked back and closed his eyes. "Blakemore here!"

"Can we meet today, Mister Blakemore?"

He smiled. *Oh, that voice.* "Sure. Any time you say. I'll be in the office all day."

"No. I mean.... No, that won't work. Would you consider meeting me at the Lincoln Memorial at eleven this morning?"

He held the phone aside, murmured a curse, then said, "Oh, hell, why not. But first, how will I know you?"

"I'll be on the north side, fifth step from the bottom on the right. How will I know you?"

"Pasty white. Skinny. Short. Balding. My picture is over the column in today's paper."

"I will see you at eleven." She hung up.

Denny arrived a few minutes late, hoping she would already be in place. She wasn't hard to spot–fifth step up bottom right. He hoped that was her–the slender brunette with long velvet hair blowing in the wind. His sour temper vanished. *Wow! Gorgeous, even from here.* The impression held as he neared. *Oh, yeah, and I have definitely seen her before.*

She flashed an uneasy smile as he approached.

Denny whistled to himself. *Yep, I should know her.* He offered a hand and she took it firmly, towering over him while standing on the same step wearing flats. He stood 5' 8".

"Thank you so much for coming Mister Blakemore. "I'm really–"

He broke in impatiently, waving off the requirement for formalities. "My pleasure." He raised his sunglasses, squinted and then said, "I hope you don't think this is a come-on, but I'm pretty sure I should know you."

Her strained smile faded. She nodded. "Yes. We met some years ago. That doesn't matter now."

"Well, maybe not to you, but I–"

She looked pained and cut him off. "Please, Mister Blakemore, the past really isn't important. Maybe someday we can relive old times. Please, not now."

He shrugged and said, "Okay, it's your ball game. So, what now?"

"I have a cab waiting. Will you feel comfortable coming with me? To Arlington, if that's acceptable. The National Cemetery?"

How dangerous can she be? "What the hell. Let's go."

She called someone and said, "On the way." They didn't speak during the ride. She seemed troubled and gazed out the side window, away from him. The cab crossed the Potomac and turned toward the cemetery. The woman radiated an appeal Denny didn't understand but felt intensely. He sneaked glimpses to reaffirm his initial impression of her.

Elegant.

They walked into the cemetery and up a hill through geometrically perfect rows of white stone markers. Denny noticed the guy long before they reached the bench he occupied. He stood as they approached, solemn and tall.

She smiled and reached for his hand, then turned to Denny and announced, "Jim, this is Denny Blakemore. Denny, Jim." Her partner gave Denny's hand a Mid-West firm handshake. He stood inches taller than the woman.

Denny wrote in his notes later, "The archetypal American male as we Americans like to regard ourselves. Tall, athletically lean with neat, short graying hair. Not really handsome. Rugged. Pleasant enough to look at. Face creased with permanent smile wrinkles. About forty-five."

The man's eyes impressed Denny. He had the coldest, hardest, bluest eyes Denny had ever seen; eyes that lost that hard edge when he looked at her. All of Denny's adolescent fantasies about having the woman for himself evaporated. He didn't have the inclination or ability to love a woman the way the tall man's eyes loved her.

Denny said, "Jim? That short for James?"

The man turned to face Denny, eyes cold and hard again. "Yes, but Jim works."

Denny nodded. "Okay. Well, Jim, about the call yesterday. Interesting. What can I do for the two of you?"

Jim gestured to the bench. "Have a seat. This may take some time."

Denny sat and the woman took a seat beside him. He still didn't know her name but figured it would surface if they ended up doing business. Jim stood in front of them for a moment, glancing watchfully both ways, then said, "First, let me thank you for coming. You won't be sorry. We are going to tell you a story that may well change the course of American history." Denny's amused smile caught his eye. "You will soon learn that I do not exaggerate. We desperately need your assistance. However, even if you agree to help, there will be conditions."

"Whoa! Whoa!" Denny said, frowning, waving both hands. "Agree to what?"

Jim waited until a jogger passed before continuing. "The information we have might possibly be...no, it will definitely be dangerous for you. It is far more sensitive to our government than anything you can imagine."

Denny hated theatrical buildups. "Don't be too sure of that, friend. I have a rich imagination and I've heard just about everything. Let's get on with this."

Jim nodded. "All right. Think back if you will, two years ago. Remember the Flight 8109 crash in Rome?"

"Of course. Go on."

"My son, his wife and my grandson were passengers on that airplane." He announced it matter-of-factly, eyes boring into Denny, watching for reaction.

"Sorry to hear about your family."

Jim nodded. "Thanks. Now, do you remember Abdel Hafez? Anything about him?"

"A little. Somewhat hazy there."

"How about the Arab Terrorist Alliance he organized? Anything about that?"

"Yeah. Okay, I'm with you. Go on." Denny could remember the bombing of Flight 8109 vividly and had tracked the Arab alliance Hafez organized after ISIS power faded.

Jim went on, "Okay. What do you remember about Ahmed Hazam?

Denny shook his head. "You have to help me there."

Jim didn't hesitate or smile. "He assassinated Abdel Hafez and escaped. Made world news. Remember that guy?"

"Oh, yeah. I definitely remember that. Still looking for him, I believe."

Jim looked around, covering all directions, then moved close and leaned next to Denny. Through fingers spread over his mouth, he whispered, "I am Ahmed Hazam."

Denny winced. Millions of synapses in his brain snapped shut all at once. The impact of that name and the chaotic day it shared with history smashed into his mind. He protested, "Wait just a damned minute. You're jerking me around, right?"

Jim didn't smile and those cold blue eyes did not waver. "I am sincere. Hazam was my mission identity."

Denny didn't think anyone alive over the age of ten at the time would ever forget. "Oh, come on. This has to be a joke, right?" He looked around for a camera crew.

"No, I'm dead serious," he insisted. "No pun there. Leslie and I have proof if you want to hear the story. Everything you need."

Ah, so it's Leslie. Denny stood and paced in front of the bench, letting the information sink in. *Now what? If this guy's claim is valid, I am standing face-to-face with the most wanted and quite possibly one of the most lethal men on earth.* He stopped and snapped, "Wait!" He whirled to face Jim. "Seriously. You cannot expect me to believe any of this!"

Chapter Two

THE WHISTLE BLOWER

The couple had chosen Blakemore as their contact because most of the reading public knew him. Denny Blakemore, better known as *The Whistle Blower,* was a journalist celebrity known more for his inclination to pry and meddle in the affairs of the mighty than his ability as a writer, though he could write well enough. Twenty years ago, Denny broke into the big time with an acclaimed weekly syndicated newspaper column dubbed, appropriately, *BEYOND THE NEWS*, a reveal column that he still wrote and people still read.

Denny's particular calling as an investigative reporter set him apart from most journalists, that and his uncommon appetite–some called it a mean streak–for blowing the proverbial whistle. His credits include two NYT best-selling books. In *THE SMELL OF TREASON,* he unveiled the truth behind a major political party's Russian money connection. His second book, *THE GOOD OLD BOYS,* won the Pulitzer Prize, uncovering abuse of public funds by Congress. Both books cost powerful men their reputations and livelihood. Denny is not loved in high places, but he is feared. He will blow the whistle.

Denny's considerable clientele consists chiefly of political victims; betrayed subordinates; abandoned wives and mistresses, and a few ambitious behind-the-scene operators. His reputation is such that he no longer needs to look for yarns. Tales gravitate to him naturally, unsolicited, by phone, over the transom and in the mail. Myths, lies and truths have always reached Denny, often from the hands and mouths of complete strangers. Refined women press neatly folded napkins with scribbled phone numbers into his hands at cocktail parties. Most contacts are bitter people with an axe to grind; people who expect him to wreck someone and happily provide the necessary information. Denny usually weeds out and disregards agenda-driven revenge seekers. He has accrued enough legitimate leads to keep him in business for years without having to sink into the shadows of some poor slob's personal life. However, he will use almost any lead to undo a crooked politician; he is passionate about that.

Denny's office is located near most of the action–Washington D.C. Edith Samuels, his receptionist-secretary, is also his most loyal friend and vocal critic. She terrifies him. They almost had a thing once just after she came to work fifteen years ago. No big deal–nothing more than a combination of office familiarity and a weak moment. They drank quite a bit one evening to facilitate the preliminaries and ended up on the floor laughing and impotent. They have been good friends since.

Edith is the only person who can endure Denny's eccentricities, barely, and serves as the perfect counterbalance to his lifestyle. He pursues every waking moment in frenzy while she never hurries–ever. He is obsessed with time: saving time, gaining time, using time. Edith cares only about quitting time. He screams and curses, smokes nonstop, talks on two phones and works on the next column all at the same time. Edith blithely drowns the commotion in the next office with ear buds and music. She provides a constant reminder of just how bizarre his behavior is, not that it does any good. Edith is also the only woman he knows who can stand his misogynist perspective of women in general. She doesn't care what he thinks. He pays well.

As he sparred with Jim at Arlington, though he didn't realize it at the time, Denny was engaged in the pivotal moment of his life, facing the worlds' most sought after man. If the man's claim proved true, he was a ruthless assassin. Denny still wasn't buying it. "No way! Who the hell–"

Jim stopped him. "Everything I have told you is true. I...." He turned and said to her, "Sorry, Leslie." Her smile forgave him. His attention returned to Denny. "We. We want to tell you what happened and why they want to eliminate us."

Denny scowled. *We?* "Is she part of this?" He glanced at her, struggling with the knowledge. *Please, not Aphrodite.* "Her?" He pointed to Leslie

"She is. Yes. Definitely."

Denny held up a restraining hand, stalling for time, organizing his thoughts. "This is all too much and way too fast for me. You'll have to slow down. How did she–"

Jim interrupted again, "Accidentally. She got caught between me and the people trying to kill me. Leslie knows the other half of the story, though–the government side. Look, I know this seems sketchy, but we are not willing to provide more information until we know where you stand. There is no reason to go on unless you want to hear the story. I guess we need your answer to that. Are you interested?"

Denny shrugged and looked away. "Maybe. What's the catch?" *Leslie who? I really should know who she is.*

Jim nodded. "There is a catch. You cannot write the story without our approval, or unless we are killed." His eyes bored in.

Denny's reservations peaked again. The whole thing struck him as preposterous–to hear a story and not be permitted to write it. He responded in typical gruff fashion. "This is a crock! You two are going to tell me a great story and expect me not to write it? Who put you up to this anyway?"

His outburst didn't faze them. They waited patiently–parents waiting out a rebellious child.

Denny paced, reservations forming. "Okay," he said. "What's in it for me, then? What's the catch? Come on, I have work to do. You're losing me here."

Jim didn't falter. "It's quite simple. We tell you the story; you present a tape recorded copy to the President and you become our insurance policy."

Denny froze, looked up at the twosome and said, "Whoa! Now you just hold it right there. As in, *the* President?"

Jim nodded. "Correct. After he listens to the tape, we are confident he will call off the search for us. That simple."

Denny turned away, surveyed the bleached rows of crosses, trying to think. After a moment he turned back and said, "Nothing is that simple in politics, friend, even assuming your story has that much clout. Now, humor me here. What search?"

Leslie interceded. "Mister Blakemore, we sympathize with your impatience, but what we have to tell you is momentous, as I'm sure you must surely recognize by now. As for what search? I can only say, be assured you will know when we tell you the story and you will have every opportunity to check the validity of our claims before entering into any agreement, if we reach an agreement. Today is preliminary."

"And just how, may I ask, do I manage to check all this out? And you?"

She established eye contact with Jim before continuing. He didn't nod or give any perceptible signal, but she obviously sensed his answer. She smiled a we're-in-this-together smile for him, a smile Denny would have killed for, then turned and said, "We will be placing our lives in your hands, Mister Blakemore."

"Oh, for Christ's sake!" he groaned. "Would you two get off the Mister crap? My name is Denny! Hell, we might as well be friends, because I'm pretty damned sure we're going to do business."

She recognized the breakthrough and smiled. "Denny, then. I like Denny."

He imagined what happened from here on would definitely be interesting. "Let's press on. First, why me?"

Jim nodded to Leslie and she said, "Your reputation and ethical standards attracted us, Denny. We have faith in you. But we would like assurance that you will preserve our secret until we are safely away if you decide not to help us."

"My word is good, folks. Everyone knows that. Confidentiality is everything in my business. Okay, you have my word. Now, what happens if I decide to help you?"

She smiled at him, this time just for him. God, he thought, she is sensational. Like no woman ever.

"If you agree to our terms," she said, "we will become co-conspirators. The problem is, in a court of law, if this ever goes to court and it very well could, you could be considered culpable, Denny. Aiding and abetting after-the-fact." She forced a grim smile. "Just so you know, you can get out at any time."

Denny stared, first at one, then the other. A profound moment. They had neatly placed the ball squarely in his court. It seemed, if he picked up the ball and played the game, there was an awfully good chance he would not come away the better for it. By that time he felt confident that they were genuine and their story would be legitimate. He had a penchant for recognizing pivotal opportunities, at least for anything newsworthy, and felt certain that they held the key to something possibly staggering.

"Okay. I want to hear the story. We are now officially in business."

Leslie took a document from her purse and handed it to him. "Not quite. Read that tonight, Denny. Sign both copies if you still want to hear the story. We will call in the morning. You can give your decision then. Now, is there anything else?"

He took his time, folded the paper without reading it, then looked up and said, "You damned right there is! I'm not about to take off on a wild goose chase. Who the hell are you?" He looked directly at Leslie. "And how do I check you out? I mean both of you!" He glared first at one, then the other.

Jim nodded when she looked at him. She turned to Denny and said, "My name is Leslie Reardon."

The name struck a familiar note. *Leslie Reardon? On the tip of my...but not quite.* "I need more than that. You said we met once."

"Yes, briefly at a party. I worked the crowd for Senator Charlie Collins at the time, as one of his legal assistants. He fired me because I uncovered the story we are going to tell you. Is that enough?"

Denny snapped his fingers. *Bingo! That Leslie Reardon. How could I forget? Been a couple of years, though. Seems like we even spoke for a moment. Leslie Reardon. A damned lawyer.* "Okay, Leslie, that will do for a start. I remember you now."

She didn't let it go. "I hope you will be prudent about knowing me. As you will soon learn, our lives are in extreme danger. Some very determined people are pursuing us."

"I am always discreet. Now, how about you?" Denny directed his attention to Jim.

She answered, cautious, like an attorney. "Jim's information is too sensitive right now, but we promise that it will come out with the story, Denny, if you decide to sign the contract."

He recognized an impasse. "Okay, I'll be in the office by nine in the morning. Call me."

They both shook his hand and walked away. Denny sat on the bench staring after them long after they disappeared. *What in the hell am I into?* He tingled all over.

He confirmed her identity after a few calls that evening. His contacts remembered her activities and described her exactly. *Okay, she's legit.*

He didn't have much luck with Ahmed Hazam, or whoever the hell Jim really was. Hazam still held worldwide interest. He was an international mystery according to Denny's Reuters and AP contacts. And, yes, he was still the most wanted man on earth.

He signed the contract well after midnight. A fairly straight-forward document. They agreed to tell him the story and he promised to record it and make copies. He would then hand one copy to the President of the United States, along with their demand for amnesty. He acquired exclusive rights to write a book revealing their story if the President refused to comply with their demands. He also received authority to write a book if they failed to contact him on the first day of January and July each year thereafter, forever.

Ridiculous, Denny thought. I have nothing unless the President blows them off and they decide to publish, or get themselves killed, or if they decide, for whatever reason, not to contact me according to the arrangement. Only then can I publish. Of course, I could simply go ahead and write the book anyway and say they didn't call. Visions of those cold, hard blue eyes acted as a deterrent. *Yeah sure, like I would cheat on him.*

Denny didn't have much to gain, but nothing to lose other than a little time listening to a story. His news instinct said the time would not be wasted.

*****

Leslie picked him up on the street two blocks from his office the next day at noon. They stepped from the cab five minutes later, walked through the Smithsonian, called an Uber ride on the opposite side and found Jim waiting in a little neighborhood park a mile to the north. Denny addressed the ground rules.

"I want everything," he told them. "From Day One in chronological order. We will start at the beginning and end...well, whenever the hell it ends. I want complete freedom to ask questions. I want assurance that you will answer everything without hesitation. I expect absolute cooperation without exception and without deception from both of you. There can be no secrets between us. None."

Leslie protested." Surely you don't expect us to reveal our private lives."

"Oh, but I do. Yes indeed. Absolutely everything."

Jim had frowned all through Denny's little soliloquy, and then intervened. "What are you, a voyeur or something?"

"No, I'm a journalist and a damned good one. Look, you two, if I'm going to be your insurance policy, then I want complete honesty and candor. Forget your hang ups about privacy. Anyway, what the hell difference will it make if you're dead? Why should I miss a chance to profit from this if the opportunity ever comes?" He sat back, arms folded. "Okay, now, the damned ball's in your court."

They both sighed at exactly the same moment and looked at each other, brows wrinkled. He didn't see anything pass between them, no signal, no eye movement, nothing, but something happened again. They could understand each other by communicating on a subliminal level that Denny was unable to detect. She nodded and they stood. She spoke. "Sorry, but I guess we weren't prepared for this, Denny. We will have to think about it and call you back." They walked away holding hands.

She called the next morning and consented to his demands.

Their story took two weeks to tape. Sometimes they both attended the sessions; sometimes they came alone. Denny never saw them again after they finished. How much did their story affect him? After he listened to the completed tapes, Denny took a six-month leave of absence and devoted every moment of his life to the story. Edith and Denny interviewed every person associated with the story and visited every geographical location. They re-lived and checked every aspect of their account.

Denny discovered more about people and events involved in their story than Jim and Leslie would believe possible. He visited hometowns, work places, schools and family graveyards. He talked to their friends and enemies. He listened, taped and wrote. He journeyed back to the beginning and explored their story minute by minute, location and event, all without assurance the story would ever be published. Denny did the unthinkable and became personally involved. Nothing in his life prepared him for what he discovered or how much he learned to care.

He heard from Leslie twice after the taping sessions. She called on the first day of January and July, according to agreement. They exchanged routine pleasantries. He thought she sounded happy. The last time they spoke, she said, "I don't believe we are being followed or spied upon any longer, Denny. I'm sorry about your story, but I think our strategy worked. The President apparently took your tape seriously. I wish we could see you again, but you know how it is. Thanks again for everything."

He wondered at the time, *Was that goodbye? Are they going to let me publish?* The third call should have reached Denny the first day of January.

It didn't.

According to agreement, he began writing the final draft, preparing to publish. The requirement to write their story saddened Denny more than anything in his entire life. The obligation to write signaled the possible death of Jim and Leslie and the end to what had become his most treasured friendship. What Denny Blakemore published generated more national suffering than even he could imagine.

In the beginning, what Jim had done struck Denny as primitive, savage and morally indefensible, and far too extreme for any civilized man. What Jim did moved Denny's opinion against him. In the beginning. He listened, checked the facts and circumstances, then changed his mind, concluding what Jim did was appropriate. Jim did what ordinary American males would like to do under the same circumstances, in their fantasy world.

Denny understood the enormity of the story. If it ever went to print, the impact would almost certainly destroy the executive branch of the American government, and probably alter the course of world history.

Jim was not the typical American citizen, whimpering impotently after being violated by forces of terrorism. He did not shelve his anger. He refused to accept the usual inept bureaucratic government responses Americans have learned to expect. He took action and exacted a dreadful vengeance. He did the unthinkable.

Jim and Leslie left an agonizing dilemma for the rest of us to ponder, balancing our own strengths and weaknesses against theirs; whether we would or wouldn't; whether we could or couldn't; whether we measure up. Their story is not a story about victims to feel sorry for or someone to hate. Their story is about what can, could and will happen. Their story is about the inevitable. The love they shared is part of the story. Leslie became Jim's link to the world and his reason for living; his sanity and purpose; his everything.

This is a love story. We Begin:

Chapter Three

THE BEGINNING

Leslie and Jim remained extremely cautious throughout the taping period, inventing new ways to meet each day. She phoned the first day and said, "Wait on the corner of Seventh and New Streets tomorrow morning at nine." The next morning a cab driver stopped and yelled, "Hey, buddy! Your name Blakemore?"

"That's me."

"Get in!"

The driver dropped on the top level of a parking garage with instructions to start walking down the ramp, adding, "It's already paid for, bud."

Jim intercepted him one level down.

"Sorry about all the sneaky tactics," he said. "Not that we don't trust you, but we need to–"

Denny waved him off. "Don't worry about it." Jim came alone, much to his disappointment. After that, Denny ever knew who would meet him. "Is Leslie okay?"

"Yes. She probably won't join us until later, after the story is well along. You did say you wanted the story in chronological order, right?"

"Yeah, I know. I'm disappointed, that's all. You're a lucky man."

His wry smile dismissed the comment as unimportant. They walked to a rental car and Jim drove around for thirty minutes, constantly checking the rear view mirror. He pulled over and stopped by a vacant lot on a shaded side street near a little park.

"This is the office today, Denny. Make yourself comfortable."

He stretched, reclined the seat and relaxed. "Let's do this."

Denny opened his briefcase, placed a recorder on the seat and said, "It's running. I'm going to tape every word, no matter whether it deals with the story or not."

Jim glanced at the recorder, eyebrow lifted, then said, "So I gather." He waved off the offer of a cigarette but signaled permission.

Denny said, "Let me lead for a while, until you are familiar with the routine."

"I thought you might do something like that, Denny. I know the story. I don't need prompting."

Denny ignored him. "Where were you when it all began?"

Jim nodded. "Oklahoma City. That's where it started for me. On the Twenty-Fifth of May just over two years ago. That's when I got news of the crash, and that's what kicked everything off for me. But first, I think you should know my name is not and never was Ahmed Hazam. My name, for your record at least, is James Colby. That will show up in your research."

"Okay. Let's go back to Oklahoma City. Tell me how you lived and what you were doing."

"Sure. I lived in an old red brick quadraplex in the western outskirts of Bethany, an older western suburb of Oklahoma City. Cheap living, Denny. Two rooms furnished. Really shabby and isolated. A second-rate bachelor pad. Neat and clean, though." He glanced over and smiled. "Orderly habits are a carryover of twenty years in the military. FYI, I retired on twenty from the Corps. Much more about that later."

Denny made notes, but didn't look up. "No doubt. Why were you in Oklahoma?"

Jim rested his head on the seat again. "Right." He sighed deeply. "Divorce. Been divorced a couple of years by then. Bad scene at home. More about that later. Actually, I was broke on that day in May. Broke and essentially homeless. Been on the run from life for two years; separated from everything and everyone. I severed all home ties and left the area. Seemed like the only way at the time. My emotional state was pretty ragged after the divorce. I couldn't stop long enough to plan the next day, let alone a future. I spent precious little time thinking or doing anything positive until the Twenty-Fifth of May in Oklahoma City."

"Why the divorce?"

"Figured you might ask." He shifted in the seat and stared through the window on his side for a few moments. "We were married twenty-five years before it fell apart." He looked at Denny, snorted and smiled grimly. "I'll give you my version. I expect hers would be different. Leah. Leah Kelly. All the way from high school. She loved the military life: bridge, club activities, compatible friends, travel and golf. Leah made a great officer's wife. After my retirement and against her wishes, we moved back to my hometown in Missouri and started cattle ranching. I bought several small farms adjacent to my father's farms during those twenty years in the Corps. Leah was unhappy on the farms. Hated the isolation. Things began to collapse between us." He sighed. "Our relationship went from borderline to rotten shortly after she got mixed up with religion."

He rubbed his face savagely at this point and groaned. "God, what a horror story that is. She threw in with a bunch of Jehovah's Witnesses. Gone all the time proselytizing, Bible study, building churches. You name it. She became someone I didn't know and didn't enjoy. She hated that I had once been a Marine. Eventually, she wouldn't let me touch her. I gutted it out for three years and got out. In reality, we were both completely different human beings and no longer well-suited. No love. No fun. No happy. I filed for divorce the week Jimmy graduated from high school." He frowned. "She asked for everything, the house, the farms, and I didn't fight it. Signed over most of my retirement. I lost everything and didn't care. I was free.

"I toyed with the idea of borrowing money to start another cattle operation. The banker, an old college classmate and pretty good friend, helped decide against that. I'll never forget the conversation. 'Cattle prices are going down.' he told me. 'I'd sure like to make the loan, Jim, but you are fresh out of collateral. Sorry, but I have to advise against it.'

He sat up. "You talk about confusion. My entire life shot to hell. I got up and walked out. Stopped on sidewalk, bent over, holding my knees, sick to my stomach and disoriented. I must have looked crazy, bent over there in the blazing sun."

He paused, breathing heavily as bitter memories surfaced. "Couldn't even remember where I parked my damned truck.

Anyway, I hung around the area a while after that. I don't know what my ex passed around, but no one would have anything to do with me. When I went to the house to get my things, she wouldn't let me in. Called the damned sheriff. I lost my head when he arrived and told him to mind his own business. Known the guy all my life. He threw down on me and called for assistance." His brow wrinkled. "Jailed my ass. Kept me locked up for two days. Said I was dangerous. Never been in jail before, Denny. When I got out, I left the area.

"The idea of starting over appealed to me at first, but that notion faded as I drifted away from home. My new lifestyle included too much whiskey, that's for damned sure. The worst part, though, was the alarm." He twisted in the seat and looked at Denny. "Let me tell you about the alarm. An inner alarm. Every time the danged thing went off, I moved on—someplace—any place. I expected the next town would settle me down. Didn't happen. The alarm would ring and I would keep right on moving on. Two years passed that way, Denny. Wasted years." He looked relieved after the confession. "Those years blurred into one confused, obscure stopping place on the road to nowhere."

"How did you get along financially?"

"Sold cars when I needed cash. Selling fit my nomadic lifestyle. I was a transient—most car salesmen are—but I could sell. Selling cars provided enough money and the freedom to leave again when the alarm went off. Do you know what the secret of selling is, Denny?"

"No idea."

"If I could, would you. Seriously, that's it. When a buyer objects or balks, just say, 'If I could get him to meet you in the middle, would you?' Or, 'If I could get him to extend the loan, would you? Almost always works. Keeps the sale going."

He stared at the steering wheel for a long time, lost in thought. "What do you think, Denny, is that enough background? I really want to move on."

"Okay. Let's get back to the afternoon of May Twenty Fifth—at the apartment."

"Yeah." He deliberated a moment, and then sighed deeply. "All right. Let's do this. I was sitting in the apartment in the dark after running for an hour. Running, not jogging. I didn't have enough sense to take it easy. That's the exact moment it started. "I heard a car door slam and approaching footsteps. I got up after a violent knock and threw the door open. This overweight sales buddy of mine was poised to knock again. I said, 'Jesus, Doc! You in a damned hurry or something?'

"Doc Holliday shifted uncomfortably and looked nervous. 'You're out late, Doc. What's going on?' My initial irritation receded rapidly as the look on his face revealed that something was definitely wrong.

"Doc just stood there, scratching the back of his neck. I figured he must have been thrown out by his old lady. Wouldn't have been the first time. He finally said, 'I got some real bad news, man. You better sit down.'

"Doc pushed by me. 'I mean it. Sit, dammit!' He motioned toward a chair. It's really strange to think back on it now, Denny. Do you know how I responded?"

Denny shook his head and motioned for Jim to go on.

"I got mad. Isn't that odd? I must have sensed something. 'What in the hell is going on, Doc? I've never seen you act like this. Whatever it is, it can't be that bad.'

"I sure sounded confident, but the perception of doom was already spreading. Doc couldn't seem to find words and that bothered me. Finally, he said, 'Yeah, man, it is that bad. Your ex just called the agency. Look, I hate to be the one to tell you this, but....' He mouthed words, but made no sound.

"The news that my ex had called shook me up. Doc looked miserable, trying to form words. He finally looked up and said, 'There just isn't a good way to say this.'

"My patience ended. 'Just say it, dumbass! For Christ's sake, out with it!'

"He turned away, I suppose to collect his thoughts, then took a deep breath and faced me. He held both palms up to fend off my anger. 'Okay.' He cleared his throat. 'Your son's been killed, man.' His mouth was quivering, so I knew it was true. 'I'm really sorry, man.'

"Nothing happened, Denny. I didn't feel pain, or grief, or anything. Nothing. I heard what he said and understood the words. I saw the sad look on his face, and yet nothing happened. I don't know what I expected, certainly nothing like...well, nothing. I searched his face for clues, for some evidence of credibility, then collapsed into the seat Doc had suggested earlier. I kept watching him, hoping for something–a reprieve. Then the shivering. Emotional stress always makes me shiver. Look at me. I'm trembling now. I need to take a break, Denny. You mind?" He opened the door and stepped out.

"Go ahead. I could use a smoke."

"There's a john in the park." He steered my attention to the little community park down the street. "I'll be back directly."

Denny began sorting through notes to spare Jim further embarrassment. He flipped the recorder off, lit a cigarette, got out and leaned against the car. Jim returned ten minutes later and reclined again. Denny reminded him where they stopped.

"Right. Doc took it hard. Poor devil looked guilty, like it was his fault. I said, 'Okay, Doc, tell me what happened.'

"He seemed relieved and heaved a sigh. 'It happened in Rome this morning. Your ex called couple of hours after you left work. Said some Arab terrorist outfit bombed the airplane just before it landed. There were no survivors.' He shook his head sadly. 'Three-hundred-and-twenty-six people, man. Can you believe that?'

"I stared at the floor, chilling violently. I needed to vomit. I lurched to my feet and stumbled to the bathroom. Several minutes later, still perspiring and weak, I returned to the living room and took a seat opposite Doc, 'I'm okay. Tell me about his family. Were they with him?' I remember closing my eyes, waiting for the inevitable axe to fall. Like sitting in a road waiting to be run over by a truck'

'Yeah, they were.'

"Doc turned to leave. I know he wanted to help, but at the same time desperately needed to get away. I placed a hand on his shoulder. An onlooker would have thought our roles were reversed and I was the one offering comfort. 'I'm sorry you got tagged with this business, Doc. I know how tough it is. I did it a few too many times in the Corps. I'd like to be alone now, if you don't mind.'

"He gave me one of those woeful undertaker smiles, patted me on the back and got the hell out. I turned out the lights and stood at the door for a long time, staring into the night. That's when the tears came, Denny, ran down my face in torrents. The full impact of what happened came in stages, each a step higher up the scale of pain than the previous. My throat and chest hurt. I dropped to the floor on my hands and knees and rocked back and forth trying to hold back the pitiful sounds of an amateur crying. I had forgotten how to cry. Crying hurts worse if you don't practice occasionally, you know that?

"Anyway, much later, after the initial onslaught wore off into sadness, I balled up on the floor and lay there all night staring into the darkness. After calling the airline the next morning to confirm everything, I packed and drove to the funeral services in my hometown. My ex still lives there. She remarried." He laughed and shook his head. "Married the damned sheriff. I suppose that's why he was so quick to park my ass in the slammer. The graveside services were simple and short. No caskets to bury. Nothing but a granite stone to mark the passage of three innocent people.

"From newspaper photos, I could tell the aircraft had burned completely. The fire made individual passenger identification impossible. My son and his family, everyone on the airplane had to be identified from a passenger manifest the airline had to reconstruct manually. Some computer problem. The results didn't change anything. My son was still dead.

"I lingered beside the grave long after everyone left, sitting by the marker bearing his name, sifting fresh dirt through my fingers. My life changed during those moments, Denny." He sat up straight and looked at Denny with a puzzled expression. "Did you ever reach a definitive fork in the road of your life, Denny?"

"Probably, but I can't think of anything."

"Did you ever have the opportunity to make a choice that you knew, with absolute certainty, would be the major turning point in your life?"

"Does anyone ever know that until later in life?"

He nodded. "I did, and I knew it. I made that choice, Denny. I knew exactly where each fork on that road led, and they were diametrically opposed. I knew the road of least resistance probably meant a life of bitterness and regret for me, but it was also the practical road leading to accepting and getting on with life. I knew the other fork led into the unknown and probably toward an unattainable goal. I had the opportunity to choose between living with a danger and probably an early death, or dying from old age in a rocking chair. I expect you can guess what choice I made."

"I can guess."

"I forfeited my life, Denny. Jim Colby vanished that day. I didn't pray to or seek solace from a god. I sat there beside my son's marker and cursed. Cursed and cried and then deliberately chose the fork in the road that was a clear path to danger and death. My death."

He relaxed, body tension melting as he slumped back in the seat. Denny noticed his eyes and cheeks had recessed perceptibly during the past ten minutes. He looked tired and older. Denny recognized that the session was finished and shut the recorder off. "You okay, Jim?"

"Yeah, but I think Leslie should probably jump in at this point."

"When do I see her?"

He grinned sheepishly and glanced at the clock on the dash. I never saw him wear a watch or ring. "About as soon as we get to your office."

"I see. So, I guess the two of you pretty much have things all planned?"

Jim detected his discomfort and said, "This is not fiction, Denny. What we have to say doesn't require any direction from you. We don't have to speculate about what happens next. Anyway, I'm pretty strung out and need to burn it out of my system. I'm going to find a place and jog until I drop. I promise tomorrow will be a better day, longer anyway. I'll drive you back to the office. Leslie will join you there."

Jim surprised Denny by coming up to the office. Denny complimented him on the session and offered a cup of coffee. Jim refused, looked around a moment, shook hands and departed.

Chapter Four

LESLIE

Denny already knew that Leslie Reardon had been popular in Washington during her stay with Senator Collins. She had the reputation of being a brilliant attorney and a much sought-after guest in the capitol social whirl. Each informant told him that she was extraordinarily beautiful. Most truly beautiful women defy accurate description and Leslie fit that picture. She stands nearly six feet tall, not including heels, and measures probably 38-24-38. She looks to be about thirty. Leslie is forty-two. During her stay with the senator some lurid tales circulated involving her relationship with him and other powerful Washington men. None of the stories are true.

She stepped into Denny's office shortly after Jim departed, smiled warmly and he fell in love all over again. That's the way Leslie affected him. No other woman ever moved Denny the way she did–not ever.

Leslie came directly across the room and offered her hand, confident, businesslike and in control. He stammered, "Have a seat"

"Good afternoon, Denny. Nice to see you again. How did the meeting with Jim go this morning?"

"I think we got off to a respectable start."

The arc of her eyebrow warned that "respectable" wasn't good enough. He quickly added, "Actually, we are off to a great start."

She smiled again, a smile reflecting pride. A woman like Leslie never once flashed such pleasure over Denny's accomplishments. She might just as well have said, "Well, of course he did, Silly. I knew he would."

Then, much to his surprise, she suggested they do the taping in his office.

"Aren't you concerned about…well, you know…that someone might…?"

"I will be more cautious in the future, Denny. Shall we?" She motioned to the chair by his desk.

"Oh, sure. Have a seat." After she sat he ventured, "I suppose you spoke to Jim before coming up?" She may have blushed. He wasn't sure.

"Yes, for a few moments." Her chin rose slightly, daring him to press the issue.

"Then I presume you must know the drill with the recorder?"

"I am prepared, if that's what you mean, Denny."

Just another way of letting him know they planned to run the show. He stuffed the outline he had written into a drawer and turned the recorder on. "If it's all the same to you, I would like to start on the Twenty-Fifth of May, three years ago. That's where I started with Jim."

She looked surprised. "Oh? I thought we would begin at a somewhat later date." She frowned. "You want me to go all the way back? No personal history first?"

He could tell the date threw her off. "I will ask for information about your personal life later. For now, if you can remember, I would like to know how the Twenty-Fifth of May went for you. What do you remember?"

Her eyes glazed. "Oh, I will never forget the day of the Rome crash. My life changed that day." She looked unhappy, but sighed and said, "First, I had to take a cab to work. Car in the shop." She paused, eyebrows raised, half expecting him to intercede. "Is that too detailed, Denny?"

"No. Remember, I can always omit. Anyway, this will help loosen you up."

"I remember staring through the water-soaked cab windows on the way to work, mentally conditioning myself to the gloom, the prospect of a huge repair bill, and another dreary day at the office. It wasn't an ordinary day on the Potomac for me. I was unhappy, having recently fallen out of love with the Washington scene. I expect that had quite a bit to do with my mood. Everything was working against me: car trouble; the cab ride; rain; wet hair; the umbrella didn't work. That's how the day started.

"I cringed entering the Senate office building, despising the requirement to smile and nod dutifully to each of the artificially cheerful secretaries as they tracked my way through. 'Good morning, Miss Reardon. Good morning Miss Reardon.' "I sound like a bitch, don't I? Really, I'm not that touchy, but their conduct always reminded me of a little nationwide breakfast establishment where everyone yells, 'Good Morning!' when you enter."

Denny asked for a description of her office. He wanted to be able to see where she worked, starting with the door.

"Let's see. The door had an opaque window, one of those shower door things with bold black six inch lettering proclaiming my position: LEGAL ASSISTANT. Sounds important but I was not the only legal assistant subject to the whimsy of Charlie Collins, senior senator from Colorado. I was his only female attorney, though. I am certain my status as female had everything to do with having a private office. Charlie was nothing if not a male chauvinist. Was is past tense and wrong. Is. He still is. He had ulterior motives right from the start but I was too preoccupied with the opportunity to work for him, that and the Washington scene, to notice. More about that later.

"Once inside, I checked the IN-basket. Empty. My only work that day, and a recent string of days, were copies of *THE WASHINGTON POST* and *NEW YORK TIMES*. Actually, my problems were much worse than that. Senator Collins had not found favor with me for quite some time. Both papers headlined the Rome crash and international terrorism. For some reason the news held me captive. I cried. Yes. I cried like someone close to me had been involved. Odd, don't you think, particularly with how things turned out with Jim?

"The door opened, as it did every day about that time, and my savior walked in. Portia. A happy, full-figured little black woman. My best friend at the office. I think she befriended me to neutralize the collective disdain of the other women office workers. I believe the staff looked upon me as Senator Collins' pampered hussy. Portia was one of the few pleasant constants in my life. She moved a chair into position beside my desk and settled in for what had become our customary morning chat. She lowered her ample body carefully, groaning and puffing, then said, 'Well, what do you think will happen now, after the airliner thing?'

"I put all pretense of work aside and gave her my full attention. 'Well, knowing our revered president as we do, I feel safe guessing President Denning will do something that ends up making loud popping noises, don't you? Seems to be his nature.'

"Portia chuckled. 'Yes Ma'am. Wesley is sure going to do something about this Hafez guy, either that or risk the wrath of all them xenophobic redneck constituents he caters to.'

"Portia's façade of earthiness camouflaged an excellent education from Stanford and a penetrating intelligence. She was a fraud, considerably ahead of her contemporaries in ability and knowledge. I knew she used me to snoop on the Washington social scene. She liked gossip. I enjoyed her anyway. She said, 'Can't you just see Wesley pacing in front of a captive audience in the White House war room?' Portia had splendid teeth and a contagious smile. 'Yes, Ma'am. Them ol' boys will be busy noddin' agreement and keeping they mouths shut.'"

Denny interrupted. "Tell me, what do you think about President Denning, Leslie?"

Leslie brightened, welcoming the challenge. "Wesley Denning? Oh, I believe all the bad things anyone ever said about him. He a loose cannon. That backwoods façade he cultivates may fool some, but he is smart enough, if way too arrogant. And the lies. Why? Almost nobody believes anything he says. Wesley came along at the right time, though, after a long series of leaders selected and programmed by corporate America. America was primed for Wesley's brand of Old West arrogance and toughness. His Montana background and disregard for moderation helped him gain instant popularity with the working man. His base loves him. Behind the scenes, I believe Wesley is a ruthless, cold-blooded scheming politician. He loaded every cabinet position with sycophants. Almost no one has the guts to oppose him. Wesley had more power than any man in Washington long before he decided to have it all. He loves power. I'm sure none of that is news to you."

"No, but I like hearing it from you, Leslie. Now, tell me what you really think."

"I had the opportunity to be around Denning on occasion and believe all you need to know about him is vested in those shiny cowboy boots he wears, even at funerals. I think Wesley Denning is exactly the man he presents to the public. If he says he is going to do something, then, as he would say, You can bet, by God, he will. He is an arrogant, overbearing bastard. I despise everything about him."

Denny laughed. "I think I knew that was coming. Okay, let's finish with Senator Collins."

"Right. Charlie Collins. In the end, and it took much too long to sink in and I am embarrassed to admit it, I realized that Charlie hired me away from the ACLU for reasons other than my legal talent. Quite simply, he killed four birds with one stone by placing me on his staff. He gained a lawyer, a woman, a bleeding-heart liberal to match his own political views, and a woman attractive enough to fill in socially for his homely wife. He did not want me as an attorney. That reality still hurts. That assessment of his intentions didn't surface until late. I didn't want to think poorly of Charlie, or myself for being duped, but I finally came faced the fact that he was not the man I wanted him to be.

"In the beginning I had some nice assignments and plenty of heady social contacts with dignitaries and celebrities. But Charlie...." She rolled he eyes and groaned. "Charlie spoiled everything by making sexual overtures. At first I managed to steer our relationship around some weakly veiled proposals and innuendoes, but his overactive adolescent libido overcame common sense. He, literally, and I am serious, backed me into a corner." She shook her head sadly. "Charlie forced me to do the politically unthinkable. I spurned him, and harshly. That certainly changed everything. My value to the good senator evaporated and I found myself with nothing to do but read the morning papers. He never gave me another decent assignment. In retrospect, I know he led me on with just enough interesting work to keep me on board. I occasionally accompanied him to social events, certainly not in the way prevailing gossip of the time would lead you to believe. I didn't complain much early on about the too-easy work load, but when I began asking for more challenging work, nothing changed. I hope you don't think me vain, but I knew by then the senator enjoyed the notoriety he gained by being seen with me in public. Portia clued me in on that. Charlie loved gossip associating him with an attractive woman. Any attractive woman would have done.

On the Twenty-Fifth of May, I planned to give Charlie one last chance. Either use me as an attorney or lose me. I was going to give him a couple of weeks and then resign. I felt better with that settled. Washington once held great promise and I admit enjoying the atmosphere, just not enough to waste my professional life. I needed work that led to realizing my life goals."

Denny stopped her with a hand motion and said, "Wait. I need that. What life goals?"

"Really, only one. I wanted to be a federal judge, like my father." She studied Denny's face for signs of cynicism. Finding none, she continued. "This may seem somewhat calculating to you, and I admit it. The truth is, I came to Washington because I needed a powerful sponsor. I had a pretty good idea by then that life in public is all about who you know. I remember thinking that the Washington scene would provide opportunities I could only dream of in Denver. By the end of May, the dream was over. Charlie was never going to forget or forgive and I would never change my principles for the likes of him."

She threw up her hands. "That's it. As you have probably surmised, I did not become a federal judge."

"Good stuff, Leslie."

"I want to stop now, Denny. You know why I came to Washington. What Jim has to say absolutely must come next. I probably won't see you for a few days, depending on how you two fare. This much I will say, Tomorrow will be a big day for you." They shook hands and she departed.

Chapter Five

THE AFTERMATH

Jim and Denny met in a different place each day. Sometimes, to Denny's delight, they met Leslie for lunch. Leslie and Jim planned everything. Denny just came along for the story. Jim had a great sense of humor and laughed easily. Denny believed he was genuinely happy. The ready smile only faded when he recalled some particularly grim event. Denny thought it would be easy to label him nonchalant if he didn't know better. He believed Jim would make a great buddy and began treating him like a good friend.

Denny learned to admire the rare affection Leslie shared with Jim. They weren't silly, never touching or leaning on each other like lovesick adolescents, but their feelings were transparent. Their eyes and body language conveyed clear messages.

Jim often poked fun at himself, describing foolish, embarrassing things in his past. It didn't take long for Denny to understand what Leslie saw in him. Jim impressed Denny as a decent guy; easy to be with; usually witty and interesting; always attuned to everything around him. He was part of his surroundings, never an outlier.

"Where did we stop yesterday, Denny?"

"Right after the funeral."

Jim's cheerfulness faded. "Right. The funeral." He sighed, scooted down in the seat, closed his eyes and began. "The ceremony left me in a depression much worse than the divorce. No one hung around after the ceremony. I remained for hours, sitting by Jimmy's marker. Darkness settled long before I left." To make a point, he looked over at Denny. "That's when I came to that fork in the road I told you about yesterday. I hung around the old hometown for a couple of days, shut up in a small motel, grieving and depressed when I was sober, grieving and depressed when I was drunk. I suppose, looking back, leaving the area would have translated to something like desertion–like willingly accepting my son's death. I couldn't leave."

Denny waved for a stop. "Tell me about the drinking. Drinking seems out of character. Am I wrong?"

He laughed. "No, you're right. Never much of a drinker." He looked pensive. "The drinking always made things worse the next morning." He chuckled. "Like that's something new. But, no, I never was much into alcohol, if that's what you mean. Anyway, on the morning of the third day after the funeral, I woke up on the floor needing to get to the bathroom. I couldn't stand up or walk. Seriously. I had to crawl like a damned back alley drunk. Diarrhea. Oh, man, messy business. Pathetic. I think that may have been the low point. I lay there on that cold floor nursing a splitting headache and despising myself. The room reeked of crap, vomit and alcohol, and I couldn't stand up without being sick. Much later, it seemed like hours, I pulled myself off the bathroom floor, cleaned up and poured the whiskey down the drain. That ended the drinking. Never took another drink after that. Well, maybe a glass or two of wine with Les.

"Anyway, I forced myself through some half-hearted calisthenics and jogged out into the countryside about as far as my legs would take me." He smiled and told on himself again. "Brilliant idea, huh? Get up off my deathbed to go jogging. Anyway, the results under those circumstances were predictable: cold sweats, nausea, sprawled in a ditch puking my guts out. I eventually got up and headed back to the motel. Didn't make it far before collapsing again." Jim didn't say anything for at least a minute, just stared, jaw muscles working.

Denny almost turned the recorder off. Jim shook his head slowly, obviously still lost in thought, and then looked up at Denny, smiled feebly and said, "I just laid there, sick to death, feeling sorry for myself. I hadn't thought about the decision I made at the grave for a couple of days, but that was all I could think about then. I didn't have the strength to get up and go on, just laid there, seemed like for hours, until well after dark, chewing grass and thinking. I thought about the fork in the road at the cemetery but really hadn't chosen which road to take. I took the first step down the road lying in that ditch.

"Later, after staggering back to the motel, the depression was gone. Like magic, Denny. My entire outlook changed. I didn't sit around anymore wishing for a damned drink. Sadness and grieving began taking second place. I was utterly fixated on a purpose. Sleep came without the aid of alcohol that night.

"I stuck around for a couple of days, reading and listening to news about the Rome disaster and talking on the phone to State Department representatives. Those conversations confirmed the newspaper reports that a known team of terrorists were traced into England shortly before the crash, and after the crash they were filmed heading for Libya. American Intelligence agencies spotted the attack orders electronically, leading to a camp in the desert in central Libya.

"I expect you remember, Denny, President Denning launched war planes from the Sixth Fleet to bomb Libyan military targets, including that isolated camp identified as the origin of the message traffic. The world was appalled as Libya had not actively supported terrorism in years. America attacked on the day of my son's funeral. I don't believe military retaliatory strikes have ever accomplished much, except gain sympathy for terrorists."

"That surprises me, Jim. I figured you to favor military retaliation."

"I think retaliatory air strikes against Libya were a waste of gunpowder. President Denning's all too predictable reaction proved nothing. We bombed Libya for political reasons, a transparent attempt by a weak politician to placate his base. American intelligence reported that a terrorist group led by Abdel Hafez was responsible for the Rome bombing. Actually, he took credit before the world knew who he was. Hafez disappeared and waited for us to forget, and he damned sure had historical precedent on his side. We always seem to forget.

"The Hafez bunch was a spin-off from ISIS, we knew that much by then. They were not connected to any particular Arab country, so America really couldn't do much. Hafez patterned himself after bin Laden, as an independent renegade, a loner. He deliberately left an electronic trail to taunt us, leading to that empty camp in the desert. Libya, probably with good reason, denied any knowledge. Hafez wasn't exactly a new name as it turned out. At one time he served as one of Muammar Khadafy's trusted lieutenants. Hafez and Khadafy came from the same Libyan Berber tribe. Probably distant cousins. No one at our State department seemed to know exactly when he dropped out of the Libyan government. Hafez resurfaced as the leader of a terrorist group after the Rome bombing, becoming an instant champion throughout Islam.

"I got busy reading at the local university library, devoting every waking moment to the study of terrorism. More specifically, my interests focused on Libya–Abdel Hafez in particular. I traced his trail back years, starting at age twenty with PAN AM 103. Surprised, Denny? That's right. Abdel Hafez helped orchestrate the 103 bombing over Lockerbie, not those two unknown lackeys Khadafy finally delivered to a Scottish court. I didn't know where my interest in terrorist activities would lead at the time of my son's death, but I remember the exact moment my curiosity changed to hatred. That happened one evening as I searched for news on television, watching a reporter interview two Libyan diplomats, Assad Jalloud and Omar Jimmoudi. The reporter asked if they belonged with the Libyan mission to the United Nations.

'Yes, we are proud to be Libyan.'

'Would you care to comment on the UN air strikes against your country, Mr...I'm sorry, I don't know your name.'

'I am Assad Jalloud,' he said. 'Infidels do not understand the power of Allah.' He turned to a gathering crowd and shouted, 'Allah will avenge Believers! America and her western toads will pay for atrocities against my country!'

"The reporter pressed on. 'Excuse me, Mr. Jalloud, but I believe the retaliatory strikes against your country were sanctioned by the United Nations.'

"The other Libyan joined, 'Allah will raise his sword against The Great Satan!'

'Excuse me, sir,' the reporter said. 'Who are you?'

'I am Omar Jimmoudi. America is The Great Satan. America will pay for the death of our women and children. One thousand infidels will die for each Muslim life!'

"Police hustled the Libyans away for their own safety and the interview ended. I didn't realize it at the time, Denny, but that's the exact moment I began planning. That television interview opened the floodgates for me. Nothing remained but hatred and anger. I didn't care if I lived or died. I left home with a pretty clear plan about what to do next. The decisions I made that day were as calculated as any I ever made. Inhumanly cold, I know, but I no longer believed the American political system would do anything, or couldn't. I could, and would.

"I called Doc Holliday at the auto agency in Oklahoma City and told him I wouldn't be back. 'Hold what money I have coming, Doc. Let my apartment go and store my gear. I'll come back sometime and make it up to you.'

"I wanted a good nine millimeter pistol, one I could buy without a permit. Believe me, that took very little time and effort. You wouldn't believe how easy it is. I found the pistol at a gun show in Joplin Missouri. Not inside the show, mind you. A crippled old man stopped me outside and showed me the gun. I bought it, no questions asked. The gun came equipped with four boxes of hollow point shells, but I needed a silencer. You probably can't get a silencer at gun shows. Locating the silencer proved to be more difficult than buying a gun unlawfully. Anyone can get a gun in America, Denny. Anyone. Silencing devices are tricky. Any overt attempt to locate a silencer could draw attention from authorities. I simply used Google and found some fundamental religious right wing survivalist groups located in the Missouri Ozarks. The FBI had long since shut down the most radical organizations and arrested the leaders, but some camps were still open.

"I found and spoke to members of three survivalist organizations. Some surly men at the first two camps ran me off. Survivalists are generally hostile to strangers. Then, while talking with the pretty if not too intelligent wife of a jailed member of a Neo Nazi group called The New Order, she mentioned a couple of guys who might make parts for guns. She said, 'I don't know much about their business, though. You'll just have to ask them.'

"I found the men in a rundown backwoods camp that, according to some unhappy neighbors, specialized in training civilians for combat. The neighbors all complained about constant gunfire and explosions. The entire camp membership looked like a collection of unwashed social rejects, probably living off welfare. The number of dirty, tattered, shoeless children playing at home during what should have been a normal school day puzzled me.

"Two men, both bearded and wearing desert camouflage military uniforms, came shuffling out to meet me. They were more than a little suspicious to say the least. I figured they would run me off and I would have to try some other tack. They refused to talk at first, but the smaller and most vocal of the two finally spit a stream of tobacco and said, 'Lookee here, mister, why don't ye jist pack yer ass rat on back where ye come from. We ain't gonna do nuthin' fer ye. Just pack rat on outta here.' Jim laughed, realizing how much he sounded like a hick.

"You do a great redneck imitation, Jim, or is that really you?"

"Yeah, I suppose the dialect is part of me. Southern Missouri you know. I was part of it for years. Anyway, I tried to gain their confidence by showing a copy of the newspaper article about the Rome crash. 'Did either of you by any chance get to read that?'

"The smaller man took the paper and pretended to read. Tobacco juice had stained a permanent brown streak down the middle of his beard. He spit and said, 'So what?'

"I told him that my boy and his family died on that airplane. I moved closer and pointed out my son's name and the article about the funeral. I flashed my military retirement ID card and Oklahoma driver's license. The little one spit out his cud and reloaded while the other sharpened a stick with a Bowie knife the size of a machete. They were in no hurry. Just getting ready to do business, Denny. I sold cars and know the signs of a deal in progress.

'Look, fellows, I could really use some help,' I said, begging shamelessly.

"The larger, up to then silent man, spoke for the first time, 'Look, friend, we are sure enough sorry about your son, but that don't concern us none out here.'

"I sensed the larger man to be the leader. 'I want you to make a part for me. Wait here for a second. I walked to the truck, got the pistol and handed it to the small man and five-hundred dollar to the big fellow. 'I need a silencer,' I said, cringing at what I expected to happen next. "The little guy spit and pawed at the ground. Neither man would look me in the eye. The big guy said, 'Well, friend, I guess you got yerself a little problem. What made you think you could get one here?'

"He tried to hand the money back. I stepped away. The little guy almost swallowed his tobacco, but recovered and choked out, 'Ye must be outta yer friggin mind!' He had a high pitched, whiny voice. 'A silencer?'

"I stepped farther away so they couldn't hand the gun or the money back. 'Don't misunderstand me. I don't know if you men do this type of work, but from what I hear you could probably find someone who does. Tell you what. I'll come back here in two days. If there is no silencer…. Well, I'd appreciate getting that gun back, and the money. But, if there is a silencer, then there will be another five hundred dollars in it for you. What do you say?'

"Tobacco juice streamed from both men. They shuffled and looked at each other. The big guy spoke first, 'Hell, man, they ain't no damned silencer worth that much.'

"I had them. 'It is to me, friend. It damned sure is to me. What do you think?'

"The big man then said, 'Anyways, this here gun ain't no good for a silencer. Damned automatic. Might be you ought to be thinkin' about a revolver.'

"Of course he was right. 'Isn't my pistol more valuable than a revolver?'

"He balanced the gun gingerly and said, 'Reckon so.' He studied the gun for a few moments, then said, 'Might trade you.'

"I breathed a sigh of relief. 'Okay,' I said. 'Something like a 357?'

"He smiled and patted the holster on his hip, then said, 'Right here. I'll trade you this piece right here even up. Still five-hunnert for the silencer, though. Won't take no less.'

"I countered, 'No way. You can buy two 357's with that pistol of mine.' He pawed the ground, spit and looked off into the distance.

"I know the rules, Denny. The first guy who talks after a closing pitch, loses. I decided to lose. 'All right, my gun now and five-hundred more when I get the silencer.' He nodded and handed the money back, then said, 'Same time here in two days, friend. Two days.'

"I breathed a sigh of relief and headed to the truck as fast as I could, returning to the camp two days later with little hope. I figured the men and my gun would probably be long gone. My suspicions were soon confirmed. Not a man in camp. The place looked deserted, just a bunch of kids and two or three beat up women living in a couple of even more beat up mobile homes. The women wouldn't talk to me. I started to drive away, loathing myself, figuring I wasted time and lost my gun in the deal. Just as I closed the door, a skinny, teen-aged girl with bright red facial sores rode a rickety bike close by the truck and said, 'If you got five-hundred dollars for me, I might have something you want. I need to see the money first.' Her face hardened when I hesitated. 'Lookee here, Mister. If you don't do right you won't get nuthin.'

"I thought a moment, gave up and handed her the money. She straddled the bike and counted it. After pocketing the money, she said, 'You just wait right here exactly thirty seconds, then follow me down this here road.'

"I wondered if there would be someone waiting down the road, or if the girl had simply taken me for five-hundred dollars. She materialized from the greenery as I drove around the turn, placed a brown paper sack on the hood of the truck and faded back into the brush. The sack contained a Smith and Wesson 357 pistol and a three inch blue steel cylinder. They fit together perfectly. Several shots into a nearby stump confirmed that the silencer didn't affect the gun's operation.

"I used my last day in Missouri to make final preparations. Two days later, I arrived in New York City and took a room close to the Arab Missions near the United Nations."

Chapter Six

OPEN SEASON

═══════◉═══════

The sleepless drive to New York seemed to last forever. Jim spent hours thinking about the morality involved. Weighing right and wrong didn't help. No way to justify what he planned to do. He discarded even the pretense of rationalizing and shifted time and energy to a plan of action. Jim's core plan consisted of a gun and silencer. Not much. It didn't take long to realize the details would have to be worked out on the scene. The miles drifted by after that, his mind in a stupor, no longer thinking about right or wrong.

Memories of his son held sway over all else. The more he thought about Jimmy, the less he cared about conscience, or justification, or anything other than getting it over with. When he managed to pry thoughts away from Jimmy to his own life, he didn't find much pleasant to recall–only the bad times, never the good. The nagging requirement to justify his intentions troubled him, but even that faded. Nothing mattered. He had lost a wife, the ranch, his son and grandson–everything.

My son is dead. End of that story.

*****

Jim spent the first days in New York hanging around the Libyan mission to the United Nations, watching for Jalloud and Jimmoudi. He picked them out late the second day, decked out in traditional Mid-Eastern robes and turbans. He later concluded that their attire must have been for a ceremony as he never saw them wear it again. The two young diplomats, apparently inseparable, regularly dressed like young Americans.

He followed for three days before discovering a constant pattern to their daily habits. Jimmoudi and Jalloud left the Libyan Mission each evening, strolled for thirty minutes, then slipped into a multi-level parking garage. They drove an expensive late model American luxury car from the garage and didn't return until well after midnight. He followed them twice in his truck, ending up at what looked like a cheap cat-house to him.

His daily routine changed to accommodate their nocturnal habits. He spent most of the early afternoon hours at a public library, reading and researching. His interests at the library included every detail he could gather on Arab customs and culture. Abundant news about terrorism helped cement his desire to exact vengeance.

Jim wasn't thinking about stopping with Jimmoudi and Jalloud. He planned to go on and on until someone killed him. He tired of study and thought, Okay, that's enough. It's time. No reason to wait.

He retrieved the truck from a paid lot the next morning, drove it to the Libyan's parking garage and left it on the level beneath their car, thinking it better to run downhill than up if it became necessary to run. After taking the pistol and silencer from beneath the seat, he transferred them to a briefcase and then to the hotel room.

The following hours weighed heavily, waiting for nightfall in the drab little room. He brooded about his son's family, murdered along with other innocent people to bring attention to a cause so alien to Americans that few knew or cared about it. He didn't think the average American would give a damn about terrorist causes even if they understood. His son lost his life to a group of radicals who struck without fear of death. Their religion promised to martyr them after death, providing dozens of celestial virgins, or raisins, depending on your source. A small part of their religion was so extreme that the more ardent followers willingly strapped explosives to their bodies and died for the cause. They came from societies conditioned to regard America as The Great Satan, where young men and women are trained from birth to hate Westerners, Americans more than others.

Jim thought, Americans might not be considered such easy

targets after tonight. Of course they regard us as easy prey. Why wouldn't they? We rarely display anything close to righteous indignation, at least not for long.

His thoughts turned to Juliet, his son's wife. One of the prettiest women ever, and one of the brightest. The background events leading to his son's death were not noteworthy, with the possible exception of Juliet. She had worked as a petroleum engineer for an American-based, Iraqi-owned petroleum company in Houston, Texas. She was Iraqi. She met his son in Houston where he oversaw some civil engineering work for her company. Their relationship advanced rapidly, culminating in a happy marriage and the birth of James Colby III. The arrival of a grandson sealed his son's death warrant. Jimmy made a promise the day his son was born, a promise to take Juliet, the girl from Iraq, home to visit her family. When time came for their journey, terrorism, which had been fairly quiet for years, lulling people into a false sense of security, was increasing.

Jim remembered calling. "I don't think the trip is a good idea, Son. I will help with funds if you send ticket money for her family and avoid travel to the Mideast." Father and son exchanged heated words prior to the journey. "If you want to get yourself killed, that's your business, but don't take my grandson. Hell, Son, a three year old kid won't remember anything anyway. I'll come down and stay with him while you and Juliet visit."

"Dad, the boy is the reason for going in the first place. There is no point contesting the issue. I promised Juliet. We aren't dealing with a variable here."

His son kept promises. Jim barely spoke to Jimmy the day he called from New York to say they were boarding. Afterward, he felt guilty for not being more forceful. *My fault. I should have been more persistent.*

*****

A slender, dusty ray of sunlight penetrated the dingy hotel room. Jim watched the spot of light inch across the floor and up the wall as evening approached. When the light lost its source and vanished, he took a cold shower and got ready. He dressed in dark clothes and soft-soled black shoes, then unconsciously began looking for signs of nervousness. His hands were steady and dry–pulse rate, fifty-five. Nothing abnormal. *No jitters? Odd. No pre-game jitters for the first time in my life.*

Jim packed and made a final check of the room, leaving no trace of evidence if something went wrong. He stood at the door before leaving, mentally reviewing the plan*: Room paid for another week. Weapon checked and loaded. Wearing nothing light colored. I'm ready.*

He pulled his shirt tail out, shoved the gun beneath his belt and left the room. During the walk to the parking garage the thought about getting the truck and driving away hit him. The notion to bolt, to get out, to end the madness, entered right on schedule as he knew it would. The idea of deserting was not new; he had been pushing it back for several days. Jim knew all along that abandoning the mission would have to be dealt with when the time came to act, and sure enough, right on schedule.

Too late. No amount of second guessing is going to stop me.

He knew his initial grief had changed considerably since the day of the crash. Sadness and grief had changed to rage, and rage to madness. He realized the whole affair was quite insane and thought, No sane person would even think about what I'm going to do.

He sat in the darkness at the parking garage, taking in the surroundings, counting and observing seven other vehicles on his level. He sauntered by each one, checking for occupants, for anything suspicious. *What the hell am I looking for? Bad guys in trench coats watching through binoculars? Dumbass.*

He lingered in the shadows for ten minutes, allowing his eyes to adjust, quelling a disturbing new feeling that he couldn't shake.

Something doesn't feel right.

Jim needed to deal with the new sensation and walked the entire level burning off nervous energy. He went down the ramp to the level below to repeat the procedure, checking every vehicle. Exercise helped. His breathing and heart rate slowed. He stood again in the shadows listening, and then swiftly climbed two flights to the top level. The Libyan's car was parked in its usual place. He took position in the shadows forty yards from the car. Jim knew he couldn't hit anything from that distance with the silenced pistol and planned to move closer when the time came.

One hour and fifteen minutes later, Jimmoudi and Jalloud showed up, either extremely drunk or under the effect of some marvelous drug. They giggled and shoved each other like teen agers, fumbling with the car keys, so involved with the lock that they didn't notice him inching forward in the shadows, one concrete pillar to another. *No reason to worry about being detected. I could walk right out in the open and they wouldn't notice.*

He stopped at the last pillar before encountering the Libyans, now only twenty feet away. They were practically falling over themselves trying to unlock the door. First one would fumble with the keys, and then the other would wrestle them away and jab at the lock. He couldn't help smiling. The scene reminded him of similar instances in his youth after a great fraternity party or some memorable Marine happy hours. He knew exactly how the two men felt. And then it was over.

Can't do it. Not now. Not ever.

He didn't feel hatred for those men–no rage–no madness– nothing at all. Their death would prove nothing. They weren't responsible for his son's death. He sighed deeply, stepped back into the shadows and slipped the gun under his belt. He didn't feel better, just defeated, even though a tremendous weight had lifted. He rested his forehead against the cool concrete and waited, unable to see through the veil of tears washing down his face, draining the last of pent up hatred and tension. All he felt was foolish, standing in the dark crying.

Jimmy's death will probably never be avenged, certainly not by me. I don't have the courage or enough hatred for vengeance. This is incredibly stupid.

He desperately wished the comic figures on the other side of the column would get in their damned car and leave so he could get out of town. Any place outside of New York City would do. Just out. Nothing else in the world existed except the frenzied antics of the two giggling, boneless shapes and the floundering comedy with the car keys.

Two hollow explosions rang out. Jim flinched.

Gunshots?

The Libyans clutched their chests, jerked, reeled drunkenly and fell, sprawling beside the car. Jim held his breath, pressing close to the dark side of the pillar, paralyzed, watching them die. The stricken men thrashed and cried out briefly but soon lay still. Jim pulled the pistol from his belt and peeked around the pillar at the Libyans now face down in spreading pools of blood. He couldn't see or hear anything unusual. The background hum of big city noises filled the night. Nothing moved. No running footsteps. He desperately wanted to change position, to withdraw into the darkness, but assumed whoever shot the Libyans knew of his presence. He felt real panic for the first time in years. *Get out of here! Two dead men yards away and I'm armed and dressed like a jewel thief.*

He darted into the shadows farther back in the garage, paused to catch his breath and listen, then ran to a drainage vent in the floor, removed the perforated cast iron cover and dropped the gun down an eight inch drain pipe. He had scouted the garage previously and figured the pipe connected directly to the city sewer lines beneath the parking garage. *No one will ever find the gun, not in a thousand years. I damned sure don't want it..*

Jim had killed in combat without feeling guilty, but for some reason felt responsible for the deaths of the Libyans, probably because he came so close to killing them. He broke from cover and sprinted headlong down the stairs leading to his truck. Nothing seemed more important than to separate from the area and the reason for his presence there. He stood in the shadows for several seconds upon reaching his truck's parking level, attempting to control breathing. Jim had been in enough dangerous situations to understand the effect of excitement and need to maintain control in tense situations.

His eyes moved rapidly, attempting to take in too much at once, not really seeing anything. He took slow, deep breaths to calm his racing heart, trying to concentrate on the next move. *Calm down. Walk the hell out of here and sin no more.* He grimaced at the thought. *Humor at a time like this? Focus.*

He noticed a dull light green van parked two spaces from his truck, a vehicle just like a thousand other work vans, without windows in the back.

That truck was not here earlier.

A quart of adrenaline poured into his bloodstream. Every alarm in his body went off like rippling explosions. He began to shiver in an automatic attempt to bleed off the turmoil. Every instinct to turn and run surfaced. He couldn't move. His body trembled and he remained rooted to the spot. He began analyzing the situation. *Don't go near the truck. Turn around. Get the hell out of here.* He backed slowly toward the stairwell and turned to reenter, then heard footsteps coming down the steps. *Go! No choice now.*

He turned back toward the garage, took a deep breath and faced his truck. It had taken on the ominous appearance of an enemy. *My imagination may be working overtime, but those footsteps behind me are getting closer, and fast.* He took a deep, uneven breath, almost a sigh, and headed for the truck. The sound of the green van's sliding side door slamming open nearly deafened him. Two men materialized, crouching, pistols aimed.

"Freeze! You're under arrest!" The voice didn't come from either of the two men now cautiously inching their way toward him, guns aimed at his chest. The voice had come from beyond a pillar like the one he hid behind only a few moments before. His breathing stopped. He glanced around for an avenue of escape. *I am so screwed.* He straightened slowly and let his arms relax. *No way out.* The first trace of suspicion pricked at the recesses of his mind. *Who are these people? How did they....*

Another man sat up in the bed of his truck, holding a short-barreled shotgun aimed directly at his head. The mystery voice stepped out from behind a pillar holding a shotgun. All four men closed from different directions.

Professionals.

Two men roughly handcuffed Jim while another completed a thorough body search.

Experts.

Another man emerged from the darkness of the stairwell carrying an M-16 rifle with a night vision scope and attached flash suppressor/silencer. Jim knew who shot the Libyans. One of the body searchers reported to the man with the scoped rifle, "He doesn't have the gun."

Jim tried to think of something to say but couldn't piece the puzzle together. The entire sequence of events happened within seconds.

The man with the rifle placed the weapon in the crook of his arm and said, "We won't need his gun. No time to look. Get the keys to his truck and follow us."

The little man giving the orders stepped into full light. Jim couldn't take his eyes from the rifle and night vision scope. After a series of clipped orders, the scope-carrier jerked a thumb toward the van and the other men dragged Jim to the sliding side door and forced him inside.

"There's been some mistake," he protested, finally gaining a voice. "I haven't done anything. Who the hell are you people?"

One of the men holding him said, "Just keep your mouth shut, buddy. You'll find out soon enough."

They departed the parking garage barely a minute after the shots. The Libyans, sprawled grotesquely in pools of congealing blood, would still be there in the morning to gross out some unsuspecting attendant. The guards forced him to lie on his stomach facing the rear door, which, as with the sides, had no window. He tried to plead his case to the guard and received a heavy foot on the back of his neck and a firm warning: "There isn't a damned thing I can tell you, buddy. You just lay there nice and quiet and keep your mouth shut."

Jim eventually resigned himself to wait until someone with authority took control. *Must be taking me to someone who can straighten this mess out.* He could tell by road sounds when the van departed the rough city streets in favor of a freeway. No stoplights. No one said anything to him during the next four hours. The van never slowed or stopped.

Chapter Seven

A CHANGE OF POLICY

The men holding Jim captive were members of a joint covert anti-terrorist FBI CIA team. Three such teams had been formed to locate foreign terrorists within the United States. Two of their prime suspects happened to be the Libyan diplomats Jim selected as targets.

Less than a week after Jim began trailing Jimmoudi and Jalloud, the New York team detected his presence. The four members of the joint team normally met at 2:00 each afternoon to compare notes and schedule activities. CIA agent Carl Owman, a stooped little man prematurely past his prime, typically started the daily meeting by reviewing film obtained from a remote camera installed in a hotel room window directly across the street from the Libyan Mission. The camera ran twenty four hours a day, scanning a panoramic view one-hundred feet either side of the mission entrance.

Carl ran the film FAST FORWARD, pausing only to identify people exiting and entering the target building. Two days before Jim Colby entered the garage with intent to assassinate the Libyans, Carl slowed the film to normal speed as the suspects appeared on film in the Mission doorway.

"Come on down!" he yelled, imitating the announcer of a daytime television game show. "Here they are. Looks like the boys were running a little late last night." He held the FAST FORWARD switch down until the Libyans walked out of the picture.

"Whoa! Hold it!" FBI agent Steve Shirley commanded. Shirley, the group's practical joker, a ready-for-retirement, somewhat overweight dry-hacking chain smoker who could barely speak without provoking a coughing fit. When he regained control of the cough, he said, "Yo, Carl. Run that sucker back to our friends and let's watch it again from there–at normal speed if you don't mind."

Carl didn't protest. The interruption meant nothing to him. He wasn't going anywhere. After re-setting the film, he ran it forward at normal speed.

Steve held up his hand. "Whoa! There! Freeze it right there." He stepped to the screen to more closely examine the blurred images. The other men exchanged questioning looks and resumed their usual banter. Steve turned and spoke to Carl. "Do we still have results for the past two days?"

"You know I do. Right there in the safe. I've already patched it, though. Why?"

"Not sure yet. I think maybe we better take a few minutes and look at it. How about four or five days in a row, up through today," He motioned toward the screen. "Can you do that?"

Carl sighed and lumbered to the safe. "Easy enough. Will a week work?" Steve studied the version intently while the others waited to see when he would share his thoughts. Steve suddenly pointed to the figure of a walking man and said, "Freeze it! Okay, now pay attention, people. I want all of you to take a good look at this guy. Ready? All right, now wind it back to the start, Carl. Run it again. This bird is hanging around way too much to suit me."

To their collective surprise, the team found Jim on three of five days' film. Each day he crossed the camera's field of vision ten to fifteen seconds after the Libyans departed the picture, possibly– more like obviously following them.

"No doubt in my mind," Steve declared. "The timing and frequency of his appearances are not random. He's trailing our guys."

The team's schedule of activities altered at that moment to include watching for the stalker to determine if Steve's suspicions about his movements were viable. Two days later, the team not only concluded that Jim was probably following their Libyan suspects, but they knew where he resided. Paul Sells, the nervous CIA agent in charge of the team decided it was time to establish the new man's identity. That evening, while two agents trailed Jim, the other two gained access to his room. When they met later that night to review their findings, Paul spoke first: "Okay, fellows, we may have a problem here. This guy looks like some kind of a nut to me. He has newspaper clippings pinned all over the walls of his room, and every single one of them deals with terrorism. Most of the articles are fairly recent, but they all have something to do with Libyan terrorists. There is one article about last spring's Rome crash posted over the headboard of his bed, sort of like a centerpiece. I think…." he paused and gazed deliberately from one man to another. "I think we may have ourselves an anti-terrorist terrorist here."

Steve chuckled. "Careful, Paul or you just might coin a new word. Anti-terrorist terrorist? How in the hell did you come up with that?"

Abe Savage, a balding FBI agent on his last assignment before retirement, said, "I don't think this is a damned joke, Steve. This is serious stuff. Pay attention for a change, would you?"

Steve didn't take anything seriously. He shrugged and said, "Hey, Dogbreath, I spotted the damned guy. Lighten up!"

Carl intervened. "Okay. Okay. Let's move on. We dusted a couple of drinking glasses in the room and got some clear prints. If we get these prints to the Bureau tonight, we might know who this guy is before noon tomorrow."

Paul Sells isolated Abe with his eyes and motioned to the door. Abe got up and left with the print evidence without a word. The next day's 2:00 meeting proved interesting. Abe started. "His name is James Colby. He is–get this–a retired United States Marine Lieutenant Colonel."

Steve whistled. "Wow! That is interesting, Abe, but why is he following our boys?"

Paul Sells leaned back and blew smoke expansively. "Relax, Steve. Abe and I have been up practically all night putting this thing together. Just sit back and reap the benefit of some professional police work." His face spread into a self-satisfied smile.

Abe sat on the coffee table in front of the other three men and continued. "We are dealing with the All American kid here. A freckle-faced farm kid with a fishing pole. He went to a small rural school; belonged to all the clubs; played on all the teams; went to the local college; married the local girl; had a kid, yada, yada. Boring, right? Wait for it. He joined the Marine Corps right out of college and had a great career. Made Lieutenant Colonel beneath the zone. Was a battalion commander, retired on twenty and started cattle ranching. Nothing all that interesting, but wait. What is interesting is this: He served in several top secret operations while in the Corps, all associated with Force Reconnaissance."

Steve whistled again. "Recon? Ricky Recon. So, we are dealing with a super grunt."

Abe nodded. "Correct. He served in Recon for six years, then to intelligence, and then got his infantry battalion. Couldn't get all the info on the classified operations he took part in, but he saw some pretty sticky stuff and has medals and ribbons plastered all over his chest. According to the Defense Department, there is not one single thing in his record to detract from what they call, 'An illustrious and outstanding career.' Okay, it gets better. Listen carefully, because what comes next is more than just a little bit interesting. He just happened to be a member of the Marine rifle and pistol teams for two years as a junior officer." Abe looked up to observe the expressions of the other three men.

Shirley let out another long, deflating whistle. "Man, are you thinking what I'm thinking?" He glanced from one man to another. "We could have a serious problem here, don't you think? Hell, there is only one logical reason for this jarhead to be following our boys." When no one responded to his perceptiveness, he gestured helplessly. "Come on, guys. Think. We might be interfering with something official."

Abe held up his hand for silence and said, "Before you jump to conclusions, Steve, there is more. Colby ran a cattle ranch for several years after retirement. Apparently lost everything in a divorce settlement. After the divorce, it looks like he drifted all over the western half of the United States doing a little bit of everything–everything but settling down. We have copies of W 2 forms from Houston, Denver, Seattle, Las Vegas and Oklahoma City. He hasn't stopped moving since the divorce."

Steve, still miffed by the slight, asked, "Why is that important?"

Abe took a drink from a stained coffee cup that clearly needed to be discarded. "Just background for what comes next. We believe the most noteworthy item of information we were able to piece together is this: Colby's son, his daughter in law and only grandchild, were killed in that airliner crash in Rome last month. In other words, he is here on his own dime. Revenge, maybe? Whatever he ever owned or loved, he lost. So, nothing to lose, right? I'll check it out with the head shed, though, so we don't mess up something."

Abe paused for a moment and closed the folder. He looked supremely confident. "Paul and I believe he is planning to take our Libyan friends out. No, actually, we are convinced. Colby is no nut, gents. Think about this, He has all the tools: the experience; the ability; no roots; and finally, and this is most important, he definitely has a motive. Gentlemen, we have a crisis."

The room remained silent for several seconds while each man reevaluated the stunning information. Paul Sells broke the silence. "Okay, this is clearly beyond the scope of our mission. Someone up top needs to be informed, and damned quick."

He walked to the window and watched the street traffic below, considering the next move. The other men sat quietly and waited. Paul turned from the scene below and spoke with an uncommon air of authority. "All right. I'm leaving immediately for Langley. You men will need to work out a schedule. I want to keep this office manned and Colby under surveillance twenty four hours a day. Now listen carefully. From here on no information about Colby may be released except by me, and I mean exactly that. I trust you can understand." He looked directly at each man long enough for them to nod agreement. "My appointment as team chief has not been important up to now, but there can be no question about responsibility. We are faced with a crisis. Responsibility for this little incident, whether important or not, belongs to me. Okay, let's divide tasks and get on with it. I need all the information you have. I'll be leaving for Langley this afternoon."

*****

Two weeks earlier. Washington D.C.

A large, round, black framed government clock on the battleship gray wall indicated fifteen hundred hours. Two armed Marines stood at parade rest in front of an unmarked door, occasionally stealing glances at the clock, then down the hall toward the elevator. The Marines, on the second basement level of the White House, were both highly experienced staff noncommissioned officers with lofty security clearances. The senior man, a burly Gunnery Sergeant, held a clipboard featuring five boldly grease-penciled names at the left margin. Four of the names already had check marks placed adjacently.

According to the clipboard, the Secretary of State, the Director of the Federal Bureau of Investigation, the Director of the Central Intelligence Agency, and the Director of CIA operations waited inside. The men were subdued, their expressions reflecting inner turmoil. Each man appeared lost in his own thoughts. No one spoke, no one smoked, and no one took his eyes from the door. All four stood respectfully as the President entered, then discreetly waited for him to be seated.

"Seats, gentlemen!" he ordered. They sat without waiting for him to take a seat because they knew he wouldn't. He never sat down when he was upset, and he had good reason to be troubled. The select group knew exactly why the meeting had been called–no preliminary briefing necessary. Each man had been personally contacted by Denning's secretary and she left no doubt in their minds about the great man's frame of mind.

"The President wants to see you this afternoon at fifteen hundred in the war room. I would advise you to be prepared for dialogue on the Rome crash. And, for your information, I have never seen the President so distraught."

The staff knew her to be an excellent barometer of his various moods. The President came into the room head down, arms folded behind his back. He did not acknowledge their presence after ordering them to sit. He paced back and forth across the front of the room without taking his eyes from the floor. He appeared to be furious. Everyone present recognized the symptoms: wrinkled brow, pursed lips, contorted facial muscles and the pacing–the damned pacing. They had seen it before. He only paced when angered.

Wesley Denning always got exactly what he wanted, but not that day. That day, the Twenty Fifth of May, brought impending political disaster to him. Terrorism threatened the very fiber of his regime and the core of his honor, for he had repeatedly and confidently promised voters that only he could deal with terrorism. The four men knew when he finally stopped pacing all hell would break loose.

Denning stopped suddenly and leaned across the table, balancing on his knuckles, glaring fiercely at the captive audience. The weight of his upper body rested heavily on the table. He slammed a huge, white knuckled fist onto the green felt top and looked straight at Adrian Burt, the CIA Operations Director.

"I am not directing these first comments at you, Mister Burt. Your part comes later." He pushed back to a standing position and gazed from one man to another until they all felt the sting of his eyes. He pointed at each man, his arm fully extended. "Three years!" he shouted. "Three goddamned years! I have listened to you, disagreed with you, and in the end I deferred to you. No more!" His hands clenched and unclenched repeatedly during the diatribe. "No sir! No more!" He began pacing again. His wary entourage shared glances.

"If I just went on ahead with what I damned well knew was right three years ago, those people in Rome would still be alive. I'm to blame. I knew better! Yes, this is on me. I damned well knew better." His voice lowered. "I'm not mad at you people. You gave good reasons–good enough to sway me. No, I'm mad at myself. I knew the right thing to do and let you talk me out of it. Now, by God, we are going to do things my way! I don't give a damn, not a single tinker's damn what you fellows think! And I don't give a damn what the rest of this goddamned planet thinks cither! This terrorist crap is coming to a screeching halt, and I mean right now!" He reinforced the words by slamming his fist on the table again. He paused and studied their faces. Denning did not expect nor did he detect the slightest hint of dissent.

"Now, Mister Burt! Now is where you come in."

He took a seat across from Adrian Burt and propped his shiny western boots on the table and casually lit a cigar. He shoved the gold plated cigar box across the table. Each man gratefully helped himself. The harangue was over; the stage set for his next move. Everyone breathed a sigh of relief and waited for Denning to get down to business.

When he spoke, he did so without a trace of rancor. His anger had run its course. "Not one word of what we say here today will leave this room, gents. Ever. What we decide to do here today might leave the room, but we are not going to talk about it again, not ever. Nothing we decide here can be associated to any of us. Let me make dead sure you know how serious I am about that. If one of you ever mentions a word about this meeting, or what took place here today, I will personally hunt you down and kill you. This is life and death stuff."

His expression left no doubt. His reputation as a ruthless politician was as well-known as the personal image he cherished. Wesley thought himself a hell for leather, hard riding outdoorsman–a modern Teddy Roosevelt. He lived by the code of the Old West and took great pride in being compared to Roosevelt. Denning never went back on a promise. He had just promised to kill anyone who leaked.

"What happens here today will be life-defining for everyone here. Now, does anyone want out before I say anything else?"

No one looked up.

"Look, gents, if you want out, just get up and walk out. But, if you stay, then by God you will be irrevocably committed. If you stay, your life may never be the same. I'm going to stop this terrorism bullshit, gents, and it isn't going to be pretty. I'm going to do whatever is necessary to stop it. If that means playing dirty, then so be it. If it means World War Three, so be it! They don't follow rules, gents, and neither will I. Not from here on. I'll tell you right now, I intend to break some rules. So, here's your chance to get out. I won't hold it against you if you leave. (They all knew he absolutely would.) That's a promise, gents. Okay, it's decision time. I'm going to break rules. Some bad people are going to die. In or out?"

He waited several seconds before speaking again, giving each man time to digest the situation. "All right then!" He stood and leaned over the table. "I don't know exactly how to stop terrorism, gents, but after three years, I know for damned sure you fellows don't. Now, here is what I do know: I am not going to talk to the sons of bitches anymore. The talking part is over. I won't ever try to deal with the bastards again! But I'll tell you what I am going to do! I'm going to kill their asses!" He pounded the table again.

"And something else! There will be no negotiating! There will be no warning. You can't deal with some jerk holding a plastic key to heaven. I will not martyr a bunch of religious nuts or give them an international incident they can use against us. No sir! And I will never turn the other cheek again, or roll over and let some third rate bunch of camel herders dictate one damned thing to me!" He turned to Adrian Burt. "Are you starting to get the picture, Mister Burt?"

He didn't wait for Burt to acknowledge. "You, Mister Burt, are going to come up with a plan. I know all about your work and I think you are the man for the job. When you do come up with a plan, let me know and we will have this meeting again. "The rules are simple. There are no rules. That's the rule. You have a blank check. You can ask any man in this room for any kind of assistance. I personally guarantee you will get it. Anything, Mister Burt. Let me repeat, There are no rules, no restrictions, no boundaries and no damned treaty or alliance you need to respect. I am going to stop terrorism against American citizens. I want every would be terrorist to forget about screwing with America and Americans. I want terrorists to die, Mister Burt. I want terrorists to suffer. I want a plan that works and I want it soon! I'll give you two weeks! You don't need to worry about how your plan will be received by Congress, or anyone else for that matter, because we are going to run it ourselves. Just us. If every man in this room doesn't buy your plan, then I won't use it. So clear your mind and give me something quick. Is that vague enough for you, Burt?" The President smiled. Burt didn't move a muscle.

"Okay, Mister Burt, think about it this way, What would you do if you were in my place and could do anything you damned well wanted to about terrorism? That's what I want from you. So, what are you going to do? What can you do? Hell, I don't know. But you know I already have military options, so don't dabble in their business. I have diplomatic, trade, backdoor channels and IOU's. "He paused, lowered his voice and said, "I have almost everything, Burt, and none of it works. I want something that works. I want to stop terrorism. I don't ever want to be awakened in the middle of the night again with news that another American has been killed by terrorists."

He smiled at Burt congenially. "Now, that's not asking too much, is it? Good. All right, pull the bureaucratic plug and do some free thinking, Mister Burt. I don't care how weird your plan is as long as it works." He turned to the others and said, "Now, gents, we should probably get back to work."

The President, followed by his trusted lieutenants, filed out of the room leaving Adrian Burt alone. Not one man had spoken during the meeting. By not disagreeing, they were committed. Adrian felt scant relief, other than his boss was at the meeting and he wouldn't have to explain himself at work. He stared at the table top and idly drummed a pencil. The enormity of the assignment staggered his imagination.

President Denning had just declared an all-out, no-holds-barred covert war on international terrorism. The men in that room had agreed by not disagreeing that undeclared covert actions would become the main thrust of the president's strategy against terrorism. Overt military operations would still be part of national policy, but only as diversion to the new emphasis on covert operations.

The proposed anti-terrorist operation's classification clearance rated such rigid secrecy that much later, when Denny Blakemore tried, he discovered that nothing he had access to recorded anything of value.

*****

Paul Sells returned to New York City from his meeting with Adrian Burt a sober and determined man. A changed man. He returned with an assignment few of his kind ever dare dream of, at the end of a less-than-celebrated-career. He certainly did not suffer from a lack of direction or emphasis from Langley.

What happened during Sells' visit to CIA headquarters at Langley that day was never officially revealed, and there were no written records of his trip. Paul Sells, by nature a nervous man, suffered from high blood pressure and alcohol abuse. The new mission placed him under tremendous pressure, a once in a lifetime dream come true. It had taken Sells twenty nine years of faithful service, but he finally had a juicy assignment with teeth.

Sells' visit to Langley came shortly after Adrian Burt received his secret marching orders from President Denning. Sells' timely report about noticing Jim following the Libyans found a ready audience at CIA headquarters, and gained for him an extraordinary meeting with Adrian Burt. His orders came directly from Burt. The MAN. The Operations Director's words still rang in Paul's ears the morning he returned to New York: "Paul, as of this moment, you are on the cutting edge of history. No, by God, you are the cutting edge. Nothing you have ever done or ever will do compares to the importance of this assignment. Don't let anything or anyone maneuver this mission off track. This is your career, Paul. Hell, this is *my* career."

Sells' orders included automatic dispersal of the team upon completion of one final all important task. He and the other CIA agents received verbal orders to report directly to the CIA Operations Director himself when the mission terminated. The FBI agents had similar orders within their club.

"Everything depends on you, Paul," the Director told him. "Don't let this slip through the crack. Our national interests are at stake here. We, you, me and the agency are under the gun here. Do whatever you have to do, and I mean exactly that–anything–but don't you dare fail me. I'm giving you a blank check. Do you know what that means? It means that you do what you have to do and I will back you one hundred percent. There are no rules. Get the job done, Paul. I'm depending on you. The president is depending on you."

Those were the Operations Director's last words to Paul at Langley. Adrian Burt himself followed Paul to the waiting helicopter and clapped him on the back. Adrian Burt did that.

Chapter Eight

AMNESTY

━━━━◦━━━━

Jim lay in the back of the van for four long hours, hoping every change of speed meant an end to the journey. His body ached after hours on cold steel. He needed to take a leak in the worst way. The guard didn't say anything, but kept the pressure of a booted foot on the back of his neck.

As the van sped on through the dark, his fears and anxieties receded somewhat. He began forming realistic conclusions about the situation. *They are probably not going to kill me. They could have done that at the garage. There has to be some mistake.* His analysis really wasn't that soothing, and like most instances of wishful thinking, didn't solve anything. He had recovered from the catatonic state of shock that paralyzed him during the capture. He couldn't reason and gave up trying, dozing intermittently.

Reflecting back later, being able to sleep under those circumstances seemed odd– speeding through the night, captive of complete strangers. During alert times, his thoughts drifted inexorably back to the same perplexing questions: Who are they? What are they doing with me? Why is it taking so damned long? Where are we going? Who in the hell are they? Even if I get the opportunity to prove my innocence, how can I? Will they be able to find the gun if I need it for evidence? Will they even bother looking for it? Was I set up?

His mind raced through the maze of events. *I never once gave thought to the possibility of being caught.* He felt foolish, lying on a steel floor wondering why he ever considered doing anything so reckless. Jim took some comfort knowing that he had chickened out of killing the Libyans at the last moment, but shuddered, thinking of how close he came. His thoughts raced. Did these people know what I was going to do in that parking garage? Have to assume they do. Oh, they knew. They had a night vision scope.

He couldn't come up with any good answers and finally gave up. *Nothing left to do but wait. Someone will come along sooner or later and take charge. This has to be a mistake.* More elemental problems pressed in on him and the luxury of speculation began losing the power to compete with reality. He was freezing and desperately needed to take a whiz. The brutal, chilling effect of the metal floor had numbed his entire body, and the rancid air in the van reeked from at least ten packs of cigarette smoke.

I need to deal with reality. Even in my most deranged state of mind, I had to know death or life in prison would be the best I could hope for if I got caught. He began facing his situation with a positive mind-set, even though he didn't think whatever came next would be good. *And I don't have any idea what comes next.*

Naps came in fitful intervals, interrupted only by the incessant thumping of the tires against regularly spaced, tar-filled cracks of a concrete highway. *Probably an interstate. Interstates are the only Eastern roads with concrete surfaces without stoplights or toll booths.*

He awoke when the van left the concrete surface in favor of an asphalt road. The rushing noise of wind against the van changed perceptibly as it slowed to a more moderate speed. The change in speed heightened his anxiety and the break in monotony provided reasonable hope that the journey would soon end. The van slowed further several minutes later and lurched while negotiating a sharp turnoff onto what sounded like a gravel surface. Within moments they came to an abrupt halt.

Every nerve in his body jangled as he listened for cues. All three guards gathered in the front part of the van, and then sat in total darkness smoking cigarettes, whispering in hushed tones. The ordeal continued. Later, much later, Jim heard another vehicle creeping down the road and stop nearby, followed by sounds of a car door opening and closing. Time dragged on.

"Hey!" he yelled. "I really need to take a leak!"

"Tough shit, buddy." They all laughed.

Jim groaned, surrendered and wet his pants. He heard footsteps on gravel approaching the van. A voice from the darkness barked, "Okay, people. It's clear. Get him out."

One of the guards answered, "About damned time! What took you so long?"

The sliding side door opened and two guards eased Jim through the door. He stepped from the van into what appeared to be the front yard of a well-lit and manicured estate. His surprise at the unexpected surroundings turned quickly to misgiving. The grounds and buildings bore no resemblance to a prison or anything official. He didn't know what he expected–certainly nothing like an elegant country estate. He balked and said, "Will someone tell me what in the hell is going on here?"

One of the guards yanked him toward the lavish dwelling. "Don't ask questions, friend. If we knew the answers, which we don't, we wouldn't tell you. So don't bother."

His legs were stiff and didn't respond naturally to the simple task of walking. He hobbled along as they hustled him into the house and directly to a room without windows. They took the handcuffs off and left him alone, standing on a bare wooden floor by a steel military barracks bed featuring a neat stack of army blankets and sheets.

"Get some sleep, pal," the last guard said on the way out. "You don't have much time."

Jim listened to a bolt lock slam into place after the door closed. The only other door in the room led to a small bath with minimal supplies of creature comforts. *No windows.* He tapped on the walls. *Metal. No chance for escape. This is a prison.*

Jim took advantage of the bathroom to wash his trousers, then made the bed and flopped down to wait. He didn't know how long he waited before the thump of approaching steps drew his attention. He assumed it to be midmorning. Footfalls approached and stopped at the door. The lock rattled. He sat up at sounds of the door opening and squinted as light poured into the room. The invasion of light backlit two men. One carrying a gun, the other a tray of food. The gun bearer, the same guy with a foot on his neck all night, flipped on the overhead light.

"You got thirty minutes to eat and clean up, buddy. Thirty minutes." They left the food tray just inside the door and backed out, the gunman in a defensive crouch, gun leveled, cautious and prepared.

Jim listened again to the unmistakable sounds of a bolt lock slamming home before their footsteps faded. The next time the door opened, thirty minutes later, a tall, well- dressed man entered. He appeared to be middle aged with splendid wavy, silver tipped hair. Jim thought he looked like a television evangelists. From the time he entered until he left much later, the man never stopped smiling, and never took his eyes from Jim's face. The gun bearing assistant protested when dismissed, but when the preacher guy's eyes narrowed, the guard nodded and got out.

Jim's visitor yelled, "Lock the door!" He then walked directly to Jim and offered his hand, smooth and confident. "I hope you are feeling well enough," he said, still smiling.

Jim was infuriated, half naked, wet trousers still hanging over the bedstead and in no mood for polite conversation. He refused the offer of friendliness. "Maybe you wouldn't mind telling me what the hell is going on," he said. "Maybe you better tell me!"

The visitor retracted his hand, unfazed by the slight, and kept right on smiling, unaffected by the hostility. "Yes, I suppose it is time, Mister Colby." He raised an eyebrow and watched for a reaction, to make sure Jim noticed the disclosure. "That's right, we know exactly who you are."

Jim flipped the covers back, sat up and pulled on his wet trousers, thoughts confined to the name revelation. The man fairly reeked of authority and self-importance. An aura of command and influence flowed from every word and every gesture he made, even his posture promoted authority. Control came naturally to him. Jim had functioned as a commander for years, associating with people who instinctively assumed a bearing to promote the image of authority. Most managed without intent. This man fit that mold.

He stepped closer to the bed and placed a brown leather briefcase on the floor, still smiling. Jim could detect no external signs to assist identification; no rank insignia; no name tag. His visitor took a seat on the other end of the bed and made an indulgent show of preparing and lighting an expensive looking cigar. After the tobacco leaves fired, he blew a huge cloud of thick white smoke directly toward Jim. A man holding all the good cards.

"I would offer you one, Mister Colby, but then you don't smoke, do you." It wasn't a question–simply another statement to let Jim know that his identity wasn't all they knew. He proceeded without waiting for an answer: "The conversation we are about to have, Mister Colby, is going to be extremely one sided, I'm afraid. So, if you will please excuse my impoliteness, I will do the talking and you listen. When I finish, you will have an important decision to make. Please, for the sake of brevity, try not to interrupt or miss anything."

He sucked on the cigar like an edible delicacy, and then blew another immense cloud of smoke toward Jim, never once taking his eyes from his captive, clearly enjoying the dominant position in the drama unfolding at his command. "Last night...." He paused again to puff on the cigar, to drag out the mystery even more. "You killed two Libyan diplomats in cold blood, Colonel Colby."

Jim could not suppress facial evidence of his surprise. *They know my rank?*

The visitor noticed the surprised look and said, "Yes, that's correct, sir. We know exactly who you are, Colonel. I also have proof of your guilt. Irrefutable proof. And I also know this: If you are brought to trial by our government for murdering those men, you will be convicted and in all likelihood spend the rest of your life behind bars. However, should we choose to extradite you to Libya, as that government will no doubt demand, I suspect you will be killed by having your head lopped off. You, sir, are a murderer and it does not make one iota of difference that your son and his family may have fallen victim to Libyan terrorism. Even if they did, you had no moral or legal license to take justice into your own hands. Those two innocent men you killed were in no way connected to your son's death, Colonel. And, by the way, did you know they were both princes? That's correct, Libyan princes." He paused to puff on the cigar, watching for a reaction, enjoying himself immensely.

Jim was too stunned to react. Not only did they know his name and rank, they also knew about his son's death. He tried to suppress surprise and allowed his growing anger to surface. "Okay, the two of us need to get a couple of things straight, pal," he said. "First, if you blow that damned cigar smoke in my face again, I'm going to put the stinking thing out on your tongue. You got that?"

No effect. The emotional outburst seemed to amuse his visitor.

He pressed on. "Look, I did not kill those men, princes or not," he said. "I admit being at the garage, but I didn't kill anyone and you know that. I don't believe for a moment that any of this farce is coincidental. This is a setup!"

The visitor smiled condescendingly and blew another cloud of smoke, this time to the side, and waved his hand for silence. "Colonel Colby, please. You are wasting time. All right. I expect you should probably be apprised of a couple of conditions new to your life. First, you, sir, are no longer within the American legal system. There are no rules protecting you here. My organization does not play by the same rules you apparently are counting on to deliver you from the dilemma you are in. It doesn't make any difference how much you complain. Complain all you like. Nothing is going to change. Your course was set the moment you decided to take the law into your own hands. You no longer have citizen rights. There is no recourse for you now, except through me. Accept that and your future will be greatly simplified. Save your anger and energy, Colonel. Nothing you can do or say makes the slightest difference, nor will it change anything. Your course is set."

He opened the briefcase and took photo copies of newspaper clippings Jim had thumbtacked to the hotel room wall in New York City and laid them in a neat line on the bed. His next announcement stunned Jim.

"You see, Colonel, we have been monitoring your activities for some time. Oh, and you were quite correct when you said this matter is not coincidental. It is no accident that you were captured."

Jim recovered and said, "I can prove I didn't kill those Libyans. All you need to do is compare the bullets that killed those men to my gun. Sure, I had a motive, and I admit being at the scene, but I didn't kill anyone."

Another puff of smoke. "Colonel Colby. Really. I'm disappointed. What do you take me for? What makes you think I'm interested in proving you are not guilty? I truly am disappointed. No jury in the world would believe you under the circumstances, now would they? Even if we had the ability to find your gun, and I am advised your method of disposal would preclude such an event,

I must inform you that we are absolutely not interested in finding it. No, we have all the proof we need. Motive and presence. What else must I say to convince you? We will not waste time trying to prove you are innocent. We absolutely-do-not-care. Look at the facts. You were on the scene. Here is photo proof of that." He slapped another photo down at the end of the line already on the bed, like dealing cards. "Also," he motioned to the photographs on the bed, "you certainly had ample motive. Oh, and here is a photograph of you in possession of a weapon with an illegal silencing device." He dealt yet another photo. "We have days of visually recorded proof that you were following those unfortunate Libyans. So, you see, Colonel, there really is no good reason why I should waste time attempting to corroborate your pathetic alibi. No. Now, let's get back to the business at hand, shall we?"

Jim couldn't tolerate any more of the man's patronizing demeanor. He stood and snapped, "Forget it! I want out of here!"

"Tsk tsk, Colonel. Temper, temper. Remember, I talk, you listen. What little I don't know about you isn't worth knowing. Suffice it to say, we have done our homework. Now, suppose we terminate the menial patter and get to the substance of my visit, shall we?" When Jim didn't answer he continued. "Very good. I have been authorized to grant you complete amnesty for last night's unfortunate misconduct." He watched Jim's reaction. "Ahh, I thought you might find that interesting."

Jim didn't try to stem the anger. "Amnesty? Is this some kind of a joke? If it is, I'm getting damned tired of it. Amnesty for what?"

The strength of his voice attracted attention from the guard who opened and rushed in, gun at the ready. The dapper man seated on the bed only smiled and waved him away again. The guard nodded and ducked outside and the bolt lock snapped into place.

"Sorry for the interruption, Colonel. This is no stunt. There is no subterfuge involved in anything I have told you. You are not yet connected to last night's bloodshed, and, up to the moment, there have been no charges placed against you. You just might be completely exonerated of all charges without ever being brought to trial if…if you play your cards right. Of course you must do something for me in return for such favor." His face smiled but his eyes were cold.

Jim recognized that his visitor had just set the hook.

The smiling man studied Jim's face, watching for clues to his feelings. After several awkward moments, he leaned over, pulled the briefcase onto the bed, opened and spun it around so Jim could see the contents. He smiled confidently. "Not only am I authorized and prepared to relieve you of blame for last night's...oh, how do I say this without being crude? Let's just say, unfortunate circumstances?" He lifted a bundle of money from the case and casually flipped it toward Jim's end of the bed. "I am also in a position to make you a very wealthy man. I also know you could use it. "

Jim hesitated before reaching for the money–a stack of hundred dollar bills. He tossed the money back into the briefcase, stood and stepped away. "I haven't denied being there last night, but you can't prove I did anything because I didn't. You can't buy me, either, for whatever you have in mind. You need to find yourself another man. I'm not going to play your game." He still didn't know who the guy was.

His visitor exhaled another cloud of smoke and leaned back on an elbow. He looked completely satisfied, gazing at the cigar lovingly. He looked up and spoke with an air of complete indifference. "Let me assure you that this is no game. There are five hundred thousand dollars in that briefcase. Normally a bit theatrical for my taste. Nonetheless, a genuine effort on our part to convince you of our sincerity. If you choose to work with us, there will be an additional five hundred thousand upon completion of the assignment. If you decide not to work with us...." He shrugged. "Well, I suppose I have already covered those options, haven't I?"

"You keep mentioning we and us. Who do you represent?"

The cigar moved without assistance to the corner of his mouth. His cheeks sank inward and his eyes partially closed in concert with another effort to draw pleasure from the tobacco. He gathered the money and photographs, closed and locked the briefcase, then removed the cigar to answer. "I don't want to appear rude, Colonel, and if I sometimes seem less than candid, please bear with me. But, in answer to the question, You will never know who we are. Any attempt to learn will be a complete waste of time. Now, let me say this one more time so there can be no chance of misunderstanding. If you do not choose to work with us...." He gestured in a manner to indicate there would be nothing he could do about the consequences. "You, sir, will most assuredly be transported to Libya in chains and a certain and gruesome death, of that you may be absolutely sure. There is quite a clamor taking place between our governments as we speak."

Jim fearlessly announced, "You can't extradite me for something I didn't do."

He shook his head sadly and groaned. "Would you listen to yourself? What must I do to convince you? Oh, this is all so unfortunate." His expression changed for the first time, exhibiting signs of annoyance. "Very well then, Colonel, let's try it one more time, shall we? It's quite simple really. With me, you have a chance; without me you are a dead man. That's as simple as I can make it. Now, I'm tired of fencing with you. Make up your mind."

Jim wanted to duel. "Make up my mind to what? I'm not about to make any decision based on the information I have." Then, unwilling to call a halt to the conversation, he said, "But, just for the hell of it, what would I have to do?"

His visitor nodded, obviously pleased, raised both hands, as if celebrating a score. "Ahh! There now. That's more like it. We have finally arrived at the core." He picked up the briefcase and walked to the door before facing Jim again. "You must do exactly the same thing you did last night, Colonel Colby. The only difference is, this time we select the target, and this time you get paid for it."

Jim started to answer, but closed his mouth and thought, This really cannot be happening. The whole thing suddenly struck him as humorous. He started laughing. "You want me to be a hit man? Is that what this is all about?"

The caller's expression remained stoic. "Hit man is not a term I am particularly fond of, Colonel. I much prefer something a little more refined."

Jim laughed. "Call it whatever you like, partner. If you are suggesting I kill someone, it's all the same, isn't it?"

The man stopped smiling and looked stern. "I assure you, this is serious. Entirely."

Jim was still laughing. "Sure it is. Pardon me all to hell, but I find this conversation amusing. The whole damned thing is a joke. And by the way, I'm no longer a Colonel. And while we're clearing things up, I'm really tired of all this crap!"

The visitor didn't blink. After another patronizing smile, he said, "Nevertheless, I require an answer."

Jim stared at him for a moment before sitting on the bed to review their conversation. His dilemma was somewhat clearer. *If I believe this guy, and I am beginning to, they've got me. I don't have anything left to do but play out the hand.* He decided to lay out his cards. "Look, I'm no hired killer, partner. If I couldn't kill for myself last night, don't you think I'm a hell of a lot less likely to do it for you? If you are serious, and I'm not about to believe you are, what makes you think I would consider something so utterly ridiculous?"

"Ridiculous, Colonel? That's a good one coming from you. You must remember, I know everything about you. I know for instance that you have the best of all motives. No one would deny the justice of your motive. And I also know that you have the training and ability, the appropriate skills and experience, and ... and this is the most important thing I know: You really don't have any choice. You must either work with me or die. That is the only choice you have." He smiled warmly. "It could be a lucrative arrangement."

"Assuming what you say is true, and I decide to work for you, who am I supposed to kill?"

"Very well. Your target assignment will be the man directly responsible for the death of your son, and for the deaths of hundreds, perhaps thousands of other innocent people. I know you are familiar with the terrorist leader, Abdel Hafez. I can and will provide conclusive proof that his group is responsible for the bomb that killed your son. We know that beyond doubt. We have traced the execution orders to him. And, by the way, Hafez publicly took credit for the bombing yesterday. I'm not sure you know that."

Jim believed him. The man appeared to be dead serious. "Hafez? I know all about that bastard. But to even think about assassinating him is damned silly. Do you really expect me to consider something so idiotic! In the first place, he is in Libya, and that alone makes it all but impossible to get to him. He has Libyan government protection. What am I supposed to do, just fly over there, walk right up and shoot him? Who in hell dreamed up this harebrained scheme?" He didn't try to hide his annoyance.

The visitor stood motionless throughout the diatribe and waited.

Jim wasn't finished. "What you have suggested is impossible, but I suspect you already know that."

The visitor brushed an imaginary speck from his lapel and said, "It may well be impossible, but that will be entirely up to you. Whether or not you succeed will also be entirely up to you, but you will try, sir. You have no choice, either practically or emotionally. You see, I am absolutely convinced that you will take this opportunity to avenge your son's death. I know you that well. Now, let me summarize some things you probably should know before you reach the only rational conclusion possible." He held up a finger and started counting, adding another finger with each number. "First, we can offer any assistance you need, but the conduct of the mission will be your responsibility. Second, there will be some physical restrictions, should you accept this assignment, and you will. Third, you must accomplish the mission alone. Fourth, if you are captured, there will not be one shred of evidence to connect you with our organization, or the American government. We would, as I'm sure you must know by now, disclaim any knowledge of you or the mission. Fifth, you will have sixty days to accomplish the mission. And finally, upon completion of the mission, you will be provided a new identity and moved to a safe area of your choice."

He paused to catch his breath, turned and knocked on the door. The door popped open immediately. The guard rushed in prepared, then relaxed and grinned foolishly when he saw Jim sitting on the bed. The dignified caller said, "I shall return at noon for your answer. If the answer is negative, you will be on the way to Libya before nightfall with photographic evidence against you, drugged and in chains. Good day, Sir"

The sound of the door slamming ended the conversation as firmly as a gunshot. Jim paced the room for thirty minutes before reclining on the bed, reviewing every word of the morning's conversation with perfect recall. If everything the man said was true, he couldn't see any way out.

They have me.

He tried to think of possible options. None, unless he decided not to believe and test the strength of the man's threats. *He is offering amnesty for a crime I did not commit. I believe he could turn me over to the Libyans if I refuse the assignment. It looks like I either have to accept the mission or they will use me to quell an international incident. Not very appealing. If I accept, I might find an opportunity to escape.* He agonized over how to resolve the problem for several moments. Then, in a flash of insight, confusion lifted and the incredible sequence of events during the past day no longer seemed so much like a bad dream. He began to laugh, to himself at first, then out loud. The incredible events of the past day no longer seemed like a bad dream.

Epiphany!

For several days, nothing had mattered except revenge. He planned and prepared for revenge, and yet, when faced with the prospect of murdering innocent men, he couldn't do it. He wanted to avenge his son's death in spite of risks to his own life. He had not cared about living as long as he could exact revenge.

Just because I couldn't murder two innocent men, neither associated to my son's death except by accident of birth, doesn't mean the desire to avenge my boy's death is gone, does it?

He realized nothing had changed–nothing except someone was going to pay him a million dollars to kill the bastard responsible for his son's death.

Why should I care who they are? They are willing to pay me to do something I was ready to do for nothing yesterday. Maybe I reneged when faced with the prospect of killing innocent people. This time I won't turn back. Hafez is no innocent.

His decision synthesized in a flash. The reservations and moral dilemma of past weeks dropped away like sun burning through fog. He lay back to wait, smiling for the first time in days.

*****

Adrian Burt helicoptered from the meeting with Colby directly to the White house lawn.

President Denning met him in the basement war room. "Have a seat please, Mister Burt. Hope you don't mind if I stand." He waited for Burt to settle. "Now, how did it go?"

"Very well, Mister President. We have our man."

Denning slammed a fist into an open palm. "That's great news! Great news! Now, Mister Burt, answer me this: Are you sure he will do it?"

"We believe he will, Sir. We have done what we can to build a psychological profile on him. We are satisfied that he will."

"Good. Now tell me why."

"He is perfect, Sir. Farm kid. Ex Marine. Very familiar with weapons. His father was a gun nut who taught him to shoot early in life. There is much more if you—"

Denning waved his hands irritably. "No, I don't mean that, Mister Burt. What I want to know is, Why you think he will, not why he can. Hell, almost any ex Marine probably can."

"Colonel Colby has nothing to lose, Mister President. We believe he may be somewhat psychologically disturbed by grief, but certainly not incapacitated. He has lost everything of value, and I mean everything: his wife, his ranch, his self-esteem, his path through life, and now his son and grandson. We don't believe he is ready yet, but we judge that he can be induced, provided we apply the right stimulus, and most of what we need has already been done by terrorism."

"When will you know for sure?"

"Noon today, Sir."

Denning pounded fist to palm again, said, "Sounds good. Let me know. Call me direct. Just say yes or no. Thank you, Mister Burt. Thank you." He rushed out.

Chapter Nine

PREPARATIONS

Noon.

Opening sounds of the sliding bolt crashed into the vacuum of silence, amplified by Jim's jittery state of mind. The overhead light snapped on. He sat up, squinting, eyes adapting, focusing once again on the smiling face of his genial visitor.

High noon. Ironic. High noon, just like the movie. Judgment time. Life-defining time. Decision time.

He rolled over and stretched, fingers interlinked behind his head. "Let me get this straight," he said without waiting for the visitor. "You are going to pay me a million dollars to assassinate Abdel Hafez. Is that correct?"

The man rapped on the door and the bolt lock clicked. "That is correct, Colonel Colby. One million dollars. Half now and half upon delivery."

Jim took his time, to let the man stew more than anything. He already knew the answer. "Please, no more of the Colonel routine. How do I know you are trustworthy? How do I know you will keep your promise? And what makes you think I won't skip out the first chance I get?"

"I can only answer that we don't know everything about you, just enough to believe you are the man we have been looking for. When you couple the information we do have about you with your present compromised circumstances…well, I think you may begin to understand our faith in you. As for doubts about us, I appreciate your concern. I just don't think there is much we can or will do about that."

Jim nodded matter-of-factly. He really hadn't expected much. "What am I supposed to do, just walk up and blow him away?"

The cigar lighting performance again lasted too long, Jim presumed in an attempt by his visitor to demonstrate lack of concern. Clouds of rich, white smoke nearly obscured the performance before he spoke again.

"You, sir, according to your records, were once a very successful military officer. So you see, I am fairly confident that your idea of how to consummate such a plan will be effective and well thought out, possibly as good as anything we might concoct. I believe it imperative that you devise the plan, however, since you will be executing it. Therefore, how you accomplish the mission will be left mostly up to you. We will provide guidance as needed and assist if you ask of course, but only in ways that will not associate us to you. Equipment, training; maps, documentation–you name it and we will make arrangements for it."

Jim took a few moments to think before asking, "What makes you so sure I can do it?"

"We aren't fooling ourselves. The prognosis for success is not exceptional. However, after due consideration, we believe you will probably attempt the mission and that you have as good, perhaps better chance of success as any. Couple with that the knowledge that we presently do not have a better prospect. Frankly, I doubt there is a better prospect."

He puffed on the cigar and fanned the smoke away to clear a field of vision. "Now, I would like to have your answer, sir. Are you in?"

Jim laughed, attempting to sound scornful. "You know what I think, partner? I think you and your organization are probably more demented than I, which isn't saying much for you. If you know as much about me as it seems, then you must know I would probably do it for nothing. So, why pay me?"

The dignified man smiled pleasantly, reached into his vest pocket and retrieved a plain white envelope. Before he could hand it over, Jim interrupted the order of events by saying, "I will need proof of Hafez's involvement in the Rome crash. Absolute proof. I must know, for a fact, that he was responsible. Can you arrange that?"

His visitor squinted through the smoke to look him straight in the eye and said, "Absolutely."

"How soon?"

"Within the hour if you like. I take it then your answer is affirmative?"

"Do I have a choice?"

He stepped closer and handed the envelope over, then said, "None whatsoever. You are a dead man if you refuse. My guess is that you will probably die during the attempt, but at least you will have a chance to survive, depending on providence and how effective you are. I hope you do succeed. If you do, you will be purging the world of the worst kind of vermin." He directed attention to the envelope by pointing the cigar. "Inside that envelope is a receipt for five-hundred thousand dollars, ready to be deposited to an account number assigned to your new identity at a bank of your choice. The remainder will be made available upon conclusion of the mission. However, this money will not become available until sixty days from today. The name we use–the name you will be assigned–will remain unknown to you until that time. If you are unsuccessful, we will recover the money."

"No deal. I want the money in cash."

"I see. I will need to get back to you on that."

Jim thought for a moment. "What about my identity?"

"The Marine Corps and the Defense Finance and Accounting Service will be advised of your death tomorrow. We have devised a plan to use the body of some unfortunate, probably a homeless derelict, and arrange the fabrication of a death certificate for you that should satisfy all administrative requirements. We will satisfy the monetary requirements of your beneficiary–your ex-wife–and you will be given a military funeral ceremony at Arlington with full honors. That, I am advised, will officially be the end of the you the world has known. Sometime within the week you will officially cease to exist."

"Who will I be between now and mission completion? Who will I be after completion of the mission?"

"Between now and then?" He shrugged. "I suppose that depends on who you need to be, if there is a need. Hardly matters, does it? Before you leave on the mission, we will have a permanent identity for you in a bank box with you in possession of the key."

"No deal. I want possession and control beforehand. That request is not negotiable."

"Again, I will get back on that. About the money, though. We cannot meet your requirements with cash, other than enough to get you by immediately after the mission. How much will you need?"

"Fifteen-thousand dollars cash in my possession before the mission."

"Done. I can and will provide the accounts in your new name before the mission, certified accounts only accessible by you with your account number. You will be able to contact the banks and verify the money before leaving this compound."

Jim thought for a moment. "I absolutely demand to check the accounts before the mission."

"Done. Now, I need your plan as soon as possible. The plan you intend to employ is necessary, sir, so we can get to work. First we must build your mission identity and arrange other necessary administrative and support details. Between now and then, you won't need credentials for anything, particularly since you won't be anyone. As I said, you will cease to exist sometime this week."

"Okay. Now I am going to tell you how this is going to be done. This arrangement is not a one-way street, partner. I won't work with you unless you agree to meet my requirements."

His visitor smiled benignly. "Don't forget. I hold all the cards."

"I don't think so. Look, I don't believe for a moment that you would turn me over to the Libyans. That would be like admitting American complicity. So forget about using that ploy. It was a nice touch, though."

"Don't underestimate me, sir, and don't be too sure about what I will and won't do. I will attempt to accommodate you for the moment, however. What do you have in mind?"

"You blew this off, but I must also have in my possession, before the mission, the identity I will assume after the mission. I want everything that I presently have: driver's license, social security number, work history, education, the works—full identity and history in my possession before the mission, along with money."

The visitor looked surprised, then appreciative. He said, "I'm impressed. You are thinking ahead. Why the documents?"

"That's not all, friend. I also want those dollars you promised in cash, one-thousand dollars each. I want the fifteen-thousand in hundred dollar bills. I will also need enough time away from here, unescorted, to place the money and identification in a safe place, a place of my choosing."

"No chance. That's asking too much and you know it."

Jim enjoyed the feeling of being in control. "That's bullshit and you know it. If I do things your way, I could lose everything. I need reliable compensation and I must have it ahead of time."

The demands seemed to stump his caller. His brow furrowed as he thought about the unexpected twist. He recovered nicely, smiled and said, "You are quite right, of course. Very well, what state will you want your new identification papers registered in?"

"Colorado. You may also place the remaining five-hundred-thousand in a Colorado bank, under my new identity. Make it Denver. I will take possession of the Four-hundred and eighty-five thousand remaining initial money before I leave here in a certified account only in my name, and we must agree to all the identity and monetary terms before the mission. Understood?"

He nodded thoughtfully. "I will concede that, but I'll need to be able to retrieve the initial five-hundred-thousand in the unfortunate circumstance that you don't make it back. So, we'll just have to make some–"

"No deal. Forget that."

Another long pause followed before he smiled blandly and said, "Your way, of course. Four-hundred and eighty-thousand dollars in a local bank of your choosing and fifteen-thousand cash. The remainder at a bank in Denver in a certified account you can monitor. We have a deal then?"

Jim sat up and offered his hand to seal the bargain and said, "Yes. If everything is as you say and as soon as I get the paperwork you promised: my new ID, the information about Hafez and the money, then you can count me in. I don't know who you are, partner, or even if I should trust you, but I won't go back on my word."

The clearly delighted man stepped back from the hand shake and said, "I knew that about you from the beginning, Colonel Colby."

"Okay, when do I start?"

His facial expression changed from sociable to business. "As of this instant. You are now in complete control of the mission. You will never see me again or the men who brought you here last night. Your only contact with our organization will be through a representative who will introduce himself immediately after I leave this room. However, I will be on-call, available to you throughout the mission."

He started to knock on the door, hesitated and turned back. "You are never to reveal anything about this mission to anyone, sir. What you are going to do is classified beyond Top Secret. I know you are aware of the responsibilities of secret clearances. If anyone ever happened to learn of the assignment, or your target's identity, or anything about this mission, we would be forced to reconsider our position concerning your well-being. I hope I'm not being too subtle and that you understand what I mean. What we are involved in here pertains to national security of critical importance. Secrecy is mandatory." He remained at the door for several seconds, apparently lost in deep thought, then evidently decided there was nothing else to say and rapped on the door. The door lock snapped and two guards entered.

The visitor held a hand up, almost like a wave goodbye, then cleared all expression from his face and said, "I am...We. We are deeply sorry about your family, Colonel. What happened to you is against the canons of humanity. We sympathize with you entirely. The sole purpose of this mission is to stop such terrorism. The covenant you and I are now part of binds us with many others and permits any measure necessary to stop terrorism. I believe you share our interest. I wish you great success and a fair wind. I also sincerely apologize for the necessity of burdening you with this device." He tapped on the door and motioned toward a flat metallic band one of the guards produced upon entry.

Jim offered no resistance as the guard placed a radio tracking device on his ankle. An intricate clamp clicked into place, snug and secure.

His visitor said, "That device is absolutely foolproof. If you tamper with it we will be alerted. It is extremely sensitive. I think it is attractive, though, don't you?" He smiled, turned and walked away without looking back.

*****

A short, dark complexioned, middle-aged man with severe facial scars of unchecked adolescent skin disease stepped into the room. He stood, feet apart, arms folded aggressively, staring at Jim with open contempt. "You will call me Kareem. I am from the Middle East. I am an American citizen. I work for the American government. I have been assigned to assist you. Those are my instructions. You don't need to know anything else about me."

Jim recognized immediately that they were off to a poor start. He knew enough about the sullen man in those few seconds to know they would never be friendly. "Kareem, is it? I don't give a damn what your real name is and don't you ever walk again into a room I am in without knocking. If I need anything from you, I will call. Now, when do I get food?"

Kareem's arrogance suffered only momentary deflation. He stifled a rejoinder and jerked a thumb toward the door. "I only assist with the mission. You must prepare your own food."

Jim walked to the door half expecting some form of reprimand. Kareem must have detected his misgivings.

"You are no longer prisoner. We are alone. This building is located on a very large farm. No other persons live nearby. I am directed to instruct you that the agency commands you do not leave the farm until it is necessary to accomplish the mission. The device on your ankle will alert if you cross farm boundaries. Your movements here will be closely monitored and people have orders to shoot to kill if you try to leave. If you need anything from the outside, I will be your messenger."

Agency? Well of course. Everything I do or say, every breath I take from here on will be tracked and recorded. Probably sensors in every square foot of this compound.

Jim stepped into the hallway and spoke without looking back. "Follow me, Kareem. I may have questions." He toured the house, noticing that the furnishings seemed complete, indicating a recent occupant, or perhaps someone was permitting use of their home. After lunch, Kareem brought a golf cart to the house and the two men spent part of the afternoon exploring the grounds. Jim didn't see a neighboring building. The property probably consisted of more than a thousand acres. Among other things, he found an indoor firing range and a fully equipped gym.

He spent the remainder of daylight hours in a well-equipped study making notes and studying packets of evidence a courier delivered late that afternoon. Kareem also brought the information promised about Hafez and his involvement with the Rome crash. After reading the material, Jim no longer harbored doubts about charging Abdel Hafez with his son's death. According to the letterhead, the classified information contained in the packet came directly from the CIA. The Agency letterhead sealed his suspicions.

The report provided conclusive evidence that Hafez had personally trained the team of terrorists responsible for the bombing. Only Hafez could have known the information provided to news media when he took credit for the bombing. He disappeared into the interior of Libya after the bombing. CIA information pinpointed him at a desert location near the town of Sabha, three-hundred miles inland from Tripoli. Jim snapped the papers down and rage returned. He would kill Hafez.

At six that evening, he yelled for Kareem. The absence of an intercom and phones left no option. Kareem took his time and the relationship took a turn from bad to worse. He handed an envelope to Kareem. "Get this list of supplies on order tonight."

Kareem tore open the envelope before Jim could stop him and started reading the contents, frowning and muttering the whole time. He looked up and said, "Why do you want two of everything?"

The little man's attitude angered him. "You don't need to know. Just get it on order. Tonight! Now!"

Kareem's self-importance ran unchecked. "I will tell them we have been all over the farm, that you ask many questions about the boundaries. Maybe too many? He smiled like a tattle-tale kid. He apparently thought the sponsors would object to the requests. "You will not be allowed to make trails for motorcycles. They will never agree to these requests." He waved the envelope.

"Okay. Now listen carefully, Kareem. What I do is none of your damned business. Don't you ever question me again. And," he closed the distance, his face within inches of Kareem's, "Don't you ever open another envelope containing communication between me and whoever they are. You got that!"

Kareem backed away. "I must go," he said. "You will not need a language instructor, however," he pointed to the envelope. "I am sure that is why I am here. I speak all Arabic languages." Kareem, still seething from the rebuke, gritted his teeth openly. Jim had fixed him as an unimportant subordinate and he didn't like it. "Your possessions are upstairs," he said, barely containing his anger. He glared, then to strike back said, "They will shoot you if you try to escape."

"They won't have to. Move all of my stuff into this room, and move a bed in here. Inform the person in charge that the rifles, motorcycles and associated materials must be here no later than noon tomorrow. The other supplies can arrive a day or two later, no more than that. And tell them I want a metal security carrying case with combination locks–good locks."

As Kareem turned to leave, Jim added, "You will meet with me for language study in the sauna at eight-thirty every morning and twelve-thirty every afternoon." After Kareem departed, Jim changed into workout clothes and went directly to the gym and posted a schedule of exercise routines programmed to increase in difficulty at a steady pace for the next seven weeks. He turned the sauna temperature to 115 degrees, humidity valve off, imagining the 115 degrees needed to be dry to simulate the midsummer Libyan environment. He believed there would be no chance to survive without being in great physical condition. He pulled an exercycle into the sauna before leaving the gym, planning to ride the bike during language study every day thereafter.

Kareem is going to hate the sauna.

Jim's daily schedule began each morning at five-thirty. He went directly to the gym for calisthenics and then ran for thirty minutes over a three-mile course that Kareem resentfully helped cut through the woods. The same trail would serve as a motorcycle track later on. His schedule demanded something every minute of the day.

After breakfast, he joined his recalcitrant tutor in the sauna for an hour and a half of language training. Kareem exploded the first time Jim ordered him into the sauna.

"No! I will not!"

"Look, sport, it doesn't make any difference to me who does the teaching, but this is where it's going to happen. I don't have time to sit someplace nice and comfortable to accommodate you. If you can't handle the job, then get out."

At ten-thirty each morning, the silence of the quiet countryside ended with the earsplitting sounds of high-speed motorcycle engines. Motorcycles were familiar friends to Jim. During his son's teen years, they rode practically every weekend. As they departed on Sunday morning rides, his son would say, "Remember, Mom, the family that bleeds together stays together." She hated motorcycles. The love affair with motorcycles provided a pleasant time in his life. His fondness for dirt bikes helped through the five week training period as he pressed himself and the bikes, skidding, jumping and scrambling around the rugged course.

He ordered new gas tanks, each providing a bonus two gallon capacity. According to his calculations, the additional fuel would provide an added forty miles in the desert, still well short of his destination. *Have to figure something out when the time comes.*

Each morning, after riding and cleaning the bikes, he showered and went to the study to rest. His mind wouldn't stop and there wasn't enough time to waste it napping. Lunch came next, then two more hours of language study with Kareem. They only spent the first thirty minutes in the sauna, much to Kareem's relief.

Jim spent from three till six each afternoon in the study, examining maps along the Mediterranean shoreline, Tripoli and Benghazi, eventually covering every open spot on the wall of the study with maps and photos. His benefactor, undoubtedly the CIA, provided up-to-date aerial photographs, infrared imagery and geographical maps. He read the World War Two battles for North Africa several times. Montgomery, Rommel and Patton maneuvered and once fought over the area he planned to use.

*****

He asked for an in-depth personal briefing on Hafez. The briefer, a tiny man wearing a permanent worried expression, arrived one evening and lectured until late the next morning.

"I have been directed not to tell you who I am or where I work," he announced, smiling wistfully. "I hope you don't mind." He seemed surprised when Jim offered his hand and they got off to a friendly start.

Jim said, "The only thing I care about is the information you have on Abdel Hafez."

The briefer beamed proudly. "I know more about Hafez than any man alive. I have been closer to him than his shadow for the past three years. Hafez is the focus of my life."

"Why? Do you mind?"

He wasn't the kind of man who could look you in the eye, always anxious and uncertain, but made himself look directly at Jim. "Abdel Hafez murdered my wife during the embassy bombing in London three years ago. She was there on business. He killed my wife and twenty-three other innocent people. Hafez doesn't care who dies, only that people die to promote his cause. I swore to get even." He glanced up again and said, "And I will."

"Well, then we have something in common."

"Oh? What is your interest?"

Jim almost went too far, but collected himself and said, "That doesn't matter. I would like to know Hafez as well as you do."

He laughed. "That would take years."

"I don't have years. I have less than three weeks. Give me a comprehensive rundown on him. Make it as complete as you can."

The little man smiled, content, a man in his element. "Very well. First and foremost, you should know that Abdel Hafez is a member of the same Berber tribe Muammar Khadafy came from. In fact, they are distant cousins. I suspect you now understand why Libya is protecting Hafez."

Jim nodded. "That helps."

"No, that explains everything. Hafez and his tribesmen are trained from birth to despise all things Western. They are devout Sunni Moslems with a long history of terrorism and violence. Now, and this is important, Hafez fervently believes he is Allah's messenger. His followers also believe he is a prophet. I know that sounds radical, but true nonetheless. I caution you not to permit his fundamentalist persona to distract you. Hafez is extremely intelligent and very crafty. He is a determined man on a religious mission, which makes him even more dangerous."

The lesson continued throughout the night. The little man with a dead wife and a bone to pick helped assemble a probable/possible list of travel that Hafez might pursue. Jim needed to determine a likely time and place to strike.

*****

At six each evening he changed into athletic gear, repeated the morning physical training program, took a quick shower afterward and arrived at the study for more study by eight. He dedicated evening hours during the first two weeks to ballistics, taking time to calculate the exact weight and type bullet necessary for the mission. After selecting the bullet, he compiled powder selections based on bullet weight and target distance, selecting the best powder with painstaking attention, leaving nothing to chance.

The 308 caliber target rifle he chose enjoys a reputation for accuracy and dependability. Many long distance shooters, snipers in particular, favor a 308 capped with a superior target scope. The bullet he selected for the mission would explode on contact, not because of any explosive charge, but rather because it would be traveling at such high speed. His calculations called for less than a second to travel from the firing position he selected to the target, a quarter-of-a-mile distant.

He fell into bed too fatigued, sore and nervous to sleep at ten each night. Two weeks passed before his body toughened and adapted to the rigors of the schedule and he was able to get by without using sleep aids. Jim lost fifteen pounds during the first two weeks. The weight came off involuntarily. He looked skinny, almost emaciated, but felt more energetic than he had in years.

Jim's light complexion presented a problem. His sponsors provided two bottles of a suntan mixture containing CANTHAXANTHIN. He also ordered dye for the beard he began growing the first day. Fifteen days after beginning heavy doses of the pigment-stimulating chemical, his skin deepened to a shade dark enough to preclude use of cosmetics for the mission. He became dusky enough to pass as a Mediterranean native.

He was directed to choose an identity for the mission from passport copies of three American oil company employees, men who flew in and out of Libya regularly. He found it odd that anyone representing American interests could still be working in Libya, but discovered that the Libyan government is tolerant of oil experts, even though our government maintains minimal diplomatic ties. He selected the passport of a dark-skinned, forty-year-old man with a mustache and beard, feeling confident that he could eventually simulate the man's appearance, particularly since the candidates were already pre-selected for likeness. The man he planned to impersonate was a Libyan-American technical advisor. Even though getting into the country promised to be much easier than getting out, Jim wasn't confident about getting in. He didn't have talent for languages. His greying hair also needed coloring to match the passport photo. After testing several dyes, he chose one that turned his hair a dusky black. His new beard and mustache grew rapidly.

Ten days into training, Kareem reminded him that twenty-four hours remained in which to produce a plan in writing. He met the deadline and sent Kareem to tell his sponsor. A man with credentials arrived the following day. The plan called for departure on the tenth day of August. At that time, fifty-one of the sixty days allotted for the mission would have elapsed. The plan included prepositioning the motorcycle, rifle, and a small van secreted in Benghazi Libya, the van loaded with the motorcycle and escape supplies. Most importantly, a specific room in a specific high-rise apartment building in Benghazi.

The identification papers and passport arrived, featuring Jim as Ahmed Hazam, a Libyan-American petroleum technician.

Chapter Ten

CHARLIE COLLINS

Charlie Collins was a third term senator when Leslie came to Washington–third term and well positioned on the senate power ladder. Washington watchers knew him as a stuffy little man with an extremely high opinion of himself. Most of the legislators he worked with considered him a royal pain in the ass. Collins also had the reputation of pestering women–a notorious toucher. Charlie probably never made it to first base with any A-Team woman, but that didn't keep him from trying. He combed his silver hair in an Elvis pomp, wore a corset and faced the world with a listless, contrived smile. Charlie could not suppress a nervous laugh around a long list of people he considered his betters.

Thirty five days after retired Marine Lieutenant Colonel Colby began training as an assassin, Charlie Collins stumbled, quite by accident, onto evidence of the CIA/FBI super-secret assassination operation. More accurately, a member of Charlie's staff did. An ambitious young aide discovered discrepancies in expenditure figures of the CIA's accounting division. Solid evidence indicating that the agency had been spending considerably more money than Congress allocated for secret operations. He also found signs of possible money laundering. The CIA had undoubtedly obtained funds from an unknown, unauthorized source and transferred the money internally to bolster a congressionally authorized account. He speculated that the agency was using money seized while assisting sister agencies, probably the DEA, with overseas drug busts. After a cursory investigation, the staffer reported his findings to Charlie, additionally revealing the probability of an illegal internal slush fund.

Charlie didn't take the young man seriously. "Hell, that's nothing, Ray. Forget it. We have to give the spooks some elbow room to operate, don't we?" He winked and smiled slyly, his way of letting the young man know that Charlie Collins knew secrets. Institutional looking-the-other-way is not unusual for some powerful congressmen. Charlie's abnormal behavior surprised the hard-charging staff member. Ray had been certain the senator would not voluntarily miss an opportunity to expose the abuse of public funds. Charlie had the well-earned reputation of being inflexible, particularly when he perceived any opportunity to see his name in the news.

Collins won his first term by a landslide, but barely squeaked by the second time around. His political advisers recommended an emergency infusion of media exposure to insure better voter recognition for the third election. Charlie took the advice seriously. He needed a gimmick, something to make headlines, something to appeal to folks back home. He found it with a strategy of watching over the common folks' tax dollar.

Charlie begged an appointment to the powerful Budget and Finance Committee, a sure way to discover where the government's operating money originates and where it is supposed to go. He hired a staff of young, dedicated lawyer/accountants and unleashed them on government agencies with his congressional authority. In short order, Charlie Collins uncovered and exposed several significant cases of bureaucratic fiscal mismanagement, garnering some headline making, senate seat-saving news. He loved the limelight. Charlie Collins, the working man's champion. His determined troops vigorously traced every wayward dollar wasted or misspent by the government. He exposed, disclosed, revealed, tracked down, smelled out and reported fiscal discrepancies with gleeful dedication. Reelection assured.

"Excuse me for pressing the issue, Sir," the aide persisted. "But I don't think we can afford to look the other way on this."

The senator didn't look up from paperwork. "Really? And just why is that, Ray?"

"This mystery fund could get to the media, Senator, and if it slips out...well, we could end up looking pretty bad. We are involved, Sir, because we have knowledge."

Charlie looked up, squirmed uncomfortably and frowned. "Damn, Ray! Have you opened a can of worms and backed me into a corner?" He sat back and took a deep breath. "Okay, what the hell is going on? Let me hear it again. You don't have a bone on for someone over there, do you, Ray?"

"No, Sir. I don't usually have any problems with those people, but they are deliberately stonewalling my investigation this time."

Charlie sighed, cleared his desk, and said, "Okay, let me see what you have."

He scanned the report, still not convinced the list of discrepancies constituted a major inconsistency–nothing he could sink his teeth into. He ridiculed the aide's suspicions of drug money laundering and nonchalantly assigned the agency's excess finances to an unconventional, not-so-secret fund that he already knew about, a fund commonly sanctioned by Congress, if only by indifference.

"Oh, hell. It's nothing, Ray. Congress traditionally allows the spooks considerable latitude concerning that damned fund. We have to let them have a few little secrets, don't we? What would a CIA be without secrets? Let it go. Don't be that picky." He slid the report across the desk toward the puzzled assistant.

"I appreciate what you are saying, Sir, but I really don't think you can afford to ignore this much money." He tapped the folder. "This is a lot of money, Sir. I think this amount of unauthorized money is dangerous–particularly for you."

"Well, let's don't start worrying about it too soon, Ray. We can always expose it if the damned thing starts to generate any media interest, can't we?"

Charlie Collins and his contemporaries belonged to the congress that failed to anticipate international drug expansion, the same congress that ignored opportunities that flourishing drug traffic provided to law enforcement and intelligence agencies that could secure enough money to fund significant operations without congressional knowledge. Charlie couldn't convince the worried aide that he had discovered nothing more than a not so secret fund.

"The idea of a slush fund, even one this large, does not disturb me, Senator. What does bother me is that no one over there will cooperate. They clamp down tight when I ask questions. Nobody will admit anything. I don't think they are ignoring me, Sir. I think they are scared. If it's such a well-known and recognized fund, Senator, then why are they stonewalling? I smell something wrong here. They have never been this evasive."

The slush fund didn't upset Charlie. He could easily get to the bottom of that if need be, but the aide's report of evasiveness irritated him. The determined aide finally had the senator's attention.

"Did you talk to the Operations Director about this, Ray? Does Adrian Burt know you are having difficulty?"

"I have not, Sir. He won't see me. I cannot get an appointment with Burt. I think something big is going on over there, Senator. Even if the fund is a recognized channel, I really don't think you can look the other way this time, not when we are implicated by association now that we know that we are dealing with millions. Millions, and all unauthorized. We would definitely be implicated if this were to surface, Sir."

"You say Burt won't see you?"

"No, Sir. I can't even get him to stop in the hall."

Charlie swelled. "Well, no pissant agency guy is going to dodge my authority! How long have you been trying to get with him?"

"Nearly two weeks, Senator."

"Two weeks? Hell! They ought to know better than that. Has Burt been on vacation or something?"

"No, Sir. I see him around almost every day. He just won't make time. He is deliberately dodging me."

Collins nodded and pursed his mouth grimly. "Okay, you let me handle this, Ray. I'll call Burt's boss, and then by damn we'll get to the bottom of this business real damned quick. But first, tell me again where you think the money is coming from."

"Well, Sir, I'm pretty sure it's laundered drug money. Lots of it."

Charlie frowned. "Jesus! Drug money? Do you have a feeling for how much?"

"Not precisely. Well up in the millions, though."

"Millions? Damn them! Well, I guess we better look into it then. Who is running that damned mystery fund over there?"

"Operations, Sir. Adrian Burt."

Charlie scanned the open folder again. "You better be sure of this, Ray. I don't want to go off half- cocked and get swallowed up like a fart in the wind."

"I am certain, Senator. There is some guesswork involved in the source, I will admit that, but they are way off on the audit. What they are doing smells a lot like the Iran/Contra affair. Well, maybe not that big. Not yet. I am not sure where the money is coming from but my bet is, and what I hear is, they are hoarding money from overseas drug busts."

"The CIA is into drugs? These are serious accusations, Ray. You better be damned sure."

"Well, Sir, that's not exactly what I meant. I don't know that they are into it in any operational way. Maybe they just aren't turning over captured money. It's probably something like that." The aide began to waffle under the senator's probing.

"Okay, one more time, Ray. Are you sure they are playing with unauthorized money?"

"Absolutely sure about that, Sir." He placed a finger on the paperwork. "Here are the figures. They don't come close to matching what congress authorized, as you can see."

"This is no place for mistakes, Ray. I have to have a definitive answer."

"Yes, Sir. I am sure."

Charlie sat back. He knew the young man's reputation for accuracy. "Well I'll be damned. I'll be double D damned. Wouldn't you think those sons of bitches would learn? Wouldn't you think? Well, okay, Ray. I will get to the bottom of this for you."

Senator Collins didn't get to the bottom of anything, but he did get a speedy lunch with CIA Director, Ed Bagley. Their food cooled and spoiled during a bitter verbal exchange and eventual stalemate. Collins stubbornly refused to let Ed sidetrack or humor him away from the issue. "You are avoiding me, Ed. What's the big secret? If the fund is for something super sensitive secret, just say so."

"You know that already, Charlie."

"Look, Ed, we have done business before. We go way back. I know the damned ground rules. I back off if this is sensitive national security stuff, you know that. But I have to decide that for myself. If you won't tell me...well, I'll convene a damned investigation and announce it to the press. I will, Ed. You know I will." He sat back. "All right then, your ball."

Ed's face turned mottled crimson. He leaned across the table and growled, "Okay, Charlie, this goddamned investigation of yours has gone too far. You are meddling in something that is more than sensitive–it is dangerous. That's all I can tell you, except you need to call the dogs off, Charlie, and I mean right now. I wish I could talk to you about it, but I can't. I will say this though–what we are doing is a matter of national security. Highly classified stuff, Charlie. Access only to those with a need to know. Trust me on this and lay off."

"Why won't you tell me? You know I'm trustworthy. Have I ever leaked? When did I ever abuse secret information? I don't pretend to understand this, Ed. We've always talked before. You also know you have to stay clean with me on budget matters. Now, what in the hell is going on? It can't be much. You cannot rat hole enough money to support anything big."

Ed stood up angrily, face flushed, fist knotted. "If it isn't much, then for Christ's sake let it go, Charlie!"

Charlie's eyes closed to slits. "That your final word?"

"Absolute and final!" He threw a twenty on the table and stomped out, leaving Charlie stewing.

Collins disclosed the details of his meeting to several of his trusted staff members and planned a counterstroke. He fumed about the rejection all that afternoon, and then dove in over his head and held a press conference. He announced to a group of clamoring reporters the possibility of an illegal CIA fund and publicly appointed an investigator. Afterward, he invited Ray and two other staffers to his office, provided drinks and sat back glibly to wait for the frantic call he knew would be coming from the CIA. "By God, Charlie Collins knows how to play hardball," he told his audience. "I bet you a week's pay the bastards will call me within thirty minutes."

The call came, as Charlie knew it would, just not from the CIA.

*****

Senator Collins didn't get invited to the Oval Office often. He and President Denning frequently took opposite sides on money squabbles, at least that's what Charlie believed. The true reason for the rift between them was that President Denning thought Charlie was a weeny and said so publicly. He detested Charlie. Denning never freely associated with Charlie Collins under any circumstance.

Denning phoned Charlie personally, inviting him to the Oval Office. Wesley handled the call with unusual cordiality–urgent, but cordial, without giving a reason for the visit. Charlie knew it had something to do with his press conference.

He turned to Ray with a satisfied smile. "Hey, we must have struck a pretty sensitive nerve. The big boy wants to see me. You are damned sure on to something, Ray."

When Charlie arrived, he found the President waiting, along with four other men. The National Security Adviser, the FBI director, who refused to shake Charlie's hand (Charlie had exposed him one time too many in the past), the CIA Director and CIA Operations.

"Come on in, Charlie!" Wesley hailed. "Nice to see you, hoss! By damn, you look pretty good for an old fart." Wesley shook Charlie's hand energetically and motioned toward a chair. "Have a seat, my man. I won't keep you long, but we need to talk."

Charlie, and every other player on the Washington scene, understood all too well the great man's ability to manipulate people, controlling the outcome of issues before anyone discovered his intent. He also recognized an unusual edginess in Wesley's voice. He noted that the other participants seemed ill-disposed.

The President was clearly disturbed, despite his show of friendliness. Denning sat on the edge of a chair opposite Charlie and leaned over the coffee table, intimately closer. His facial expression quickly lost genial warmth. When he spoke, his voice carried an uncharacteristic edge, almost a tremor. "Let's talk about your press conference tonight, Senator. Damn, man, I wish we could have talked before you said anything to the press. Ed here briefed me about your investigation." He took a breath and then, face contorted in anger, shouted, "I know about that damned money! I personally approved the expenditure. As far as I'm concerned, there is nothing more to be said about it, Senator! And for your information, nothing more *will* be said!" He stared Charlie down.

Denning then sat back and smiled, ostensibly dismissing the

tirade as unimportant. "You don't have to call off the investigation if you don't want to, Senator, but if you persist, it will eventually get back to me and I will have to admit authorizing the fund. And then, Senator, I'll be forced to invoke executive prerogative due to national security interests. That, of course, will effectively end your little investigation. The public doesn't like this sort of thing, Charlie. You know that, and I goddamned sure don't like it. If I am forced to bury this damned investigation of yours, I will, and that would end up hurting you, me, and the party. This damned investigation of yours isn't going to prove anything or do any of us any good, Senator. I want you to call it off." He changed tactics again and smiled warmly. "I realize you don't know the details, and, believe me, you better leave it that way. You are hurting me, Charlie."

Charlie weathered the storm without flinching. "You know about the money?"

"Of course I do. I authorized it." He leaned forward again and stared directly into Charlie's eyes. "I will deny knowledge if pressed, Senator." He aped Charlie's insipid smile.

"And you plan to keep it from Congress?"

"I do. This business is on very close hold, a critical national security matter, Senator. That's all any investigation will ever prove. If you push me, all you can do is muddy the water and make my job difficult, but it won't prove one damned thing I can promise you that much. Now, I am asking this as a friend. Leave it alone, Senator. Now, I'm going to say one more thing, and I want you to listen carefully, Charlie. This is damned serious business and you really do not want to jump in the boat with me on this one."

Charlie wasn't ignorant. He was out of options. He also had enough political acumen to extract himself from bad situations advantageously. Quid Pro Quo. He could get a marker for something he wanted later. "Very well. I will handle it, Mister President. But, if I call off the investigation too quickly without a decent explanation, the media people are going to ask questions. I propose to let the investigation die a natural death from lack of interest, if you know what I mean."

Denning stood and smiled pleasantly. His external demeanor transformed like a chameleon. "I knew I could count on you,

Charlie. I owe you. You just made my life much easier and that means a lot. You can feel free to call on me any time, for anything. I owe you a big one, Charlie."

*****

The next morning, Leslie Reardon asked for a meeting with Senator Collins to give him an ultimatum about work assignments. Charlie barely glanced up as she entered the office.

"What can I do for you today, Miss Leslie?"

"I hate to bother you, Senator, but there seems to be no other way." She fidgeted, waiting for his attention.

"What is it, Les? You know you don't have to mince around with me. Come on, out with it." He looked up and gave her the antiseptic smirk she hated so much, the smirk that told everyone he only pretended to care.

"I am sorry to bother you, Senator, and I hate to ask for anything. You have been wonderful to me and I am indebted to you for so much."

Charlie thought he recognized a signal of submission and reclined to enjoy the moment, hands locked behind his head. "Come on, Leslie. Out with it! Ask anything you like. Try me."

She despised him for being so damned patronizing. She lied. "I have thoroughly enjoyed my assignments here, Senator, but I am not satisfied that I have achieved anything worthwhile recently. I am asking for more challenging work."

She watched him uneasily, searching for signs of anger. Charlie had a notorious reputation for being a tyrant. He didn't appear at all disturbed, which made her wonder if he even heard what she said. He sat there, a self- satisfied smile spreading slowly. She felt like waving a hand in front of his eyes to get his attention. He looked so smug, smiling his "I-know-something-you-don't-know" smile.

"That's it, Leslie? That's all? You should have said something earlier. Well, bless my soul. I thought everything was okay. I'm sorry. It's my fault for being so damned insensitive. This concern of yours didn't come up overnight, did it? Well, of course not. I'm glad you have the courage to say something." He rocked forward and said, "Let me think about it, honey, okay? I'll get back to you no later than this very afternoon."

Charlie already knew what he would do with her. That afternoon, she received the assignment of examining CIA files for suspected misappropriation of funds. When he called her back and announced the assignment, she experienced excitement about her job for the first time in weeks. The responsibility for such a sensitive appointment surprised her. Senator Collins had replaced one of his favorite boy wonders in her favor. The thrill soon subsided as she discovered just how little information she had to launch an investigation with.

*****

"There has to be more than this." She slammed a thin folder on Boy Wonder's desk and complained. "Come on, Ray, the senator had more than this to say at the press conference yesterday. So, where is it?"

Ray's sneering smile demonstrated how much he enjoyed her frustration "I am following instructions. That's everything there is, lady. Take it or leave it."

The folder contained nothing more than a few scribbled notes. Ray's relaxed behavior and mocking smile looked rehearsed to her, like he was in on a joke and the joke was on her. He said, "I take it you and Charlie are getting along a little better? How cozy."

"Think what you like, friend," she responded. "The bottom line still says you are off the case. Thanks for nothing, Ray."

She snatched the folder from his desk and slammed the door on her way out. Later, Leslie pieced together a skimpy plan of action based on what little information she possessed, along with some wishful thinking. She didn't believe Ray. *There has to more. The investigation made national news only yesterday. I have to find out what kicked this whole thing off and start from scratch.*

She stepped into the hall and locked her office well after midnight and leaned against the door with her eyes closed, suffering a sobering moment. *Charlie is playing a game and I am nothing but a tool.*

Chapter Eleven

THE MISSION

Jim selected Benghazi as the primary target area–more precisely the Al Jamahiriyah Military Barracks. Hafez often used the barracks as a second home. The Revolutionary Guard, a paramilitary organization and Libya's version of the Gestapo, met at the barracks every year on August fifteenth to celebrate their anniversary. Hafez wouldn't miss the party as he is an honored member of the Guard. Jim reviewed Libyan newspaper articles and photographs of the celebration for the past seven years. Hafez always attended, customarily serving as the featured speaker.

Jim collected every available scrap of information on Hafez. The expert who briefed him would have been hard pressed to know more. Hafez's rise to prominence in the world of terrorism began just as hatred of everything American raged at a high pitch in the Mideast. The average Arab thought of Hafez as an Arabian Robin Hood well before Americans knew anything about him. Hafez avoided capture and death on several occasions, alerted by governments America generally considered friendly to the West. He directed a tight ring of loyal followers, none of whom he trusted.

Hafez submerged after the Rome crash, to a desert compound he believed to be secret. Jim received photos of the camp that would have stunned Hafez: two blonde women running around topless; Hafez naked urinating behind a tent, and other equally revealing shots. American intelligence knew when Hafez arrived and departed, but didn't always know where he would venture next. He never announced travel plans and his public appearances were not advertised.

Jim selected a high rise apartment building in Benghazi, just over four hundred yards from the entrance to the barracks. Room confirmation arrived the next day. That's when he knew that his sponsor were not incompetent. Everything happened at once.

He requested a current telephoto image of the barracks entrance from the window of the mission room. The next day an eight by ten glossy provided all the evidence he needed to feel comfortable with the field of fire. The distance from his firing position to the front gate of the barracks measured 420 yards. Jim rigged a practice platform sixty feet up in a tree at the compound, placed a man-sized target at 420 yards, and trained for a week before packing the mission rifle. The rifle and motorcycle needed to be smuggled into the country well ahead of time. After carefully packing the equipment, he turned the crates over to Kareem. Jim didn't know how "they" would transport the equipment into Libya, but was convinced they could and would.

He ordered a windowless van large enough to carry the mission motorcycle and supplies. The van had to be parked in a locked garage on the eastern outskirts of Benghazi within two blocks of an area he stipulated. The van and motorcycle had nothing to do with successful completion of the mission, but everything to do with his survival. He ordered a two-day supply of survival food and water placed in the van, along with a loaded nine millimeter automatic pistol.

The final two weeks of training included accelerated language study. He never did get the hang of it. Kareem bitched as time in the sauna increased. Kareem once told him, "You work like a man of twenty. What is your age?"

"Closing in on fifty."

Kareem looked astonished. "For such age, you have done well, other than your Arabic is not acceptable. Do you expect to fool anyone?"

"Not really. Let's concentrate on the words and phrases necessary to get by customs. That should be good enough, don't you think?"

Kareem shrugged. "Possible. Perhaps they don't stop you for questions. If they ask…." He shrugged. "If I knew more about the mission I could be more sure. I cannot know how to help with such small information." Kareem tried devious methods on several occasions to learn about the mission. Jim remained cautious about what he said and kept all information locked. The two men learned to get along well enough by the end of training. Once, while Jim cooled after a session in the sauna, Kareem sat beside him and asked about family.

Jim growled, "Forget about me, Kareem. You don't need to know, and for damned sure it is none of your business."

Kareem accepted the rebuke without complaining. "You are not someone I forget. No, I will not forget."

Jim let it go even though he thought the words sounded like a threat. "You need to call your boss today, Kareem. Tell him the paperwork they promised must be here soon. Nothing will happen until those papers are in my hands. They know what I mean."

Kareem brought a locked briefcase the next day. The case contained fifteen-thousand in cash and identification papers Jim would need after the mission. He retreated to the study and pored over the paperwork, learning about his new identity.

TEN AUGUST

He awoke thinking, Finally, training finished and equipment in place. Nothing left to do. He napped off and on through the day and strolled around the farm attempting to relax and recover. Late that afternoon Kareem located him and said, "You must come. There is visitor."

"Who?"

"I have no knowledge."

"How many?"

"Many men. You come now."

Here we go.

Two burly men in suits intercepted them on the way. One beckoned to Jim, the other led Kareem toward the barn.

Jim wasn't worried and smiled at the suit, "So, what's up, partner?"

The spick-and-span man in the just-right suit just smiled and motioned for Jim to follow. He led directly to the study, held the door open and said, "Leave the light off. Off."

Jim stepped in and the door closed. The room was dim, just a faint glow of sunlight seeping through a half open blind on one window.

"Over here please, Colonel Colby."

Jim turned toward the voice and noticed the top of someone's head above a swivel chair behind the desk.

The chair spun. "Step closer, please."

Jim could not make out the man's features.

"I suppose you know who I am?"

Jim stepped closer and observed for a moment, not quite sure, then stammered, "Yes Sir, Mister President."

"Good. Are they treating you well?"

"Are they.... Oh, yes, Sir."

"Do you need anything? Anything at all?"

"No, Sir."

"I was sorry to learn about your family, Colonel."

"Thank you, Sir."

President Denning stood and offered his hand. "Well, looks like the two of us are off on a great adventure. I know all about your mission. I ordered it. I wanted to see you off today and wish you Godspeed and let you know the country is solidly behind your effort, and to tell you personally how important what you are doing is. We are going to stop terrorism, Colonel, just us–the two of us– you and me for now, but many more soon. I want you to come see me when you get back. I plan to take care of you in every way. Give this mission your best. There are many things you don't need to know to be successful, but there is one thing you do need to know. I have intelligence information that leads me to believe that all the terrorist organizations in the Mideast are forming another damned alliance. This new coalition is not part of any particular country, which is going to increase our terrorist problem. Your target is the man behind all of it–just so you know. Now, I know you have your own reason to conduct this mission, and I know it's valid, but I am here to encourage you to put emotions aside, Colonel. Do this duty for your country and mankind. This is the most important thing you will ever do. Are you with me?"

Later, Jim couldn't remember what he said. They shook hands.

"I have things to do, Colonel, and I know you are on a tight schedule. Good luck."

Denning departed through a side door. Jim stood in the

shadowy room alone, feeling much better. *So, I'm the big doggy's personal assassin. No one would ever believe that and I doubt he will worry much about me telling anyone. Who would believe it?*

Shortly after the president departed, a guard gave Jim a cell phone. He immediately checked his bank accounts and found them in order, the promised money deposited in his name and account number. Kareem drove him to Dulles airport where they met three men he recognized from the New York City parking garage. "Nice to see you fellows again," he said, with more than a hint of sarcasm. No one smiled. Two of the three led him a short distance away after ordering Kareem to remain in the car with the third man. One gave Jim a briefcase and a sealed envelope containing flight schedules and tickets. The other produced a small leather pouch containing keys to an apartment in Benghazi, keys to the garage and van, and most importantly, the key to a hotel room in Tunis, the capitol of Tunisia, his destination after the mission, provided he managed to get that far.

Jim inventoried the contents, studied the itinerary and tickets, counted the promised $15.000, then placed everything in the briefcase and hung the keys around his neck on a sturdy necklace provided for the occasion.

One of the guards whistled and Kareem came forward with a bolt cutter to sever the tracking bracelet. After waving Kareem away, the oldest agent, worried and sweating, whispered instructions. "You are on your own now. If you are caught there will be no assistance from our organization. You will go from here directly into the terminal and place the briefcase with your future identity in a rented lockbox. Place the lockbox key on your necklace. After that, you will become a man without a country. If your mission is successful, additional airline tickets and instructions will be in that hotel room in Tunis." He pointed to the longest key on the necklace.

"You are never, under any circumstance, to reveal information about this mission to anyone. Such disclosure would be considered a critical security violation and we would be forced to react accordingly. Good luck." He stepped back, sighed deeply and said, "That's it. I'll be on my way."

The man sitting in the car with Kareem waved at his associates and drove away. Jim walked into the airport lobby with the other two following closely, making no attempt to be discreet. He assumed there would be more agents scattered around the airport monitoring his progress. A quick check of a clock revealed only thirty minutes until flight time–already late for passenger check in. He suspected they left so little time deliberately, knowing he still needed to store the money and identification papers and they wanted to know where.

He suddenly slowed, then sped up, then slowed again, deliberately shortening the distance between himself and the younger guy following, then whirled and buried his fist in the man's stomach. The poor devil folded and collapsed, gasping for air as Jim sprinted for the main entrance. The older guard didn't try to keep up. Crowd noise rose noticeably. He didn't look back.

Jim dove into the first available cab, handed the cabby a hundred dollar bill and spurred him to get out of there in a hurry. Two miles from the airport, he flashed another hundred and said, "You can have this, buddy, right now, if you cross the median and take me back to the airport. No speeding from here on."

The cabby didn't hesitate, snatched the bill and swerved across the grass median and headed back. Jim entered the lobby through a different door, placed the briefcase in a locker after paying the girl at the desk for a month in advance, adding that key to his necklace. He had never entertained the notion of attempting an escape. He was going to see about killing the man who killed his son. When he showed up at the flight waiting area, he noticed two agitated men whispering into cell phones and casually tapped one on the shoulder, smiled and said, "Nice day, isn't it?"

After an almost comical double-take, one man held Jim by the elbow as his partner trotted over. Jim looked at his sweating captor and with a wry smile said, "I think you can let go now, sport. I'm not going anywhere."

The nervous man released the hold. Jim identified four more sweating, deep-breathing, wide-eyed men, arrayed in a semi-circle around him.

His activities from then on consisted of the routine nuisances of modern commercial airline travel. He thought security officials paid more attention to him than the other passengers, which made him feel good about fitting the profile he needed to imitate. They took him aside at Dulles and again at the Heathrow to body search and question him before boarding, asking trivial questions about his business and destination. Their extraordinary precautions gave him added confidence that he might go undetected upon arrival in Libya. He resembled an individual western security officials are trained to look for.

Jim stowed his overnight bag and took his assigned seat in first class, comfortably located next to a window. A very attractive olive-skinned woman wearing what he considered to be Muslim apparel soon took the seat next. He groaned inwardly. The prospect of sitting beside a foreigner for the coming flight didn't hold much promise for conversation. She stowed her things, then turned to him, smiled warmly and said in perfect English, "Hello. My name is Dianne. I hope we have a pleasant trip." To his surprise, she offered her hand.

Shortly after takeoff, after a few words of friendly conversation, she casually placed her passport on his lap. He glanced down, then to her.

"Open please. Read."

What he read sent alert signals to every cell in his body. Dianne Hazam.

"That's right," she said, observing his surprise. "Your wife." She retrieved the passport, patted him on the thigh and with an amused smile said, "That condition will be temporary of course. I understand you didn't do extremely well in language study, correct? I am to travel with you to Benghazi and help with customs along the way if necessary. I don't know who you are or what you are doing, and I have been told not to ask. Here is my telephone number in Benghazi. I will be there for one week. My job is to assist in any way, but only at your request. Questions?"

It took him a moment to recover from the initial shock. He felt foolish for being surprised. *I should have known. They aren't going to let me flounder around alone.*

"Nope. No questions, Dianne. Nice outfit."

"Good. I am going to teach you a code just in case we ever need to speak secretly. From this point on, any number we use will be decoded by a base number. That number is two. If I say 'Base plus four,' you mentally add two to get the real number. For instance, look at the phone number I gave you." She motioned to the slip of paper on his lap.

He picked it up.

She said, "Now, read it to me using code."

He didn't need to meditate. He had used similar procedures in the Corps. He said, "Base plus two. Okay, that would be 458-7754."

"Correct. If you choose to go down instead of up, just say base minus and then the number. All you have to remember is the base number for your mission is two. Now, do you play chess?"

"Some. Not well."

They played throughout the flight. He lost every set. She refused to answer questions about herself or the organization. They had a three hour layover in Athens. After breakfast, he left her sitting in a waiting room and drifted around the terminal, identifying at least three men who seemed way too interested in his progress, always somewhere nearby. Their presence came as no surprise–not after the Dianne experience. He would have been amazed if they weren't there. He sauntered out the front door twice, stretching and yawning, then jumped into a cab and headed downtown. Once satisfied the security elements couldn't possibly have followed, he directed the cabby to a cross-country bus station, checked schedules, threw his carryon bag into a rented locker and returned to the airport an hour before flight time, feeling much better about the prospects of his future. They were waiting, at least three visibly exasperated men, probably professionally embarrassed. Dianne chided him, whispering, "Really, you are creating more trouble than necessary, don't you think?"

"Perhaps, but I have my own agenda. Let it go at that."

ELEVEN AUGUST

She demanded that they speak Arabic until the airliner landed in Benghazi, even attempting to engage in witty banter. By then he knew enough about his impoverished command of Arabic to keep his mouth shut if at all possible. They had to wait in line for a customs' inspection. After watching the line in front of them for several minutes, he commented to Dianne, "The customs agents are inconsistent, aren't they? They jump all over one guy and barely notice the next."

She said, "Your concern is not warranted. What they do is

child's play–just for show. They have no reason to be cautious. Libya has no history of internal terrorism. Why should they bother with security? Don't worry. Act natural. I will divert his attention if necessary."

Jim wanted to tell her that what he planned to do would probably drastically change their attitude about internal terrorism. When his turn arrived, he nodded and grunted as the customs official listlessly regurgitated a list of memorized questions. The agent wasn't looking at him, too busy ogling Dianne, her enticing smile and flirting eyes. Her little drama worked like a charm. The agent didn't search him and barely glanced at the passport, passing him through with an unconcerned wave, greeting Dianne with a leering smile. As soon as Jim found his luggage, a small overnight bag holding nothing but a change of clothes and toilet articles, he left the terminal. Dianne was history as far as he was concerned. He had not asked for her and didn't want her involved in the mission. She was one of them.

He had to restrain himself from looking back as he stepped onto the scorching, sunlit sidewalk outside the terminal. *Slow down. Take your time. Make absolutely certain no one is following.*

Perspiration seeped through his shirt, down his face, even down his legs. The temperature was well over one hundred degrees. The long weeks of sweating in the sauna helped as he walked to the street corner and sat at a bus stop, waiting until at least six buses passed before sighting one almost empty. He didn't care where it was going and bolted from the bench to squeeze into the bus just as the driver closed the doors. Sitting in the rear for an entire circuit gave him plenty of time to concentrate on following traffic. He didn't see anything suspicious but knew the people who sponsored him didn't have to follow; they knew exactly where he was going and probably had tracking devices embedded in his bag. He wasn't worried about them.

He took a cab to the downtown district and found a motorcycle shop. Weeks of study paid great dividends. He knew Benghazi as well as any city in America and rented a bike after engaging in the customary haggling. Kareem had cautioned him, "Merchants in Arab countries will not respect you if you fail to bargain well." Kareem would have been pleased. He rented the bike for one week at half price. Jim felt a rush of relief and gained confidence. The motorcycle would negotiate narrow streets and alleys. No automobile could follow him to the apartment.

The room overlooking the target area looked and felt exactly how he imagined it would: very small, drab, hot and musty. He didn't bother searching for microscopic cameras or sound sensors, but would later. Jim saw the rifle crate the moment the door popped closed and stepped directly to the window to identify the barracks compound. He squinted across an almost empty park-like square, through rising columns of afternoon heat vapors before locating a clutch of squat military buildings surrounded by a fifteen foot high brick wall. He could read the Arabic inscription over the entry arch. The proximity of soldiers and the mental image from study and photographs during training told him all he needed to know. He could see at least fifty yards of sidewalk in front of the barracks entrance from his vantage point and breathed a sigh of relief. The setting couldn't have been selected more perfectly.

He opened the rifle box, just to make sure, then left the apartment and rode the bike to the garage on the eastern outskirts of the city. Sixteen minutes. Minutes that would probably seem like forever when and if the time came. The van and motorcycle were there, as promised. He inspected and started the vehicles, then inventoried the escape supplies before returning to the apartment. Later that evening he timed himself over the possible escape routes within the apartment. His eventual departure would probably be under duress, almost certainly linked to the element of time, and not much time. He stood at the window overlooking the barracks, fired an imaginary shot, checked his watch and walked leisurely down the stairs and rechecked the time on the sidewalk near the motorcycle. The interior fire escape stairs at the end of the hall provided the quickest way out. He ran through the entire escape routine again, beginning with a make-believe shot, ending at the garage on the outskirts of town. Seventeen minutes.

Jim returned to the apartment and examined the rifle. He wouldn't be able to sleep until he knew for sure the rifle had come through in perfect condition. Everything depended on the rifle. The wooden crate looked undamaged–no dents or scratches. He had lined the box with thick sponge rubber and suspended the weapon inside on firm bungee cords to prevent it from touching anything. Threads tied loosely from the gun to the sides of the box were intact. If any threads were broken, there would be good reason to worry about the scope being knocked out of line. He removed the ten cartridges from the crate, all hand loaded to his exacting specifications.

After dark, he sighted through the scope for several minutes, tracking pedestrians in front of the barracks entrance, tripping the trigger a dozen times to experience the feel again. He had never felt more confident about anything than his ability to score a direct hit from the distance across the square. He placed the rifle under the bed and settled back to listen. Benghazi night noises sounded pretty much like those of any large city. Visions of capture, torture, failure, all took a turns as the focal point of his thoughts, aggravating his peace of mind. The thing bothering most, the one he couldn't seem to get out of his thoughts, was how unreal everything seemed: the rifle; being in Benghazi; the mission; his unruffled composure. He could have been watching a movie.

He stood at the window most of the night thinking the next day might bring some sense of reality. The night drifted by as he volleyed from bed to window. The light of morning would come far too late to suit him even though he knew the next day could only be worse. *Relax. Tomorrow will be here soon enough.* He tried, but found himself back at the window staring at the barrack's entrance.

TWELVE AUGUST

The sun rose with Jim still at the window trying to imagine what the scene below would look like when the time came. After daylight, with a vivid mental picture of the barracks entrance imprinted on his mind, he closed his eyes and tried to visualize the mission. After at least thirty mental run-throughs, he slept and awoke at noon in a pool of sweat. He dashed water on his face and left the apartment to buy a copy of the Libyan national newspaper EL FATEH. *What a joke. Me reading Arabic.* His limited reading skill relegated the exercise to nothing more than keying on particular words and pictures. He didn't learn anything, which wasn't disappointing, since he didn't think Hafez would advertise. He thought about calling Dianne but didn't trust her or the people she worked with.

He returned to the apartment and ran in place, usually his absolute last resort, but public jogging in Libya was out of the question. Jogging in the August heat, or at any other time in Libya is not normal. He figured there were good reasons why Libyans don't win Olympic track and field medals, but felt pretty sure extreme temperatures was the big one.

He bathed and left the room to look for clothes that might resemble the somewhat haphazard regalia worn by members of the Revolutionary Guard. Once on the street, he found vendors a veritable wellspring of paraphernalia. He mingled with the crowds, listening to vendors noisily hawking deliberately overpriced but negotiable wares. Each stall featured a noisy proprietor waving products at prospective buyers. Jim's shopping spree took the best part of two hours. He eventually gathered a tolerably authentic, semi military uniform to wear, a pair of black running shoes and a belt. He didn't trust anyone and had long since decided to assume his benefactors had sensors in everything he owned and felt sure they were listening to and watching every breath he took. The drab collection left something to be desired in quality and color, but favored close enough the uniform worn by the ever present Revolutionary Guards. He figured the outfit, regardless of uniformity, would probably go unnoticed on the street during a crisis.

After depositing the uniform at the apartment, he made several trips to various vacant lots nearby, filling four pair of socks with sand for use as support for the rifle. With sandbags in place, his heartbeat wouldn't cause even a microscopic movement of the scope's cross hairs. He repacked the rifle in the box and slipped it under the bed.

Jim left the apartment in the middle of the afternoon, the hottest part of the day, a time when few people stir in Benghazi, and rode the bike to the garage. He drove the van back to the apartment, loaded the rifle and drove south into the desert. He located a road identified during training and drove until he was completely out of sight and hearing. He parked the van and walked 420 paces into the desert, placed an empty plastic jug at the bottom of a dune, and returned to the van.

He listened for traffic, quickly positioned the rifle and sand-filled socks on top of the van, loaded one shell and methodically squeezed off a round. After replacing the rifle, he walked to the plastic jug. *Smack in the middle. Perfect.* He returned to the apartment, placed the rifle, sand bags and Guard uniform above the false ceiling in the bedroom. After dismantling the rifle's shipping crate, he scattered the wood in different trash bins throughout the neighborhood, leaving no clues to arouse suspicion should some intruder get into the room.

Late in the afternoon, he shopped for a pair of scissors, some shaving lotion, a fold out razor, a little radio and enough food to last a week, then changed American money for enough Egyptian money to last a few days. He couldn't risk leaving the room often or for long, possibly missing an opportunity he already knew to be speculative. Once a day, thereafter, he planned to leave the room after dark to buy a newspaper, check the van and operate the motorcycle engine for a few moments. He never left the room if anyone was in the hallway. No one would remember anything about the occupant of room 714.

Jim re-dyed his hair, mustache and beard. Without the dye, his naturally graying hair made him look too old to be a member of the Revolutionary Guard. He laid out the uniform for the next day, planning to wear it from then on. He practiced with the rifle and sandbags after dark, moving the only table in the room to a position in front of the window. He planned to leave the rifle in place on the table, muzzle just far enough inside the room to be concealed from sight by the dingy curtains. No one on the outside could see the rifle and he didn't plan to move it again. He shoved the bed against the door for safety and began yet another restless night sitting in front of the window, and more hours of Muslim calls to prayer.

Chapter Twelve

THIRTEEN AUGUST

The day literally started with a bang. Crackling, popping sounds of small explosions woke Jim with a start. He sat up on the disheveled bed, straining to listen. *Gunfire?* He sprang from the bed and rushed to the window. Complete pandemonium reigned below, sidewalks and streets teeming with milling people. Revolutionary Guards raced through the streets in vehicles of all types, civilian and military alike firing weapons into the air, creating general havoc, scattering crowds of frightened people.

What in the hell?

The crowds increased rapidly, people pouring onto the streets. Jim couldn't think of a reason for the chaos. It looked like a celebration. *I must have missed something. What in the hell is going on?*

He felt a sense of dismay and rushed to the scope to look for anything that might give a clue. The barrack's area still looked normal and that calmed his nerves somewhat. Jim needed to risk time away from the room to learn about the cause of the bedlam below. He dressed quickly, a tingling sense of urgency driving him, placed the rifle and sandbags above the false ceiling and stepped into the vacant hall with an urgent sensation of desperation. It seemed his plan was in jeopardy. He needed information. Down the stairs he went, three at a time and into the swarm of people on the streets. He drifted from one group to another trying to gain news from their animated conversations. He couldn't piece anything together.

Dianne! I can ask her. He dialed. *Come on, answer the damned phone.* Nothing. Frustration mounted. On the street, when he finally managed to decipher enough of the clamorous dialogue to interpret what people were talking about, he could hardly believe it. A new wave of terrorism swept the world during the overnight hours: embassy bombings, airliners downed and general hysteria. The people on Benghazi's streets absorbed the news with a sense of triumph, chanting joyously, celebrating a great victory. 188 dead in a downed American airliner; a lethal chemical attack on a crowded London street; bomb explosions at American and English embassy compounds throughout Asia and Africa; suicide bombers at American and European sporting events. People on the streets were celebrating a deadly wave of atrocities directed mostly at innocent civilians. The deliriously jubilant crowds were cheering a great victory.

He called again. She answered on the third ring. "What the hell is going on?"

After a brief silence, she said, "Well, husband, hello to you, too. I presume you must be talking about the news?"

"Do you know what is going on?"

"I have a pretty good idea if my interpretation of the news is accurate, and it usually is. There has been coordinated terrorism against enemies of Islam. Lots of it. The Libyan president appeared on state television early this morning to disclaim Libyan involvement."

"More, please."

"Let me quote what he said. 'Coordinated strikes against Western imperialism mark the beginning of the long awaited Islamic Jihad.'"

"Okay. What does that mean, exactly?"

"It means the promised Holy War is here, my friend. This is Islamic Jihad. And, by the way, your man Hafez appeared on Arab media all across the Middle East, not just here in Libya, taking credit for the attacks. Let me read what he said. 'I have been chosen. I am chosen to lead the Holy war against the infidels. Tomorrow, forces of The Prophet will unite with me to form a coalition of organizations dedicated to Arab sovereignty. Our brothers from Syria, Iran, Iraq, the Libyan Revolutionary Guard and Palestine will join me. The new Islamic state will not belong to any nation. We have formed an alliance responsible only to Allah.'

Jim whistled softly, thinking, My God, the president was right. He asked Dianne, "What do you think happens next?

"Your guess is as good as mine, but whatever, it probably won't be good news for America or any Western government, to say nothing of individual Westerners already in the Mideast."

"I may call you back later."

"At your disposal."

He joined the people on the street celebrating their new hero. Hafez appeared on Arab national television stations throughout the Mideast proclaiming himself leader of the final stages of the Jihad. 'The end of the Holy War has begun,' he declared into a microphone held by a BBC reporter. Hafez spoke respectable English. Street crowds roared as he repeated his message in Arabic. 'The time has come to rid our holy lands of Western imperialist mongrels. The time has come to stain the sands of our Holy Lands with the blood of the Great Satan and his infidel followers. The time has come for all True Believers to unite, to purge our lands of the pestilence of Western influence. The time has come to return to Islamic values, to Islamic Sharia, to return Islamic control of our holy lands.'

The long awaited and promised Holy War finally had a prophet. The crowds were delirious. It didn't matter to the people on the street that their country would not lead the Jihad. They finally had an Islamic hero. 'We return to the ideals of the Prophet,' Hafez promised. 'We will once again be pure, ridding ourselves of Western influence.'

Jim wandered the streets, listening and watching as the new alliance took shape. Hafez urged his brothers from all Arab nations to join, to unite in a solid front against America and all Western nations. One by one, scattered terrorist factions fell in line, broadcasting their allegiance. A meeting to organize major participants developed.

Jim sensed the cadence of pre arrangement. He didn't think something so vast and organized could evolve overnight, not without much planning. Events appeared to be unfolding in an orderly fashion. The Alliance's initial organizational assemblage would be held on Libyan soil on the birthday of the Revolutionary Guard. Jim's plan, even before the new terrorism, counted on Hafez celebrating that day.

Immediately after Hafez made the announcement, a spokesman for the Libyan government appeared to issue yet another disclaimer to ward off retaliation by the United Nations, specifically mentioning America's Sixth Fleet. "Libya is not part of the Arab alliance, although the Libyan people support the ideals of our Islamic brothers. Libya will not tolerate interference from unfriendly nations. My government wishes to inform the world that the Libyan Revolutionary Guard does not speak or act for the government of Libya. They act independently. Their voice is the voice of Islam, not that of the Libyan government. While the government of Libya agrees in principle with the objectives of the Islamic Jihad, we do not condone the use of force against any nation or the rights of innocent people. We are a peaceful nation."

Jim thought the little speech was an interesting gimmick, promoting Libya as a moderate influence. Years ago, Libyan leader Khadafy, a vocal radical on the international scene, after denouncing everything American or Western, practically vanished after America left a huge bomb crater beside his tent during the Reagan era. Before the bombing, Khadafy often slept in a Bedouin tent behind his house at the Azzizaya military compound in Tripoli, ostensibly to further his image as a desert brother. The bomb killed his fifteen-month-old adopted daughter, seriously wounded two of his sons and slightly injured his wife.

Ah, Reagan. I remember.

Khadafy, pretending to be reasonable, pulled back from his confrontational posturing after the bombing and Libyan support for terrorism receded to barely noticeable behind-the-scene activities. Years passed while Libya prudently maintained a facade of detachment. Now, with the formation of the new terrorist alliance, the Libya government, even though publicly denying support of the new organization, embraced Hafez, the Revolutionary Guard and the new Alliance.

It seemed obvious to Jim, while drifting around the streets of Benghazi that day, that Hafez and his alliance planned to shoulder the notoriety, permitting Libya and other Islamic countries to disclaim responsibility. Libya had a fresh new face to hide behind. Jim felt confident that his interpretation of events was close. He felt a great sense of relief about what he intended, though still suffering from not so vague feelings of quilt. The new outburst of terrorism furnished bonus enthusiasm for the plan. The relentless thought that after all the training, the trouble of traveling to Libya, and he still had doubts about the mission was troubling. Pretending to be an assassin seemed a better option to him in the beginning than any other choice.

Now his involvement in an arrangement that provided the opportunity to even the score for his son's death, his willing participation in planning events that placed him on the scene prepared to exact revenge, was no longer in doubt. He wasn't pretending. For the first time, he believed that he would play out the hand. He forgot, for a moment, the enormity of the new terrorism and came to peace with himself.

Truth is, I never thought I would actually do it any more than I could pull the trigger at the parking garage. I have been thinking about how to get back to the States, where to go, what to do when I get there. I never thought I would actually do this. I planned all along, subconsciously, to walk away, use the escape plan and disappear over the horizon.

An escape plan had always been part of the assassination plot, but the plan, the one he turned over to his mentors in Washington, certainly wasn't the strategy he intended to follow when the time came to get out. He had planned to abandon the mission and escape from the very beginning, to play the game until the time came, then get out. He didn't think anyone could catch him and he would be a million dollars better off.

Now, Hafez, murderer of his son, had altered his intentions in one night of terror. His determination to complete the mission was fixed. Jim roamed the streets watching crowds of people dodge careening vehicles driven by high-spirited members of the Revolutionary Guard. The rampaging Guards rejoiced wildly over the deeds of their new leader, firing weapons, chanting his name: "Hafez! Hafez! Hafez!" Jim strolled past the jammed marketplaces and into the suburbs. Even there excitement and joy radiated from the typically stoic inhabitants. People clustered in groups on corners and yards tried to keep children off the streets and close at hand. Even the old people appeared to be joyful, though perhaps somewhat anxious about the calamitous changes taking place. He thought the more composed were probably worried about the possibility of American retaliation. They had seen it before.

Later that evening he lay in bed mulling over the day. Hafez had given another speech on television, making inflammatory comments about "Western influence," which he vowed to exterminate. His raging hostility surprised Jim. The little man bore an almost inconceivable enmity toward the United States, swearing to 'Teach the imperialists what terrorism is all about!' His studio audience responded, 'Satan! Satan!' People on the streets echoed. 'Satan! Satan!'

Hafez pledged to 'Eradicate all Western mongrels from the holy lands. The Great Satan's clothes, Satan's automobiles, everything of Satan will be vanquished from our glorious lands.' Later, he shocked the entire world by outlawing every person in the Arab world with Western heritage. 'Close your borders, brothers. Arrest them, man, woman and child. They are all spies.' He called for the nationalization of Western businesses. Shortly after his speech, according to reports from Western media shown on Libyan television, American and Western diplomats, businessmen and innocent tourists were arrested and carried off by bands of terrorists throughout the Mideast. Libya, Iran, Iraq, Syria, even the Egyptian government, long considered friendly to America, seemed helpless to stop the chaos.

A Libyan government spokesman once again appeared to disclaim responsibility. 'The Jihad is not a Libyan government affair. The Jihad is the concern of all Muslims. Libya denies knowledge of the events we are accused of. We know nothing of hostages. We have taken no hostages.'

Hafez announced to the world, 'We have arrested Western spies. The will of Allah has prevailed! The Islamic Jihad has begun! The imperialists must pay for atrocities perpetrated against true believers.' An hour later, Hafez appeared on television again and announced, 'The first trials are complete. I am pleased to announce, ten of the imperialist mongrels have been found guilty of spying and have been executed.' Television sets throughout the world corroborated his claim by airing the gruesome sight of masked men beheading captives in an unspecified desert of an unspecified land. The cameramen took great pleasure walking from one bloody, naked Caucasian body to another while filming close-ups of the grisly scenes.

Jim could not believe the crowd reaction when the television cameras panned down the line of corpses. They cheered and danced, their hatred functioning as an emotional aphrodisiac. The people were crazed. The more Hafez reported, the wilder the crowd reaction. They loved him. From out of nowhere, they had new hope–a prophet–a savior.

Hafez ridiculed the weakness of Western governments. 'They will not strike us militarily. Who will they kill first, innocent children? No, my brothers, they will not strike. They don't know who we are or where we are. If we unite, no pack of Western dogs can penetrate our strength. The brotherhood of Islam can defeat any force on earth! Our cause is sacred.'

Jim called Dianne and asked for her opinion.

"Today has been a terrible day for history, another day of infamy. I believe Hafez is correct believing the alliance will draw nations together if America retaliates for the executions. The situation compares closely to President Carter's Iranian hostage crisis, a situation where we could do nothing right. This time, however, the entire Mideast is involved with or without their endorsement. The sad thing is, this time the world knows almost nothing about the leader or his cause. I think we are in for a bad time. Do you need assistance?"

"No. Why do you ask?"

"I can be there within minutes."

Of course she knows where I am. Dumbass. "No, I think things are on track."

Jim slept little that night. Crowd noises and gunshots resonated through his room throughout the dark hours.

FOURTEEN AUGUST

All day he listened to radio and television announcements, perceiving even more unity among the terrorist states and factions, learning about more hostages, and to top it all off, he watched another telecast of another beheading squad at work in another unspecified desert. No Arab country could be held responsible. Arab leaders wrung their hands in dismay, publicly denouncing the outrage. A PLO faction claimed credit for an atrocity; a fundamentalist Iraqi group bombed an Italian railway station and demanded recognition, some European terrorist sympathizers joined, as did an Indonesian group. Peripheral groups expanded the activities of the new alliance. The entire world started shutting down–airline schedules canceled, public events canceled, people at home from work, military forces massing.

Jim listened and watched the news reports with mounting distress. His hatred for Hafez grew. One thought overwhelmed all others: This is the man who murdered my son. He no longer harbored misgivings about the mission, sitting by the window watching, occasionally snoozing in the sweltering heat, beginning to think more about escape, having given the plan only token attention. It seemed weak.

Will it work? Will I even get a chance to try? Should have spent more time perfecting a damned escape plan since it looks like I'm going to need it. The plan is not that well thought out, probably because I never really planned to use it.

The only part of the plan that he approved of now was the fact that his benefactor didn't know it. He distrusted them and produced a plan going west from Benghazi to Tunisia while secretly planning to go east to Egypt. If they were determined to exterminate him and the possibility that he could compromise their involvement, then he was a step ahead. There was no reasonable way, he thought, that the American government wanted him to survive.

Early that evening he walked the streets again, hovering on the edge of crowds standing around blaring radio and television sets in storefronts, listening to and watching their new hero. He stood on the periphery to watch as Hafez spoke. The little man's method of speech conveyed a captivating madness, but his wild gesturing and emotional words held the crowd spellbound. Hafez looked like a windup toy soldier. His appearance struck Jim as comical. Not one person in the captivated audience shared his opinion. He discovered the one thing he needed to know. Hafez would be at the Revolutionary Guard anniversary celebration. Jim drifted away from the chanting crowd, free of all previous reservations. No doubt remained.

Back at the room, door bolted, gun in position, he sat in darkness mentally preparing. His heart beat slowed and his thoughts channelizing into an almost suspended state. He no longer agonized over morality or thought of deserting. He wasted no more energy debating reason. He felt nothing, just cold. He chilled in the one-hundred degree temperature, thinking, if he thought at all, about the flimsy escape plan.

They will be waiting for me.

Chapter Thirteen

FIFTEEN AUGUST

Jim dozed in the chair throughout the night, periodically waking to gaze through the scope. Activities in the Mideast had captured his attention all that day. The radio fairly hummed with news of the new Alliance, of more Western hostages and executions. A meeting of Alliance members was scheduled for the Sixteenth to coincide, much to his satisfaction, with the Libyan Revolutionary Guard anniversary.

I am at the right place at the right time.

Before the day ended, he knew the PLO planned to send a representative to the meeting, as did Abu Nidal's old Fatah Revolutionary Council. Emissaries from Saudi extremist Osama bin Laden's now defunct terrorist group al Qaeda planned to attend, though bin Laden was long gone. Representatives from the defeated ISIS, along with Syrian, Iranian and Iraqi terrorist factions were scheduled. Almost every known Islamic terrorist organization planned to have representatives in Benghazi. The Alliance of Terrorist States appeared to be fact, and from all indications the nightmare of organized terrorism would be terrifying.

Late that afternoon, he watched a convoy of desert-colored government trucks and vans pull to a stop in front of the barracks. A large semitrailer tractor backed a lumbering flatbed trailer into position in front of the main entrance. The moment Jim noticed the flatbed, he also recognized that it would stage his target. He had seen photos of the same truck while researching the mission. Workmen labored in the heat, stringing wires from a row of microphones on the trailer. Others placed huge speakers at strategic locations in the park between his room and the barracks.

He watched activities until the workmen finished and armed guards sealed off all streets leading into the park. Final preparations at the scene were complete, almost like the Libyans read the script he wrote six weeks earlier. The cast of characters differed but his plan could not have been drawn more perfectly. Hafez would climb onto the stage sometime the coming day.

Jim counted at least two-hundred posted guards. No person could approach within two city blocks of the cordoned area. He sat in the shadows of room 714 and thought about the bullet: Four-hundred yards across the park, twenty more to the stage, less than one second of time to right a terrible wrong.

He left the apartment one more time to buy sixty feet of slender rope, a roll of duct tape, a length of one-inch pipe, black shoe polish and a can of black spray paint, all wrapped. On the way back he stepped into the hall of the sixth floor to check room numbers–exactly the same as the seventh floor. No one answered when he knocked on 614.

He didn't plan to sleep and probably couldn't as his body tingled with tension. Every nerve cell in his body jangled with electric energy. A series of calisthenics took the edge off, but his muscles were tight enough to snap. He eventually gave up and surrendered to the inevitability of nerves. *Why fight it? There is no chance to survive tomorrow. So it doesn't matter.*

At three in the morning, he darkened the room with sheets over the window, painted over the sensors detected during his stay, then slipped down one flight of stairs and knocked on the door of room 614.

An annoyed man's voice eventually answered in Arabic, "Yes? Who is it?"

Jim offered his best Arabic, 'Manager. Open, please. This is emergency. Emergency!"

A chain rattled and the lock snapped. Jim crowded in and closed the door. An old man, possibly in his late seventies, wearing a long white nightshirt began protesting. Jim held up a hand for silence.

"Who is here with you?"

"Alone. I don't...."

He hit the old man flush on the jaw. The poor devil crumpled and sprawled on his back. Jim dumped the rope and duct tape from the sack, tied and gagged his whimpering victim, then dragged him into the bathroom and closed the door. He had to gamble, to hope none of the occupant's family or acquaintances came to check on the old man. He probably needed twelve hours.

Jim returned to room 714, covered the rifle with a blanket in case he met someone in the hall, and went swiftly to room 614. He returned to 714 and positioned the shoe polish-blackened pipe on the table, letting it protrude just past the curtains so an intent observer could see it, then hurried back to the room below with the sandbags.

He arranged the table so the rifle muzzle was slightly withdrawn into the room so no one outside could see it, then back to room 714, grabbed the radio, wiped the room of fingerprints, checked for condemning evidence, took the sheets down from the windows, locked the door and returned to 614. After checking the field of vision for obstructions, he sat back to wait.

Now I won't have to spend the night worrying about Dianne and her friends.

He sat beside the rifle, determined not to move from the window. Nothing would move him until Hafez died. He felt nothing but cold.

WASHINGTON D.C.

The phone rang in the makeshift bedroom off Adrian Burt's office at Langley. He checked the clock. 11:00. "Burt here."

"Excuse me, Sir. This is Hollis in Communications. You have a secret message. For your eyes only, Sir."

Burt mumbled, "Thanks, John. I'll be right over. He dressed and hurried to the center just down the hall. He had been sleeping at headquarters for almost a week from the time Jim began the mission. The message read: POT BOILING. ON SCHEDULE. RED SHOES OUT.

Adrian smiled for the first time in days. He left the communications center thinking, Dianne and her ridiculous code names. Red Shoes. Anyway, Denning will be pleased.

Chapter Fourteen

SIXTEEN AUGUST

The day began after Jim stumbled from the chair at dawn, splashed cold water over his face and checked the hostage, threatening death if he made a noise. Jim ate a chunk of stale bread with wine and gave the old man food and water. To his surprise, upon return to the window, a dense crowd was already assembling in the park, thousands more crowded the perimeter. Guards searched every person. The fortunate few permitted inside the park stood patiently in the scorching sun. Hours passed, the temperature soared above one-hundred degrees by noon. By three that afternoon thermometers in the shade registered one-hundred-and-five. Room 614 had to be at least that warm, and yet he chilled.

The scene below did not divert his thoughts. *I'm either exhausted or in a trance, because nothing seems real. This could be a dream.* Never in his life had he felt so alone, or so cold. The magnitude of what he intended didn't overwhelm him, nor did he think about the effect his actions would have on the people below, or the world. He didn't think about escape. The crowd in the park didn't matter, or the soldiers, or the scurrying officials. Only the makeshift stage mattered.

Activities increased suddenly in early afternoon. Four helicopters arrived and orbited overhead. His heartbeat accelerated. The Russian-made choppers descended singly to land inside the barrack's wall, stirring blinding clouds of dust. Several minutes passed before the engines revved again and the choppers departed in billowing clouds of dust. Jim couldn't see well enough through the dust to identify anyone. The helicopter passengers disembarked and ran through the dust clouds to disappear into a nearby building.

Hafez is in there. So close. So damned close.

Long weeks of waiting had dwindled to minutes. Jim still didn't feel nervous, just cold. During training, he envisioned there would be a colossal inner battle when the time came. He pressed his fingertips to a neck artery. *Whoops! Pulse over ninety. Body signs right on schedule–time for fight or flight. Only a madman wouldn't show stress.*

An insidious sense of excitement began building. The sweat-soaked Guard uniform felt cold and clammy. He sat back, stretched and took several deep breaths. The crowd noise diminished suddenly. He sat bolt upright, skin tingling, pulse pounding, hands shaking.

What in the hell am I doing here?

The thought seeped in right on schedule, just as it always had before stress-filled events. The trait showed up routinely during his life: before his first boxing match; before jumping out of an airplane; upon entering combat; leaving his family for combat and many similar occasions–all dangerous. A parade of doubts raged as he mechanically leaned forward to watch through the scope. *Just business. Get on with it.*

The activity in the park below diminished as the afternoon wore relentlessly on. Jim couldn't control the perspiring or the chilling. He watched, worried that he might not manage the shakes well enough to shoot accurately when and if the opportunity came. An officer dressed in a flashy Guard uniform occasionally took the stage and spoke to the waiting crowd. Jim couldn't hear well enough to understand. The people in the park cheered and chanted each time the official appeared. Their half-hearted enthusiasm lasted only long enough to appease the speaker. The ended all activity each time he left the stage.

At approximately five p.m., a ripple of excitement moved through the crowd and they began chanting, this time without the stimulus of a leader. The crush of bodies near the stage suddenly opened as a wedge of guards formed a human battering ram and knifed through the throng toward the stage. The crowd went crazy.

Jim stopped breathing and leaned into the scope. *This is it.*

The crowd noise suddenly increased as the Libyan president stepped onto the stage, pumping a fist to the crowd. Jim trained the cross hairs over the medals on his chest. He had calculated an eight inch bullet drop at that distance. The president's arm swept grandly toward the end of the stage and Hafez bounded up the steps to the swelling roar of the crowd. The racket pounded through the open window with a deafening resonance. Jim no longer felt cold.

Hafez paraded and the faithful cheered. He soaked up the adulation, rousing his admirers to more applause, strutting back and forth across the stage, arms spread When he lifted his arms the mob cheered, when he lowered them, they quieted–like conducting a symphony. Hafez stopped, turned and beckoned toward the stairs leading to the stage. Four more dignitaries emerged from the crowd. Two of the newcomers wore traditional Arab turbans and robes, the others wore Western style civilian clothes with Arab turbans. Jim recognized all of them.

Wait for it. Wait for it.

Hafez paraded as more celebrities arrived on stage: the PLO second-in-command stepped forward, a Syrian government official came next, then a man representing what was left of ISIS. He recognized an Osama bin Laden lieutenant, followed by one of Iran's leading fundamentalist Mullahs. Others followed, incidental dignitaries taking inferior positions behind the infamous front line. Jim didn't recognize the men in the back row, assuming them to be minor players representing lesser organizations.

Hafez finally stepped to the microphone, gesturing for silence, posing imperiously, arms outstretched, palms down, motioning for quiet. The crowd noise hushed at once. Jim reacted instinctively, took a deep breath, superimposed the horizontal crosshair over Hafez's arms and the vertical through the center of his body. He didn't detect the slightest movement of the crosshairs; no sign of heartbeat; no trembling; just dead calm.

He adjusted the sight picture, chin just above the center of his target's medal-bedecked chest. Time stopped. Noise receded. The roaring in his ears receded into a vacuum. He morphed from human to machine, an integral part of the gun. Trigger pressure increased, slow and steady, without the slightest sign of nerves.

The roar of jet engines hammered into his ears without warning. Two old Russian MIG fighter jets swooped directly over the park at rooftop level. The unexpected noise was jolting. Jim relaxed pressure on the trigger and glanced up from the scope to see two more MIGS slanting toward the park, beginning a high-speed, low-altitude pass.

"Perfect!" He said aloud. "Perfect!" He took another deep breath and leaned into the scope. Noise from the approaching jets increased as they screamed over the park. Jim waited for the sound to reach its zenith, the MIGs directly overhead, and without the slightest hesitation, squeezed the trigger. The rifle bucked against his shoulder and cheek. Pandemonium swept the stage. Horrified dignitaries scrambled over the side, diving and running, scrambling to get away from their fallen comrade. The thought of killing someone else never entered Jim's mind.

Waves of screaming people turned into a turbulent mob within seconds, a stampede of screaming terror. The harsh sounds of automatic weapon fire resonated through the park. Moments later, dozens lay bleeding, crushed, writhing and dying amid the wild dash to escape. Others fell and died of gunshot wounds from indiscriminate gunfire as the startled Revolutionary Guard fired into the crowd, striking out blindly, firing at phantoms.

Jim tore himself away, stood too quickly and nearly lost consciousness. He grabbed his knees for a moment and took deep breaths, then staggered to the sink to vomit. The sounds of heavy running footsteps came from overhead. He froze, listening as someone kicked in the door to the room above, followed by more heavy footsteps and shouting. He suspicioned all along that someone would show up. After splashing water over his head, he took a deep drink, cut the old man's bonds, warning him not to move until hearing the room door close. He stumbled to the window, let the rope down and slithered quickly out and down. On the ground, he simply walked away from something that had never seemed real.

The enormity of his circumstances soon struck with full force, heart racing, and then the nausea. Jim desperately needed to lie down, delaying for a moment at the edge of the building to control breathing before stepping into the street to join crowds of scurrying survivor, all running for their lives.

The bike sputtered to life on the fourth kick. He barely noticed the sun-scorched vinyl seat. No one in the panic stricken crowd noticed him. Everyone was running; women screaming; children crying; men jostling. Another burst of gunfire from the barracks area set him in motion. Once away from the crowd, the journey across Benghazi went smoothly. He wanted nothing more than to separate from sounds of gunfire and the nightmare of dying people. People on the streets along the way seemed bewildered by the commotion, standing in the middle of streets watching rising columns of smoke. No one paid the slightest attention to the Revolutionary Guard riding the other way.

Jim dismounted a block from the escape van, left the engine running and walked the remaining distance as casually as his wobbly legs permitted, wondering if the van could be a trap. Every fiber of his being, every part of his body tingled as he suffered a mounting alarm response, expecting bullets to slam into his body at any moment. He stood in the shadow of a vacant warehouse for a moment, observing the garage before walking by to look for the piece of string he left stuck in the door. *The string is there.*

Nothing happened smoothly at the garage. The van wouldn't start–nothing but a metallic click as he turned the key. He popped the hood and wrenched the battery cables with his bare hands. It started. After a deep, shuddering sigh, he compounded complications by backing into the half-open door on the way out.

Action at the barracks had taken place late enough in the afternoon to preclude the requirement to wait in the garage for the right time to leave. Waiting would have been near impossible in his agitated condition, particularly since he knew he had been betrayed. His thoughts shifted ahead. He needed to be at the desert no sooner than nightfall, three hours away. The escape route he presented back in the states called for use of back roads and alleys until he got out of Benghazi. From Benghazi, his purported escape route followed the main road along the seacoast west toward Tunisia. He furnished the plan as a feint, believing the road west offered too many opportunities for interception. He would drive east instead, from Benghazi to the little town of Makili. Maps portrayed the route as a secondary farm to market road, but research did not show the narrow, cluttered little lane he discovered once outside the city. Concern about being on the right road pestered until a damaged road sign finally relieved his doubts.

Makili lies on the boundary between good farm land and the Libyan desert, exactly one-hundred-and-fifty miles east of Benghazi. Jim needed to arrive at desert's edge near Makili just after nightfall, and not a minute earlier. He drove steadily, constantly fighting the urge to speed, still jittery, half sick and troubled by too many questions.

He wondered, how long before the Libyans start a search? Will they block this road? Will they be organized enough to coordinate a search? What about the Americans? Do they have sensors on the van, the motorcycle, on me? How soon will realize that I am headed east instead of west?

Makili held the next key to survival. If he made it there, he would have a chance. Prospects for survival looked better with each passing mile, better than he imagined during planning. His thoughts projected ahead in a positive manner for the first time in weeks. *I might actually get out of here.*

No formal road existed in the desert east of Makili. Maps indicated an unmaintained trail leading east across the desert. He remembered something English General Montgomery once said, 'Distance doesn't mean much in the desert. Only time matters.' *Well, Monty, I don't have much time.*

Desert and darkness were indispensable coconspirators. Everything depended on being at the desert in darkness. Jim was no stranger to desert riding, having raced in the deserts of Nevada and California with his son. Four-wheeled or tracked vehicles had no chance to catch a motorcycle in the desert. Helicopters could present a problem, but not after dark.

What about the CIA? They will probably know my position as long as I am in this van.

An hour east of Benghazi, several ragged columns of overloaded military vehicles filled with soldiers approached from the east. He pulled over and held his breath. The vehicles careened by without slowing. Each mile left him farther along the road to freedom and closer to more unknowns.

Benghazi, and the awful specter of what happened there, receded. He stopped picturing the scene in the courtyard. Miles crept by as he fought the urge to speed. *Need to hold it down. I don't want to be at Makili before dark. Damned poor idea to launch off into the desert in daylight.*

Jim noticed several produce trucks parked at what appeared to be a truck stop and turned back to approach the trucks from the rear. He threw the pistol, cell phone and belt into the produce of the last truck. *That should provide some confusion.* He hadn't worried much about being captured, mostly because he never thought there would be an escape. The evening shadows lengthened along with his prospects for escape and he was too exhausted to rejoice.

The glow of city lights glimmered on the horizon ten minutes out of Makili. Darkness approached from the east as the desert closed on the road from the south. The desert and road merged three miles west of Makili just as the sun went down, plunging the day into almost instant night. *Perfect. Right on time.* He turned the van toward Benghazi, unloaded the bike and left the keys in the van, hoping a thief might steal it before some curious official investigated.

He mounted the bike, drove a half a mile back toward Benghazi, then straight south into the desert before turning to circumnavigate the town. Jim rode cautiously without the luxury of a headlight. He didn't plan to turn the light on until well east of Makili, headed away from town. Jim could see nothing unusual in town. No flashing lights. No sign of roadblocks.

He rode five miles east of town before finding the road, discovering it to be nothing more than a couple of ruts. Only then did he feel secure enough to turn on the headlight and begin concentrating on speed. The plan called for an average of thirty-five miles an hour across the desert, but the trail was rough and indistinct, blending into rocks and sand, almost invisible at times. He rode faster than common sense dictated, pressing hard with almost one-hundred-and-eighty miles to go before daylight and safety of the Egyptian border. The rutted trail compounded handling problems and the constant exertion drained his strength.

Eight hours to Egypt.

Jim needed to locate at least two more gallons of gasoline somewhere along the route.

There would be two opportunities to find the necessary fuel. Without the added gas he planned to ride east as far as possible, cover the bike with brush and start walking. If walking became necessary it would probably cost him at least two more nights in the desert.

His final destination, the small Egyptian town of Qattarah, is located nearly fifty miles inside the Egyptian border and forty miles south of the Mediterranean. Once in Egypt, navigation would be easy. No roads or trails to follow across the desert there, but Qattarah is on a road running perpendicular to his route and would be easy to find, even at night. A good desert racer can average up to fifty-miles-an-hour, but good riders don't race at night.

Jim increased speed as the moonlight brightened and the desert shimmered. He pushed the bike to fifty-miles-an-hour over long, straight stretches. His confidence, the bike's front fender and hopes of an uneventful ride disintegrated in a split second. He crashed violently, slamming head first into the ground. Later, lying semiconscious in the sand gasping for air, sounds of the bike motor running wide open spurred him to action. He crawled to the bike, pressed the "KILL" button, and then flopped, almost afraid to investigate the cause of blood in his mouth. After recovering strength enough to try again he rode cautiously, resolved to stick to common sense speed.

Cold desert night air soon became his primary tormentor, requiring periodic stops to revive blood circulation. All dirt bike riders know that the numbing of exhaustion is universal. Winners overcome physical pain and fatigue to outlast the also-rans. He was drained and not half way to the finish line.

The Sarir pipeline leading south into the desert from the Mediterranean loomed in the darkness three hours and fifteen minutes east of Makili. Jim turned off the headlight and rode slowly toward the scattered lights of a little pipeline town. The village had fewer than five-hundred inhabitants, mostly workers on the pipeline. He rode along the pipe until finding a place to drag the bike beneath, then carried the empty fuel cans toward the sleeping town. The pain of walking felt better than riding.

Got to make Egypt before sunrise. Move it. Move it.

He located an old American pickup with a gas engine, slid under and poked a hole in the tank with his survival knife. After filling both containers, Jim plugged the tank with cloth ripped from his shirt and returned to the bike and then made another trip for more gas.

Four gallons of additional fuel should be enough.

He smiled at the good fortune. The smile cracked open his damaged mouth and blood flowed freely. By then he had regained enough feeling in his fingers to permit examination of the wound.

The main damage seemed isolated inside the lower lip. He ate and rested while the bleeding ebbed.

The journey to the Egyptian border promised to be easier, but far more dangerous. The plan called for riding a seventy mile stretch of paved road to another small town astride the Libyan/Egyptian border. He didn't pass or meet another vehicle. His fear of crashing receded as tiredness desensitized the demand for caution. His mind, affected by exhaustion and a desire to end the interminable day of torment, functioned in a haze. He rode much too fast, fighting conflicting urges to pull into the desert and sleep, or press on and put an end to the punishment. Village lights emerged from the darkness an hour and a half later.

He pulled off the road and into the desert again, bypassing the town lights off by positioned the lights ninety degrees to the left, making a gradual semi-circle around the last obstacle in Libya. Just as the lights of town passed a position to the north, he ran headlong into a five-strand barbed-wire fence and crashed. He didn't care.

The border.

Jim lay on the ground for several minutes after the fall, too tired to get up and too delighted to care. He eventually staggered to his feet, checked the fence to see if it might be connected to electrical intrusion devices, and then spent the last calorie of energy pulling the bike under the fence. After resting, he swept signs of motorcycle tracks from the crusted earth before leaving the scene.

He smiled despite exhaustion and pain, blood dripping again from his smashed mouth. He thought about riding a short distance into Egypt, hiding the bike in a gully and sleep. Tempting, but good sense prevailed. He pressed on to the east, maintaining course by positioning Polaris off his left shoulder. He needed to be at the road to Qattarah before sunrise. Jim lost control of the motorcycle frequently, running headlong into obstacles that normally required little effort to avoid. The falls weren't particularly violent but ate up more time and energy than he had to spare. He no longer felt pain.

He drew the motorcycle to an abrupt halt just as the first rays of daylight broke through darkness, straining to identify an irregular object on the eastern horizon. Something ahead didn't fit the pattern of desert topography. Jim blinked to clear dust and sand from his eyes.

The road to Qattarah.

He rode back into the desert, away from detection, dumped the bike into a depression, covered it with brush and walked to the road and saw village lights to the south. *I am standing on the road just north of Qattarah.* Time passed. His legs were numb from fatigue. He was so cold that he could barely move, and when he tried to walk he staggered like a drunk. Improved circulation rallied his mental and physical condition. He began to think about little things. He took off the olive drab shirt and turned it inside-out to present a non-military appearance, threw the knife into the desert and then used the remaining water to wash blood and dust from his face. The water snapped him back to full consciousness.

Qattarah's inhabitants were opening shops and conducting morning chores as he staggered into town. He bought bread and fruit from a wrinkled street vendor who told of a bus going all the way to Cairo every other day. Good fortune continued. The bus was scheduled to arrive the next hour. The bus, an old American school bus, arrived early already filled with people and animals, mostly chickens. The human occupants screamed back and forth incessantly, yelling to be heard, causing the next speaker to yell even louder.

The noise level finally diminished as rising temperatures tired the crowd. Jim couldn't have cared less. He slept in a near coma. The noisy people and stinking animals had no effect.

Chapter Fifteen

CAIRO

━━━━━● ━━━━━

Jim arrived on the outskirts of Cairo well after dark. The dilapidated, creaking old bus pulled off the road in a run-down section of town. The driver took the keys, stepped out and walked away. After waiting until the other passengers disappeared, Jim slipped down the dark side of the street and headed toward the glow of bright lights of downtown Cairo.

Food. Food first and then think.

Once in an area of modern buildings, he stepped back into the shadows to observe a cafe down the street. Once established at an isolated table, he ordered red wine, bread and cheese while studying the customers, mostly tourists and foreign businessmen grouped according to nationality. Muted discussions reached him from every direction, all centered on news from Libya. The magnitude of what he did in Benghazi began to sink in.

The whole damned world is fixated on me. Half the world wants to kill me and the other half wants to glorify me.

The conversations jerked him back to reality. Headlines of assorted newspapers lying on nearby tables blazoned type three times normal size in red ink. The headlines read simply:

ASSASINATION

He picked up an English language paper featuring two photographs of Hafez across the front page beneath the headline. The first, a blurred photo taken sometime before the Sixteenth of August, featured Hafez in uniform. Next to it, a gory full color layout displaying Hafez lying in a pool of blood on the stage in Benghazi. The pictures of Hafez held Jim's interest until he noticed a smaller photo on the bottom half of the front page. A photo of him. He snapped the paper closed and glanced around the room, half expecting everyone to be staring at him.

My picture? How did they get the photo on my passport? The caption beneath read: AMED HAZAM–ASSASSIN. In the text below, Libyan authorities identified Hazam as a technician from America. Jim understood. Only a select few knew about Hazam, or that he was the assassin, and they had betrayed him. *That's pretty damned interesting. Only one possible way the Libyans could know. Those miserable son of bitches.*

Overwhelming tiredness and desperation swept over him. He noticed a more complete English language newspaper lying on an nearby table and casually stepped over to secure it. After reading every account of the assassination and the associated after-effects, he was amazed by how much world attention the assassination had already received. *What a hell of a mess I'm in. Might as well have shot the Pope. The Libyan government is offering ten-million and my own government wants me dead.*

The newspaper reported that police authorities throughout the world were searching for him, but also confirmed the one thing he most wanted to know: The shot was fatal. He was surprised by world reaction to the assassination and saddened to know that so many people died in the panic or were victims of indiscriminate gunfire.

Didn't see that coming. If the Libyans knew, then why didn't they stop me? Hmmm. Probably got the tip too late but not too late to catch me. They would have if I stayed in 714.

According to the newspapers, Libyan officials reacted to an anonymous phone call and arrived seconds too late at the assassin's empty room but found the rifle in the room below minutes later.

I always knew the CIA would try to get me killed–an unacceptable liability–a loose cannon who knows too much.

All Libyan airports, transportation centers, seaports and main roads were closed within thirty minutes of the assassination. He closed his eyes and thought back. The escape was more than luck. The decision to take back roads after losing confidence in the CIA made it feasible. Misgivings about Dianne; worry about being electronically tracked, and the decision to move down a floor probably helped.

The newspapers reported that Hazam had called immediately after the assassination, demanding credit in the name of a spinoff ISIS organization. *Nice touch. Setting Arabs against each other. The guys who hired me didn't want to bring down the wrath of Islam on America.*

His thoughts raced through a tangle of possibilities until only one acceptable course of action remained. He needed credentials and money. *I am a man without a country and no credentials. I need to get to Athens and that bus station locker.*

He studied the customers. A tall, thin man speaking English soon held his interest. An English civilian wearing a white dinner jacket and bow tie. The Englishman was speaking in hushed conversation with two British airline pilots and didn't notice Jim move closer.

Definitely English. About my size.

An emerging escape plan focused on the tall man. Jim's concentration settled on the Englishman. The three men eventually stood and shook hands. The pilots departed one way, the Englishman another. Jim breathed a sigh of relief and followed. Three minutes later, outside a small hotel, he backed into the shadows and watched as the focus of his attention stepped inside, checked messages at the counter and then pressed the elevator button for the third floor. Jim crossed to the other side of the street to observe third floor windows, watching for a light to flick on. Nothing. He hustled to the rear of the hotel and noticed one light on in the second to last room on the third floor. He returned to the street, watched five minutes longer to see if any fresh lights came on. No lights.

He returned to the alley to look for a weapon and found a two-foot steel rod. Jim didn't have difficulty entering the hotel as the clerk didn't remain behind the counter. He ran up the stairs to the third floor, tip-toed to the second-to-last room on the alley side and knocked.

"Who's there?"

"Bradley, is that you?"

"Yes. Who is it?"

"It's me, old chap, Allen. I believe you left money at the cafe."

A lock clicked. The doorknob turned. Jim rammed through as

the door cracked open. "See here!" the startled Englishman complained, backing away.

"If you so much as make a noise, partner, I will kill you! Get your hands up!" He brandished the rod menacingly.

"I say," Bradley complained, holding his hands up. "If it's money you need."

Jim's ragged appearance and the pipe presented a suitably intimidating image. "I'm not kidding, friend. I am desperate. Sit there!" He pointed to a wooden chair. "Don't do something stupid. I'm in serious trouble, friend, but I don't want to hurt you."

Bradley sat. Jim locked the door, checked the apartment for signs of additional occupants, then grabbed some ties and belts from a closet and tied the Englishman to the chair.

"Hate to do this to you, but I have to make sure you don't do something silly. When does your maid service come?"

"I am permanent. There is no maid service. See here now."

Jim located rolls of adhesive tape and gauze, rolled the gauze into a ball, stuffed it into Bradley's mouth and taped it securely. He found a passport, a driver's license, two-thousand dollars in cash, insurance identification cards, and best of all, an American Express card.

Jim shaved the beard and mustache and washed his hair in a scalding concoction of every soap in the apartment. The scrubbing turned his hair color several shades lighter. Bradley's clothes fit loosely, but close enough. He filled a small overnight bag with spare socks, underwear and a few toilet articles.

He called the airport and made reservations in Bradley's name on the first available flight to Athens and remained in the room until 3:30 A.M. before taking a cab to the airport for a 5:00 flight. He arrived at the airport at 4:00, checked in, then left the lobby to pace in the shadows outside until the last minute, fearing to expose himself again. Nothing suspicious happened to drive him away; no car screeched to a stop; no one rushed into the lobby; no one seemed to be searching.

The last call for boarding sounded at 4:45. He took a deep breath and hurried through the lobby to board an old Boeing 727 converted for express with only ten passenger seats. The airliner departed right on schedule. None of the seven passengers exhibited the slightest interest in him. The flight to Greece took less than two hours.

He hoped the Athens airport would be crowded. The airplane parked on the apron well short of the passenger terminal and the steward announced in broken English, "All passengers must deplane and walk to the terminal. You will be responsible for your own baggage. Please walk between the yellow lines until you are inside the passenger terminal."

The ground crew shoved a rickety loading ramp against the aircraft, not unlike a builder's scaffold on wheels. The passengers deplaned immediately and scurried for the terminal, giving Jim a moment to examine the surroundings from a vantage point at the fuselage door. Seventy-five yards of apron separated him from the main terminal. The distance to the terminal looked like a long distance run.

He trailed behind, walking within the yellow lines, watching for any unusual movement. Then he saw them and hesitated. Two men in an observation area on the second level of the main terminal, faces pressed against the window. *Here we go. They are looking right at me. Damn! Damn!* He kept walking, head down, glancing up to keep track of them. Half way to the terminal, the two men spun away from the window and began running.

Okay, slick, you don't need a script to know what's going to happen next. Someone behind him, probably the steward, yelled as Jim crossed the yellow line and sprinted across the apron toward another wing of the terminal. He stopped to catch his breath at a service entrance and turned to see the two men from the observation window running toward him across the apron. He darted through the open door and slammed it.

No lock.

He vaulted a counter and frantically twisted the knob on the door leading into the main hallway.

Locked!

Jim could see into the hallway through a small, wire-mesh window, but saw no other way out of the room. He scrambled back across the counter and picked up the heaviest weapon he could find–a metal tool box. He peeked through the window and saw both men only a few feet away, pistols drawn.

He remembered the first guy–the man with the rifle and night vision scope from the New York City parking garage. As the door burst open, Jim swung the box, striking the leader in the chest, stopping him cold. A pistol dropped inside as he fell outside. The other man fired three times as Jim reached for the gun. A searing pain burned across his forearm as he snatched the gun inside and slammed the door. After pausing to think, he fired a shot upward through the door to discourage pursuit, scrambled over the counter, blew the hallway door lock apart with one shot, pocketed the gun and stepped casually into the hall. Several puzzled passengers stopped to stare. He stepped briskly toward the interior of the terminal and said, "Just an air valve folks. Nothing to worry about." After the first turn in the hallway, he began running, slowing to a brisk walk before entering the main terminal. Several police cars were parked haphazardly in front of the terminal, rotating lights on. More sirens approached as police converged at one of the middle entrances. A portly man in civilian clothes handed each cop a piece of paper, urging them into action.

No chance to make it to the side doors before the police get there. He placed a hand over the gun beneath his shirt and made it to a side entrance as a pair of officers took position, heads together, bending over a picture. *My picture, I bet. I'm dead.* The picture portrayed a man with black hair, mustache and beard. *That's Hazam, not me.* Jim covered the bullet wound with his hand, smiled confidently and walked through the door.

"Parthenon," he ordered the cabby. *Parthenon? Is that the only place I could think of?*

He vacated the cab minutes after leaving the terminal to buy a wallet and briefcase, departing the store by a back door to hail a cab to the bus terminal. Jim patted the last key, the key to the locker containing the cloth belt he had fashioned from a shirt during training in the States. The belt containing the money and ID secreted there during the wild cab ride from Dulles at the very beginning of the mission. He hoped his sponsors believed the contents were in the now empty briefcase stored in the locker at Dulles. He opened the locker and breathed a sigh of relief.

It's still here. Now all I have to do is keep moving.

He had two-thousand dollars from the Englishman and now fifteen-thousand cash in the makeshift money belt. He sat at an isolated table at a nearby outdoor café and opened the money belt to check the contents; new ID, work and education history–his new life.

Jim used Bradley's phone to call the bank holding the promised $485.000. No record of him or the account. He sat back, stunned by the turn of events. *How did they...? Ahh, of course. They withdrew the money after the mission.* The smug feeling of well-being of moments before collapsed. After ordering a beer, he thought. Well, at least I have enough to get back to the States.

Jim finished the beer while using the Englishman's phone to call the Athens police. "Do you speak English? Okay, this is important. Write it down. A man's life is at stake. His name is...." He gave the necessary information to free Bradley. That done, he walked to the bus station and took the first bus out of Athens, traveling all that day and most of the night. After stopping at a small town on the northwest coast of Greece, he took a room in a tourist hotel and slept fifteen straight hours. The next morning he boarded a twice weekly ferry from Greece to Italy using the Englishman's passport.

After a long day at sea, he arrived in Otranto on the east coast of Italy, rented a room and spread everything on the bed, taking time to study each article. First, a current American passport with his new identity, Michael Allen Stokes, fifty year old salesman from Denver, Colorado. No next of kin. *How convenient. No one knows anything.* He found diplomas from a Denver high school and the University of Colorado, gaining some satisfaction that the college degree matched the degree in marketing he graduated with twenty seven years before. He placed most of the money in the cloth belt, retaining two thousand dollars in the wallet.

I can get back to America and last a few months before needing work. The initial disappointment diminished as new challenges intrigued–like starting life all over. He stuck around Otranto for five days, regaining strength. The beaches, good wine and food replenished his spirit.

I need to move on. Someone will surely track me down if I wait.

The trip across Europe took ten days; ten days of small towns, crowded buses, sneaking by customs, eating cheese, bread and drinking wine. Ten nights of sleeping in the woods and run down hostels. He crossed the English Channel on a ferry from Amsterdam to Hull, keeping with the plan of using least traveled routes. Once in England, he traveled by rail to Liverpool using the

Englishman's passport to book a tourist cabin on an old Dutch cargo ship sailing from Liverpool to Halifax, Nova Scotia.

"The cabin ain't much," the First Mate declared, handing the passport back. "But if you're willing to pay hard cash, I guess that's all we require. I don't suppose the cops are looking for you, or anything like that?"

"No. I'm traveling around the world as cheaply as possible."

"Well, Laddy, if it's cheap you're looking for, this old tub won't disappoint you. You won't go anywhere as cheap as this. You play chess?"

Oh, great. Chess again.

Months of nervous tension and strain drained after the ship weighed anchor. The voyage took two weeks, two weeks of sleeping from one side of the Atlantic to the other. He felt fit and vigorous before docking in Halifax. An American cruise ship took him from Halifax to Bar Harbor, Maine using the Englishman's passport identification one final time. He bought a used phone and a four wheel drive pickup, then mailed Bradley's papers, money and cell phone back to the address in Cairo.

Doesn't matter. They will soon enough know I'm back.

He hadn't spent much time thinking about Benghazi; too many other things to worry about. However, the blood-spattered spectacle in the courtyard pestered his thoughts during the two day and all-night drive to Denver. He wanted to arrive before anyone tracked his use of Bradley's ID. He started thinking and feeling like a fugitive. He wanted to check his account personally to dispel any doubts about the money. A phone call would alert someone to his presence. He stalled until the noon business picked up, then walked straight to the Collections/Exchange window and asked for the account balance. The teller smiled and made polite conversation as the computer digested the numbers, then frowned and leaned forward to study the screen.

Uh oh. Trouble.

Her brow furrowed. She glanced up and said, "Would you please give me your account number again, Mister Stokes?" He repeated the number. She checked again. "I'm sorry, Sir. Would you mind having a seat over there, please?" She pointed to a sitting area.

"Look, Miss, I just want to know the balance, that's all. That shouldn't be a problem. Please, just give me the balance."

"I'm very sorry, sir, but I need to check with…. Please have a seat." She forced a strained smile and headed for the back offices. Jim turned and headed to the front door. An alarm rang within the bank as he stepped outside. He stopped acting nonchalant and ran around the corner to his truck.

Well, they damned sure know I'm back now.

The future could not have looked bleaker than it did at that moment. He had no financial security. He couldn't use his new identity. He need to find a place to live and some way to make money.

I am a fugitive.

He drove south from Denver in search of an isolated place to live. He stopped at small airport near Colorado Springs and bought aerial maps featuring contour lined topography and significant man-made objects. He circled several promising locations, all isolated and mostly uninhabited. During a brief stop in Alamosa in south central Colorado, Jim purchased a cheap camper top and enough provisions to last several weeks. He studied the maps for hours, then drove west into oblivion with no plans, no friends, little money, no family, no past and no future.

Chapter Sixteen

WASHINGTON

Jim made news in Washington the moment he arrived in Colorado. Officials at the Denver bank reported his visit. Stokes, the banker told the feds, managed to catch a relief girl at the Exchange window during noon break. She hadn't been briefed well enough to handle the situation discreetly. Stokes became alarmed and vacated the premises. Bank cameras confirmed his identity.

Robert Hensley, appointed as CIA Operations Director after Adrian Burt's departure (a withdrawal hastened by his inability to locate and remove Jim from the President's list of national security risks), was a precise man with no tolerance for mistakes or confusion. Hensley received the appointment as Operations Director the day after Adrian Burt received his pink slip. Hensley's frustration mounted steadily during the baffling days following the Benghazi assassination, and now he had to deal with news that the assassin was back in the States running free. An unacceptable liability.

Hensley fumed at a gathering of his lieutenants, pounding his desk, yelling, "Well, gawddammitall! He is really loose now, isn't he, people? You should have been there waiting for him, gents! What the hell happened?"

Jack Hamm, Hensley's assistant and old college buddy, shifted, cleared his throat and said, "Our team was looking for him in Italy. Otranto, I think it was. We had solid–"

Hensley interrupted. "Well, maybe he was there, but I think was is now the operative term, isn't it? He is damned sure here now. The bottom line is, we have a problem, fellows. Think about it.

What would you do in his place?" He glanced around. No one volunteered to answer. "Well, I sure as hell know what I would do in his place, and that scares the hell out of me. What if he decides to come after us? That's what I would do. We sure screwed over him."

Jack said, "No problem, sir. He doesn't know who we are."

Robert rolled his eyes. "Oh, shit! No one is that damned stupid, and I can tell you damned straight, this guy sure isn't stupid. He can put two and two together with the best of us and has proven it. Matter of fact, he is a whole bunch better than we are if historical patterns mean anything. How in the hell do you think we ended up in this mess? He beat us at every move, that's how! Nope, you can bet your life–and by the way, that's exactly what we may be doing–that he knows exactly who we are. Oh yeah, he knows.

"Now, gents, I think we better start planning and living like he just might come after us. We hung him out to dry and he damned sure knows it. We ratted him out. He did everything we asked and we double-crossed him. I would sure give revenge some thought in his shoes. Yes sir, some damned serious thought. What do you think, Jack?"

Hamm, classic brownnoser, middle-of-the-road player and yes-man, doodled with his pencil and tried to look thoughtful. "You could be right, boss, but, like you said, he isn't an idiot. I doubt he will surface around here. Then again, we know he has a penchant for squaring scores, don't we? So, I have to agree with you. Maybe we should consider some precautions. Check our six, as the fighter jocks say. I don't think he will go for any underlings, though."

"Yeah, you're probably right. Damn, he's slick, isn't he? What a piece of work. Too damned bad Burt didn't use his head. We could have handled this guy better. No wonder they fired Burt's ass. What a screw job. Well, there isn't much we can do about that now except get a handle on him, and quick. I've got to tell the old man the good Colonel is back and still on the loose. He's gonna pee his pants. Denning is going to demand that we solve this in a permanent way, gents. Permanent."

Hamm stood. "I suppose this means it's time to pack?"

Hensley nodded sullenly. "Yep. There isn't much doubt where we begin, is there? Well, Jack, the aspens are changing. It's pretty in Colorado this time of year."

Chapter Seventeen

THE LESLIE CONNECTION

Senator Collins furnished Leslie with verbal orders to investigate the possible use of illegally obtained and unauthorized CIA funds. Her excitement soared. Leslie could not wait until the next morning for appointment credentials. She hurried across town to the CIA's Washington offices that afternoon where she encountered no trouble gaining immediate access with her standard senate staff credentials. The office superviser, however, refused to provide the records she asked for. None of the office workers wanted anything to do with her, or any other meddling Senate investigator. At first she thought they were just being evasive, but soon understood that they had strict orders not to cooperate.

Their inhospitable attitude changed, but slightly, after she presented Charlie's written authorization the next morning. They were polite, producing every piece of documentation requested without hesitation, but when asked about the fund she wanted to investigate they balked and no manager had time to talk.

Her first day on the job ended as a complete bust. The next day started the same way. Late that afternoon she stumbled onto the same evidence her predecessor had uncovered to trigger the investigation. The clue resided in an innocent looking financial ledger–OF 5930. Her spirits soared after discovering a puzzling five-hundred-thousand-dollar transaction from an entry tabbed "OP FUND." The money came from a unidentified source, and without congressional authorization.

This must be it!

She took OF 5930 to an empty conference room, locked the

door and began examining the document in earnest. The money popped up from nowhere on June 15. Then on June 16 it shifted to control of none other than the Operations Director himself, earmarked for classified project OF 5930. Leslie made a list of questions to ask, reports to check, and a reminder to look at news items for significant events during the month of June–anything the CIA might be using money to finance.

"Where did this money come from?" she asked, pointing the entry out to Hal Drieling, the deputy department administrator and duty scapegoat appointed to assist and divert her during the investigation.

Drieling, oily, sweating, and much too fat to do anything but office work, answered, "Let me see that, Miss Reardon." After he read the folder label, he said, "Oh that." He covered his mouth, coughed and turned away to hide a startled expression.

Leslie noticed his astonishment and sensed an opening. "Come on, Hal. I don't want to subpoena you. This fund does not have the required source codes. Why? Where did this money come from, Hal?"

He moaned and rubbed his eyes, buying time to think. "I don't believe we have originating codes for that project, Miss Reardon. OF 5930 simply means, Operations Fund 5930. All I know is that project has been here since I started work thirteen years ago. It's a slush fund. That's about all I can tell you. The money doesn't come from normal sources. That's probably why it doesn't have an authorized source code."

"No source code? All right, how can I find out where it came from, Hal?"

He shrugged and looked away. "Don't ask me. I sure don't know where it comes from. But I can tell you this: Congress knows all about it, Miss Reardon. You aren't the first to ask. Hell, we aren't trying to keep it a secret. If we were, it wouldn't be out here in the files where you could find it. The fund itself isn't secret–only where the money comes from and goes to is secret."

"I see. Perhaps you can give me a general idea."

He stalled for a moment, thumbing through the folder. "Well, I think the Agency uses it for projects too secret for public disclosure. That's why Congress doesn't ask questions." Drieling developed confidence and droned on, regurgitating a rehearsed response. "The legislative finance committees know about the fund and tacitly agree not to ask too many questions. We need some latitude to do our job. Some of what we do is too secret to pass around. Congress knows that and apparently agrees."

Leslie exhaled unhappily and stopped listening. Her big break was vanishing, buried beneath his rambling discourse. By then, she understood that the coded information had probably deliberately fallen into her hands. *Too easy. They wanted me to find it. 5930 is where they want me to stop, or be stopped.*

Hal's voice intensified to get her attention. "Shoot, Miss Reardon, OF 5930 isn't a big deal. As I said, everyone knows about it. I don't want to say you're wasting your time, but...." He held his hands up, signaling helplessness. "Our big guys will just stonewall and congress won't push."

She snapped the folder closed angrily and said, "Never mind, Hal. I get the picture."

He persisted, reminding her that the fund originated from sources that didn't need budget authorization. "Yep, Congress knows all about it. You don't need to take my word for that, though, Miss Reardon. Ask around."

She did. No one bothered to deny the fund. They all smiled condescendingly, gave the same corporate answer, and went about their business. OF 5930 was an in-house joke. She returned to Drieling.

"Good grief! Does everyone here know about the fund, Hal?"

"Pretty much. Yeah, we all know about it. But once the money goes through that door," He pointed to the Assistant Operations Director's door, "that's when it gets to be none of our business. Don't even bother to ask, Miss Reardon. National security interests, you know." He smiled, shrugged and said, "And that's the end of that story."

Leslie stifled a groan. "You have been very helpful, Hal. What would I ever do without you?"

She had nothing, only knowledge that the money originated from a secret source and vanished beyond the Assistant Operations Director's door. Both origination and destination of the monies were unknown. She checked with the Senate committee monitoring CIA finances and learned, once again, that OF 5930 rated TOP SECRET with an ancillary classification of

NATIONAL SECURITY INTEREST. NEED TO KNOW ONLY.

Okay, she thought, end of story. No one in the CIA Operations will talk to me about it, not officially. No one on the staff, other, maybe, than Adrian Burt, knows anything about the business of OF 5930.

She discontinued searching through ledgers and files and decided to take her questions straight to the Assistant Operations Director himself, but try as she might, she could not catch Adrian Burt in his office. Leslie tried to catch him in the hall. She didn't have any problem arranging an appointment–that part was easy– she scheduled several meetings. Burt always waited until she arrived for the meeting, rose from his chair, shook her hand warmly, canceled the engagement and ran out to yet another important emergency meeting. "I'm really sorry, Miss Reardon. Would you mind making another date? Check with my secretary."

Leslie's frustrations mounted. When she complained to Senator Collins, he seemed remarkably composed.

"Aw, hell, don't worry about it, Les. Things will eventually open up. Hang in there, kid."

She could have sworn he was enjoying her difficulties. *How odd. He would normally jump all over something like this. I am being hung out to dry.*

Then, in late August, to complicate things even more, Adrian Burt disappeared. No one at the agency would talk about it. Hal Drieling said, "All I know is he ain't here no more. Zip, pop, he's gone. Hensley has the helm now. That's all anyone knows about it around here, Les. Anything else I can help you with?"

"No, Hal, I guess not. Oh, who did you say is Burt's replacement?"

"Robert Hensley. You probably heard of him. He was the Assistant Ops Director once before several years ago."

"Yes, I am acquainted with him." She didn't care for Hensley, boasting of a Harvard education while hiding behind a dumb, good-ol'-boy country facade. His duties before involved running interference for upper management with media and congress.

She asked Drieling about Burt's fall from favor and the mysterious lack of information.

"All I know is we aren't planning to make a big deal out of it around here, Miss Reardon. No standard play-it-down press releases sincerely regretting his departure. No media handouts. Nothing. Nada. It's in-house business."

"Why, Hal? Did he just disappear?"

"Naw. Nothing like that. Been reassigned, that's all. And before you ask–yes, it's secret. The big guys just decided to swap horses in midstream I think, and Hensley is an old experienced hand."

Hensley, she already knew, had a well-earned reputation for being expert in covert activities. He had discreetly resigned from the position of Assistant Ops Director several years before, allegedly for a shady venture during an infamous arms deal with a central American country that then used American weapons against American troops. Rumors about Hensley's activities circulated through Washington at the time. The Attorney General absolved him and Hensley dropped out of sight in the shadowy framework of CIA bureaucracy.

Leslie's problems escalated. Hensley was even more difficult to capture than Burt. He had a shifty way of hiding everything, making everything secret, including his whereabouts.

She complained to Senator Collins again. "They are all stonewalling me, Senator."

"What? You haven't got anything yet? I would prefer you didn't bother me with an incomplete investigation, Miss Reardon. If possible, I wish you could have something a little more positive before you approach me again."

She thought, Miss Reardon? He has never called me Miss Reardon. Oh, I get it. Charlie is getting even. He knew this investigation was a dead end. I can't get the information unless he backs me and he won't. That's why he took his fair-haired puppy boy off the inquiry. He planned to let this investigation die from the very beginning.

"Do you mean to tell me, Sir, that I cannot expect your assistance? I need some pull. This investigation requires your support, Senator. Hensley won't talk to me unless I have your active sponsorship. He has forbidden me to talk to anyone on the Operations staff again without his permission. He is deliberately side-tracking this investigation, Senator, and I can't talk to Adrian Burt. I can't even find Burt. They are hiding him. I need help. Your help."

He held up his hands, warding off further requests. "It's your baby, Miss Reardon. If you want out, just say so. I can find someone else."

She left the office more frustrated than ever. *Charlie is getting even. I would bet anything he's in there laughing his ass off right now. He doesn't care if this damned investigation fails. He wants it to fail.*

She changed tactics the next day. The money from the suspect fund had moved to the Assistant Operations Director on 15 June. *So, what happened on the Fifteenth of June, or thereabouts? Why did they need the money? What for?* Leslie proceeded directly to the city library to study world and national news for the month of June. She made copies of several pertinent stories that might relate to the CIA, including the death of two Libyan diplomats in New York on June Sixteenth. *I wonder...coincidence? No, that's inside the country. CIA responsibilities are external.*

She waited until late that evening when Hensley and his department heads wouldn't be at work, and strolled into agency headquarters with intentions of learning about the location of CIA field operatives during June. The young watch officer, impressed by Leslie's Congressional authorization papers, her air of official importance, and perhaps the view down her deliberately sagging blouse, relented and led her onto the dais in the operations control room. Leslie felt some embarrassment about the blouse, fumbling with the neck opening to draw his attention. Never before in her life had she deliberately exploited her body to gain something from a man. She read the list of operating teams grease-penciled on a clear Plexiglas wall board labeled: SPECIAL OPERATIONS. Her interest narrowed to two field teams located within the continental United States, one in Los Angeles, the other in Chicago.

She turned to the watch officer and caught him staring at her legs. "I didn't think CIA responsibility extended to operations inside the United States?

He flushed. "That is normally correct. At least it was until these teams were formed."

Leslie asked to see copies of the team reports.

"I am sorry Miss Reardon, but I cannot open any of our active files to unauthorized personnel."

She thought a moment, and then said, "Of course. Would it be all right if I looked at dormant or past reports from the teams? I need to get an idea of what they are doing here in the States. This is an official congressional investigation, you know that, right?"

He grimaced. "Well.... I don't...." He appeared to waver.

She leaned over the counter seductively. "I won't take notes and I would much prefer that you stay with me."

"Let me take a look first, just to check to make sure we aren't into something...you know, something unauthorized." He searched through a file cabinet behind the main dais and located a single file containing old reports from the two stateside teams. He scanned them quickly, pretending to read as his eyes kept drifting to her breasts. "I don't see anything classified here, but the existence of the teams is classified information, so you will have to sign an access slip."

She signed the form and he gave her the folder. Leslie discovered something even more interesting than the two internal operating joint teams. Another team, not listed on the wall board, once operating in New York City had ceased reporting on June Seventeenth.

Close to the Sixteenth. Coincidence? Leslie tried to memorize the New York team member's names and handed the folder back. "You're right. There is nothing there for me. Are those joint teams still operating, and if so what are they doing?" She pointed at the board, all the while repeating to herself, *"Paul Sells. Carl Owman."*

"Those are experimental teams, Miss Reardon. We use them along with FBI counterparts to track suspected terrorists within the United States. Yes, the two teams you see on the board are still operating."

"What happened to the New York team? I see they stopped reporting in June."

Sells. Owman. Sells. Owman. Sells....

He shrugged. "I really don't know."

She believed him. "Okay, I want to know what the New York team was doing from the first of June until the Sixteenth."

Sells. Owman.

The possibility of a breakthrough excited Leslie. She pressed the watch officer for every shred of evidence, knowing she wouldn't get another chance. If Hensley ever discovered the leak, he would probably fire the helpful young man and ban her from further access.

"Sure thing, Miss Reardon, but I'll have to get the information from an inactive file in the other office." He returned shortly and said, "The New York team was trailing suspected terrorists up until the time they were disbanded. They stopped reporting on the Sixteenth of June," he announced. "The team was disbanded the next day."

Well, well. The Sixteenth is sure eye-catching. She thanked him and departed, rushing to her car repeating the New York team member's names over and over: *Paul Sells. Carl Owman* until the names were recorded in a note book, then breathed a sigh of relief. *Finally, something to work with. Dates and names.*

Early the next morning, armed with the names, she returned to the agency just as the doors opened. Leslie breezed into the Operations Department's outer offices and presented her credentials to the office manager. "I want to know where these agents are located." She handed the receptionist the list.

The receptionist dialed a pre-set number, reported Leslie's request to a watch officer, then smiled and said, "Sorry, those men are out of town on assignment, Miss Reardon."

"Wrong. I know they are not assigned duties at the present."

"All I know is what I'm told. They are on temporary assignment to the Assistant Operations Director. I could let you know when they return."

"Are they out of country?"

"They are on special assignment with the Assistant Operations Director. You know what that means?" An insipid smile let Leslie know it didn't make any difference if she did or not.

Leslie recognized another dead end. They were not going to let her talk to the agents. "No thanks. You needn't bother." She flopped into a seat in the lobby to brood and think. *Too many coincidences. First, the New York team broke up on June Sixteenth. Second, the team members all went to work for Hensley afterward. Third, Burt disappeared mysteriously and the Assistant Operations Director has been avoiding me. And fourth, the suspicious money transaction happened shortly after the New York team broke up.*

Leslie couldn't ignore the number of coincidences, including the murdered Libyan diplomats. She found the name of one of the agents listed in the Fairfax phone directory. Sells. The onlky Sells in the directory.

"Mrs. Sells, this is Peg Jergens," she lied when a woman answered. "Agency Operations. I'm trying to contact Paul."

"Well, honey, he went to work on time this morning. That's all I can tell you."

"Then he must be here somewhere. Sorry to bother you. Good bye."

Leslie didn't ask Hensley's permission, she scheduled a conference room that afternoon and asked the Ops section administration chief to page the two agents from the New York team. She pretended to be from administration, ordering the agents to the conference room for a review of their retirement benefits program. They became evasive the moment she produced her congressional credentials. She questioned them one at a time. The first, Carl Owman, gave the company answer to her questions about the New York team, "Sorry, Miss Reardon. Field operations are classified."

She knew what to expect, probably nothing, but had to do something. Owman said he didn't know anything about the missing money, which didn't surprise her. She finished questioning Owman, admitting that her only lead was starting to look very weak.

Then it happened.

Paul Sells, the team leader, turned ashen white and began perspiring when she asked what he had been doing on or about June Sixteenth. She pressed the opening and questioned him relentlessly, flaunting her authority. "What do you know about five-hundred-thousand dollars missing from OF 5930, Mister Sells? Remember, this is a Congressional inquiry. Rules of perjury and obstructing justice are in effect."

He hesitated, trying to think of his options before answering. His jaw muscles worked nervously. "I don't know anything about OF 5930, Miss Reardon. I'm just field operative."

She steered him through a list of questions concerning the team's activities, all of which he refused to answer, deferring to secrecy. She finished the interview by asking, "Didn't your team leave New York about Sixteen June, Mister Sells?"

"I don't remember the exact date."

"That's quite okay, because I do. Now, I want to know exactly what you know about the two Libyan diplomats killed the night you departed?" A shot in the dark.

The question clearly stunned him. His eyes widened and glazed over. He swallowed hard and avoided her eyes. "I...that must have.... I don't know."

Owman had not reacted to the same questions, but Sells nearly passed out. Leslie had served as a prosecutor long enough to detect a rupture in someone's defense.

He is lying. Anyone can see that.

Sells regained self-control and finished the interview without breaking, but Leslie had a clue. An enraged Robert Hensley barged into the conference room only seconds after Sells wobbled out. "What the hell are you trying to do? I want to see your damned notes! You have stepped over the line this time, Reardon! You are way off limits!"

Leslie handed him the notes. She had not written Sells' comments. That night she decided to concentrate on the disbanded New York FBI/CIA anti-terrorist team. Too many indicators pointed toward them.

Senator Collins came to her office early the next morning. *Is this a coincidence, or what? Charlie hasn't been inside my office in a year. Ah, he knows what happened yesterday. How word gets around.*

He smiled benignly and opened the conversation by asking, "How are you, Les? What's happening with the investigation? Are you making any headway?"

I get the first decent lead yesterday and he pops in today. "I'm terribly sorry, Senator. I should have kept you abreast. The truth is, there isn't anything to report yet. I'm working on some possible leads, but it's slow."

"I see. Well, the Agency complained to me about you this morning. They are upset about a fraudulent meeting you set up. Entrapment, I believe they called it. Anything to that?" He looked up from an idle inspection of the papers in her in-basket.

"I did what I had to do, Senator. They are not cooperating."

"I see. Your tactics do seem to be a bit questionable, Miss Reardon. Well, what's done is done. Do keep me informed from now on. Oh, by the way, I need this brief completed before the weekend. Make it your top priority. I need it no later than Friday afternoon. No more than five pages." He placed a thick folder on her desk and departed.

Leslie worked day and night to have the brief turned in on time. When she presented her work, Collins didn't so much as thank her for the effort and assigned yet another priority chore, appropriating her time for the next two weeks.

I get it. He is deliberately sidetracking the CIA investigation.

Late that night, at home, the phone rang as Leslie labored over Collins' latest assignment. The call came from Paul Sells' wife. Sells, the New York joint team chief.

"I don't know how to begin, Miss Reardon. Paul came home last night and disappeared. I suppose that's as good a place to start as any."

Leslie knew exactly who she was talking to, but had no idea why. "I'm sorry to hear that, Mrs. Sells. Is there some particular reason you called me? But first, How is your husband?"

"He was found murdered this morning, but that isn't what I want to tell you. Paul obviously knew something bad was going to happen. A few days ago, he gave me some information to give to you if something happened. He asked me to talk to you, Miss Reardon. That's how I know you and that's why I am calling?"

Leslie didn't hesitate. "Where can we meet?"

"Come to my home, please." She gave the numbers.

Leslie drove fast, a thousand thoughts racing through her mind. *Something momentous is about to happen. I can feel it.*

Mrs. Sells looked haggard–puffy eyes; stringy, matted hair; scratching her arms; sobbing and unable to sit for more than five seconds. She wiped her eyes and began. "You should probably take notes, Miss Reardon. What I have to say is terribly important. I think Paul's death must have something to do with your investigation. He didn't blame you and neither do I. I knew something was wrong with Paul long before you questioned him. He hasn't been able to sleep or eat for a long time. Paul's health has been going downhill for weeks. I didn't know what to do for him. He's been that way for at least two months, but after he talked to you it got much worse. I have never seen Paul so distressed. I'm not blaming you. Paul told me some things you have to know, though. Only you, he said. No one else."

She fumbled through her purse and found a rumpled piece of paper with penciled notes. "This is all extremely important, Miss Reardon." She blew her nose and sniffled. "It's all so terrible. Paul thought the money you are looking for went to a retired Marine Lieutenant Colonel named James Colby. Paul had something to do with Colby. He wouldn't tell me more than that. He thought you could figure it out. Colby now goes by the name of Michael Allen Stokes. That's important, Miss Reardon–Michael Allen Stokes. Paul helped to fabricate Colby's death. He wanted you to know that Colby is still alive. Paul thought he might be living somewhere in Colorado. He knows all about Colby because he helped develop Colby's new identity. Michael Allen Stokes. Please, write that down."

She paused and her brow furrowed. "I really think you should take notes, Miss Reardon. This goes on and on."

Leslie didn't argue. She wasn't about to forget a single word, but dutifully prepared to take notes.

Mrs. Sells continued. "From what I could gather, Paul thought this Colby fellow was going to kill two Libyan diplomats in New York City, that was back in June. He thinks you might know something about that?"

"I am familiar with the incident." *So, the Sixteenth was no coincidence.*

"Paul wanted you to know that Colonel Colby didn't do it, Miss Reardon. Things get pretty messed up from here on. Paul wouldn't tell me everything about those two Libyans. He said I wouldn't want to know what happened but something must have gone very wrong in New York and Paul is implicated. I think, Miss Reardon…. I think Paul did it.

Leslie looked up. "What? Excuse me. Did what?"

"I think Paul may have killed those Libyans. He didn't exactly say that, but I know him better than anyone. He talked in his sleep. Things like, 'They made me do it. I pulled the trigger.' Things like that. I can't think of any reason for the way he was acting lately, other than what I suspect. Whatever, it must have been dreadful. He wanted me to tell you that he was responsible for what happened in New York, Miss Reardon. He was the team leader. He told me that he didn't have any choice. No one else knows about the Libyans except you and me–not even the other team members.

Paul told me they believe Colby did the shooting. Paul said he thought Colby was going to kill the Libyans, but didn't. I don't know for sure what happened, Miss Reardon. Now, and this is most important, Paul said to make sure you know Colonel Colby didn't kill those men. He wouldn't say more than that, except he arrested Colby for killing those men and turned him over to Agency officials."

"You honestly believe your husband killed the Libyans?"

"Yes. I lived with Paul Sells for twenty-six years, Miss Reardon, and I know he did something terrible. I believe the guilt was killing him. He couldn't live with what he did and didn't want to die with it on his conscience. Paul wanted you to know the truth."

Mrs. Sells studied her notes for a moment and then faced Leslie again. "Paul thought the Agency may have blackmailed Colby into something after that night in New York. He and another agent were sent to Athens to eliminate Colby."

Leslie stopped writing and looked up again. "What? My, God! Do you mean to kill him?"

She nodded miserably, tears dripping from her nose and chin. "Yes, but they failed. Paul returned from that assignment with a horrible bruise on his chest. He said Colby hit him with a tool box."

Leslie couldn't absorb all the information fast enough. "Just a moment. Did your husband believe Colby was working for the CIA?"

"Yes"

"And the CIA tried to eliminate him?" Leslie cocked her head slightly to indicate skepticism.

"Yes. That is exactly what Paul told me. Yes."

"It doesn't make sense. Why would they do that?"

"I don't know. Oh, and something else. Paul thinks the Libyan government is also trying to find Colby."

Leslie thought for a moment. "The Libyan government? Good grief! Anything else?"

"Yes. Colby, or Stokes, is probably in Colorado. I already told you that, though, didn't I? Paul didn't know that for sure. He said the Agency couldn't find him."

"You mean the Agency was still looking for him? Are they still trying to–"

"Yes. Paul said they wanted to eliminate Colby. Oh, he also told me to warn you to be careful. You, Miss Reardon. He thought you were already or soon would be in great danger. Paul thought you had already discovered too much. He wanted me to convince you that you are involved in something so serious that you wouldn't believe it, and that whatever it is puts you in great danger."

Leslie didn't try to hide her astonishment. She took notes furiously while the distraught woman waited. Finished, she looked up and asked, "Is that all?" She paused and said, "Good grief. What am I saying? I can't believe I asked that. I really can't believe there could be more. This is all so unthinkable."

"There is more. You asked Paul about the use of illegal money and he didn't answer. He believed the CIA is hoarding money from confiscated drug shipments, but didn't know that for sure. One more thing, and this is probably most important of all, Miss Reardon. The CIA is not acting alone. Paul told me to make sure you knew that this business with Colby and drug money goes all the way to the top and the CIA is caught in the middle. Paul believed the orders come from the top–the very top, Miss Reardon."

Leslie departed in tears. She made notes and stayed awake all night and briefed Collins the next morning. She told him almost everything about the illegal fund, the diplomats and Colonel Colby. She couldn't bring herself to relate Mrs. Sells' story about the possible involvement of President Denning. She still couldn't quite believe that.

Collins displayed what Leslie thought to be less than sincere astonishment. "Leslie, I must say this comes as a tremendous surprise to me, if true. I really don't know if I believe any of it, though. Do you?"

His performance wasn't convincing. Leslie watched him closely and felt sickened. *He has known all along.* "It is pretty far out, Senator. I'm still not quite sure what to make of it. The implications are certainly disturbing. I still have much to do–loose ends."

"Well, you have done some good work here. Let me know immediately if anything else turns up. And, Leslie, you must know we are dealing with some mighty sensitive information here. I'm sure I don't need to remind you to be discreet. Do not speak of this to another living soul."

"Yes, Senator. Would it be asking too much to have someone else finish the report you asked for so I can get back on the investigation?"

"Oh, that. No. I wish I could assign someone, Leslie, but I can't. No, you stick with it for now and we'll worry about the investigation later. That thing isn't going anywhere. Don't worry yourself too much about it."

I just gave information that could blow the lid off Denning's administration and Charlie wants me to sit on it.

"Not a word about this to anyone, Leslie. Not a word. Do you understand?"

"Yes, Senator." She stood, prepared to leave.

"Oh, and Les, thanks for keeping me abreast. Remember, I'll need that report on time."

She rushed from Charlie's office directly to Marine Corps headquarters, presented her credentials and followed an orderly to the retired officer's section to look for Colonel Colby's file. The file had a red tab to signify deceased. The deceased classification didn't take Leslie completely by surprise. She ordered a copy of Colby's service records. The records chief, a comely red-headed gunnery sergeant, spoke freely about Colonel Colby.

"Too bad about Colonel Colby, isn't it? Sure was a nice guy."

Leslie stopped breathing and looked up. "Oh? You knew him?"

"Yes Ma'am. I served on a staff with him once, in Norfolk. Just long enough to know I liked him a lot. Great officer."

Leslie held up a photograph. "Is this his latest picture?"

"Yes ma'am. That's his last promotion photo. Let's see...taken two years before he retired."

"He would have been how old?"

"It's right here. Let's see...forty-two."

"Eight years ago?"

"Yes. He hasn't changed much."

"Oh? How do you know that? Have you seen him lately?"

"Well, not all *that* recent. I did work with him three years ago, though. He wrote an article for the *Marine Corps Gazette* about a controversial artillery piece. The Corps wanted to buy the gun and Colonel Colby didn't agree. He was summoned before a

Congressional committee to testify for Senator Whisenant who wanted to kill procurement."

"And?"

"The Colonel's testimony must have been convincing. The Secretary of Defense canceled the contract."

"Did you know him well?"

"Well? No, not really, but sort of. I had to follow him around for a couple of days. Keeping track of his contacts, making arrangements for him, getting copies of the hearings, things like that. His admin assistant."

"Sounds like you were an informant?"

"In a way, I suppose." She hastened to add, "It was all above-board, though. You see, I was assigned as his driver, to secure his quarters, coordinate itineraries and provided necessary supplies. Colonel Colby knew I had to report to Headquarters. He filled me in on everything. Like I said, a nice guy."

"What did he do before and after the hearing, in civilian life, I mean?"

"I really don't know."

Leslie hesitated a moment before leaving. She didn't want to dismiss this contact before gaining every possible scrap of information. "Would you mind giving me a physical description of the Colonel?"

"Tall. Six two or three. Very nice to look at I would say, in a rugged sort of way." She suddenly brightened. "Very polite. Never came on to me. Seemed maybe a little sad. He is pretty damned smart, though. Got into a shouting match with a senator at the hearing. The senator came off looking pretty stupid as I recall. I would say the Colonel is—was—the sort of guy most women would like to know better. Too bad about him, isn't it?" She fingered the red tab on his file and shook her head sadly. "Him getting killed in a lousy automobile accident in New York City, and after all he went through in the Corps."

Leslie read the copy of Colby's service record carefully on the taxi ride back to the Senate offices.

Lieutenant Colonel Colby, according to his latest promotion photo, appeared to be a relatively decent looking man. The file contained mostly standard information: IQ: 146, College graduate, a long list of military schools, military occupational—infantry officer with numerous citations and awards, including a Silver Star and Purple Heart. Divorced. One son. Four years overseas duty. Two years in combat. Fitness reports all outstanding. Some man, she thought. Been everywhere and done everything.

Leslie called the Marine Corps Finance Center upon return to the office and asked them to FAX all information on Colby after retirement. The data arrived that afternoon and she shuffled through copies of his old W-2 forms until finding one coinciding to the year of his visit to Washington. He had been a car salesman in Oklahoma City at the time. She traced his wanderings around the country after a divorce, to the time of his alleged death in New York City. Deceased, June 15. *June 15? Another coincidence? Not hardly.*

The records chief hadn't known the circumstances of his death, but the death certificate was signed by a coroner in New York City. The government buried Colby in Arlington National Cemetery. His next of kin, a son, had not replied to contact attempts by the Marine Corps before the funeral. Leslie wondered what happened with the wife. The dead Colonel's last address was a suburb of Oklahoma City.

She called the doctor who signed his death certificate in New York and discovered that Colby, allegedly, died in an automobile accident. She then dialed the NYPD. They didn't know much. The administrative sergeant had some difficulty acquiring a readout on Colby's accident.

"I'm going to have to call you back, Miss Reardon. This readout is incomplete."

"Really? What's missing?"

"Well, for one thing, it doesn't say here where the accident happened, nor does it give any of the usual details. Let me get back to you on this."

She had just replaced the receiver when Portia stuck her head in the door and said, "Big doings, honey. The Senator just got himself paged by President Denning. Something big is up!"

Leslie knew President Denning didn't like Charlie, and Charlie didn't have any important business pending in Congress that might be of interest to Denning.

So, Mrs. Sells might just be right. This investigation may go all the way to the top.

Chapter Eighteen

POLITICS

Leslie sensed "big doings" probably meant far more than Portia realized. She had a nagging suspicion that Senator Collins' new importance with President Denning had much to do with her investigation. A worried expression wrinkled her brow. The President and Senator lived on opposite poles, both politically and socially. Denning's arch-conservative politics and roughshod methods chafed Collins' liberal viewpoints. Charlie looked weak and effeminate by comparison. The President regularly and deliberately embarrassed Charlie publicly by referring to him as "My little accountant buddy." He invented other equally demeaning observations for people he considered enemies or competitors, all eagerly soaked up by headline-hunting reporters and his far right conservative base. Charlie retaliated by exposing the administration's fiscal improprieties to the nation, sometimes deliberately to infuriate Denning. The two men fought as if they were political opponents from opposite parties while leaders within the Republican party hierarchy struggled constantly to play down the embarrassing rift.

Leslie mentally reviewed Charlie's recent, uncommon popularity with Denning and came to the conclusion that the curious relationship had been gaining strength for several days.

Denning's call is no coincidence. This is about my investigation. Charlie's sudden popularity with the president provided Leslie with more reason to suspect that Paul Sells' wife had been correct when she warned that the investigation would lead to the very top. Leslie intuitively determined that Denning and

Collins already knew the answers she was looking for. They were using her to shroud whatever they were hiding. *"Of course. I'm caught in the middle."* She pondered before saying aloud, "And Charlie is going to trash me."

She gathered every scrap of information about the investigation, stuffed the paperwork into a briefcase, walked briskly through the building to another senator's outer offices and made two copies of everything. She walked up two flights of fire escape stairs to a friend's office where she presented a set of the copies.

"I desperately need you to put this packet in your safe for a day or two, Cheryl. This is material is vitally important. Don't let anyone see it no matter what happens. And for God's sake, don't you open it. You don't want to become implicated, believe me."

Cheryl, an old college acquaintance took the package without hesitating. "Okay, but you make it sound so serious, Les. Are you in trouble? Will I get–

"No. Still too soon to know about me, though. But no, you won't get in trouble. You won't be involved even if something does happen to me. Just don't open that packet, and I mean for any reason. I can get someone else." She knew Cheryl would be unable to resist.

"Oh, Les, you know damned well I'll do it."

"Thanks. I'll pick this up sometime later, hopefully today."

Leslie returned to her office and waited nervously for the inevitable call. *Something is going to happen, and soon. I could stand a stiff drink.* She puttered around all afternoon waiting. When the intercom finally buzzed, she breathed a sigh of relief, braced for the summons and answered.

"Miss Reardon, would you step in here please, and bring that file on your investigation. I want to see everything you have."

I'll just bet you do. "Yes, Sir. On my way."

She picked up the folder containing all original notes, newspaper clippings, Colonel Colby's Marine Corps records, her CIA notes, including the record of Mrs. Sells' conversation. She didn't overlook anything.

"Have a seat, Les. Right there." He motioned to the chair beside his desk.

Leslie couldn't shake the feeling of impending doom.

"Let me see what you have." He patted the desk.

"Of course, Senator. It isn't much, mostly speculation, but there are some very recent notes I haven't shared with you yet. Speculation, mostly."

She placed the folder on his desk and waited patiently as he casually scanned the pages. He wasn't reading anything, only pretending, just going through the motions. Finished with the charade, he closed the folder and looked up, smiling in a way that always irritated her–the same way a parent smiles at a troublesome child.

"This everything?"

"Yes Sir."

"You're sure?"

"Well, yes and no, Sir. That file does include all of the information I have, but I do have a copy."

The Senator shoved the folder to the other side of his desk. A bag of vomit wouldn't have been more repulsive to him. Leslie noticed that he positioned it well out of her reach. "I'll need your copy, too, Miss Reardon. If you don't mind."

"It is identical to the information in that folder, Senator. There is no difference."

"Miss Reardon, please." He looked pained. "I know what a copy is. Please don't waste my time. Bring it in, and I want it immediately. As in, right now." He waved her away with the back of his hand.

Leslie's thoughts raced all the way to her office. *I can play games, too, Charlie. I know you are going to discard everything and discontinue the investigation. I wonder what simple assignments I'll get from here on?*

When she returned, Senator Collins idly thumbed through her copy, placed it on the original, spun his chair around and stared directly into her eyes until she started to fidget.

No. Don't flinch.

"Leslie, you have been a good, loyal worker. I'll see to it you get the best references. I do sincerely appreciate everything you have done."

The shock couldn't have been more staggering. Her breathing stopped involuntarily, gulping to clear her throat before attempting to speak. Her voice sounded feeble. "Did you just say what I think you did, Senator?"

"I'm afraid I have to let you go, Miss Reardon. It's a fiscal thing. Don't take it personally. I must cut staff and we both know you aren't happy here. I think it's best if you resign and go on back home. I need to be able to count on your continued loyalty and discretion. Hell, I really don't have to say that, do I? I have always been able to count on you."

You dreamer.

She forgot about being accommodating. "Just like that, Senator? That's all there is to it? I'm out? What about the investigation?" She knew there would be no changing his mind, but couldn't let go without some objection.

"Oh, that," he patted the folders. "I'll put someone else on it." His face lost all expression. "Now, about this investigation. I think it would be a very good idea if you forget all about it, if you know what I mean." Another flat smile.

Leslie still hadn't recovered from being "let go." The swelling roar in her ears surged as anger spread. "Why can't you just come right on out with it, Senator? Do you think I am dim and can't read between the lines as well as anyone? I was getting too close to something important. That's the real problem here, Senator. I wasn't supposed to find anything and now you are going to cover it up by dumping me. You are going to make sure my investigation is never completed, isn't that right, *Senator?"* She wasn't conscious of speaking sharply until the last word escaped.

Charlie listened without interrupting. "I'm not going to fence with you, Miss Reardon. The investigation is my problem, not yours. How I handle it is my business. Now, we've had a nice relationship, so don't spoil it. These things happen, Leslie. You are not at fault, so don't take it personally. Business is business. Don't make things difficult for me when I need your cooperation most. I can still be of great value to you. Take advantage of my friendship. I understand the importance of loyalty and I so do you. You want to be a federal judge, Leslie, and I can promise an appointment, if you don't.... Well, I'm sure you know."

Her anger spiraled out of control. Being fired by a pompous ass stung. Leslie was fully aware that plans for the future hung in the balance at that moment, that there would be no judicial appointment if she burned Charlie's bridge. A seat on the federal bench could evaporate in one angry moment. Years of work and planning could all go to waste if she didn't control the anger.

"I don't understand why it's necessary to fire me, Senator. Surely there is something else. Oh, hell!" She stood suddenly and glared at him, thinking, Why fight it. I really don't need him. "Very well, Senator, I'm fired and that's all there is to it. I know you well enough not to ask why, but I want you to understand this: I know exactly why, and it sure as hell doesn't have anything to do with fiscal constraints. You may think your recent meetings with the president have gone unnoticed. Let me assure you that they have not! I know what is going on, Charlie, and I would bet anything that you do not. You, Sir, are in way over your head!"

She turned to leave, hesitated a moment, then faced him again. The future faded into a red mist as anger overpowering rational thought. Leslie consciously burned the bridge.

"You really should get an airhead with big tits to squire around in front of your drooling cronies, Senator. Don't screw up someone else's life like you have mine. And just for the record, what do I tell the nosy reporters?" She loathed herself for being bitchy.

Charlie stood, signaling an end to the conversation. "You don't tell them anything, Miss Reardon! Not one goddamned thing! I would prefer, after you resign, that you convey to the public that it was for personal reasons. Family. Whatever. You should go home and forget about the investigation. The investigation is over! Dead! And let me add one more thing just to make sure you aren't confused: you were involved with something here," he patted the folders, "that was way over your head, not mine. I want to caution you against saying anything to anyone about this investigation. I will have this information classified TOP SECRET the moment you leave my office. If anyone asks, I think it would be prudent on your part to deny knowledge of any kind. I will have you arrested and indicted if you ever disclose the slightest information concerning this investigation. Is that clear, Miss Reardon?"

So cold.

"If, in fact, Miss Reardon, if someone asks, which they probably won't, you are not to comment. You have been around long enough to know how to handle the press." He then smiled disarmingly and said, "Now, I'll expect your resignation on my desk today. And I also think it would be wise if you do not associate President Denning with the investigation. That would be most unfortunate, Miss Reardon. Most unfortunate."

She wanted to scream. He had just destroyed her life. She turned to leave. *Don't stop. Just get out before you say something else you will always regret.*

"Miss Reardon!"

She stopped at the door, her back to him, sighing audibly.

"Leslie, take my warning about disclosure seriously. I don't want to see you hurt. I can't tell you how dangerous this business is. Take my word for it."

She thought, How utterly ridiculous. First, Mrs. Sells' warning about danger, and now this. She turned to watch his expression and said, "Are you threatening me, Senator?"

"No. This is not about you and me, Leslie. I'm warning you as a friend, that's all. There are some extremely critical details that you don't know about concerning the investigation. Believe me, there are matters you don't want to know about. Just go home and forget you ever heard about it. And, despite your little outburst, I would still like to part on a friendly note. I can be a great asset to you, Leslie. We both know how much you could benefit from an enthusiastic endorsement from me. You take care now."

Leslie emptied the desk and submitted a letter of resignation that afternoon. After good byes to friends and the staff, she retired to the apartment, broke down and cried. Everything had happened too fast. Collins destroyed her life in an instant for reasons she barely understood. She moped around the little apartment trying to decide what to do next, pausing at a window to stare down at the darkened street. Her confused thoughts cleared the instant she noticed two men sitting in a car directly across the street. *Is this even possible? Two men watching at this hour?*

Leslie barely slept, peeking through the window a dozen times. Another car replaced the first with fresh men. They, in turn, were relieved about 9:00 a.m.

She called a cab, slipped into the back seat and said, "Anywhere, please. I just want to ride."

The cabby adjusted the mirror and glanced at her uncertainly. "You ain't goin' to work today, Miss Reardon?"

"Oh, hello Ephram. Sorry I didn't recognize you. I am so distracted. Sorry. No, not today. Just drive around. Anywhere. Please, just drive."

She watched the car across the street pull away from the curb and follow, taking position across the street again when they returned to the apartment fifteen minutes later. Leslie noticed a phone company van parked on the street later that morning. Two electricians worked inside the building for thirty minutes. She concluded that they didn't care if she knew they would soon be listening. They obviously weren't trying to hide anything. Her house phone was no longer private, that was a given, and she knew enough about cell phones never to trust one again.

They want me to know. Scare tactics. She picked up the phone and said, *"Testing. Testing. Does that help?"*

She walked down the street to a pay phone, pausing before entering the booth to wave and smile at the two men across the street, then turned away from them and covered her mouth.

"Hi, this is Leslie. Would you do me a big favor?" She waved at the men again, despising them for being there.

Later that afternoon, a taxi stopped in front of her apartment and the driver delivered a briefcase. The briefcase held only a key to a local gym locker. She hid the key and walked directly to the phone booth across the street again. "Got it. Thanks."

They met for lunch a few days later. Cheryl confessed relief about losing possession of the mysterious paperwork, particularly in view of Leslie's sacking. "What happened, Les? I'm hearing some pretty weird rumors about you. Rumors everywhere."

"Not rumors, Cheryl. Charlie did fire me."

"Why? What's going on?"

"I'll tell you about it sometime. Not now. Thanks again. You have been a good friend."

"Have been? Have been sounds so permanent."

"It is. I'm going home, but I'll be in touch. Well, sometime."

Leslie hugged her friend and crossed the street toward the stake-out car. She opened the back door and slid in. Both occupants recoiled and spun around, eyes wide.

She smiled brightly and said, "Hi, guys. Take me to the Senate office building. Would you mind? Hey, you might as well. It will save me cab fare and I expect you would probably be going my way anyway, right?"

The driver looked to his partner for guidance. The man in the passenger seat shrugged and said, "What the hell."

None of the surprised secretaries dared utter their customary, "Good afternoon, Miss Reardon" greetings. She walked by Charlie's bewildered receptionist and straight into his office, slammed into the chair beside his desk and said, "Oh, I failed to mention one thing to you yesterday, Senator. I thought you might like to know that there is yet another copy of the investigation. Don't look so surprised, Charlie. Of course I kept a copy. I'm really not that stupid." She leaned forward confidentially. "Now I want you to listen carefully. I have made arrangement to have my copy opened by the Washington Post should anything happen to me, no matter what. Can you remember that?"

"Surely you jest."

She sat back. "Jest? None of this crap is all that humorous to me, Charlie. No, I'm dead serious. Now you call off your damned sleuths and stay the hell out of my life! I don't like being followed, or listened to, or bothered in any way by that bunch of goons you have out there. Do you understand?" She thought his surprised expression was genuine.

"I honestly don't know what you're talking about, Leslie. I swear to you, I have nothing to do with anyone following you. You have to believe that."

"That may be true, Senator, but I'll bet you can damned sure stop whoever is following me!" She stormed out of the office leaving the door open.

Charlie Collins and President Denning met again that night.

Chapter Nineteen

DENVER

Leslie's agonized over the crushing finality of separation from her professional life. The idea of pursuing the investigation independently appealed, but ended when balanced against the possible consequences. *The facts are frightening. I have been warned, followed, phone tapped, taken off the investigation and fired. Only an idiot would ignore the signals. Go home. Forget about it.*

She packed and flew to Denver and sat for days alone in the darkened house, brooding about the circumstances controlling her life. She felt used and betrayed, insignificant, a disposable pawn in the political arena. Disappointment turned to bitterness. She worried about being followed, sneaking furtive glances over her shoulder, checking the rear view mirror, peeking through curtains at odd hours.

Senator Collins popped into her thoughts, as did the conversation with Mrs. Sells. Leslie couldn't stop thinking about the investigation. Nights provided nothing but time to worry and stew. And then someone entered the scene to complicate her life; someone became the new fixation. Only a peripheral impression at first, someone soon surfaced as her primary tormentor: Lieutenant Colonel James Colby–Michael Allen Stokes.

Before leaving Washington, Leslie made additional copies of his records and returned the original copy to the bank lock box she planned to share with the *WASHINGTON POST* if.... She now studied his picture and leafed through the folder of military information trying to piece together the mysterious events surrounding his disappearance. *I know he is implicated in my dismissal. NYPD says he is dead. Mrs. Sells says he is alive. The Marine Corps says he is dead. Paul Sells said he is alive and hiding in Colorado. He is alive. I know it.*

Colby's name change, the unauthorized money, the murdered Libyan diplomats, suspension of the joint CIA/FBI team, and the dates: Fifteen, Sixteen and Seventeen June popped up everywhere. Leslie impulsively placed a call to Mrs. Sells. "Mrs. Sells, this is Leslie Reardon. Do you remember me?"

"Of course, Miss Reardon. How could I ever forget."

"I would very much like to talk to you again. Would that be possible?"

A long pause, then rapid, uneven heavy breathing. "Oh...I don't...that might not be such a good idea, Miss Reardon."

"Just a few questions, Mrs. Sells, now that things have settled down. I really would like to speak with you. We could do it over the phone. I could come to your home."

"No! No, I told you everything. There isn't anything else to talk about. I'm sorry."

"I see. Has anyone said anything to you about what you told me, Mrs. Sells?"

Another long silence. "Look, Miss Reardon, I can't talk to you now or ever again. I'm sorry. Please don't call again. Good bye."

Mrs. Sells unwillingness didn't bother Leslie near as much as the likelihood that someone had probably listened. *She can't talk because she knows they are monitoring. And now they know I'm still asking questions.* She worried, even with her secret copy of the investigation dangling over their heads, and began watching over her shoulder for phantoms again.

The futile call to Mrs. Sells didn't stop Leslie's quest for more details. She handled the next venture with more discretion, asking a police officer acquaintance to call the state license bureau and ask about Stokes. He called back the next day.

"Yes, Michael Allen Stokes does have a current Colorado operator's license, Leslie. He lives at 916 Forness street, right here in beautiful downtown Denver."

Leslie's heartbeat accelerated as she drove to the address.

A vacant lot!

She flopped back in the seat and breathed a sigh of relief. The fake address didn't upset her near as much as finding him at home would have. She placed a mental stopper over the notion of resuming the investigation after that, deciding to let go. Her good intentions lasted almost over the weekend. She called the license bureau again Monday morning to ask about a possible address correction for Stokes, but hung up before they answered. *What am I trying to prove?*

Leslie dreamed about him and awoke trembling, the pillow soaked with tears. *What is happening? Can I be emotionally involved with someone I don't even know?*

She decided to do something about the bourgeoning obsession and packed early the next morning and drove fourteen hours nonstop to Springfield, Missouri. She arrived late that night, sleeping as close to his hometown as she could get. The next day she drove thirty miles north to Colby's hometown, went directly to his school and walked the hallways inspecting class pictures until she located his–ten boys and fourteen girls. Most of the boys sported flattop haircuts, Colby included.

She studied the picture, memorizing his face. "What happened to you, Jim Colby? Where are you?"

"Did you say something, Ma'am?"

The voice startled her, so engrossed with his picture that the elderly janitor arrived unnoticed.

"Oh, no thank you. I always talk to myself."

"Well, anything I can help with, Ma'am?"

"Yes, perhaps you can. Would you happen to remember Jim Colby?" She pointed to the class picture.

"Oh, sure. I been here near on forty year. I know all of 'em. Yep, Jim Colby. Good kid. In fact , I'd say about the best we ever had. He's dead now, you know. Got kilt in a car wreck in New York City." He shook his head and clucked. "Shame about what happened. Oh, yeah, I remember all of 'em and their parents before." He caught himself talking too much, grinned sheepishly and said, "Sorry. I get carried away. You a friend of his? You ain't from around here, are you?"

"No. I read something about him and thought I might write a story."

"Oh. You a reporter for the *News-Leader* in Springfield?"

"No, just a freelance writer looking for a story."

"Well, his is sure some story. A sad story, though, that's for sure. Beats all I ever heard. Had everything a man could want, then things just sort of blew apart. Yep, beats all. Too bad about him getting kilt like he did, what with all the wars and everything he lived through, then go and get hit by a danged car in a big city."

Her quest for information led to the school superintendent's secretary who supplied photo copies of pages she wanted from Colby's yearbooks. Leslie located the home of his youth, the ranch he lost, his ex-wife's home where she waited and watched from the car. A woman left the garage open and drove away late in the afternoon. Leslie followed to a local grocery store.

Attractive. Perhaps a little matronly. Good grief! I resent her! How odd.

She drove slowly through his home town the next morning, and then sped back to Denver, arriving late that night, anxious to examine the new material and paste clippings of his high school and college athletic achievements in the growing folder.

Leslie called the New York police records department and the same sergeant she had spoken to during the Senate investigation, reminding him of the previous call. "So, Sergeant, what did you conclude."

"The circumstances surrounding Colby's death are abnormal, Miss Reardon. I am responsible for recording all deaths investigated by the department and I did not enter the data on your man Colby. It appears official–I'm looking right at it–but his record is incomplete. Lots of required information left out; time and place for instance. I never record a death the way this one was logged. Not ever."

"Who did then?"

"I don't know. Someone had to insert the information about Colby into the files. I brought it to my supervisor's attention. He promised to get back to me. Do you want me to call you back?"

"Not unless you find out who did it and why." She gave her phone number and hung up feeling euphoric. *That seals it. He is alive.*

Leslie realized the CIA investigation no longer mattered and had stopped caring about exposing Charlie Collins or the President. She needed to know about Colby for no other reason than to satisfy what had become a deep-seated personal curiosity. Her consuming fascination about Colby took precedence over everything. She consigned data about Colby to a flourishing file of information and pictures, all in chronological order. He had a decent academic background, mostly A's and B's. He had been the student body president and three sport star athlete. The All-American boy. Leslie library of Colby's life stopped at the end of May, barely four months past. She could only speculate about what happened after that. *What am I doing? This has got to stop!*

*****

She called Anne Crowely, lifetime friend from first grade through high school. Leslie discarded Denver after high school for Stanford Law while Anne stayed home to marry her high school sweetheart. Years later, Leslie comforted and guided Anne through a messy divorce and their renewed relationship flourished. They had been close friends since the divorce, until Leslie left for Washington. Anne served as Leslie's antithesis: bouncy personality, big hair, snow white complexion, springy breasts shamelessly featured in low-cut clothing, and to top it off, a pink Cadillac, the product of her cosmetics business.

"Meet me for lunch, Anne?"

"Sure. Anything wrong?"

When they met, and after several minutes of friendly chatter, Leslie introduced the topic of concern. "Anne, I am in deep trouble."

Anne looked properly shocked, covering her cleavage. "Good heavens! That bad?"

"Yes and no. I desperately need to talk about it. Okay, him."

"Well, honey, you can count me in. A him? Really? Great! You were there for me when I needed you, remember? Go."

First, she revealed everything about being fired–almost.

Anne listened, intent and silent, then sat back, covered her mouth with one hand, her forehead with the other. "For heaven's sake, Leslie. So that's why you came back to Denver. What are you going to do now?"

"About the investigation? I'm through messing with that. My problem now is a Marine Lieutenant Colonel named James Colby." She revealed almost everything, including her obsession. "What am I going to do about him?"

"Do you have a picture?"

Leslie produced Colby's promotion photo.

Anne nodded, humming to herself. "I see. Well, it would be easy enough for me to be curious about someone like that." She returned the picture. "Well, well, well. I think maybe you've got an old fashioned adolescent crush on the man, that's what I think." She gave Leslie her best coy look. "Leslie Reardon, of all people, fascinated by a man, and a complete stranger at that. Let me get this straight–you have a crush on some guy you have never even seen before? Is that right? A mystery man. Wow. That's not at all like you, Les."

Leslie smarted from the merciless teasing. "Just what is like me, Anne? And try to be compassionate. I have feelings you know."

Anne reached across the table and took Leslie's hand. "Of course you do. All I meant to say is, I have never known you to be all that attracted by any man. I have to tell you though, an obsession with a complete stranger seems just a teensy bit peculiar to me. That is what isn't at all like you, Les."

"Maybe you don't know me as well as you thought."

"Guess not. And maybe you haven't told me everything? Look at it from my perspective, Les, then you tell me, what am I supposed to think?"

"Oh, God, Anne. Why do I think about him at all? How can a man I have never met affect me so much?"

Anne looked over the top of her bejeweled pink Ben Franklins. She knew Leslie's life history as no other person. She knew that any man in her friend's life would have to be marked as highly irregular. She alone knew that two prison escapees had broken into the Reardon home when Leslie was fourteen, beaten her father into a coma, raped and beaten her mother and then molested Leslie for two days before a suspicious neighbor called police. Leslie's mother died within days. Her father never recovered emotionally or physically and spent the remainder of his life in physical rehabilitation facility or in Leslie's care. Years of psychiatric therapy had done little to cure Leslie of her anxieties concerning men, even though the two criminals had not raped her..

Anne said, "I didn't think any man would ever have an effect on you like this, so suppose you tell me why this one is. Hmmmmm?"

Leslie considered the challenge. "I have thought about nothing else for days. Actually, for weeks. The honest truth?" There is no way, logically, to justify it. I am emotionally involved with him, Anne. I do understand that. I know curiosity is the driving force, but I do not understand why he seems so important. Why can't I put him out of my mind? I think the truth is, I don't want to. Is he alive? Does he live in Colorado? Was he associated with the investigation? If so, why? How? On and on I go."

"Damn, Leslie! There has to be more to this."

"No." She fibbed unconvincingly.

"Well, I think there must be, and I think it has everything to do with what you know about this guy Stokes that you are not telling me. Honestly, I didn't think anyone would ever get through that defensive veneer of yours. I hope it is about the man, not the circumstance."

"Oh, Anne, that's silly. Let's get back to the subject. Have I gone off the deep end?"

"Of course you have, silly! That's what I just said! Look, I can understand why you would be upset about what happened to you in Washington. I would murder anyone who treated me like that. But this mystery man is a whole different something else. Maybe he is just some emotional escape mechanism, and maybe you are subconsciously insulating yourself from the trauma of what happened in Washington by fantasizing about him. Perhaps he is interesting, maybe even attractive, but maybe you are using him because you are safe from him. Possible?"

"I honestly don't know what to think. Sometimes I think I am walking a line between sanity and insanity. Is it so crazy to think about him?"

"Maybe. Maybe not." Anne leaned closer and whispered, "Do you ever have premonitions? Have you ever reached for the phone just as it rang to find the party you were going to call is on the line?"

Leslie started to protest, but Anne pressed ahead. "Don't answer. The reason I asked is because all those things happen to me."

"What's the point, Anne?"

"The point is, maybe he is your destiny."

Leslie recoiled angrily, glaring at her friend. "Oh, for God's sake! You know better than that. And you know me better than that." She squirmed and looked away.

"Apparently I don't. Maybe you intuitively know intangible and psychic things about this Colby fellow."

Leslie rolled her eyes. "Anne, really. That's just marvelous. I'm psychic. Psychotic would be better."

Anne could see her logic wasn't finding a receptive audience. "Oh, get back to work, Leslie. You don't need me. Get your job back. Stay busy. Everything will work out."

*****

Leslie broke from self-imposed exile and reclaimed her old position with the regional ACLU. She received a high-profile assignment to represent the Southern Ute Indian tribe in the final stages of a mining permit lawsuit against the federal government and her daytime thoughts drifted from Colby. She threw herself into work, laboring long, hard hours, almost but not quite drowning her illusions with work.

The worst times for Leslie came at night, just before and after sleep. She always thought about him during quiet times. She didn't think about Senator Collins, or Washington, or the CIA, or the investigation. She thought about *him.*

Chapter Twenty

KAREEM

The day after Jim boarded the airplane at the beginning of the mission, his tutor, Kareem, arrived at Langley. He arrived with two men dressed in casual attire. They followed him from the agency car to the office of his regular contact.

A young man stood and said, "Ah, Kareem. Nice to see you again. You have been out for some time." He nodded to the two men standing behind.

Kareem was so ready for relief, finally free from demands of the exacting American's torture sessions in the sauna. "Yes, the assignment was difficult." His eyes flashed anger. "Now, why am I here? Why am I being detained? I have been loyal."

The contact, unsettled by Kareem's anger, looked away and cleared his throat. "The Assistant Director wants to see you. These gentlemen will escort you."

Kareem, by then more apprehensive than angry, for although he despised Adrian Burt, he also feared him. Burt came around his cluttered desk to shake hands. The two men operated in a frosty alliance, an awkwardness promoted by Burt's suspicions even after a three-year association.

Three long years had elapsed since Kareem approached the Agency upon arriving in the States, volunteering his services to the United States government for the privilege of a Green Card and promise of future citizenship. He knew a great deal about Libya and the Agency wanted him. Three years and his citizenship papers still had not progressed beyond the probationary stage. Burt never quite believed the legitimacy of his defection. Kareem identified

Burt as his nemesis. He was indignant that the Ops Director had never used him without cumbersome restraints, always on trial with the Agency. Adrian didn't believe Kareem's story: escaping Libya to save his life, or that the Libyan government wanted to try him for treason, or that he hated Libya and would do anything for America, betray any trust and abandon every connection to his birthright, anything to endear himself to his new country of choice. Burt had obtained valuable intelligence information from Kareem on occasion, information that always proved accurate and helpful, so the alliance endured.

Kareem had visited the States as a military exchange officer before Libya became an enemy, attending the War College at Fort Leavenworth in Kansas. He seemed to adapt well to life in the United States, spoke English fluently, understood American slang and accepted Western fashions and habits. Nothing could have been farther from the truth.

Kareem's tribal name in Libya was Kareem Alef Assid. He belonged to the tribe of Musa Abdul-Hafez, Abdel Hafez's father. Kareem was Hafez's first cousin. His mission in life and sole purpose in America was to engineer his cousin's rise to power. He believed, and had been promised that the day his cousin took power would be the day he would return to Libya as a national hero.

Abdel Hafez, with advice and backing of his father, revitalized the Revolutionary Guard and rose to a position of power second only to the head of state. The Libyan leader at that time, Muammar Khadafy, another desert kinsman, represented the last obstacle to the Hafez plan for complete power. Hafez sent Kareem to America to serve as a listening post and to infiltrate a branch of the American government posing as a defector. Hafez found Kareem's reports favorable and believed that America would not interfere when the time came to take control. American oil interests in Libya would sway the government not to interfere in Libyan politics.

Burt forced a smile and said, "Your work during the past two months has been commendable, Kareem. I have good reports. The Agency would like to reward you. Some members of the Washington office are going up to our mountain retreat this weekend. I want to offer you the opportunity to go along. How would you like that?" He smiled and winked at one of the attending guards.

Kareem started to object. His immediate plans did not include spending time with Americans. Safia, desert princess and current female fixation, waited. His anxiety escalated. The mountain retreat held infamous status within the agency, often used to hide and protect important defectors and fugitives. The sanctuary lay well inside a national forest in the Smoky Mountains. Few outside of the Agency knew of its existence. It was little more than a peaceful hangout for recuperating agents and a glorified prison for guys like Kareem who needed to be restricted. Once inside, no man could get out and outsiders could not get in.

Adrian Burt recognized Kareem's dilemma and gleefully bored in. "Well, what do you think? Should be a good time."

Kareem studied the Director's face for a clue and resisted answering.

Burt went through an almost ceremonial process, step by exasperating step, of lighting one of his loathsome cigars, and said, "Well, come on. What do you think? Sound good to you?"

Kareem shrugged. "Do I have a choice?"

The Director's face hardened. He snapped a lighter open, sucked on the cigar until a cloud of rich, candied smoke filled the space between the adversaries. "None whatsoever. Have a good time." He waved the little troupe out.

One of the men behind Kareem tapped him on the shoulder and jerked his thumb toward the door. The Director threw his head back and blew smoke rings as Kareem backed away, leaving the building between two humorless agents, one he recognized as the driver from Dulles the day his language student left the farm compound. Paul Sells. He remembered speaking to Sells at an applicant lecture during his first week at the agency.

Kareem spent the following days at the mountain retreat, bored and frustrated, thinking of Safia and hating everything American. On August sixteenth, the little group boarded a plain white windowless government van and traveled back to Washington. Kareem worried about his destination and safety. The driver unceremoniously dumped him on the curb in front of his apartment and drove away. Kareem suspected all along that his incarceration at the retreat had everything to do with the recent assignment. While watching the van vanish, he thought, So, the mission must be complete. Will I ever know?

Safia didn't answer. With nothing to do, he watched the late-late news. The commentator wasted no time reporting breaking news from Libya. "First, today's shocking news. Abdel Hafez, Libyan terrorist leader, has been assassinated in Benghazi. Hundreds died in the ensuing panic. More after these words from our sponsor."

Assassinated?

Kareem stared at the television, bewildered, furious, tormented and sick, all at the same time. He leaped to his feet, glaring at the television. The commentator reported that, 'An anonymous Arab terrorist group has taken credit for the assassination.'

Kareem knew better. *I aided my cousin's murderer! They used me to kill my own cousin!* He kicked the offending television into shards of plastic and glass, raging and screaming. After regaining control, he sat on the couch, closed his eyes and thought. He flew to Libya the next day, downhearted and furious. His champion had been destroyed on a bloodstained stage in Benghazi. His life dreams perished the instant his cousin died. He no longer had reason to play the part of defector. He no longer had a cause to live and sacrifice for. His purpose in life was destroyed. He would seek guidance.

Kareem didn't trust anyone in the Libyan government enough to reveal the secret of Hazam. They would treat him as a traitor. Some would probably identify him as a defector, not as a patriot. No, he would say nothing publically about Hazam. Kareem had traveled to America to do his uncle's work and would now seek his counsel in time of need. Musa Hafez lived in the desert, hundreds of miles inland from Benghazi.

One day after entering Libya, after an all-night automobile journey and short helicopter flight, Kareem sat astride an Arabian horse along the crest of a great sand dune ready to descend into the oasis containing his uncle's village of goatskin tents. He reined the horse to a stop and inhaled the late evening desert air. The irony of his immediate circumstances did not escape notice. *I have come all the way back–hundreds of miles into the desert and two-thousand years back in time. Home.*

He didn't remain long in the tents of his family, departing in two days with two trusted relatives, both educated in America and fiercely loyal to the tribe. Three days later, after entering the United States through Mexico, he reclined in the rear seat of a rental car parked in the shadows across the street from a two story colonial home in the suburbs. Paul Sells' home.

The Agency had assigned Sells to nonessential jobs after the Athens' debacle, stationing him deep within the bowels of the intelligence center with no real job, disenfranchised, disheartened, unhappy, nothing more than a burdensome liability. Sells was emotionally drained, listless, unable to break the torment of memories and too bewildered to reason. He wanted to retire. His pride lost a battle of wills to his wife's panic-stricken plea for security. "You have to stay, Paul. You won't get full retirement benefits now. Only one more year, Paul. You owe me that much!"

His spirit spiraled steadily downhill. He withdrew into an alcoholic cocoon and toyed with suicide. Depression consumed vitality from his life. He slept, seldom feeling well enough to connect with family and drank at the office. The numbing benevolence of alcohol helped him through the grim hours of wakefulness. He no longer even pretended to work. After work, he stopped at a neighborhood bar to fortify himself for the predictable encounter with his wife's wrath.

Later, after stumbling from the bar, girded for her anger, he sat in the car entertaining a plan of ending it all. He couldn't think well enough to devise a painless way to do it and drove home to her. He could recite her sniping from memory: 'Clean up before you come to the table. Take off your coat for Christ's sake! You smell like a damned brewery. If you go to bed again without a shower, I swear, Paul, I'm going to leave!' She would be terrible. He steered onward because he didn't have the energy to think of a better place to go.

Sells sat in his drive wrestling with thoughts of returning to the bar. He gave up, switched the ignition off and stepped from the car directly into the muzzle of an automatic pistol. The depression he felt only moments before shifted to fright, and fright to panic. He recognized the intruder as the guy who had driven with Hazam to Dulles. Since the assassination, Sells had worried that something like this might happen.

Kareem waved the pistol toward a car parked across the darkened street and said, "Go there. Make no mistakes."

Paul stumbled to the car, reacting without thinking and saw two more men. They drove to a small country house somewhere west of town and tied him to a sturdy wooden chair in the center of an otherwise unfurnished, windowless room. Kareem turned on an overhead light.

Sells really didn't care what happened next. Nothing mattered. He watched the proceedings as a disinterested observer. He didn't speak and never once offered resistance. Paul knew from the instant he first saw Kareem that the Arab would kill him. He accepted the finality of his plight, summoning long-lost inner strength, not strength to resist, but the strength to be dignified. He yielded to the inevitable and surrendered to death.

Kareem wasted no time, ordering the others outside to serve as sentries. He then turned his attention to Sells, demanding information concerning the assassin. "Who was he? Where is he? What name does he use? I have many ways to gain information. I will know or you die."

Sells refused to answer or even look at Kareem. The silence infuriated the Arab and he began pounding with a club. The beating continued until Paul lost consciousness. Kareem changed methods and ripped at the female end of an extension cord to expose bare electrical wires, then plugged the male end of the cord into a wall socket. He applied the bare wires to Sells' throat each time his perspiring victim refused to answer a question. Sells' body contorted involuntarily with each electrical shock. He crashed to the floor still tied to the chair, convulsing uncontrollably, struggling to breathe. Kareem seemed to enjoy watching Sells' reaction and played with the electricity until the room reeked of burnt flesh and electrical smoke.

Paul screamed. Screams escaped no matter how much he tried to keep his mouth closed. Kareem employed the electricity until the seizures provoked complete paralysis and ultimately blackout. Unconsciousness was an unreliable ally; Paul couldn't depend on it to last. Each time he awoke, Kareem administered the electricity. Paul Sells sensed death. The certainty of death brought peace of mind. He craved death.

Kareem recognized that his hostage couldn't tolerate more punishment–no man could. He had known from the onset that use of sodium pentothal might be necessary to prove any answers torture furnished. Truth serum became his last chance to extract information from the tormented man writhing on the floor.

Sells didn't know much: The name–Michael Allen Stokes. State of residence–Colorado. Yes, Stokes assassinated Hafez. No, he had not seen him since. No, he didn't know where Colby was. Kareem contemplated more torture, but decided against further delay. He tied the exposed electrical wires to Paul's genitals and connected the plug to the wall socket. Paul lost consciousness and died from heart failure within seconds.

Chapter Twenty-One

COLORADO

Jim headed west from Colorado Springs, steering entirely away from population centers, driving from one isolated location to another looking for a place to live. Days later he stumbled onto some vacated mine buildings in western Colorado and spent time exploring back roads between Silverton and Creed, high in the San Juan mountains.

After a miserable, cold night in the truck, he drove to Silverton, a small town in west central Colorado. Silverton once had been the center of a gold mining bonanza. The mines were now nearly all closed and deserted. The town existed almost entirely as a recreation destination. While eating lunch at a small café, he noticed a bulletin board by the cash register containing notices thumbtacked to the cork. He examined the posts and found job offerings. One appealed to him, an advertisement for a deserted mine complex watchman. Call.... He took the card and called. A woman answered.

"I am looking for a job and noticed your card. What does the job entail?"

"Just a minute. I'll get the boss."

A gruff man took over. "Yo, this is Arnold. What can I do for you?"

"I need work. Is the mine watchman job still available?"

"Where are you right now?"

Sitting in my truck in Silverton."

"Come on down to the Coffee Café on main street. Ask for Arnold Gant."

Arnold led him to a back booth. "Why are you up here? You got woman problems? Drugs? Alcohol? I can't use a man gonna cause me worry."

Jim grinned and offered his hand. "Name's Michael Stokes, and I'm clean. Just looking for seasonal work."

Arnold took his glasses off and cleaned them on his shirt sleeve before continuing. "I see. Okay then, is there anything between you and the law I should know about?" He cocked an eye at Jim. "Or maybe there's somethin' you'd druther I didn't know about?"

"Nope. I have a clean record. No dope, no liquor problems. I'm in decent physical shape. I expect I can do the job for you."

"Okay, what have you done? Just so I know what I'm dealin' with."

"I am retired from the Marine Corps. Single and honest. I don't mind hard work. You can depend on me, if that worries you." He decided to gamble. "I can get references." He couldn't, of course, but hoped Arnold wouldn't insist.

Arnold's eyes bored in relentlessly, looking for signs of weakness. "I'm a pretty good judge of only two things, partner: horses and men. I don't know nuthin' about women or money and I ain't never going to know." He laughed and his eyes glittered merrily in the shade of the worn brown Stetson. "Nope, I don't need no reference on you. I make my own mind up about men. Now look, partner, I don't want to hire no damned dude. Life up here ain't all that romantic. Okay, if you got time I'll show you the deal."

They drove east for fifteen minutes and stopped on the road. Arnold got out and motioned for Jim to follow. He stood in the middle of the road and pointed up—way up. "There she is, bud. The old Boxer mine. I represent a corporation that just leased all of it for fifteen years. They plan to make a tourist attraction out of her with all the fixin's. May take a while, though. Years maybe. Anyway, they want a reliable watchman and you might fit the bill. The job ain't much, Michael. They call you that?"

"Mike works for me."

"Okay. We loan the necessary tack and two horses. You have wheels, I guess."

"Yes. A four-wheel-drive pickup."

"That's good because it's pretty steep and the road is rough going up there. The pay is three-hunnert a week and a place to stay. You have to buy your own grub. That's it. Take it or leave it."

"What, exactly, are the duties?"

"It's big place, as you can see. Several mines all along up there. What they need is a man to keep vagrants and thieves out until the place opens, and that could be two years from now." He pointed and swung his arm along the mountain." All of those old mine buildings you see are a part of it. There are paths you can take to get around between the different mines. There is a pretty good industrial fence all the way around." He pointed to a cabin about half way up the mountain. "That right there is where you will live. I kinda like the place myself. Little rough maybe, but snug and fit. Has a fireplace. You will need some bedding. There is a working hand pump well for the horse, but you probably want to carry your own drinking water in. There is a tight shed behind the house to hold the horses and truck. You ride don't you?"

"Yes. I can handle a horse."

"That's good. A horse is about the only decent way to get around up there. Your job will be to keep the fence up and patrol at different hours a couple of times a day. That's about all there is to it. It ain't as easy as it sounds This is mighty rugged country. I'll want you to check in with me every day on the phone so I know you're okay for one thing, and so you can keep me up on things. It really is a pretty damned fine place to live if you like being alone. As I said, they ain't no electricity, but it's tight and dry. You will need to get into town once a day to charge your phone, or you can get one of them little portable generator thingys and stay up there as long as you like. If you like livin' all by your ownself, I expect you'll probably like it just fine." He squinted at Jim. "If you move anyone in, though, I'll have to approve that. So, what do you think?"

"I'd like to try it."

Arnold nodded. "You ain't gonna be up there none too long this year. I expect the weather will drive you down soon. A month, maybe less. Snow drifts over the road at that altitude from September until late spring. Be pretty dangerous to get trapped up there. Hell, you can stay up there all winter if you like. I wouldn't, though. Access by wheeled vehicle will be impossible and it will probably stay that way until sometime in April."

Jim nodded, trying to look thoughtful to hide his delight. "Think I'll just take it, if it's all the same to you."

Arnold offered his hand. "It's a done deal then. I'll save a room for you in back of the cafe during the winter if you're a mind to stick around."

Jim remained in town for two days working the kinks out of a pair of jumpy horses, then assembled a stockpile of supplies and headed for the mines. What he discovered wasn't the lean-to shack in the trees he imagined. He stopped the truck short of the cabin, draped his arms over the steering wheel and took stock. Everything about the cabin suited him, at least from the outside, and best of all, he didn't have to sign anything. His nearest neighbor lived miles away. Last but not least important for a fugitive–no one could pop in on him unexpectedly. The half mile long road up to the cabin was steep and treacherous.

Jim planned to supplement the meager salary by living off the land when possible. Small game, pinion nuts, fish and wild vegetables should be plentiful in the mountains. He didn't break out in smiles or celebrate wildly when he saw the cabin, but faced the prospect of living on the mountain with as much enthusiasm as he had been able to generate for anything in months. Life looked good and his new home came with mountain smells and sounds. He almost felt content.

Jim finished surveying the area and breathed a sigh of relief as the cabin was too far off the roads to be bothered by casual back-packers. He planned to tack "posted" signs near the road to town. His only visitors would be animals. Elk and deer would probably frequent the meadow morning and evening.

The cabin rested at the edge of a blue spruce and aspen forest. He could see Pole Creek mountain to the east, standing nearly fourteen-thousand-feet. Jim carried boxes of provisions to the front porch and placed them on the slatted swing, then turned to look back down the mountain. Looking southward, he observed the most picturesque mountain valley he had ever seen. The hollow, echoing sounds of a stream rushing over boulders far below echoed up the mountain. Along with the cabin, a small barn and corral sat next to the meadow fifty yards from the cabin. He noted, with some satisfaction, that the meadow was fenced and would provide adequate forage for the horses, at least until snow. He walked down to the main road twice to get the horses.

The first thing he noticed upon opening the door–spiders–spider webs everywhere. He drove back into Silverton to purchase insect spray and feed for the horses. Finished shopping, he noticed a commotion down the street near his truck. A police car, rotating lights flashing, blocked the street. A crowd of interested sightseers gathered. He walked down the opposite side of the street to observe and winced at the sight of a tourist bus butted against the rear of his truck. He took a deep breath and crossed the street.

"That's my truck."

The officer on the scene extracted a small notebook from his shirt and prepared to write. "I don't think the damage amounts to anything, Mister...?" He looked up, waiting for a name.

"Stokes." Jim agonized over the requirement to furnish his name, but thought, What the hell. I'll probably only be here a few weeks.

"And the name of your insurance company, Mister Stokes?"

Jim thought quickly and lied. "United Services Automobile Association, but I'm not going to make a claim for that little ding. I won't be asking for insurance money."

The officer stopped writing, cocked an eye at Jim and said, "Well, if you say so, but the bus company insurance will sure pay if you want it fixed. They ran into you after all. You sure that's the way you want it?" He was already putting the notebook away, thankful to avoid the hassle of writing up another fender-bender.

Jim tried to appear nonchalant. "It doesn't amount to anything. Yeah, I'm sure." The crowd dispersed and he left town immediately, relieved that the incident hadn't been important enough to record.

There are few roads leading into or away from Silverton, other than the north/south highway descending into the valley from eleven-thousand-foot passes on both ends of town. Jim enjoyed the challenge of driving the challenging mountain road and returned to the cabin in good spirits, prepared to battle spiders. He spent the next day cleaning the cabin and two night sleeping on the porch, away from insecticide fumes.

He decided to adopt the name Jim when dealing with neighbors. Michael Allen Stokes was too easy to remember. He didn't plan to see, let alone talk to many people, but anyone who came to know him would call him Jim. When he arrived at the cabin in early September, the aspens were losing leaves and winter had already sent out early scouts. The aspen leaves had long since changed to a yellow and his horses were developing thick winter coats. The average night-time temperature fell a degree or two each day. He still hadn't given much thought to where he would spend the winter months when it became necessary to leave.

He arrived on the mountain less than a month after the harrowing escape from Libya. The hatred and grief that once controlled and ruined his life had diminished. When feeling anything at all about the assassination, he felt remorse. Visions of that day lurked and lingered in the shadows of his mind, churning to life during quiet times. Quiet nights on the mountain only heightened the spectacle of carnage trapped in his memory. Death and violence coiled in darkness. Jim struggled with memories as silence and time vied to ruin what prospects he had for peace of mind. He worked feverishly to keep from thinking and gradually achieved at least some semblance of peace, even occasionally pondering the prospect of a future. The illusion of a future always perished, smothered in the ashes of his past. He couldn't break the bonds of Benghazi.

I have become one of Thoreau's mass of men leading lives of quiet desperation.

His daily activities settled into a vigorous routine of work, only occasionally did he notice the beauty of his surroundings. His life stabilized emotionally, yet he never laughed or smiled. Days became tolerable if he didn't think too much; the nights demolished him.

He began writing in spare time—scribbling notes, jotting ideas, sometimes in the saddle, sometimes late at night. The ticking bedside clock, once his enemy, lost importance to the rhythms of high country. Time became an asset. He still alerted at unusual sounds, pausing to listen and determine the source. His emotional state had improved to such an extent that sleep no longer ended in sweat drenched nightmares. His thoughts drifted from the past to tomorrow and days to come.

Chapter Twenty-Two

THE MOUNTAIN

Leslie's work for the Indian tribe kept her running from one government agency to another, from the state capitol offices to archives. She worked steadily, sunup to sundown, day after day, accumulating facts to support the tribe's case against the federal government. Leslie navigated the musty halls of bureaucracy until she had the necessary information to press for settlement.

With a nudge from the national ACLU office, the judge shoved her claim ahead on his docket. When the government defense lawyers encountered her evidence, they asked for a recess, bickered amongst themselves, conceded impending defeat and settled out of court. The Southern Ute Indian tribe profited from a substantial payoff. The federal government reimbursed the tribe for minerals taken from the reservation illegally over the past fifty years. The princely settlement astonished the tribe and helped restore Leslie's confidence. She felt good about herself as an attorney for the first time in years, treasuring the wave of professional recognition and personal fulfillment.

However, even in light of glowing success, time didn't pass her by without a measure of weak moments. She still couldn't suppress depressing thoughts about Senator Collins and the aborted CIA investigation, or the disturbing memory about Mrs. Sells and the likelihood that the last call had placed her very high on the CIA skyline.

Relentless, sleepless spells resurfaced after dreams about Colby, dreams that raided her nights with increasing intensity, leaving her always more distressed. The same dream shattered her sleep night after night: dusky men with guns pursuing the man locked in the center drawer of her desk. The dreams left her feeling powerless and frustrated. She could not exorcize Jim Colby from her life, waking from the dreams to battle the relentless obsession with his folder. She seldom went back to sleep without surrendering, and once again opened the drawer to spend hours combing through his records. Leslie found little solace in the file and never discovered anything new. She would sigh and lock the records away.

Why can't I let him go? He has become part of me.

She had other issues, not so pressing or important. Washington still plagued her, as did painful memories of Charlie Collins and the aborted investigation. Leslie received an unexpected opportunity to learn more about Colonel Colby in early September. A member of the Colorado Attorney General's staff assigned to monitor the Indian tribe claim provided the opening.

"Don, if I asked you to find out something for me, something quite unofficial, would you consider it?"

He didn't look up from his work, but grinned mischievously and said, "Depends, Les. I am a married man you know."

"Very funny." She tapped a pencil on the desk, considering the wisdom of proceeding with the idea. "If I gave you the name of a Colorado resident, could you get information about his driving history for me?"

Don's eyebrows rose, but his eyes remained fixed on the paper before him. "Oh, probably. Why? Is this associated with the case?"

"No, nothing like that. Let's just say I've lost track of a friend and I'm curious. It's personal, Don, nothing connected to business, so if you don't want to...."

Don closed his eyes, raised his forefinger to indicate enlightenment. "I am to serve as a private investigator, right?" He looked up and smiled slyly. "This couldn't have anything to do with your notorious nightlife, could it, Les? Some old boyfriend?"

She recognized an opening and smiled demurely. "Maybe. Would you?"

He nodded. "Sure. What do you want to know?"

She started typing to conceal the importance of her request. "Oh, just the normal things you get with license plate readouts. Where he lives will do for a start. If you can get his address, I can take it from there."

He grinned, then frowned and said, "Wait a minute. You mean you don't even know where this guy lives?"

Leslie cringed and stopped typing. "Not exactly." She decided to play the game Don's way, as an attempt on her part to peek in on a romantic interest. "He's sort of an enigma to me. Plays hard to get. A confirmed bachelor. I do know the address he gave me is a vacant lot. If I can locate him, I intend to give him a well-deserved surprise." She gave Colby's name and address.

He scanned the information and said, "A vacant lot? My, my, you are mysterious. Okay, Les, let me ask around. When do you need to know?"

"Today would be fine." She laughed nervously. "Really, no hurry, Don. It's no big deal, really. I'm just curious."

Don called the next day. "There isn't much on your mystery man, Les. All I could find is that he got rear-ended in Silverton early in September. That's on his driving record. Not his fault. No charges placed against him. No traffic points deducted. No injuries involved. No insurance involved. That's all the license people have on him."

"Did you happen to get his address?"

"Yep. Care of some realty outfit in Silverton."

Leslie's heartbeat accelerated as she scribbled the numbers. She absently replaced the receiver, forgetting to thank Don, and then spent yet another sleepless night.

So close.

The following Monday, she drove the eastern route, south from Denver through Alamosa, then west to Durango for the final meeting with the tribal chiefs. After the meeting, she departed Durango immediately after noon Tuesday, planning to drive home the western route, north through Silverton, Ouray and Montrose, then east to Denver.

Silverton

She pulled off the road five minutes later on the northern outskirts of Durango, suffering from an incriminating barrage of confusion and thoughts of turning back. *Why am I even thinking about this? I'll just drive right through Silverton and get back to Denver. Enough of this!*

She headed north, up a steep, winding mountain pass, down, then back up to eleven thousand feet, her thoughts on Silverton.

She had known for at least a week that she would drive through Silverton and deliberately sacrificed two valuable days to make the journey in a car instead of flying. Leslie continued north, struggling with condemning thoughts about common sense and wisdom. An insidious foreboding escalated with each mile, spoiling any chance to rationalize innocence. Each new turn in the road generated mounting excitement.

Silverton.

Her heart beat wildly as the road descended into Silverton an hour later. She caught fleeting glimpses of the town on the way down into the valley–a toy town in the bottom of a bowl. The road forked at the bottom–one way to Ouray and common sense, the other to Silverton and.... She turned down main street and drove directly to the sheriff's office, just as she always knew she would.

"What can I do for you, Miss?" An enormous deputy let his feet drop from a desk as she stepped into the little office.

"I'm from Denver, officer. I'm looking for a man named Michael Allen Stokes. He lives around here somewhere and I need to contact him."

"Well, I'd need more information than that to be able to help you, Ma'am. What's his address? What does he do? But first I should probably ask why you want to see him? Are you related?"

She tried not to act too interested. "The only thing I can tell you for sure is that he was rear-ended here in September by a tourist bus. He's an old acquaintance, officer and I've lost contact. I have a personal message for him and would deeply appreciate your help." She hoped a feeble smile and fluttering eyelids might work in her favor. Her severe, courtroom business suit certainly wouldn't.

"Let me look." He thumbed through a file drawer and pulled out a folder. Moments later, he waved the folder and said, "Here he is. September the Seventh, this year. Fender-bender right here on Main Street."

The door behind her popped open as another officer entered. The deputy with the folder shook his head slowly and said, "There isn't much of anything here, Miss. He don't have no address, other than an in-care-of. Hey, Ed, you know this guy? Stokes. Michael Allen Stokes?"

The other deputy nodded to Leslie, looked at the folder for a moment. His face lit up. "Oh, yeah. I don't exactly know him, but I know where he lives." He glanced at the other deputy for permission.

"Yeah, it's okay, Ed. They're old friends."

"He's the watchman out at the Boxer mines. Lives in the old superintendent's cabin up on the site. Yep, that's him all right. Stokes. I remember him. Took an insurance refusal statement from him once. Didn't seem none too upset about the dent. Didn't plan to file, so I just filled out the form. Yeah, that's the guy all right. Stokes."

"Could you tell me how to find him?" Leslie asked, smiling warmly. "I would love to drop in and surprise him."

Both men started laughing, looked at each other, and then laughed again. "Oh, sorry. Yes, Ma'am, it's easy enough to give directions, but that ain't the problem. That's why we're laughing. You see, the problem is he lives miles back in the mountains. That's the problem. It's easy to find his place, though. All you have to do is go east out of here to Howardsville, then turn right on the first side road to Stony Pass. Road sign points the way. Once you get to the turnoff it's...oh, maybe five miles on the left-hand side of the road. Can't miss it. His place is the only house on that side until you get to the pass. A big sign on the left reads, Boxer Mines." He frowned at her, squinted and said, "You ain't thinking about driving up there, are you?"

Leslie's chin rose imperceptibly. "I certainly am. That's why I came." The confident response surprised her more than the deputies. She had not given thought to the notion of making an attempt to see him.

The deputies exchanged skeptical glances. The big man said, "You wouldn't be driving a four-wheel drive vehicle, would you, Ma'am?"

"No. Do I need one?"

More exchanged glances. The big man scratched the back of his neck and grimaced. "Well, yes, Ma'am. Either that or a horse."

"If I could rent such a vehicle, how long will it take to drive to his cabin?"

"Well, if you're not afraid of a pretty bad road, about half an hour I reckon."

Leslie's calm expression didn't expose her mercurial thoughts.

"Fine. Is there a rental agency here in Silverton?"

"No Ma'am, not exactly. There is this fellow who rents out some old Jeeps on his own, though. Kinda like a rental agency, I suppose. Might have to catch him at home."

Leslie scribbled the name and address and located a rundown house on the outskirts of town with a back yard filled with rundown World-War-Two Jeeps.

The proprietor refused to rent for less than a full day.

"But I will only need it two or three hours at the most."

"Don't matter. I ain't changing the rules. Take it or leave it."

After paying what she considered an exorbitant price, and after minimal instruction on the intricacies of manual shifting and four wheel drive, Leslie hiked up her skirt and climbed in.

If I have it right, it should take half an hour each way. That leaves an hour of daylight to spare. I need to hurry.

The road was rocky, dusty, narrow, twisting, but worst of all, there was a sheer drop on her right–straight down. The Jeep's wheels spun and chattered as the grade steepened. There were no side rails, no warning signs and no signs of human life. The adventuresome spirit that furnished the momentum for her journey soon faded. She would have turned back but couldn't find a place wide enough. The thought of backing down was ridiculous. It took longer than she thought to arrive at the Boxer mine sign.

PRIVATE KEEP OUT.

She rested, looking up the steep little trail leading up to the mines. Time flew and shadows lengthened. Leslie began worrying about the requirement to drive back after dark, all the while staring up the little side road. *This must be it.* She dismounted and walked a way up the extremely steep side road until coming to an opening in the trees. *Buildings. Has to be it.* She could see a barn and pickup truck at the edge of the meadow, and the outline of a cabin beyond, blending indistinctly into the trees.

Now what? "I'll tell you what, Leslie Reardon," she announced. "You get back in that Jeep and drive straight back before it gets darker." Her heart was beating wildly, not all from the effects of altitude. She didn't move, staring at the complex of buildings, lingering. *What if I.... No! I can't just drive in on a perfect stranger.* After moments of indecision, she walked back to the Jeep, lecturing all the way, "Anyway, what could I say? Hi, I'm

Leslie Reardon. You don't know me. I just happened to be in the area and thought I'd drop in."

She stood by the jeep looking up the mountain. *I really didn't plan to meet him anyway. Just want to know if he exists. Now I know.*

The Jeep started after several panic-stricken moments of grinding away on the sluggish starter. The shadows had already pushed daylight far up the mountain. The main road sloped downhill away from the little side road. Water rushing from the meadow had washed across the road, eroding the downhill side. She turned up the side road far enough to back down and turn toward Silverton on the main road, stopped and struggled to get the gears into reverse. The foot brake went all the way to the floor. She couldn't manage everything at once. The Jeep lurched backward, gaining speed as she stabbed at the squishy foot brake.

Leslie jerked at the gearshift, fighting to shove the unfamiliar mechanism into a forward gear. Any gear! The Jeep, free of engine compression, plunged backward, picking up speed as she fought the gears, steering and pumping the brakes simultaneously. Things went from bad to worse as the Jeep careened downhill. The brake pedal went all the way to the floor. She panicked, pumping the pedal furiously. Resistance began to build, just not enough to slow her flight downhill.

Leslie had enough presence of mind to turn the Jeep as it lurched onto the main road. The top-heavy vehicle skidded sideways toward the edge. She had no option remaining other than to keep pumping the brakes. The Jeep swerved drunkenly, skidded across the main road, teetered on the edge of the canyon for a moment on two wheels, and then slipped over the edge, rolled and crashed down the nearly vertical, rocky slope in a cloud of rocks and dust.

Leslie saw light, then dark, light, dark, as the vehicle rolled. She felt each blow as boulders tore the little vehicle apart, clinging to the steering wheel with all her strength, her body alternately being thrown against the seat belt, then back into the seat as the rolling motion accelerated and the Jeep gathered momentum in a ball of metal, rocks, dust and noise.

The roll bar protected her from jagged boulders until, with a glass-breaking metallic crash, the Jeep slammed into trees and stopped, ripping the seat from its anchors. The steering wheel struck her forehead and she tasted blood. No pain. Nothing, just the pleasant taste of blood, then coughing and choking. She regained a foggy level of awareness, enough to know she was hanging upside down, watching blood drip steadily from hair hanging in front of her face.

Consciousness faded in and out. The smell of gas revived her during a lucid interval.

Gas?

Leslie began tearing at the seat belt. She couldn't feel her right arm and her left arm flopped uselessly. She drifted peacefully back into the comfort of darkness. When consciousness returned, it came with a new sense of urgency demanding her attention, and it came with flames, heat and smoke. She clawed frantically at the release mechanism until it snapped open. The next impression lasted but a short time–weightlessness. Impact with the ground didn't seem as violent as the initial crash. She rolled and tumbled until with a final paralyzing jolt, slammed face first in something soft and cool. Moss.

Later, much later, eons of time later, she regained consciousness just long enough to identify the glow of fire and she couldn't move. Nothing mattered.

Chapter Twenty-Three

JIM

The clock read 4:45 a.m. Jim seldom rolled out of bed before six and couldn't think of a good reason for the restlessness. Daylight wouldn't break the eastern horizon for another hour. He groaned, threw the cover back, hung his feet over the edge and sat up.

This is ridiculous. Must be the change of seasons. I'm getting anxious to leave.

Recent weather signs proclaimed the arrival of autumn and near the end of time on the mountain. He stepped onto the porch and stretched, reviewing his plan to spend the day inside, cleaning house and resting. He dressed and clattered around the kitchen preparing breakfast, then stepped back onto the porch to look and listen at least three times before sitting down to eat.

Something out there? Maybe the elk. Every sound, every movement drew his attention. He said aloud, "Damn, I'm wired. What is it? Am I just antsy or is something out there?"

The snap in the crisp morning air carried a hint of seasonal change. He loved cool air and didn't think the weather accounted for his nervousness.

A smell? A noise? What? Something is not right.

After breakfast and several more visits to the porch, he decided to pack the saddle bags and spend the day in the wilderness away from the cabin and the odd restlessness. He saddled the bay and struck a course east into the depths of the national forest. Jim often rode just to get away from the confines of the cabin, well away from the chance of meeting another human. Riding didn't monopolize his thoughts, not astride the gentle bay mare. He carried a notebook to make a list of things he needed to do before leaving. While riding, his thoughts usually ranged widely through a variety of subjects: war and death, despondency, life as a fugitive, and, on occasion, women. Women still held the place of honor in his musings. Women were the foundation for the few pleasant thoughts he entertained. His mind roamed freely during the escape rides, lost in reflection of the past, seldom focused on the future. During the mind-cleansing thought sessions, Jim permitted the horse to choose the direction, speed of travel and when to come home. The bay would return to the corral on her own, to stand patiently waiting for him to return from preoccupations.

On this morning, he directed the horse's course for the first hour, then sat back and permitted the animal to pick the route the rest of the day. They maintained a heading generally northeast until noon, away from the cabin. The bay stopped in a small meadow, shook her head, rattling the bit, sighed heavily, tired of the journey, and waited for guidance. Jim hobbled her in tender grass near a stream, pulled the saddle bags off and stepped into the shade to find a pine needle bed. He loved being in the deep woods, leaning back on the saddle bags, enjoying the scenery, the noises and smells and a lunch of cold beans and sardines. His thoughts settled on the grim reason he lived without the comfort of even a single friend or relative. A touch of solitary living had always appealed, but only for short periods. The long weeks of seclusion on the mountain made him think too much about what prison would be like. *It's not natural to be this alone without a plan for the future.*

He ate, took the 30-30 saddle gun from the scabbard and wiped the weapon clean with an oil cloth. Jim was in no hurry to get back to the cabin. Benghazi had changed his lifetime of ease with guns, constant companions from the time he could remember. His father kept guns and had a far-reaching reputation as a champion shooter. He gave Jim a single-shot twenty-two rifle for his tenth birthday. Jim could shoot with the best long before joining the Marine Corps. His brow furrowed as he thought, I don't think I ever felt sorry for an animal I killed during a hunt, but I hate to shoot anything now. Why do I even bother carrying a gun when I'm not hunting? I wouldn't shoot a rattlesnake. Not now.

He walked back to the mare, shoved the gun into the scabbard, still brooding about the events leading to his presence on the mountain. Killing was not an option in the Marine Corps. He understood the purpose of the profession and why he chose it. He had never once rationalized the requirement to kill another human being in combat. He could justify almost everything he had ever done with a gun. One undeniable fact always popped up to cancel any attempt to defend his actions. *It really didn't require much pressure to convert me into an assassin. My motive for killing might have been just, but what about the chaos in that park. I was the right man in the right place with the right skills and the right motive. My entire life prepared me for Benghazi. It wasn't worth it. Not now. Not then. Not ever. I must have been out of my mind.*

He let the horse pick its way back through the wilderness, too engrossed in thoughts to care. He didn't return to the present until the horse stepped into the meadow east of the cabin late in the afternoon. The meadow shimmered in golden translucence, basking in the final rays of twilight as waning beams of sunlight lit only the top of the highest peaks. The air carried a new, invigorating crispness, conveying the chill of autumn.

Time to go someplace warm.

Some snow had already fallen and melted. Time on the mountain couldn't last much longer. He faithfully cleaned and fed the mare, wiped the saddle with oil and turned the horse out before heading toward the cabin, gun in hand. Half way to the cabin, he suddenly stopped to listen, cocking his good ear toward the muffled sound of an engine. *Someone on the road to town?* He stood still, holding his breath, listening. The uneasy feeling he experienced at daybreak returned. His scalp tingled. *Someone is out late.* His brow furrowed. The sensation of something alarming escalated. *Ah, probably just my damned imagination. Whatever, it probably isn't....* He heard it again. The sound did not fit the pattern of normal mountain traffic. He turned and faced down the mountain, toward the road.

Someone is down there.

Jim turned his head slightly, giving his good ear a better opportunity. His left ear had been permanently damaged from too many gun shots through the years. Then he heard it again, the unmistakably the sound of a racing engine, followed immediately by a series of metallic crashes.

That's trouble.

He sprinted back to the corral and opened the gate, bridled the gelding, jumped on bareback and kicked him into a full gallop toward the downhill end of the meadow. The horse had covered little more than half the distance when a fireball bloomed above the trees and winked out. Jim reined the horse to a walk, attempting to soothe the skittish animal, now prancing sideways, shying from the fire. Jim wanted to hurry but the frightened horse resisted.

That was one hell of a crash. Anyone in that fire will be dead before I can get there.

He tied the trembling horse to a branch at the edge of the road after first determining the spread of fire wouldn't endanger the animal. The forest floor was wet and soft from recent rain. He ran to the edge of the main road and looked over the rim toward the fire and saw the eerie silhouette of a Jeep lodged in the trees, dangling upside-down on a narrow ledge thirty yards below. The mountain dropped away vertically beneath the Jeep, seventy-five feet before another ledge projected. The burning vehicle appeared to be bent nearly double. He slid down the incline creating an avalanche of small rocks and dust, finally arresting the pell-mell descent several yards above the fiery wreck. He waited for the stream of rocks to stop rolling and moved closer to investigate the jeep. *Empty.* The fire had diminished so he circumnavigated the site while the remaining firelight could provide light for a search.

Clambering around the fire on the periphery of the light pattern, looking inward, offered only a fair chance to detect whoever came in the jeep. He slid twenty yards farther downhill, beyond the wreck. Something shiny caught his attention, a gleaming object shimmering in the forest darkness outside his intended track. He figured the glare probably came from firelight reflecting off glass from a broken window and approached to discover blood oozing from a mound of twisted flesh lodged gracelessly against the mossy base of a tree.

A woman?

Jim desperately wished for a flashlight. The fire was nearly out. He touched her, patting, exploring, finding it almost impossible to determine the extent of her injuries, carefully turning her body away from the tree. *She's still alive. I need to stop the bleeding.* Most of the blood oozed from a wound on her forehead. He searched for other serious wounds, examining her arms and legs, then tore strips from the hem of her blouse and applied a pressure compress. After checking for obstructions in her breathing passages, he noticed her pulse was extremely rapid and faint.

Oh, not good. Probably shock. Keep her warm. He stood, stripped off his jacket and shirt, placed them over her body and continued applying pressure to the wound. *I need to stop the bleeding before moving her.*

The bleeding subsided to a less alarming rate after a few moments and he left to search the remainder of the crash site for other survivors before the firelight abated. Jim returned to the woman, relieved not to find more bodies. He checked her pulse, applied another compress and began worrying more about shock than the bleeding. *She's trembling. Is that a bad sign? Shock could kill her.* He took off his undershirt and trousers and placed them over her legs. Moments later, after the bleeding subsided somewhat, he knelt, lifted the bloody bundle in his arms and began climbing the boulders one at a time. The climb to the road took twenty minutes and most of his remaining strength. He slipped and fell several times, managing to spare the woman more injury by insulating her from the jagged rocks with his body. Upon reaching the road, he collapsed gasping for air, rested, then picked her up and stumbled on.

The horse spooked and reared as he approached. He turned it loose. It would be at the corral in the morning. He lifted the woman and staggered toward the cabin, stopping several times to stem her bleeding and recover enough strength to continue the journey. He arrived at the cabin thoroughly spent, floundered into the living room, placed the unconscious woman on the floor by the fireplace and flopped beside her. He tried the cell phone.

Dead.

Chapter Twenty-Four

DESTINY

Very little time elapsed before the chill night air and penetrating cold of the rough wooden floor revived and propelled him into action. He pulled the quilt from the bed, rolled the woman snugly into its warmth and began the essential task of building a blaze in the fireplace. When the fire no longer needed constant attention, he filled a cast iron kettle with water, hung it over the flames and turned toward the woman, uncertain where to start.

What a mess. Start with those wounds.

He rested near the fire, too tired and cold to think clearly. An aching tiredness from the all-day horseback ride, lack of food, the exhausting trip back from the crash carrying the woman, all joined to temper his enthusiasm for the task still facing him. He couldn't remember ever feeling so exhausted. He stared at her a moment longer, then stripped off his bloody shorts, studied them for a moment, and then tossed them into the fire. He settled on the only logical plan possible while watching the garment burn. *She will sure die if I don't get on with this.*

A wretched, keening noise emanated from the bundle. He turned to see the woman struggling to sit up, staring at him, eyes and mouth wide open attempting to form words with her mangled mouth. He couldn't understand anything, just strangled, raspy noises and blood-flecked coughing. She struggled to hold her head up, then fell back and lost consciousness. The entire sequence took place before he managed to get close enough to understand her murmured words. He checked vital signs. *Pulse seems stronger. She's shivering. I think that's a good sign.*

He tucked the blanket around her. "Oh, good grief," he declared, looking down. "No wonder she passed out again. I'm completely naked with blood splattered all...." He ran from the cabin, towel and soap in hand, to the horse watering tank to wash away the blood. The frigid bath and being naked in brisk night air put the finishing touches on his revival. He rushed back to the cabin, pulled on dry clothes and moved her to his bed to begin tending injuries.

Wounds first. Cleaned and disinfected or she will eventually die from infection if shock doesn't kill her first. Get some of this dirt and blood off, then take a look.

The soapy water gradually dissolved enough of the congealed blood and dirt to permit a better assessment of her injuries. *Damn, what a mess. Cuts and abrasions all over. Head wound looks like her only serious injury. I don't think she's hurt as much as I thought earlier. May have a concussion, though, and lost a lot of blood. Get her cleaned up.*

Jim concentrated on the head wound, shaving a strip of hair above the wound over the gash and washing the caked accumulation of dirt and blood. She moved when he poured whiskey into the wound, moaning, tears spreading over her face. *She's coming back.* He bent close and said, "Can you hear me? You're safe now. Don't worry."

She whimpered while he used a makeshift butterfly bandage to hold the jagged edges of her torn scalp together. "It's not much," he remarked, standing back to appraise his handiwork. "But maybe it will reduce the scarring." He decided not to wash her hair, even though it was bloody and matted. *Wait on that. Don't have enough hot water.*

He carefully removed the woman's torn, oil and gas soaked clothes, meticulously disinfecting a number of scratches and small cuts as he went, working steadily for almost an hour, doctoring wounds until the supply of anti-bacterial whiskey ran out, whiskey left over from a previous occupant. She wavered in and out of consciousness. When he finished and stood back, he noticed for the first time, despite the bruises, blood and swelling, she lived in a remarkably feminine body. Slender with firm breasts and a flat stomach. Slender women with generous breasts had always attracted his attention. He experienced pangs of guilt for taking advantage of her condition and hastened to tuck the quilt around her body.

Damned pervert. Well, whoever you are, beautiful body and all, you are going to be the sorest human on the face of the planet tomorrow.

He located a long flannel shirt and woolen socks, and with careful attention to duty, gently drew on the makeshift nightgown, then sat beside her on the bed, too spent to go on.

The bleeding had stopped and shock no longer seemed to be a problem, but she remained comatose. Jim discarded the idea of moving her down the mountain that night in favor of warmth and rest. While sitting on the bed watching the woman, he realized how long it had been since lunch.

He drank soup directly from a can without taking time to warm it, then moved a chair to the side of her bed and resumed the vigil. He wiped the tears on her face, whispering, "It's okay. Don't worry. You're safe now." He stroked her face softly and held her hand. Her grip tightened. She whispered something. He leaned close and said, "Say that again. I couldn't hear you."

"You look better with clothes on, Jim."

He sat bolt upright. *She knows my name? How is that possible? Do I know her?* The reality that she called him by name disturbed him more than the fact that she had spoken clearly. He thought, at the time that her mouth almost formed a smile, but the swelling and cuts on her face apparently wouldn't permit even such a simple function. Her eyes remained mostly closed.

He leaned close again. "Can you hear me?"

She squeezed his hand and whispered, "I have been so worried about you."

Worried about me? What the hell is going on here? "Do you know who I am?"

She mumbled something and slipped back to sleep.

How does she know me? Do I know her? Jim couldn't dispel the nagging feeling that he should know her. She began trembling violently. *Oh, man, here we go again.* "Please, not shock," he muttered. "Come on, don't do this to me." He watched her quake for a moment, then decided to provide additional heat the only way he could, by pulling the covers back, slipping into bed and drawing her into the warmth of his body.

She moaned and then whispered, "I thought they would catch you, Jim. I'm so glad you got away."

She does know me. That comment didn't spring from delirium. "No, they didn't catch me. I'm here."

*****

Leslie tried with all her might but could not force her matted eyes open. She ached all over and her arms and legs wouldn't move, but worst of all, she couldn't open her eyes. She floated helplessly in a sea of pain, in a spinning world of semi-consciousness. She didn't feel anything but pain for an eternity it seemed, then a gentle brush of something cool and damp on her face.

Mother?

Her jumbled thoughts cleared enough to detect the warmth of a body against hers. That startled her. She couldn't open her eyes, drifting in and out of consciousness, dizzy, aching and frightened, but her overwhelming and foremost thought was, Somebody is holding me. She panicked, desperate to break away but couldn't move under the smothering weight. She forced an eye open and saw fire. *Fire?* She remembered the crash and the fire. *Fire!* Panic fed energy and she fought the suffocating weight pinning her arms and legs. Her eyesight cleared enough to see fire in a fireplace.

A fireplace. A fireplace?

A warm arm slipped from her shoulders and the warmth behind her separated. She heard creaking noises of bed springs as somebody left the bed, then sensations of a blanket being tucked gently around her shoulders. She saw him then, a bearded face in the distance somewhere behind the hand wiping her face with a moist towel.

"You're okay now," he said. "Everything is all right. Don't be afraid. The worst is over. Just try to relax and go back to sleep. I'll be here."

The voice sounded like her father's, so soothing. Gradually, lucid thoughts emerged along with attendant sensations of nausea. Her first conscious words since the crash were, "Do you have something for pain?"

He leaned close. "Where do you hurt?"

She couldn't answer, trying to time a response to coincide with the labored rhythm of breathing "My head. I think my head is going to explode."

"Sorry," he said. "I used the pain killer to disinfect your wounds."

Her eyes cracked opened again. She stared at the ceiling for a moment before turning toward him. "Am I going to die?"

He stroked her forehead. "No. You are going to be okay. Can you see?"

She didn't answer. The friendly face looked very familiar. "I know you, don't I?"

"Not that I'm aware of," he replied. "Who are you?"

She squinted, straining to focus on his face, unable to see through the shroud of tears screening her vision, but felt certain she knew him. "Where am I?" she asked, trying unsuccessfully to sit up.

He pressed her back gently. "My house. Just lay back and try to relax. Do you remember the wreck?"

Her mind functioned more efficiently by the moment. "Oh, yes, I remember. How long have I been here?"

"Let's see...nearly three hours now. Was anyone in the Jeep with you?"

Confusion cleared rapidly. "No, just me." She lay back and whispered, "Three hours? That's amazing. It seems like it just happened. Who are you?"

"Just call me, Jim. Can I get something for you?"

Jim? It is Jim. "Yes, please. Water."

He returned and gently raised her to a half sitting position, holding the glass to her lips. The simple act of drinking drained her strength. Leslie fell back exhausted. "Thanks. What is that smell?"

He chuckled. "We both smell. Gas, oil, blood, whiskey all mixed together. It will wear off."

Leslie watched his every move. No doubt about it, she thought. Definitely Jim Colby. Needs a shave. She remembered him standing by the fire, naked and bloody. The vision was very clear, and very disturbing. *Was he in bed with me?*

When he sat beside the bed again, she asked again, "Am I going to be all right? Please don't deceive me."

"Best I can tell, you're going to be just fine. You have a head wound, but I don't think it's serious. There shouldn't be any visible scars if that's what you're worried about. I didn't find any broken bones. Other than that, how do you feel?"

"Awful. I think I'm going to vomit. Don't you have anything for this headache?"

"I don't think I should give you pain killer for a head wound. If you take a sedative, I'll have to keep you awake until it wears off. Can you do without it?"

Leslie's swollen eyes closed. She found it difficult to breathe through her mouth and her nose was swollen and blocked by congealed blood. Her breath caught suddenly and she tried to sit. "What did you say?" She had fallen asleep. "Oh, I'm sorry. My eyes won't stay open."

"I think it's probably okay to sleep now. Don't worry. I'll be right here. You go on to sleep. I will be right here." He darted back and forth to the kitchen, watching her, preparing broth and tea to have nourishment handy when she woke again. She slept fretfully until daylight. Jim stayed awake tending the fire, checking vital signs, watching her breathing.

Pain woke Leslie. She lay perfectly still trying to remember. The sounds and smells in the cabin seemed real enough. She was almost afraid to open her eyes. When she finally did, he was sitting in a chair beside the bed, head down, snoozing, and didn't notice her.

"I must still be alive," she announced.

He started at the sound of her voice, placed the tablet on the floor beside the chair and smiled. "Well, good morning. How do you feel? No, don't answer that."

She groaned and touched her head, searching for the source of pain. "I hurt all over." Her head throbbed at the slightest movement. "I would take some aspirin now, if you don't mind." She attempted a feeble smile, only to flinch at the resulting pain. Her swollen, battered mouth began bleeding. She tried to sit up when he returned with a glass of water and aspirin.

"Whoa! Wait for me," he cautioned. "Let me help." He put an arm around her shoulders as support while she drank. "The aspirin is already dissolved," he said. "Drink all of it if you can."

She drank with great difficulty, pausing periodically to gasp for air. Finally, lay back and said, "I'm really weak. Do you know what I need worse than anything?"

"I have food heating," he said. "What else can I do for you?"

"I can't stand this awful taste in my mouth. Could I please brush my teeth?"

"Certainly. You can either use my toothbrush or I can get a washcloth."

She tried to smile, then grimaced and replied, "A cloth will do fine."

He came back with a pot full of warm water and a cloth. She refused assistance. He stood by and watched as she dabbed at her mouth, rinsing blood from the cloth, then finally covered her finger with the cloth and washed her teeth. Afterward, he spooned broth, tea and honey until she begged him to stop. When he returned to the room after washing dishes, she seemed much stronger and began asking questions.

"Have you called the authorities? Will someone come for me today?"

"I will answer all of your questions, but I need to know a couple of things first. For starters, Who are you?"

"Why, I'm…. She hesitated, seeming surprised and puzzled. "I'm sorry, I thought you…." She regrouped, suddenly realizing there was no way he could know anything about her. "My purse? Did you…."

"No, I didn't find a purse. I'm almost sure it burned, but I'll look for it again when it's light. What were you doing driving around up here all by yourself at night?"

She collected her thoughts and gave an evasive answer. "Oh, just sightseeing. I rented a Jeep in Silverton. I guess Jeeps are out of my element. Weak brakes. I couldn't get it in reverse. I imagine you know the rest better than I do. The Jeep must be ruined."

He laughed. "Oh, much worse than ruined. It burned after the wreck. There's not much left." He studied her for a moment, and then suddenly exclaimed, "How do you know who I am?"

She looked away, unwilling to face him. "I have never seen you before in my life. Why do you ask?"

The look on his face said he didn't believe her. "Just something you said last night while you were semi-conscious. Forget it."

Her mind whirled. *Did I say too much?* Then, "What did I say?"

"Nothing, really. Don't worry about it."

"Have you called the authorities yet?"

Jim shook his head solemnly. "No. There is no electricity up here and no telephone service. My cell is out of juice. Sorry."

The announcement disturbed her. "No phone? Well, could you call from a neighbor's house? There must be some way to inform the authorities." She was shaken by the extent of their isolation, even though she knew beforehand how far from civilization he lived.

"Believe me, Miss, there is nothing to be done short of taking you down the mountain in my truck. My nearest neighbor is several miles away. Frankly, I'm afraid to leave you alone for the amount of time it would take me to get to the neighbor's place and back. Anyway, I'm pretty sure they don't have a phone."

"I'm sorry to sound so pushy," she said. "but I just thought there might be a search taking place and we could stop all the trouble, that's all."

"When you are strong enough, we'll go down the mountain. Don't worry about the search party or the expense. There simply isn't anything we can do about that. I know you're worried about your family and friends, but try to think how happy they will be, not how sad they are now." When she didn't answer, he realized she was asleep. Her eyelids had been drooping for some time. While she slept, he left the cabin to feed the horses and gather firewood. A cold front with low clouds and drizzle had come in the night. He studied the sky. *Snow coming. Just what I need.*

She woke again in mid-afternoon without the throbbing headache and ate without his assistance. Jim looked in on her from the kitchen and saw her trying to sit up.

"Do you feel that good?"

She had pushed the covers away until they only covered her legs.

"I feel much stronger. If this mess of hair was clean I would nearly feel human. I hate to ask, but would you please cool the house down a bit? I'm smothering."

Uh oh, she's hot. It's not that warm in here. He sat on the bed and placed a hand on her forehead. "You are running a temperature and I don't have medicine to deal with infection. So, that's it. Ready or not, we are going to get off this mountain."

"I would like to wear my own cloths, if you don't mind." She held the blanket securely around her shoulders, embarrassed because she knew he had stripped her clothes to tend wounds.

"Sorry, but your clothes belong to the same paragraph of history as the Jeep. I threw them out. I'm sorry. Your return to civilization will be in my clothes. Here." He tossed an old pair of jeans and flannel shirt on the bed. "Will you need help?"

"Thank you, no. I think you have done quite enough."

He reached for his jacket and paused at the door. "Take your time. Don't exhaust yourself getting dressed. I'll be back in a few minutes."

While waiting on the porch, the sudden turn of events left him unaccountably depressed, suffering a feeling of loss that revealed all too clearly a fondness for her company, brooding over the requirement to deliver her to civilization. Her infection was not too alarming, that could be remedied easily enough with medical attention, but losing her so soon.... *How odd? I don't know who she is or even what she looks like. One sleepless night with a beat-up, sick woman and I already miss her.*

He returned to the cabin, solemn and determined, banked the fire, turned out the kerosene lamp, and against her feeble protests carried her to the truck. The trip to Silverton took too long. She tired and slept most of the way, moaning when the truck bounced. He stopped and pulled her gently across the seat and laid her head on his lap. They stopped at the first gas station in Silverton and asked the attendant to call for medical assistance. A sheriff's deputy arrived first with an ambulance close behind.

Leslie received a cursory medical examination from the ambulance attendants while Jim answered the deputy's questions about the accident. He couldn't avoid giving his name and stiffened when the deputy said, "Oh yeah, you live in the superintendent's cabin out at the Boxer mines, right?"

How in the hell does he know? Oh, yeah, that bus accident. Jim furnished details of her accident while juggling contrasting emotions about revealing too much. He needed to be forthright, but information could lead enemies into his life. He felt vulnerable for the first time since arriving in Silverton. *I have to get out of here now, that's for sure.*

*****

After the attendant fastened Leslie into the gurney, her eyes shifted to Jim standing with a deputy sheriff nearby. As the attendant began to close the doors, Leslie said, "Please, would you get that man talking to the police for me? I must speak with him."

She didn't care that tears trickled down her face, or that her lower lip trembled. She reached for his hand and held securely. "I don't know how to thank you. You saved my life. I'll never be able to repay you."

He gently pushed the hair away from her forehead with his other hand. "That's right," he said. "You cannot repay me and you don't need to thank me. I wish.... I'm glad you're going to be okay." He stepped back.

"Good bye, Jim. Thank you for being there."

*****

He watched the ambulance disappear and ached. His heart ached. The woman in the van had touched his life more in a few hours than anything he could remember. *Why so melodramatic? Am I that lonely?*

The deputy interrupted, asking for more information.

*****

The slam of the ambulance door added to Leslie's sense of loss. She had lost control of her life only to be saved by a man she knew more about than any other person on earth. She watched helplessly as the gentle man vanished in the distance. Watching him disappear hurt more than anything Leslie Reardon could remember.

Chapter Twenty Five

DESPAIR

Leslie received a strong sedative and slept throughout the journey to Durango where doctors diagnosed a low grade infection that capitulated readily to powerful antibiotics.

"You are in no clinical danger, Miss Reardon," the doctor explained the following morning. "However, you are considerably weakened from loss of blood and susceptible to infection. You should probably remain here a couple of days as a precautionary measure."

Her thoughts during hospitalization seldom strayed from the man on the mountain. Leslie now understood all too well the peculiar depth of her preoccupation with him, but rationalized by thinking, He saved my life. Why wouldn't I think about him? Her thoughts seldom strayed. Never before had another person affected her so profoundly. Leslie couldn't stop thinking about him.

Well, at least I am no longer in doubt. I know the investigation would have led me to him if Charlie hadn't called it off. I really don't want to associate Jim with the investigation, though. I'm not sure I want to know everything.

She didn't want to think that he might be involved in something sinister. And yet, the more she thought the more convinced she became that he probably had been involved in something she would find at least unpleasant. *More to the point, Why am I entangled in something that I'm pretty sure won't end well?* Her mood shifted from the elation of finally finding him to a deepening sadness associated with the grim likelihood of never seeing him again. Hours of questions and counter questions plagued her thoughts. Leslie tried to form a plan to follow after release, recognizing that the most practical plan would be to forget about him. *Forget him? Oh, sure, like that's going to happen.*

Her brooding silence created concern for the doctor. "We are worried about you, Miss Reardon. You have survived an extremely harrowing experience, no doubt. You are very fortunate to be alive. However, it seems to me that you would be delighted about your good fortune. Your behavior is inconsistent with what I expect under these circumstances. You appear depressed and that bothers me. I think we need to talk."

"I am certainly not trying to argue with your diagnosis, Doctor, but you are overstating the problem. I'm just not the bubbly type."

Leslie sat at the window gazing north. Always north toward Silverton. She didn't eat, couldn't sleep and resented the annoying swirl of interruptions by concerned staff members. The doctor was right, she was despondent, but for reasons she couldn't share with anyone.

The doctor returned that evening. "I want to prescribe a mood altering medication, Miss Reardon. I think it might perk you up a little. You will feel much better."

She responded immediately. "Absolutely not! I will not take medication, Doctor. I fully understand the cause of my problems and it is personal. I won't take drugs."

He stepped back, folded his arms and studied her over the Ben Franklin's habitually crowning bridge of his nose. "Really? Then perhaps you wouldn't mind sharing your diagnoses with me?"

"I do mind. It's very personal."

Leslie knew her symptoms were related to post-traumatic shock as the doctor had every right to think. She decided to shove the entire matter of the man on the mountain from her mind and concentrate on doing whatever she needed to be released. The next morning, she thanked the doctor for his assistance and begged for dismissal. He agreed reluctantly, but persevered, "I am convinced the source of your distress is too complex to be cured by the superficial means we have employed up to this point, Miss Reardon. So, with your permission, I'm going to refer you to a psychologist I know in Denver."

"Don't bother. I won't go."

He signed the release.

*****

Jim broke away from the deputy as the ambulance disappeared and took a meal in town before returning to the cabin. Eating out served as an excuse not to go back immediately. It would be lonely on the mountain. He stopped on the road and climbed down to the jeep and found her purse. It had burned almost beyond recognition. No identification survived. He drove back to town and asked the Jeep owner for her name.

"I just took her money, buddy. Cash money. She left her car keys with me as collateral. I suppose she will send someone for it."

Jim brooded about the deputy knowing about him all along, thinking, Too many people have known where to find me from the day I arrived on the mountain. I have to leave. Why was she looking for me? She sure didn't come up here by accident. Who is she? Even after conceding his exposure and making the decision to leave, he didn't. He sat on the porch and thought, but he didn't leave and knew why.

Her.

At first, he thought, imagined would be a better word, that she might come back. She couldn't find me if I leave, though. I don't know for sure that she was even looking for me? Nah, she won't come back. I would like to know why she came, though. Gave her the opportunity to confirm or deny being married by addressing her as Miss. No ring. She either ignored me or she's single. Stop it! There is no place for a woman in my life. Not ever. He sat on the front porch, staring across the valley, procrastinating, craving a fantasy he could never have.

Her.

His discontent and loneliness filled the following string of days and nights. An overwhelming sadness defeated even the trace of peace the mountain had provided. He couldn't escape the awful reality that her presence generated. He didn't exercise; he didn't work; he brooded about the future and hated the past. He gave in to the hopelessness of life and cried the bitter tears of defeat.

Her.

Tears washed away despair and reason returned. He resolved to stop thinking about her, about yesterdays and tomorrows.

I need to get the hell out of here.

He began a frantic routine designed to drive away the consuming lethargy, and still he thought about her.

I'm in love with the idea of being in love. No woman can ever be part of my life. I would rather die than live like this, though. At least I learned that much from her.

With no plan, other than to move on, Jim began the last chore on his list, cutting logs to replenish the supply of firewood. He would pack and disappear as soon as the task was finished. His stay on the mountain had come to a merciful end.

Chapter Twenty-Six

REVELATION

Leslie's associates at the ACLU stopped working and whispered as she walked through the door on Monday a week after the accident. Her assistant, a tall, dreadfully thin young man with an out-of-style ponytail haircut stepped closer and whispered, "Gee, Miss Reardon! Should you be here? You look so pale."

"I'm fine now, Gary. I know what you must be thinking, but I look worse than I feel. Thanks for being concerned."

When members of the staff finished asking the obvious questions about her health and the wreck, they gathered, formed a friendly alliance and approached the director. He agreed with their concern and directed Leslie to stay home until she healed.

"Go, Leslie. There really isn't that much going on around here right now and you are worrying everyone. Go home."

She reluctantly yielded to the pressure. "You are probably right, Don. I'm in no frame of mind to work anyway." At home she sat in her father's darkened study and thought about the man on the mountain and the disruptive effects he still had on her life.

During the weeks after Senator Collins's dismissal, Leslie considered continuing the investigating the CIA on her own. The outrage and need to expose whatever Collins and his cronies were trying so hard to hide had something to do with Jim Colby. She knew that. Now that she knew Colby, the opportunity of doing something that could implicate him restrained her anger at Collins. She hoped Jim wasn't involved and her initial suspicions were wrong, but intuitively knew they weren't. *He is involved. Too many indications to the contrary. What did he do?* She also knew, beyond doubt, that her present emotional dilemma was linked to him. On one hand, she desperately wanted to know more about him, on the other she didn't want to discover something damaging. Time alone left her progressively more disturbed and emotionally involved.

I can't go on like this. She sat in the shadows analyzing the preoccupation with him; combing through every instant of time with him, then started over, wondering at her own sanity. She wandered about the house for hours, unable to settle down, powerless to think of anything to divert her curiosity, gazing through an upstairs window–the only window facing southwest toward Silverton. Sometime after midnight, with assist from a near overdose of sleeping pills, she curled up on the couch in the study and slept only to awaken from a nightmarish dream, drugged and tired. With a show of determination uncharacteristic of recent behavior, Leslie decided to forget everything else and end, once and for all, theorizing and worrying about him.

I'm satisfied with my knowledge of his life up to the falsified death certificate in New York. I don't know anything from that day until he found me on the mountain. The problem, obviously, must be somewhere between those dates. I need to find out what went on in his life from June until now. She formed a rough plan to exploit old and reliable contacts. Decision made, Leslie rushed to the bath to freshen and leave for the office at once. She left a path of strewn clothes across the floor and made a wide-ranging mess of the bedroom and bath. Finally, hairbrush in hand, she glanced in the mirror and recoiled from the wretched, pitiful woman staring back. *My, God! I look dreadful.*

The haggard, black-and-blue image in the mirror startled her. After splashing cold water on her face, barely glancing into the mirror to run the brush through the tangled mat of hair, she daubed lipstick on and rushed from the house. Under normal circumstances, Leslie Reardon would never appear at work looking worse than a high-paid fashion model. Her usual choice of clothes favored assorted tailored business suits. Leslie arrived at the office dressed in the clothes she slept in, barely noting the surprised stares of the staff as she rushed through the building.

The director, informed by Leslie's alarmed friends, stepped into her office and closed the door. His voice halted her frantic search through file cabinets. "I thought we agreed you should take some time off, Les." He was not pleased.

Leslie turned, smiled contritely and begged. "Please, Don. I'm not here to work. Please don't fuss. I'll just be a few moments. Please, this is very personal and important." Her woeful expression appealed for understanding. She turned back to the files. Don sat on the edge of her desk and sighed. "Come on, Les. Tell me what in God's name is going on? And pardon me all to hell for saying so, but you look like death warmed over." He sighed a why-me sigh and said, "Look at me, will you? Tell me what I can do. If you are in some kind of trouble, I want to help. This behavior isn't what I have come to expect from you. You have to admit, this is all pretty weird. Look at me!"

She paused, straightened and said, "You're right, Don. I desperately need help." She took a seat behind the desk, held up a restraining hand and said, "Let me think for a moment." *What about Jim? Is this the right thing to do?*

Don listened attentively as she revealed the entire story. When finished, he smiled and said, "If I didn't know you better, Les, I could almost be persuaded there might be some personal interest involved here. Am I reading you right?"

She didn't retreat from the challenge. "I know this may sound silly to you, Don, but yes, it is personal and vitally important to me. I can't explain everything. I know you must think I'm–"

He held up a finger to stop her. "It doesn't matter. How long has this been going on?"

She groaned and collapsed into the chair. "Oh, God. Much too long. I need answers, Don." She noted his raised eyebrow and added, "I'm sorry. I really can't explain." She smiled thinly and said, "Yes, I need help. Please?"

Don looked to the ceiling and gestured helplessly, appealing to heaven with upraised arms. "After all she has done for me." He let his arms drop and said, "Honestly, Leslie, I'm embarrassed that you haven't asked before." He spent the next ten minutes listening to her requests, then stepped to the door and shouted, "Staff meeting! In here!" Two attorneys and four legal assistants filed into Leslie's office. "Okay, people, I want you to drop everything this morning and give full attention to a new project. I want you to drop what you are doing and help Leslie with a little investigation. This is not official and hopefully won't take much time."

Don briefly reviewed the information Leslie had given, then concluded, "The only thing we know for certain about this guy is that he lives somewhere in the mountains near Silverton. Leslie believes he works for a corporation that is leasing the Boxer mines. He's about fifty and lives in a cabin east of Silverton. The cabin doesn't have electricity or phone service. Uses the nickname, Jim. Your best lead, Gary," he glanced toward Leslie's assistant, "is a deputy in Silverton who has spoken to this Jim character. And by the way, Jim is a nickname. He is Michael Allen Stokes."

The director gave verbal assignments to each staff member. Before releasing them, said, "Do your best work troops. This is for Leslie. Let's get hopping!"

He turned to Leslie and pointed to the door. "Now, dammit, go home, and that's an order. I will call." His stern expression demonstrated that she didn't have a choice.

By mid-afternoon, a confused staff confessed to the director that they had reached dead ends. Leslie rushed back to the office to find Don waiting in her office, alone, his expression an ominous picture of concern and foreboding.

He sat on her desk and said, "I'm not so sure you want to know what we discovered."

She placed a blank sheet of paper on the desk and picked up a pen. "Maybe not, but I need to make that decision."

"Okay. We learned enough about your Jim guy–Michael Allen Stokes–to know that something is seriously amiss, and I do mean serious. This Stokes fellow has a valid Colorado driver's license, but, as you already know, the address just happens to be a vacant lot. The state motor vehicle bureau gave us some sketchy information about a bus accident late this summer. Nothing there other than when and where. Our credit card investigation turned up no record of a credit card. The same bogus address appears on Stokes' high school and college degrees.

"None of those things are too weird, Les, but our investigation uncovered some information that I find to be very disturbing. It seems all of your Michael Allen Stokes' records just happened to originate on the exact same day this past June."

She frowned. "The Sixteenth, right?"

"Yes. So, his records are fabricated, Les. Stokes is fabricated. We think he could be in a witness protection program–something like that. Anyway, by tracing Stokes' high school and college diplomas, we uncovered some pretty bizarre information. The schools listed on his diplomas have records to prove that he graduated, but there is no evidence of him in school yearbooks, nor do any of his alleged classmates exist–nothing at all other than bogus paperwork to indicate a Michael Allen Stokes ever attended those schools.

"His birth certificate came from the courthouse in Cheyenne County, right here in Colorado. However, the County Recorder's comments about unusual entries lead us to believe there was tampering. Also, our investigation failed to confirm that the parents listed on his birth certificate ever existed. He is a fake, Les. His social security number is valid, by the way, just happens to belong to a man long dead. We couldn't get any information from the feds about his work or tax history. I personally ran a check with state and federal law enforcement agencies, Leslie. Stokes doesn't have a criminal record. I know, surprise!"

She sat back and sighed. "Well, that's a relief."

He gesture helplessly. "Really? Anyway, that's it. That's all we could get on him."

"What you have just told me," she said, "is that Michael Allen Stokes seems to have been instantly and mysteriously created in June, is that right?"

"Precisely."

She sat back, arms folded, distressed by the collection of useless, disappointing details. "Tell me, who do you think is hiding him, and why?"

"We couldn't find out who or why, but obviously someone pretty high up in both state and federal governments had a hand. I think you could be meddling in something pretty sensitive, possibly even dangerous." He waited several moments before breaking into her thoughts. "Unless there is some awfully good reason, and I honestly can't think of one, I'm not going to pursue this matter, Les."

"You have done enough, Don. Thank you."

"What happens now?"

"I don't know."

"Well, my advice would be to stay the hell away from him, and I mean that, Les."

She nodded and got up to leave, only to pause at the door. "Thank everyone for me. I'll be in touch."

She walked through the door leaving a worried friend muttering to himself. "I'll be in touch? That sounded a little too much like good-bye."

Leslie's entire outlook changed the moment she left the building. Jim wasn't a folder full of papers and photographs on her desk. She had seen him. She didn't return home to wallow in depression or mope around without purpose. She whisked through the house opening blinds and windows, doing laundry, tossing food from the frig, and then slept soundly until noon the next day. She didn't think about what Jim might have done, or the extraordinary attraction she felt for him.

I know who Jim Colby was. I want to know why he isn't Jim Colby now. She believed the government was hiding him, but wasn't sure she wanted to know why. Not yet. She only wanted to know something that would reinforce the good feeling she had about him. *I'm through worrying about him being mixed up in something sinister.*

The last purple and yellow bruise on her forehead had faded, almost matching the normal hue of her skin. She packed a suitcase, closed the blinds, left a note for the housekeeper and locked the door on the way out.

Chapter Twenty-Seven

COMPROMISE

A steady rain fell all day after Jim shook the melancholy and began preparing to leave. Rain trapped him indoors, frustrated by inactivity, confined with thoughts of being exposed, and *her*. His meditations bordered on fantasy or anxiety, depending on the subject. Mostly he thought of her and about the future, or the lack of a future.

Rain continued. He decided to drive to town for a decent hot meal, choosing a little restaurant off the main drag, a place preferred by the locals, away from tourists. Several local businessmen were present. Jim ordered and began reading *THE DENVER POST*. A pleasant commotion at the door drew his attention. Everyone present greeted the towering deputy as he walked in for free coffee. Good-natured banter and backslapping followed the law man, clearly a local boy, through the restaurant. The deputy's merry eyes stopped drifting when he noticed Jim. He nodded and Jim returned the greeting.

"Hold that coffee for me here, will you Sally," the deputy slapped his hand on the counter to indicate where he would sit. He straddled the chair across the little table from Jim and sat without asking. "So, how's it going up at the mines?" he asked.

Jim, trying to appear untroubled, looked up and said, "No complaints."

"Say, did that bus company ever pay you off for dinging your truck?"

Jim kept his eyes on the newspaper. "Nope. It didn't amount to anything. Never bothered to file a claim."

The conversation lapsed. Jim figured the deputy had something else on his mind. They exchanged synthetic smiles.

The deputy fidgeted with an imaginary scratch on the back of his hand, then looked up and said, "Well, I guess it doesn't matter then." He stood and scooted the chair back under the table.

Jim breathed a sigh of relief.

"Oh, I heard about you bringing that gal off the mountain. Good job. Is she okay?"

Jim flinched inwardly. "Guess so. Haven't heard."

The deputy looked surprised. "Somehow I thought you two...." He rolled his hand." Well, I didn't know if I should tell her about you or not." He laughed and said, "I never did learn to say no to a woman. Didn't cause any trouble for you, did I?"

Jim looked puzzled.

The deputy quickly added, "She came up to the office looking for you. Said you were an old friend. What was I supposed to do?"

A multitude of questions entered Jim's thoughts, but he couldn't pursue them with a cop. *So, she was looking for me.* He collected himself and replied casually. "What do you know about her?"

"Not much, really. Said she was a friend from Denver, so we gave her directions to your place. Hope you don't mind. Real purty. Damned sure not from around these parts. Said you were old friends." His eyebrows elevated, asking for approval.

"Did she give a name?"

The question appeared to confuse the deputy even more. "Hold it. You mean you don't even know her name? Well, shit! I'm sorry, partner, but she sure seemed to know you."

"She didn't give you a name?"

The deputy scratched the back of his neck again and frowned. "Nope. Not that I recall." Then, "Come to think of it, I don't think she ever did say her name. Maybe Ed Saunders could help you. He rented her the Jeep. Lives just behind the firehouse."

"Thanks. Think I'll a word with him. She left some stuff I probably ought to send back."

"Yeah, talk to Ed. Well, see you around."

Jim went directly to the Jeep rental agent's house, there to endure several minutes of Ed's complaints bemoaning the destruction of his Jeep.

"Man, I don't know how the hell she got through it all without getting herself killed," Saunders muttered. "That sucker was nearly bent double. Burned to a damned crisp. She called me, though, said she would pay for it and by damn she did. Wired the money yesterday morning. Certified and all that. How do you know about her?"

"I brought her down after the wreck. Do you happen to keep records on your renters?"

"Why? Does she owe you, too?"

"No, but she left some stuff at my place. Did she happen to say why she wanted to go up there?"

"Not really. Just asked for directions up to the old Boxer mine. Said she was looking for some guy, an old friend, I think. Stokes, if I remember right. Yeah, Stokes. Said he works for the Boxer people. Here." He tore a page from the little tablet in his shirt pocket. "I copied information off her check. You can keep that since I already got the money. That's all I'll ever need from her. But she damned sure ain't gonna rent anything from me again."

Jim left town with her name and address. Leslie Reardon. 916 Mountain View Drive, Denver.

Now, how does she know me and what did she want? How did she find me? I guess the real problem is, she did find me.

He remembered giving his name to the deputy after the bus hit his truck, and also worrying about the possibility of compromise at the time, but nothing like the anxiety he suffered now.

How many other people know? I should have pulled my stake right then and got the hell out of Dodge.

He drove to Arnold's cafe and announced his intention to quit. Arnold wasn't surprised.

"Well, sir, that ain't exactly amazin'. I hate to see you go, though. Done me a good job. Anyway, I expect it's high time you come down off that mountain. It's supposed to snow in the high country the next day or two according to the forecast. I planned to get up there today and warn you. You can stay here and help this winter if you're a mind to."

"No thanks. Think I'll be heading south."

"You're welcome to come back next spring. Reckon I could use you."

"Thanks. I'll have to let you know about that."

"If it ain't asking too much, would you mind leaving a supply of firewood, just in case?"

"Already done. Enough to last a month." He raced back to the cabin with a new urgency to leave, and fast, and spent the afternoon cleaning the house and barn, and worrying.

Chapter Twenty-Eight

NOT AS STRANGERS

━━━━━━◉━━━━━━

Leslie's note to Maria indicating nothing more than a couple of days' vacation in the mountains to get her car. *Maria won't give it a second thought. She can watch her precious soaps without interference.* Leslie threw her bags in the back seat of a rental and after a deep sigh, drove away.

Why am I doing this?

She pulled the visor mirror down at the first stop light, smoothed her eyebrows and said, "What are you thinking?" She snapped the visor back into place. "I'm thinking that all the thinking is over, that's what I'm thinking." She sped westward until darkness and took a motel room in Montrose. The following morning, cheerful after two straight decent night's sleep, she ate an early breakfast and sped south through the mountains toward Silverton. Nothing mattered except to end the suspense, to face him and the anxieties controlling her life.

Leslie turned the rental in, retrieved her car and ate lunch in Silverton, casually engaging one of many local characters in conversation and located another Jeep to rent.

The Jeep owner, after throwing her suitcase in the back, leaned over, touching and rubbing against her while teaching the gearshift pattern, said, "I know you said you been up there before, but that road is tricky. Don't be proud. It's okay to turn back. I suppose you know they say it might snow some later this afternoon, so I wouldn't stay out too late. Might get slick up there later on." He tipped his battered Stetson, studied her skeptically, frowned and said, "You sure you know what you're doing?"

"Yes. As I said, I've been there before. Don't worry. I won't take any chances with your vehicle. The brakes work, don't they?"

"Of course. He might be gone, Miss. It's past time to get down out of the high country. I'd sure be a little surprised if you find anyone up there. Might be you ought to check with Arnold down at the Cafe. He runs that mine."

Leslie drove out of town to the east and up, and up. She didn't have the luxury of time to stew about motives, or to worry about the wisdom of what she was doing. The treacherous, narrow, rocky road demanded full attention. The bumpy road led away from civilization and inexorably upward, narrowing as it gained altitude, clinging precariously a sheer rock wall one side and a cascading stream on the other side going the opposite direction giving her a false impression of speed. She compensated by driving slower, checking the brakes, creeping along, unable to look over the side without getting dizzy.

The road climbed steadily until arriving at the Boxer mine turnoff. Some snow had already drifted across the road making the road even more precarious. Memories of the accident played havoc with her nerves. She stopped at the intersection to think and muster courage. The thin, oxygen starved air and blustering winds soon provided incentive to press on. Leslie dreaded the prospect of an encounter with him and trembled with tension.

What if he isn't here? Better yet, what if he is? The fabricated confidence of recent days faded. *I'm pathetic. Concentrate. Get on with it.*

She engaged the four wheel drive and proceeded in low gear. Frustration intensified as each sharp turn in the road disclosed nothing more than more trees and the rubble from yet another old mine. *I'll have to stay up here whether he's here or not. No way I'm going back after dark.*

The shadows of evening darkened and the air temperature had already dipped below freezing. She stopped at the edge of the meadow, within sight of the cabin still visible in waning sunlight. She didn't have the courage to drive the Jeep any farther after the last experience and started walking. Her heartbeat accelerated. An already ebbing confidence withered, merging with a spreading sense of dread. *Too late to quit.*

She got out and started walking, breathing deeply, watching for movement, listening for human sounds, wrestling with cowardice. *What will he think when I pop in?* Leslie recognized his truck and knew for sure she had the right place, then the sound of a chain saw operating somewhere beyond the cabin echoed across the meadow erased all doubt about of his presence.

She covered her face in her hands, heaved a deep sigh and turned toward the cabin, mumbling to herself in cadence with her footsteps: "Just do it. Quit thinking. You have come too far to back out now." She paused to catch her breath, patting her face, hoping to smooth the worry wrinkles, then smoothed her hair and practiced smiling. She climbed slowly through the meadow, past the barn and corral, pausing again to rest and study the setting. His cabin lay tucked into the edge of a spruce forest just a few yards ahead. She marched onward, attempting to localize the sound of the chain saw echoing from no specific direction–somewhere beyond the cabin. No answer when she knocked.

That's a relief. She often wondered if he lived alone. The thought of dealing with someone else didn't appeal to her, particularly a woman. Leslie stepped off the porch and walked around the cabin toward the snarling chain saw, brushing through snow-powdered limbs. She broke out and saw him on the other side of a small clearing, facing away sawing wood. The sight of him brought tears of relief. Seconds ticked away–a lifetime it seemed. She shouted vainly and then began walking across the clearing, cautiously picking a way through downed limbs. She was watching as he suddenly stopped working, switched the saw off and stood motionless, head moving slightly from side to side, then suddenly crouched and whirled, chain saw positioned in front of his body.

Leslie waved feebly and said, "Hi there. Remember me?" The expression on his face conveyed nothing more than astonishment.

*****

Jim took a deep breath and stood erect in stages, lowering the saw next to his leg. He felt foolish, embarrassed by the defensive reaction. There, not twenty feet in front of him, stood a tall, beautiful woman.

Her

She smiled and waved again.

Am I dreaming? His thoughts ricocheted between how good she looked and why she returned. He placed the saw on the ground, picked up a faded plaid shirt and put it on. She didn't move. Her plaintive expression puzzled him, like a plea for approval. An awkward silence fell over the scene as they stared. Jim recognized the awkwardness of the situation and stepped forward. "I'm sorry. Please excuse my rudeness. I'm surprised to see you. I see you are recovered." When she spoke, he had to strain to hear.

"I'm fine, thank you."

She wasn't quite smiling; maybe a worried smile. Jim stepped closer and without thinking, demanded, "What are you doing here?" He instantly regretted the tone of voice.

Her eyes widened. She covered her throat with one hand and looked away. "I.... I just...I–"

"Is anyone with you?" He scanned the trees behind her.

"No. I am alone."

He breathed easier. "How did you get up here this time?"

"I rented another Jeep."

He calmed, smiled and shook his head. "Really? I'm surprised anyone would rent to you after the last time." He picked up the saw. "Well, how did it go this time?"

She responded to his change of attitude and smiled. "It wasn't easy, but, as you know, I had the advantage of being here before. I didn't try to turn around this time. I left the Jeep in the meadow just down the...."

Jim could hear her voice, but couldn't understand a word. They lapsed into another awkward silence, each waiting for the other to speak. Their eyes met and held. He finally broke the stalemate, "Is there something.... Are you looking for something? Someone?"

"Nothing and no."

"Help me out here. I don't understand why you are here. Do you know who I am? Am I supposed to know you?"

"I'm sure you don't."

He noticed that she didn't answer the first part of the question. "I see. Well, it's way too late to start back down the mountain. I think it is going to snow tonight. Were you aware of that?"

The news didn't upset her. "Yes, I know. Look, I know this visit is unexpected. I hope you aren't too angry with me, but I wonder if we might...." She turned and looked toward the cabin.

He understood. "Oh, sure. Come on. We might as well. I'm finished here for the day." He led the way through the clearing.

As they reached the porch she said, "I really didn't intend to get here this late. It always seems to take much longer than I think to drive up here."

So this is no accidental visit. "If you don't mind me asking, Miss, what's the attraction? Why *did* you drive up here again?" The question obviously troubled her.

"Oh. If this is an imposition...."

He waved her off. "No, I have plenty of space if that's what you mean, and you're welcome to stay the night. I think you probably should stay. It's too late to go back, particularly with snow coming and darkness. Please stay."

They paused on the porch. Jim noticed her height for the first time. She stood almost six feet without heels. She tossed her head as a soft wind blew hair over her face. "Can I get you something? A drink?" He decided not to press for answers until later.

"Thank you. Water will be fine."

"Wait here. I'll be back in a jiffy. Need to spiffy things up inside a bit."

*****

Leslie sighed, comforted by the change in his attitude, so hostile in the beginning. His brusque questions made her uncomfortable. *Up to now, though, really not that awkward. He is handling everything fairly well, so far. Better than I deserve. I hope he doesn't ask too many questions. Oh, he is going to ask. The worst is yet to come.* When he returned with water, she noticed that he had changed shirts.

"You go on in and make yourself at home while I get your things."

Interesting. He thinks I came prepared to stay the night, or is he guessing? "No, thank you. I really think I should head–"

"No! Absolutely not. Look, if there is some important reason you need to get back tonight, then I'll drive you down, but we will both be better off if you stay. I don't bite, you know. We go back. I'm certified safe company." He smiled, a wry allusion to their previous meeting. "Really, it's okay. Stay." He gazed directly into her eyes and added, "Anyway, I expect we should probably have a talk, don't you?"

He knows this is no social visit. She welcomed the invitation, but still played innocent. "If I stay, I can get my bag later."

"No. Let me have the keys. I'll bring the jeep on up." He held out his hand.

She gave up pretense and offered the key.

"I won't be long. Make yourself comfortable inside."

Leslie had already observed more of him in the past few minutes than the entire previous visit. The scruffy beard was gone. He was much more pleasing to look at than she remembered. He looked exactly like the Marine Corps photo.

He disappeared down the slope into the darkening shadows and soon drove back across the meadow and stepped into the cabin with her luggage. Upon returning to porch, he said, "I put your stuff in the room opposite the fireplace. You hungry?"

"Starved to death." *What must he think of me? This is so bizarre.*

He held out his hand. She hesitated and took it compliantly

He pulled her up and said, "Me, too. Come on. I'll whip up something. We have plenty of time to talk later. All night."

They finished eating well after dark. By then the outside temperature had dropped well below freezing and the cabin felt cold. He produced a jacket for her and piled on more firewood.

Leslie decided to break the impasse. "I'm sorry if my presence here is troubling. I acted foolishly."

He didn't look up from the fire. "It's done. But since you are here, there is something I would like to know." He looked up then, and without a hint of humor said, "Actually, there are several things I need to know. Need being the operative term here."

She tried to hide nervousness by answering nonchalantly, "That's fair. Fire away."

He sat on the hearth facing her. "All right. Why don't we start with, Who are you? Why are you here?"

Here we go. "I am Leslie Reardon. I live in Denver. I am an attorney working with the American Civil Liberties Union office in Denver. Anything else?"

He laughed. "You answer questions–or don't answer questions–

like an attorney. I noticed that you didn't say why you are up here. And while we are at it, I also remember that you didn't answer that same question when you were up here the last time." He wasn't smiling when he turned to her and said, "So, why *are* you here?"

Leslie looked away. "I'm not quite sure. Can we just chalk it up to curiosity? I really don't have a good answer." She smiled pleasantly. "Now, will you tell me something about yourself?"

He studied her before answering. "Ah, an old lawyer trick; answer a question with a question. Okay, my answer is, That depends on what you want to know, but first, come on, be straight with me. I need answers."

She chose words carefully. "I came to thank you for helping me. I never did thank you properly."

"Sure you did. And I said no thanks were necessary." He suddenly got up and put on a coat. "Let's hold the conversation right there. I have some chores to do before I can settle down. I'll be back in a few minutes. Meanwhile, watch the fire for me and I'll leave the screen off." He stopped at the door and pointed to a door. That's your room. I like having you here, by the way." He tapped the door jamb, then said, "When I come back, maybe we can get to the real reason you came up here. See you in a few minutes."

She shivered involuntarily, breathed a heavy sigh and fell back into the chair after the door closed. *What am I going to tell him? I need answers myself. Why is he up here all by himself?* She walked around the cabin looking for clues. No pictures; no decorations; nothing lying around to suggest anything other than some writing paper, a worn dictionary, a thesaurus, an old typewriter, pencils and a notebook. Nothing else. Everything neatly in place.

*****

Jim needed very little time to feed the horses and stack firewood on the porch for the night. When finished, he sat in the barn collecting his thoughts. *She is beautiful, and I am attracted, but still don't know why she is here.*

When he returned to the cabin he found her cleaning the kitchen. They worked together, making small talk, carefully avoiding physical contact. The kitchen provided very little room for two people to move about without touching. He was intensely conscious of her. She apparently shared the same feelings and stopped talking. Their eyes met and held, much the same as they had earlier in the clearing. Her expression revealed a multitude of emotions: confusion, fright, anxiety, but mostly an appeal for understanding.

He took the cloth from her hand, hung it over the sink and stood between her and the living room gazing directly into her eyes, searching. She trembled, arms folded over her breasts, and whispered, "I'm scared to death. I really shouldn't be here."

"You aren't afraid of me, are you?"

"No, I.... I don't know." She stepped back and turned away.

"Don't be. I'm friendly." He backed away to break the tension.

She left the kitchen and stood beside the fireplace avoiding his eyes. "Thank you for being thoughtful. I'm really sorry about all of this." She offered a helpless, remorseful smile, went to the bedroom and closed the door.

Jim moved chairs next to the fireplace and sat down to wait. The kitchen encounter was too fresh, and what he saw in her eyes. She seemed so vulnerable.

Minutes later, she returned to the living room, sat down and tucked a quilted blanket around her legs. "Please don't let me bother your reading. It's cold in the bedroom."

He stopped pretending to read, placed the book aside, took off his reading glasses and stoked the fire before asking, "Are you afraid of me?"

"No, there is more to it than that."

"Tell me. What?"

"There is so much. I need to think."

He remained silent after that, eyes closed, head resting on the chair back. He could feel her eyes. *Is she as aware of my emotions as I am of hers? Am I reading her right? What in the hell brings her up here? What does she know?*

Leslie thought he might be nodding off, or was deliberately ignoring her. *I have created an intolerable situation. This is going to be a long, long night.*

"I guess you know it's snowing," he announced.

She tried not to show the panic. "Will I be able to get back to Silverton tomorrow?"

He shrugged. "Maybe. Have to wait and see. Three inches and piling up fast. Probably won't keep you here longer than two or three days."

"Two or three days? I can't...." She stood and said, "I'm going to bed. Perhaps I can get an early start tomorrow."

"Please sit. Stay with me. There really are some things I need to know. Things I *must* know. Please? This is crucial to me." He motioned to the chair.

She wavered and then sat. "You're right. "We probably should have that talk."

"Look, Miss Reardon, I hate to be rude, but I must know why you came up here the first time, and now I absolutely must know why you came back. I think you owe me an explanation."

The blunt statement ambushed her. She took time to think before answering. "If I'm honest with you, will you be honest with me?" She knew he wouldn't bargain and regretted making the offer.

His eyes narrowed. "Miss Reardon, my life is not a game and I don't want to fence with you. Please."

Leslie spoke softly. "I honestly don't have a reason that will satisfy you. I suppose I thought we might be friends."

"You're right. I cannot accept that. Why are you being evasive?"

She nodded. "I know. Okay, I'll leave as soon as possible." She started to get up, then took a deep breath and blurted, "Are you wanted by the law? Something like that?"

"No, Miss Reardon, I'm not wanted, at least not by the legal system. I don't want to seem rude, but my life is private."

Leslie thought about his answer for a moment and realized that she had no right to interrogate. "All right. If that's all there is to it, then I don't suppose we need to proceed. I'm going to bed."

He didn't protest.

She lay awake as the bitter cold seeped into the unheated bedroom, shivering in the darkness until the chill became too intense before surrendering to the warmth of fire. After settling into the chair, she said, "Sorry to bother you, but it really is too cold in there."

He placed a marker in the book, threw more wood in the fireplace and said, "Wouldn't be if you left the door open." He disappeared into his bedroom.

Leslie moved closer to the fire. The flames were hypnotizing and she slept.

*****

Jim didn't sleep, tossing and turning, unable to think of anything but her. *If things don't change between us, and damned soon, she's will leave and I won't know why she came. Maybe she came as a sincere gesture of friendship, to say thanks. That's foolish. There is still the little matter of why she came and how she knows who I am.*

Her presence bothered him in other ways. He didn't have a place in his life for a woman, and the attraction for her was unmistakable. *A damned attorney of all things.*

He went to the fireplace to throw more wood on the flames and watched her sleep. *She is truly beautiful.* His attempts to be quiet working with the fire woke her. He looked up to find her gazing at him, the flickering light from the fire penetrating the room's darkness reflected from her eyes.

"Sorry about the noise. Didn't mean to wake you. You warm enough?"

"Yes. Don't worry about me. Is it still snowing out?"

"Oh, yeah. Well over a foot now, but it won't last long this time of year."

The fire grew rapidly. Warm, flickering light illuminated the room. She loosened the blanket and sat up. "I won't be able to leave tomorrow?"

Jim shook his head. "Nope. Sorry. Not much chance we'll be able to get away for a couple of days. It's far too dangerous driving with this much snow on that steep road." He noticed her distressed expression. "Look, Miss Reardon, I'm sorry about tonight. You didn't deserve the way I acted. I wish we could start over." Changing tactics appeared to be the only way to learn more about her.

She smiled. "Good. Then you may begin by calling me Leslie."

He felt relieved. He was torn between the need to know more about her for the sake of security and the desire to know her better for personal reasons. "Leslie. I am really sorry about yesterday, and I mean that."

"My fault for coming without notice. Aren't you sleepy?"

"No. Too much to think about. How about you?"

"Same. Do you still want to talk?"

He stepped to the table and lit a kerosene lamp. Leslie's eyes followed every movement. He sat on the hearth directly in front of her and began, slow and deliberate. "All right. First, I'm glad you are here. I have thought about you a great deal."

"Really?"

"Yes. I even thought about going to Denver to look you up."

She looked surprised. "Do you know where I live?"

"Yes. The Jeep owner gave me your card. Nine Sixteen Mountain view."

"Oh." She recalled her conversations with the first rental agent and realized that Jim must know that she was looking for him even then.

"Why didn't you come to Denver?" she asked.

"I think that might have been a little presumptuous on my part, don't you?"

"Perhaps. I would have enjoyed seeing you."

"I didn't have any way of knowing that. There are other reasons. I still don't know enough about you to say much."

"You saved my life. You get special consideration."

"Look, Miss Reardon—Leslie—it's important that I know more about you. Please, if you don't mind, fill me in. Either that or we are going to part and I will forever wonder."

His candidness pleased her. Twice during the evening he had mentioned being glad to see her, even admitted thinking about her.

"Okay. I'm not married and never have been. I live in Denver alone. I'm the last surviving member of my family. I work for the ACLU as an attorney. Just your average middle aged lawyer."

"I don't want to be pushy, but your presence here is a complete mystery to me. That's really the part I want to know."

"You think I have a hidden motive?"

"I'm pretty sure you do. I cannot think of a single good reason for you to come all the way up here the first time, and now you're back." He gestured helplessly. "Hard to figure. Help me."

"I think a lot about you, too."

The admission appeared to puzzle him. "Enough to make the journey again after nearly dying?"

"Yes."

"Why? What do you know about me?"

"It seemed important to see you." She deliberately ignored the second half of his question and quickly changed the subject by asking, "Is there someone in your life?"

"No."

"Me either. Why do you live up here, so far from civilization?"

"By choice."

She pressed ahead. "Your choice?"

"Yes and no. It's a long story."

"There must be a very good reason. You don't strike me as a loner."

"I like people well enough."

"Women?"

He laughed. "A hell of lot more than men."

"But there are no women in your life?"

"No. The way I live wouldn't be good for a woman."

"And you're happy with that?"

"No. There is much more to it, and not much I can do about it."

"Why are you...." She almost tipped her hand by admitting she knew he was hiding.

A long silence before he spoke. "There is also so much that cannot be said. It's difficult to know where to start."

Leslie knew the time had come to confess her reasons. "Okay, I suppose the time for fencing is over. Perhaps I can help."

He smiled. "I don't think you understand the problem."

She replied, "I understand much more than you know, and maybe more than I should." She shifted uncomfortably, dreading what came next. "I have some things to say, Jim, that I suspect will probably be very disturbing to you. Let me explain. I know you are, at least for the present, Michael Allen Stokes. Your driver's license says you are forty-nine, as does your birth certificate. I also know your home address and your parents of record do not exist. I know you graduated from high school and college and have degrees to prove it. I contacted the schools and found there is no record of you. I know your social security number is valid, but very recent and fraudulent. All of your records originated on the same day early this year. I know your real name is James Colby and that you retired from the Marine Corps as a Lieutenant

Colonel. I don't know why, but I believe you are being hidden by the government."

She watched his expression change to astonishment. She hadn't revealed everything, wondering beforehand if the disclosure would scare him into greater caution. She had the answer. The look on his face could not have been more stunned.

*****

How does she know so much? Why does she know so much? Her voice penetrated his bewildered thoughts.

"Let me explain further." She then told him about the ACLU investigation and finished by saying, "I don't know why you are hiding, but I believe you are. None of what I have told you is clear to me. None of it makes much sense, but that isn't the reason I came up here. Please forgive me for prying into your life. I took advantage of my position. There, that is what I know." She sat back and waited for his response.

Jim collected his wits and reviewed the implications of her disclosures. Obviously, now he had to leave, and quickly. "Okay," he said. "Why did the ACLU have me investigated? I must know exactly why you are here and why you are investigating me. I cannot emphasize that too much."

She nodded slowly, and then said, "The ACLU did it for me. I still have not been completely open with you, but I expect you already know that."

"You must admit that your presence here defies reason. Why did you have me investigated?"

"What I said about wanting to know you is true. For some unexplainable reason, I am tied to you emotionally. You are the reason I am here, but there is much more than that, as I'm sure you must know. I have known about you for a long time, Jim." She sighed brokenly, steeling herself, and said, "A few months ago I got fired from a position on Colorado Senator Charlie Collins' legal staff. Do you know who Senator Charlie Collins is?"

"I do. Not in depth."

"I worked as his legal assistant. He gave me an assignment to investigate an unauthorized fund at CIA headquarters. A long story, but during my investigation I found your name linked to some unauthorized funds and got fired, I think for knowing too much. Your name surfaced associated with some of that money. Is that possible?"

He shrugged. "Possible. I don't know the details."

"I knew before I came here the first time that you were once a Marine Lieutenant Colonel. I also know a CIA agent killed two Libyan diplomats in New York and you were somehow involved, but I also know you didn't do it. I didn't learn more because Collins fired me. Apparently I was getting too close to something big. Maybe you can fill me in?" Before he could answer, she added, "Oh, and I should probably tell you that I have done a complete background investigation on you, privately."

"How complete?"

"Very. I have been to your hometown, your schools and church. I have seen your ex-wife. Not to speak with her. I know almost everything about your history until you quit selling cars in Oklahoma City."

His eyebrows raised and he whistled. "Okay, why did you come up here the first time? Were you planning to turn me in? Are you still conducting the investigation?"

"No to both questions. I'm sorry for not being completely honest with you before. If you can, please believe that I won't hide anything from you. I admit being upset that you were indirectly responsible for ruining my life–being fired–and I admit being nosy enough to keep searching to satisfy my own curiosity. But I have no ulterior motives now, other than what I must admit has become personal. I am inexplicably curious about you, but no longer part of any investigation." She held up her hands. "That's it. Everything I have told you is true. Now, it would be nice to know what I should call you."

"Jim. That's as good as any."

"Jim it is."

He studied her eyes intently. "Okay, if you aren't part of an investigation, exactly what is your motive for being here this time? My life is at stake, Leslie. I must know the truth–all of it. You should have been able to fill in any blanks in my history after your first visit. You knew enough about me then." He couldn't bring himself to believe personal interest could be her only motive.

"I suppose you could say I became emotionally involved." She couldn't look him in the eye. "But I never once thought about turning you in. I really don't know why it's so important for me to be here now. I am confused about that. Have I made a mess of things for you?"

He shook his head slowly. "Not yet. I needed to move from here anyway. I should have left the country right after you came the first time."

"Why didn't you?"

"I don't know. Maybe I'm...." He threw up his hands, a signal of frustration.

"Go on. It's your turn to be truthful. Tell me."

He smiled and said, "Maybe I've been up here too long. I tend to fantasize."

"About me?"

He laughed. "Maybe. A little."

She stepped closer and said, "I want to know one thing. Did it occur to you that I might come back?"

He nodded. "It did. I thought you came up here looking for me, but also knew that if you could find me, then I was uncovered. First the bus accident, and then you. If you found me someone else can. You were and are an enigma to me. What did you say—emotional?"

"Really? After one brief meeting, and a poor excuse for a meeting at that?"

"Yes. I get the felling there is something...." He smiled and said, "I expect you may know what I mean."

She felt the wall between them falling away. "I think I do. It is hard to understand, though. This is all so extraordinary."

"In what way?"

"Because I had to come back. I sensed that you were in trouble. Nothing could have stopped me from coming back."

He looked bewildered. "Why? You and I are complete strangers."

"Maybe I am to you, but you certainly are not to me. You have become a significant part of my life."

His smile turned to a somber frown. He sighed and looked away.

"What? What is it now?"

"Maybe nothing. Maybe everything. Leslie, as premature as this may sound, I am probably more attracted to you than any woman I have ever known. The feeling could be nothing more than the product of months and years of loneliness. Something about you has…. Well, I probably shouldn't go on."

"No! You must go on."

"I think it is time to be realistic. I don't believe it's a good idea to pursue this fancy any farther. I don't have a life, Leslie, and never will. I have nothing to share, so I think it's best if we just leave it at that."

"You sound so sure."

"I am. Beyond question. It would be all too easy to let emotions lead, but I know better. You must know by now that I live alone because I have to. I am hiding. I don't want to ruin another person's life; even considering something like that is possible."

She studied him thoughtfully. "Well, it just isn't that easy for me, Jim, because I can't stop." The words came out automatically, before she thought. "Like it or not, I am involved. Tell me why, Jim. Why are you so–

"No! I just can't talk to about it."

"Why not?"

"Because I'm in deep trouble, more trouble than you can imagine, more trouble than you should be involved with."

She didn't give in. "I have to know. This is important to me, Jim and I cannot explain it, but I have to know. Please don't shut me out."

Jim rubbed his temples, frowning. "Let me think." He turned away and stared into the fire. When he turned back, their eyes met. "All right. But first, who else knows?"

"You know about the ACLU investigation."

"You and your boss are the only ones directly involved. Is that right?"

"That's correct. Others were involved, but they only filled in the blanks. They don't know the overall picture. You can rest assured the information is safe with him. He won't say anything. I would trust him with my life."

Jim spoke softly, "And mine?"

"Your life? Are you in that kind of serious trouble?"

"Yes. There's much more to this than you can imagine, Leslie." He got up and worked feverishly with the fire, filling the bucket with ashes, and then went outside. When he returned to the room, he went to Leslie's chair and pulled her gently to a standing position.

They stood close for a moment, looking directly into each other's eyes. She appeared defenseless to him, much the same as in the kitchen earlier. He could read her thoughts as clearly as if she had spoken. What he detected concerned him all the more. Everything he dreamed about in recent years was there. Her feelings for him were as clear as his for her. He knew her trembling had nothing to do with the cold.

"I want you to go to bed and sleep," he ordered. "Leave the door open so the room stays warm. I need time alone. I'll see you in the morning. Thanks for telling me, Leslie. It is important. I need to think now." He nodded toward her room.

She turned to leave, then stopped and faced him. "I am responsible for everything, Jim, and I am so sorry. I don't know why it seemed so important to see you. Can you forgive me for intruding? I have probably ruined everything for you, haven't I?"

Jim stepped close, placed his hands on her shoulders and said, "You don't know what you're talking about." He smiled reassuringly, cupped her face in his hands and kissed her lightly on the mouth. "I don't think you have ruined anything, Leslie. I think you have unintentionally arranged it so we can know each other. As a matter of fact, you may have made it imperative." He turned her toward the bedroom and gave a gentle push.

She balked and faced him, bewildered but still curious. "Are you serious?"

He smiled grimly, but added, "Yeah. Now go to bed."

Leslie lingered, the hint of a smile playing at the corner of her mouth, then stepped close, gazed directly into his eyes for a moment and kissed him soundly on the mouth. She backed several steps toward the bedroom, the hint of a smile still tugging at the corner of her mouth, then turned and disappeared.

She woke well after sunrise to find him sound asleep in a chair by the fire. She sponged off and changed clothes before he stirred. When he opened his eyes she was sitting on the hearth, elbows on knees, chin in hand, watching him.

"Good morning," she said cheerfully. "If you will just fire up the stove, sir, I will cook breakfast."

He did outside chores while she cooked. After breakfast, back in the living room by the fire, she said, "Okay, tell me."

He turned away, took several deep breaths and stared into the fire. When their eyes met again he asked, "Can I trust you?"

"Yes."

"With my life?"

"Yes."

"I believe you. I also believe you are involved way too deep in my life now. I feel morally obligated to tell you everything, because I don't think you have any idea how serious this mess is. What I am going to tell you will probably end any thought of a relationship we may have fantasized about."

"I doubt that, but go on."

"What I say must remain secret. If you ever say anything, both of our lives will be in danger. My life is up for grabs now, and has been for a while. Now that you have unearthed so much, it is my opinion that you are also in great danger. Do you still want me to go on?"

"Yes. I need to know." Her early morning cheerfulness faded.

"My real name is James Colby, as you know. There is nothing particularly important or unusual about me, at least there wasn't until my son and his family were killed by Libyan terrorists in an airliner bombing."

Her breath drew in. "I am so sorry, Jim."

"Yeah. Well, that started everything." His voice wavered, betraying barely controlled emotions. He had to pause a moment to regain control. "I can't tell you how much their deaths affected me. Destroyed my life. Took everything I had left. All I could think about was revenge. That was more important to me than anything, and the only thing I had left. Nothing else mattered at that time; not my life; not anything." He paused to let the information sink in. "Still want me to go on? It gets messy."

Leslie's thoughts raced to keep up, trying to fill in the missing pieces. "Yes. I need to know."

"All right then. You know about the two Libyan diplomats killed in New York, I believe?"

"I am familiar with that. Remember, I told you that I know you didn't do it. As a matter of fact, I know exactly who did. He is dead now, murdered. No leads to his murderer yet that I know of.

He was the man you hit in the chest with a toolbox in Athens. His wife told me. We can talk about that later. I'm not exactly sure how you were involved, but I think the CIA used those killings to gain your services–something like that. You didn't have anything to do with killing those two men, did you?"

"No, but what you're thinking is almost true. I didn't do it, but I was in New York to kill them and got caught at the scene" He held up a hand. "But before you think too poorly of me, I had the opportunity and couldn't do it. But," he sighed. "I got caught leaving the area. Someone else killed the Libyans."

"Paul Sells did it. The CIA. So, that's why you're hiding?"

He smiled grimly. "Not even close. I would give anything if that ended it, but there is much more. I don't know for sure who my captors were, Leslie. You think they were CIA and I expect you are right. Whoever they were, they sure seemed to think I killed those diplomats."

"Jim, Paul Sells ordered his wife to tell me because he knew I was investigating. She believes he shot them."

The information pleased him. "I always thought it was a set-up. Okay, I'll try to make this short. They transported me to a hideout and offered complete amnesty for the killings, if I did something for them. Actually they didn't leave any choice. I want you to believe that. Don't ask about it right now, just take my word for it. I didn't have a choice." He stopped, waiting for Leslie to catch up.

"No choice about what? Is there more?"

He nodded. "You need to be absolutely certain you want me to continue. You will become directly involved if I do, whereas you are only indirectly connected now. What you learn will be as dangerous to you as it is to me."

She said, "Go on. It surely can't get any worse."

His wry expression indicated otherwise. "Amnesty had a price. I had to earn it. They promised freedom and a million dollars, along with a new life provided I assassinated someone."

Leslie's hand went to her mouth. "Please don't play with me."

"They were going to extradite me to Libya for killing those diplomats. They gave me the choice of working for them or being sent to Libya for trial. I didn't kill those men, Leslie, you know that, but I planned to. I had motive; I was on the scene with a gun; and most of all, I couldn't prove I didn't do it. I'm not sure it would have made any difference to them if I could have proven it. To be honest, it didn't make any difference to me at the time. I think I would have killed the guy for nothing. He murdered my son."

The color drained from her face. Leslie covered her face with both hands. "Oh, God. No. Please don't tell me that! Not you. Please, not you."

He pulled her hands away, forcing her to look him in the eye. "You have to know," he said. "Yes, I killed Abdel Hafez. That's right, but I messed up their plans and escaped without being killed myself. I know the people who hired me tried to have me caught at the scene, and I also know they tried to catch me later on in Athens. I am certain that they are still looking for me, as I expect the Libyans are. There you have it. That is the reason I hide and that is the reason you need to know. You see, Leslie, if you could find me, then they can too, and maybe through you. They will do anything to find me, and I mean exactly that, anything, including kill, to silence me. Do you know what that means to you?"

Leslie's face had turned ashen. She was almost paralyzed by the shocking disclosure. After a moment she said, "I can guess, but go ahead."

He leaned closer. "It means that you are now in as much danger as I am because you are a way to get to me. If the ACLU could find me, any decent intelligence agency can. Your boss is in danger, too. If the Libyans are looking for me and find out he knows where I am, they will force him to tell by any means necessary. Once he talks they will kill him. If the CIA learns he knows...well, you can take it from there. If the CIA is involved, then it probably goes higher up. They need to close all loose ends to the assassination. I am a tremendous liability to everyone involved. The same goes for you now. I'm sorry, but that's the way the game is played. Little people don't count."

Leslie spoke angrily, "Why did you tell me?"

"Because I'm going to leave–disappear. If I didn't tell you, you wouldn't know you were in danger."

Leslie couldn't stop the tears. The horror of his revelations seemed beyond belief, but she believed. "How could you have done something so terrible?" she demanded, angry with him for destroying her image of him. "What gave you the right to kill?"

She felt betrayed. *How could he? I counted on him being a victim, not the executioner.*

He countered with equal anger. "Who gave him the right to murder hundreds of innocent people on that airplane? Who gave him the right to kill my family? That miserable bastard killed hostages on world-wide television, innocent people unrelated to his cause. His organization has killed thousands, Leslie. Look, I'm not trying to make what I did seem right or justifiable, but the man I shot was not innocent. He was a terrorist murderer! There is no way to retract what I did, and you certainly don't need to pile more condemnation on the remnants of my life. My life was already ruined before you started nosing around!"

They glared at each other until he stood and reached for his coat. "I'm not the terrible monster you seem to think. If I had to do it all over again, I might still do the same thing, I don't know. My entire life has been out of control since Hafez killed my boy. There isn't anything to be gained by second guessing, Leslie. Hate me if you like, but I can't change anything. So, now you know." He threw up his hands and left the house before she could reply.

Leslie sat for a long time, staggered by the astonishing story. When he didn't return in thirty minutes she started pacing from room to room looking for him through the windows, thinking about his story. *Last night I actually thought he could be.... Damn him!* Her fingers traced the contours of her mouth. *We had something.* The fading promise of her trampled dream wasn't nearly as bright as the dark reality of his past. There could be no escape from his past.

Damn him!

Chapter Twenty-Nine

THE BOND

Snow fell throughout the following day. Jim left after the talk with Leslie and didn't return to the cabin until late afternoon. She also needed time to think, but stood at the windows watching for him, worrying, waiting. He came in at dusk with an armload of wood and worked with the fire before carrying the ashes out.

Leslie left the room the moment he entered and lingered in the bedroom, huddled beneath a blanket until the chill drove her back to warmth. She found him packing clothes.

"The snow is melting," he announced without looking at her. "We should be able to leave tomorrow, maybe by noon."

"I take it you're leaving?"

"Definitely. I'll drive ahead and break the drifts for you. My truck is heavy enough to plow through."

"Where will you go? Sorry. That's not my business."

He answered matter-of-factly, still facing away, unwilling to break the impasse between them. "I don't know. Haven't thought about it. Somewhere. Anywhere."

"Will you come back here?"

He turned to her. "Here? Not likely. Too many people know about me." He shrugged and went back to packing.

Silence filled the space between them. Leslie alternately watching him pack and stared into the fire. She almost shouted, "It's my fault. If I minded my own business, none of this would be necessary."

He paused, turned to her and said, "That's not true. None of this or anything else that happens to me is your fault. You probably saved my life."

"Really?"

When he stepped to the hearth in front of her, Leslie noticed that he wasn't frowning, and he spoke without anger.

"How? Because I didn't think anyone knew where I lived–not until you showed up. A misconception like that is dangerous…believing no one knew, I mean. I had a false sense of security."

"Do you honestly believe I could be in danger?"

He nodded, looking her straight in the eye for emphasis. "Yes. Sooner or later someone will probably put two and two together the same way you did. When that happens, I'll be gone and you will be a possible connection to me. At least that's what they will think."

"Why would they think that?"

"It's sensible. Because you found me; because you have been investigating me; but primarily, because you found me twice, they will naturally assume you know where I am."

She sat back, offended. "Surely you don't think I would betray you?"

His expression communicated doubt. "Probably not deliberately, at least I hope not. Their methods are extremely effective, though. I can vouch for that. To continue with your first question, Yes, I believe you are in danger. They will assume you know too much if they learn that you have been with me. They damned sure know how much I know. Think about it, Leslie, you were fired for knowing too much. Like it or not, you are not an innocent bystander. Would what you know be damaging to the government if it leaked to the media?

"Yes it would. Definitely."

"I am sure that is what they would have to think. They can't afford to assume anything."

She covered her face with both hands and moaned. "Oh, I don't know what to think. This is so hard to believe. Now I'm afraid to go back home." She looked up, eyes pleading. "Am I being paranoid?"

"Absolutely not. Legitimate concern is not paranoia–just common sense. I'm sorry for you. I wish you weren't involved."

"Not your fault. I have been involved for months, haven't I?"

She paused, long enough to draw his attention. "Change of subject, Jim. Last night you said I might have made it possible for us to be friends. In fact, as I recall, you said it might be imperative. Why?"

He nodded. "I recognized how deeply you are involved, and the danger associated."

"You seem terribly sure."

"I am. I have deliberately not let anyone into my life, Leslie. When I discovered that you were already in, I entertained the possibility of.... Well, it doesn't matter now, does it? I fantasize sometimes." He poked the fire to escape her gaze.

Leslie lashed out. "What am I supposed to do now? You say I'm in danger, and the enormity of what you did leads me to believe it, particularly if someone thinks I am a means of getting to you. What am I supposed to do, just sit around and wait to see if they find me? What happens if they do?"

The sharpness of her voice drew his attention from the fire. "I think the answer to your question would be, It depends who the *they* are. If Libyans...." He shrugged helplessly. "They are ruthless. They might do anything to get information from you. If our people find you first? I can't say. I damned sure don't trust them, though. I don't blame you for being angry."

"I'm not angry at you, Jim! I am scared."

"I don't know what else to say, except this: You are involved. You are in danger and there is not one damned thing either one of us can do about it."

She pondered his answer for a moment before replying, "I think you may be overstating the danger. I'm not going to shrink from some concocted threat. I'm going home."

He turned and started packing again. "Your decision. I don't have any choice. Both sides have already tried to kill me, so I'm not willing to bet my life they won't again. I know way too much. I could wreck the upper levels of the present administration." He turned to her. "But so can you, Leslie. You are a colossal liability to our government and a path to me for the Libyans."

"I just can't believe this is happening! What about my life? What about my work?"

Jim went back to packing. "There is nothing either of us can do to alter the facts."

Her anger soared again. "Well, that doesn't do me much good, does it? Look, I'm not very good at international intrigue, or playing cop and robber games. What would you advise? You seem to be the expert here."

He stifled a laugh and turned away to hide the smile. "Okay, I'll tell you what I think," he said, sitting on a packed box. "As I see it, Leslie, you have two options, and it doesn't make much difference which one you choose—you are still going to be in danger."

"I suppose I should be pleased to know there are options." She leaned against the sill facing him, arms folded. "Okay, just what do you think my options are?"

Jim stood and stepped closer. "What I say next may sound over-simplified, but I honestly don't think it is. Quite simply, I believe you are going to be in danger with or without me." He waited a moment for some reaction. "I think those are your options."

Her expression transformed from anger to disbelief. "Surely you can't be serious?"

He nodded to reinforce his words. "Yes, in fact I am serious. However, and I hope you don't think I am fostering some adolescent fantasy, I believe you will be in less danger with me than without me."

"Good heavens! Why would you think that?"

"Why? With me you won't have to speculate about risk. The risk would always be real enough. Risk is something I plan for and minimize. With me the reality of risk would not be guesswork, it would be fundamental. Without me, and I promise this is not rationalizing, you will always worry. I know the idea may seem preposterous at the moment, but you have very little time to decide."

She was astonished. "That's not fair!"

"Fair has nothing to do with it—not any more. Look, I'm not going to hang around here waiting to get caught. This much I know, after I leave you will never see me again. You won't be able to find me ever again. Face facts, Leslie and leave emotion out of your decision, and let me add this—It would please me very much if you decided to come with me, and I sincerely believe that is your best option."

Her arms dropped and she lashed out again, "Come with you! That is preposterous! I can't do that! I don't know you. Who are you, really? Do you know?"

He shrugged. "The idea is bizarre, I know. We aren't exactly strangers, though. Ask yourself this, Leslie, Why not? What have you got to lose?"

She laughed sarcastically. "Good Lord! Just my entire life! Have you thought this out? I have never heard anything so utterly ludicrous!"

"Why? If you decide to come with me you won't be obligated. Hell, if things don't work out you can always go home. I can't. What I'm saying is, You have two options now but only one if I leave without you."

Her anger subsided before she spoke again. "Not that I would actually consider it, but what are you going to do? Where are you going?"

"After I leave? I don't know. Someplace safer than this I hope. Start over."

"Can you ever find a safe place?

"Depends on how good I am at it. Anything will be better than rotting up here. Let me say this. You asked if I know who I am. Yes. I am the guy you saw in that class picture on the wall at school. I am the man in those reports you collected. I believe I am the man you hoped I would be when you started looking for me. I think you will find that I am exactly who you thought I would be."

She stepped closer and glared. "No. Oh no you're not. You can't be. You have done something I will never understand and I do *not* know who you are."

"What I did wasn't right; maybe not even sane. What I did made me a fugitive. My life is ruined because of what I did, and now maybe yours is too. But I really haven't changed."

She turned away. "I don't even want to think about what you did."

"You don't have to, but there is no escape for me. Living with and thinking about those memories will always haunt me. If it means anything to you, I regret what I did every day and night of my life. You also need to know this, Under the same circumstances I might do it again."

"How nice, but that still doesn't change anything for me, does it?"

"No. I wish things were different. Let me conclude by saying, I am learning to live with the past, but I don't have a choice. You have choices."

Leslie's hostility diminished as he spoke. He returned to the packing boxes and she went back to the window to gaze across the valley. Much later, when she spoke, her breath fogged the window. "All right," she said. "I agree. That's the way things are and you can't change it. Now what?" She faced him.

"What do you mean?"

"I want to know what you're planning to do with the rest of your life. Exactly what?"

He tossed the last of his books in the box. "There has to be more for me than isolation and loneliness. I will not live like this again. I'm going somewhere and start a new life. That's it. Not exact, I know, but that's it." He walked to the window and gently tugged at her shoulder until she turned to face him. "Come with me, Leslie. I won't disappoint you. I promise."

His voice, his eyes, the reassuring pressure of his hand, everything he did intensified the urgency of his appeal. Leslie turned her back. She couldn't have spoken if she wanted to.

"I think we could make us work, Leslie. It would be easy for me."

She shook her head. "I can't, Jim. I don't know you. What else can I say other than that? What I know doesn't make me want to run off with you. And what about my career?" she asked. "What about *my* life?"

"Have you thought about the options? The danger?"

"I've thought of nothing else. Oh, why do you have to be mixed up in something so dreadful?" She leaned her forehead against the window.

He could see tears in the window reflection and waited for her to regain composure. When she faced him again, much later, traces of moisture lingered on her face. A sympathetic ache lodged in his chest. He wanted to hold her but could only watch as her emotions intensified and she began crying. She didn't turn away and completely lost control and broke down, hiding her face in her hands.

Jim blinked to stem the flow of tears. They had come close to a breakthrough the night before. The potential for something between them now was nothing but a mirage.

"Is this about us?" he whispered, placing a hand on her

shoulder. After the swell of weeping subsided, she smeared the tears across her face with trembling fingers, looked up and nodded. He held his arms out, beckoning. She melted and stepped in.

Long afterward, still surprised by the desperation in her embrace, he said, "I have to leave tomorrow, Leslie. Come with me. Give me a chance. Give us a chance."

Her head rested comfortably in the curve of his neck. She didn't try to disengage. He wondered if the answer might be conveyed in her silence, in her nearness, in a shared need to seek and give comfort. She seemed content and made no effort to end the closeness.

Jim nudged the hair away from the side of her face with his fingertips and brushed her neck with his lips. She leaned back to gaze into his eyes. He could read her thoughts. The curious smile he noticed the night before played at the corner of her mouth. She explored his eyes. He took her calmness as a positive sign and kissed the remnants of tears from her face.

Fences fell away. Walls crumbled.

"I'm sorry for everything," she said. "What happened to you is terrible and I have treated it as though it happened to me. I'm sorry about your family, Jim. I'm sorry for judging you. I am so sorry for that. Forgive me."

"Done. I only wish I had known you before. Maybe none of this would have happened."

"What makes you think so?"

"I didn't have anything to live for, Leslie."

"And now?"

He held her at arm's length, searching her eyes. The grim set of her face softened as months of torment and heartache melted and the border of reserve dissolved. Tears of joy flowed; emotions spilled; neither could hide the depth of their feelings. They shared a common need and pressed together, her arms around his neck. She began kissing him, on his mouth and face, unrestrained. They reached an unspoken covenant.

More kisses exposed a passionate longing that neither would deny. He gently pushed her to arms' length, looking into her eyes, pleading for guidance. Her playful smile reinforced his growing confidence.

"What are you thinking?" she asked.

"I'd be embarrassed to say."

"I want to know."

"I want you," he said. She didn't shrink or pull away. "I have never wanted anything more than I want you at this moment," he said.

Her smile didn't change. Her eyes surrendered, sealing the bond. "There will never be a better time," she murmured.

They walked slowly to the bedroom, each with an arm around the other's waist, pausing beside the bed to kiss again and again, more insistent each time. Neither seemed surprised by the effortless familiarity. He reached for the buttons on her blouse as she unfastened his shirt. They undressed, still kissing, neither touching any part of the other's body except lips. They didn't want to ruin the magic by rushing.

Jim pushed away to observe her body. "You are beautiful. Perfect."

"And now I like you better without clothes."

They laughed easily, embracing and kissing until the burning passion returned. He pulled the covers back, placed her on the bed and began tracing the contours of her neck with his lips. Her breathing deepened and she reacted hungrily, directing his mouth to her breast. Her reaction to the stimulus could not have been more exciting to him, writhing and whimpering. She pressed against him as passion grew and the desire for consummation took over. She moaned as his mouth devoured hers, responding with insistent kisses, oblivious to everything except their shared urgency. Then, without the slightest change in desire, without a break from kissing, without any conscious effort, he shifted over her body. She tugged instinctively, hips thrusting, fingers digging into his shoulders.

They shared a need that did not permit time for tenderness and literally invaded each other. Their passion blended, neither's appetite surpassing the others. Leslie's need matched his strength; his power did not overwhelm her response. Mutual gratification happened spontaneously and mercifully. She moaned as their bodies convulsed and embraced him with all her might until he relaxed and her racing heartbeat slowed. She said, "We won't last two weeks at this rate."

They collapsed, content to lie in each other's arms, unwilling to move for fear of breaking the serene trance replacing frenzied passion, caressing, savoring the afterglow.

How quick it all happened, she thought. So unbelievable natural.

Jim propped his head up on an elbow to gaze at her. "I have never wanted or needed anyone so much." He suddenly looked serious and asked. "Wait a minute. Did you just say, We won't last two weeks at this rate? Does that mean there could be more?"

At that moment, Leslie would have risked anything to linger with him. Everything depended on what she decided.

If I go with him my life will be changed forever. There will be no legal career. There will be no home and or friends. My life will be tied to his fugitive existence.

Her thoughts lingered on the present, closing with, *I have known this would happen from the first day I knew he existed.* His question 'Could there be more?' brought her back to the present. Her eyes glistened as she thought about the incredible events controlling their lives, factors so widely conflicting that it seemed nothing could bring them together.

I need to be practical. I'm on an emotional high. Common sense should dictate what happens next. Take time. Consider everything. There are dangers. A complete life change. And yet, common sense has nothing to do with the feelings I have for him, or the ache in my heart, or the fact that I am happier than I can ever remember. Happy in the arms of a man who has done things I will never understand; things no sane person would understand. And yet, I know I will never feel like this again if I let him go.

"I have known you since I was a little girl. Did you know that?"

He smiled, thinking it an idle remark. "Really? How did I miss you?"

She wasn't smiling. "I have been in love with you from the moment I knew you were real, did you know that?"

He turned to face her. "Are you serious?"

She rolled over and with her chin on his chest, replied, "Yes. I have thought about you and dreamed about you all my life. I know that may sound silly, but it's true. I knew from the moment I first saw your picture and read your Marine records that you were going to be in my life. That's why I continued the search and that's why I am here."

He smiled, attempting to appease her sudden change of mood, a change he didn't understand. "That's amazing, Leslie."

"I know it sounds odd, but the truth is, I have been waiting for you all of my life."

His brow furrowed and the smile faded. "You are serious, aren't you?"

"Never been more serious. I have waited and watched for you, and now that you're here, there is no doubt. All of my life, Jim, thinking about you. That makes it so difficult to understand what you have done. I never thought poorly of you. You were always gentle in my dreams."

Leslie turned away to weigh the importance of her next comment. Tears spread into curtains beneath her eyes and she held up a warning hand as he reached for her.

"No. Please let me finish. You asked if there would be more. I don't think you meant more on a temporary basis."

"I didn't."

"I don't understand what you did and perhaps I never will, but I would happily trade the rest of my life for what we have shared here this afternoon. I am never going to let you go. Ever. I don't want to live the rest of my life without you." She felt the months of distress lift as the declaration replaced old terrors and inhibitions, replaced by the dream of a lifetime.

"You have to be sure, Leslie? If you are, this is too good to be true."

She derived as much pleasure from her joy as she did from the evidence of his feelings for her. "I am sure, Jim. As sure as I can be that I love you, incredible as that may seem in such short time. I have never been more certain of anything than that. I love you. Isn't that remarkable? I have never said that to another man. I have waited my entire life for you. I came back to the mountain to tell you that I love you. I regret that I didn't say it the first time we met. I knew it even then. And something else, my first impression of you was that I knew you. I believe with all my heart and soul, that my life has been focused on you for many years. I have always known that I would find you, and I have always known that when I did, it would feel like this."

She couldn't hold him away and didn't try. They rolled back and forth across the bed, never relinquishing their hold. The evening and night drifted away like a fantastic dream as they talked and touched, held and kissed, laughed, cried and joyously explored each other.

"By the way, you are never going to get this shirt back." She was wearing one of his flannel work shirts."

"That ratty old shirt?"

"It smells like you, Jim. It belongs to me now, forever."

Lovemaking that night before complete physical exhaustion claimed the last of their energy, happened as tenderly and slowly as the first experience was abrupt and fierce. They laughed, wrapped in each other's arms, complete and natural.

Just before sleep, she asked, "Did you get that money the CIA promised?"

"No. They reneged. Why?"

"It doesn't matter. My father left enough money for a lifetime."

"Guess that means I will be a kept man."

Chapter Thirty

WASHINGTON

Robert Hensley stepped into the plush office and shook hands with his boss, Ed Bagley, an old acquaintance now head of the CIA. Bagley had recently appointed Hensley as Special Operations Chief, replacing Adrian Burt. Bagley thought Burt screwed up the Benghazi mission by allowing Colonel Colby to escape. He needed someone dependable and ruthless to clean up the mess. Hensley was his man, a long-time agency pro with a history of dirty tricks experiences. The two men were also college fraternity cronies.

"Mornin' Bob. I take it you are getting a handle on this Colby thing?"

"Yes, Sir. Took a little longer than I thought, but I think we can wind this mess up in short order."

"Damn, I hope you're right. You can't imagine the grief Burt caused me. Okay, fill me in." He sat, pushed a cigar box across the desk and both men lit up.

Hensley settled into a comfortable leather chair beside the desk, blew a satisfying cloud of smoke, and began. "I believe you already know about the Englishman." Bagley's expression said he didn't. "Oh, come on, Ed, I told you, remember? Our man Colby used the Brit's ID to buy a truck in Bar Harbor, Maine."

Bagley's eyebrows raised. "Oh, yeah. Sent his credentials back– all that. That's how we knew he was back in the states. Go on."

"Right. He showed up at the bank in Denver after that and they alerted us. Got a positive surveillance ID on him when he tried to collect the money. Spooked and took off."

Bagley rotated his hand, encouraging Hensley to move on.

"That's all old news, Bob."

"Just background, Ed. I know where he is."

Bagley lurched forward." You do? Great! Well, where in the hell is he?"

"His truck–the same truck he bought with the Englishman's credentials–got dinged in a fender-bender in Silverton Colorado a couple of months ago, just a few days after we got his picture from that bank. Colby is working at a mine east of Silverton." He lingered over the cigar for a moment, letting the drama build. "Now, and this is where the good part begins. Some Libyans are in Denver asking questions, closing in on him. You remember the guy Burt had at the ranch teaching Colby Arabic? Kareem something or other?"

"Vague there. Are we in second place behind a bunch of towel heads?"

"Nope. We've been on them from the time they got to Sells. Let them go deliberately to see what happened."

Bagley didn't appear convinced. "Are you sure they hit Sells?"

"Damned sure. Sells' wife saw Kareem that night. Picked him out of our photo file. They undoubtedly tortured Colby's identity and location out of Sells, then offed him. They're in Denver right now and getting close, asking all the right questions, talking to the right people."

"What makes you think so?"

Bob studied the cigar, pleased with himself. "Because one of the people they talked to reported them. But," He held a forefinger up. "While they are getting close, they don't have the final piece. We do."

"Come on, Bob. What have you got going? You don't seem too concerned." Bagley knew the workings of his friend's mind. Hensley had set something up.

"One of Kareem's men is buttering up a clerk at the Colorado state motor vehicle offices. She tipped her boss. He called the FBI. They called us asking what we know about the Arab guy. We now know he belongs to the Hafez tribe and we have some past drug stuff on him. We have been following them and have a positive ID on Kareem. The FBI is working with us, but we have the lead. By the way, we also know where the Libyans are holed up."

"Great. Did the clerk tell them anything?"

"No." Hensley waited, watching his boss mentally sift through the information, content to let Bagley form his own ideas.

Bagley massaged his temples, eyes closed. A satisfied smile slowly formed and he said, "How interesting. All very interesting. What are you thinking, Bob?"

"Want me to pick them up, or should we try to work some kind of a trade?"

"That last part. Let me think about that for a moment, Bob. I'm beginning to see something here. Okay, try this on as a what-if. What if the Libyans found Colby? Do you think that would satisfy them? Would that even the score for Hafez?"

"Really can't say. Maybe. I doubt they will ever think Colby is equal payment for Hafez, though. We could intercede I guess, if you approve. You know, after they...." He nodded, waiting.

"Bagley started smiling. "I see where you're going. Okay, can you keep them under control until I think this out?"

"Easy enough. They're a pretty clumsy lot, and I have control over their contact. She is a player for us."

Bagley suddenly brightened. "Wait a minute! Just a damned minute! If we work this right and they do get to Colby, wouldn't that be like killing two birds with one stone? What if we happened on the scene right after they get to him. What do you think? Wouldn't that close all the doors?"

Hensley nodded. He had known all along that Bagley would come to that conclusion. "Might work. Just might work." His face broke into a victorious smile. "Yes, Sir, by God, that would take care of all of the loose cannons out there, now wouldn't it? Great idea, Ed!"

Bagley nodded, his face contorted in thought. "I am tempted, Bob. I really am. That would leave us with only two loose ends: Mrs. Sells and that snoopy Reardon broad."

Hensley held up a hand. "Oh, that reminds me. The Reardon chick is back in the picture."

The director frowned. "Damn. Not her again."

"Afraid so, boss. I should have told you. She called Mrs. Sells again recently." He held up a finger. "Wait. Before you ask, No, the Sells woman didn't talk. I have the conversation recorded. The Sells broad is running scared and knows we are listening. I also know that Reardon used her ACLU connections to track Colby through the motor vehicle people again. She called them once, and then had a cop and an attorney call. I expect she knows exactly where he is. Actually, she might even be with him. Seems interested enough."

The director leaned forward, hands on the desk, drumming his fingers, then said, "Well, well. The plot thickens. So she's part of the equation again. She should have stayed the hell out." He drummed the desk for several seconds. "Hmmm. Interesting. Very interesting." He looked up at Hensley. "You thinking what I am, Bob?"

Hensley nodded. "Think so. You're thinking we could satisfy the Libyans and suppress Colby and Reardon all at the same time if we play our cards right. That would better than two birds with one stone. Great idea, boss. Three birds."

Bagley reared back in his chair and beamed. "It might work, Bob. Why not?"

"Well, if Reardon doesn't get in the final mix, we could always have a heart-to-heart with her. You know, scare the pants off her."

Bagley leaned forward again and spoke in hushed tones. "Look, Bob, I think it will work if we do this right. Get them all at once. What do you say? I'm in favor of turning the Libyans loose. What's your reading?"

Hensley said, "We don't have anything to lose one way or the other. This is a win-win deal for us."

Bagley slammed his hand on the desk. "Let's do it, Bob. Do it."

Hensley gathered his briefcase, snuffed the cigar and said, "Shouldn't take long, Ed. I'll keep you informed."

He placed a call on a secure line that afternoon to an agent in Denver. "Okay, Frank, what we talked about this morning. The old man bought it. Thinks it's his idea. Tell the girl to give the Arabs the ACLU guy's address. Oh, and Frank, make this look good, will you? I want an update when anything goes down, and I mean immediately. Make sure to back this up with some good people, just in case. No screw ups this time. The boss wants this business to end. Don't let your troops get too close to the guts of this business, though. That is just for you and me, Frank. You and me."

Chapter Thirty-One

KAREEM

"I got it, Sali! I got it!" The woman from the motor vehicle office phoned from her car, face flushed from the unaccustomed effort of propelling her two-hundred-and-fifty pounds three blocks from the office to the car.

"You speak too fast. I cannot understand."

"I know how to find the man you are looking for! I've got it, Sali!"

"You are sure?"

"Yes. Michael Allen Stokes. Isn't that the guy?"

"There must be many men named Stokes."

"I checked, Sali. This is the guy! I want the damned stuff you promised."

"One moment. Where is he? How did you find him?"

"Oh, no you don't! I am not going to say another damned word until I get the stuff you guys promised, and it better be good, Sali. None of that cheap street-grade shit you gave me the last time. Good stuff, Sali! I'm not fooling."

"Of course. How did you find him?"

"Never mind how. You are not listening to me, Sali! Dammit, I'm serious. I'm not going to say another word until the stuff is in my grubby little hands. You hear me?"

"I must know who told you."

"Jesus! You just don't get it, do you? The deal was, I talk when you deliver. Take it or leave it. That's final!"

"Of course. We must meet."

"Bring the stuff! Come to the place in the mall we talked about.

I'm taking off early, so be there at three thirty. And you better bring the stuff, Sali. When the powder is in my hands, then we talk. I won't say one word before I get it. And come alone. I don't want anyone with you. I will have a friend nearby. A big, mean friend."

She was soaking wet from nervous perspiration when they met in the open-air lobby of an old shopping mall. She didn't trust Sali. Her mean friend was standing against the wall nearby, glaring. The FBI had placed a female agent with her at work, but she didn't know anything about the deal for drugs.

"Give me the stuff," she demanded.

Sali extended a shopping bag and started to say something.

She shushed him, checked the contents and then said, "Okay, here it is." She offered a folded piece of paper.

He took the note and hissed, "What is this? I need more than this! This is nothing!"

She stepped back and motioned to her friend. He pushed away from the wall and edged closer. "Look, you have a guy's name and address. He knows where Stokes is. That's the guy who called and asked about Stokes. The deal was, I would give you information to lead you to Stokes. Well, there it is." She pointed to the name, phone number and address.

"Who is he? Where is this place?"

She shrugged. "Some ACLU guy. Beats the hell out of me. You're on your own now." She beckoned to her mean friend and they walked away together laughing.

*****

Kareem could not see anyone through the ACLU office windows, just a desk light glowing from an upper window. An hour passed. He watched the building from a parked car near the building. One of two men with him said, "Maybe there is no one in the building. Maybe the woman tricked us."

"We will wait. There is a light and only one car in the parking lot. We wait."

Later, the three men gave up and entered the partially darkened ACLU building through the unlocked front door. "Someone is here," Sali whispered as the door swung open. The intruders locked the door from the inside and crept through the building checking offices until they came to the director's office. Kareem checked the name on the slip of paper and pointed to the corresponding name on the door. The others acknowledged by nodding.

Leslie's boss almost collapsed from fright upon sensing the presence of men behind him. He spun to face them, recovered quickly and reached for the phone while displaying an air of indignant authority. "If you come any closer, I will call the police. Who are you? What do you want?" His facade of power crumbled at exactly the same instant his bifocals disintegrated against the bridge of his nose. Blood and information ran freely as the perspiring, frightened little man whimpered and trembled.

The beating ended only after Kareem decided his bleeding captive had nothing more to offer, having babbled answers to every question and even drew a road map. Hassan felt confident his hostage was too frightened to lie.

The men ransacked the offices, spilling drawers and filing cabinets, fabricating the impression of robbery, then took their cowering hostage's wallet, shared the money and scattered the other contents on the floor.

The terrified director backed against the wall, glancing cautiously from one man to another as they formed an ever tightening semi-circle around him. The largest man, Sali, took position beside the director and draped a garrote around his neck. On signal from Kareem, he jerked. A series of convulsions signaled the end of the director's brief fight for life.

"What about the woman, Kareem? He said she is the one who wanted to know about Stokes."

Hassan studied one of the maps. "We go there now." Later that night, the three Arabs slipped through a rear window at 916 Mountain View Drive in the western suburbs of Denver.

Leslie Reardon wasn't home.

Sali speculated, "I don't think anyone has been here today. I found this note." Hassan read the message Leslie left for the housekeeper.

"Watch the front, Sali. We will search."

They found Leslie's folder of Lieutenant Colonel Colby's military information.

"That's him! That man murdered my cousin!" Hassan pointed at Colby's promotion picture and then ripped the picture to shreds. The men ransacked the house and waited an hour before departing.

"We can always come back. Let's go. We don't need her. The ACLU guy said she knows where Stokes is, so she might be there." Kareem spat at the sound of his enemy's name. He and his lieutenants departed Denver within the hour. Their arrival at Silverton the next morning coincided with the opening of business hours. They lost little time asking directions to the mines. After discovering the requirement for an off-the-road vehicle, they located the same man who rented a Jeep to Leslie.

"I rented one to a pretty gal. I think she's up to the mines now. Supposed to come back that night, but it snowed. If she ain't back today, I'm gonna have to go up there,"

He answered questions willingly and rented the Jeep. The old man didn't find anything unusual or strange about Kareem's concern for an overdue friend. "She wasn't planning to stay overnight? I'm worried. Are you sure she is still with him?"

The old man spat tobacco juice, "Well, I'd say she is. Sure seemed determined to get there. Anyway, I'd be pretty careful if I was you. It gets pretty slick up on that pass, young feller. You better wait a while before you try it. If I was you, I'd maybe wait until tomorrow. Give the snow more time to melt some."

The Libyans bought snack food and departed immediately. The trip offered more obstacles and danger than they were prepared to face. The snowdrifts progressively deepened and they stopped often to let Sali walk ahead to test the surface before driving on. Kareem had to threaten the driver.

They arrived at the meadow south of the cabin just after noon. Hassan drove slowly up the road to the opening at the lower end of the meadow and saw Leslie's rented Jeep parked beyond a small barn. Kareem assumed they were at the right place and gave instructions to his shivering assistants while struggling to control a nervous sensation so intense that he could barely conceal his excitement. The long, agonizing wait would soon be over.

Chapter Thirty-Two

DESTINY

———◇———

Leslie awoke well after sunrise to find Jim lying on his side watching her. They smiled, touched, gazing at each other, memories of the night still fresh.

She snuggled against him. "It's too cold to get up," she murmured. "What do you think we should do?" She nestled closer.

"Oh, I know what you're thinking, woman, but I'll probably be a better man after some food. But, if you insist, perhaps the old spirit could be rejuvenated."

She drew away, feigning rejection. "Oh, no. I wouldn't want you to think I'm some poor wanton thing without resources. I'll make breakfast when it's warm enough to dress, after you do the right thing and pile some wood on that fire."

"Good idea. I expect we should finish loading as soon as we can and get out of here."

"I'm excited about what happens next, Jim. Can we stop by Denver so I can–"

He covered her mouth with a hand. "No. I know you want to get some things and clear up your personal and business, but no. We'll just have to think of ways to handle all that–maybe through an attorney. We can't take the risk. Not ever."

Jim began loading the vehicles after breakfast. He fastened the old wooden stock rack on the truck, loaded the horses and returned to the cabin just before noon.

"Do you want to eat lunch here or on the road, Leslie?"

"I have a snack for now. Maybe we can stop somewhere and have a good dinner tonight." Leslie loved having someone to discuss the day's events with. She couldn't remember being so happy. Yesterday, with all the related worries and strife, no longer existed. She couldn't stop smiling.

As they sat down to sandwiches one of the horses nickered. Jim understood horse language and stopped eating to listen. His smile vanished.

"What is it?" Leslie noticed the drastic change in his appearance. "Is something wrong?"

"Not sure. Something or someone is out there. Horses only make that signal when someone, usually another horse, is approaching." He stepped to the window. The horses were craning their heads over the top of the stock rack, watching a vehicle creep up the road through the meadow.

"Get your coat, Leslie! Be quick! Follow me!" He barked the instructions while snatching his coat, and then the rifle from pegs over the front door.

Leslie darted to the bedroom and reappeared with her coat. "What is it?" Her eyes widened as Jim levered a shell into the chamber of the rifle.

"We don't have time to talk. This is critical. Just stay close to me. Come on!"

They ran into the forest behind the cabin and completed a wide semi-circle, emerging at the meadow's edge two-hundred yards east of the cabin,. They were breathing deeply when he held up hand to stop. The intruding vehicle had pulled off the road and crunched to a stop in the snow near the barn. Two men stepped out carrying guns.

"Who are they, Jim? Are those guns?"

"Shhh! I don't know who they are, but they are sure not here on a social call. They have us trapped. This is really serious, Leslie. Do exactly as I say without hesitation."

"Jim?"

He placed a finger over his lips. He could easily escape and evade in the mountains alone, but the thought of running didn't enter his mind. If the intruders were enemies, they could never catch him in the mountains, but he had to consider Leslie, way out of her element and wearing low-cut street shoes.

Jim watched as the men separated and inched around the barn, guns ready, then on to the cabin. They moved individually, one covering the other's progress with a gun, leapfrogging from one screening position to the next.

"These guys are trained, Leslie, and they definitely didn't come up here to visit." He flinched and Leslie's breath drew in sharply as the lead man kicked the front door open and fired a burst of shots into the cabin. Both men bolted inside. Another volley of gunshots echoed across the valley.

"Damn!" he exclaimed. He turned to Leslie. "We are in serious trouble."

"What can we do?"

"Play it by ear I guess. Be ready to move, and stay right with me no matter what."

He followed the gunmen's progress and reported to Leslie. "They look dark skinned to me. I expect they are Libyan. Those automatic pistols are not weapons a hunter would carry."

Shortly after the men vanished into the cabin, he turned to Leslie and said, "Okay, now listen carefully. No matter what happens from here on, don't you make a sound, and stay close to me, Leslie. We are going to move fast."

She whispered, "Are they here to kill you, Jim."

"I think that's the plan, and it won't take them long to find our tracks." He looked around trying to think of an escape route.

Leslie was frightened and confused. She whispered, "Those shots. Were they trying to kill you? This is–"

He nodded and whispered, "Not just me."

"How did they find us?" Then her eyes opened wide and she covered her mouth. "Oh, Jim! They followed me, didn't they?"

He held a finger to his lips again, appealing for silence. "Everything depends on what they do next. We aren't in a good place here, I can tell you that much. No matter what happens next, stay with me and be quiet."

The men emerged from the cabin and stood on the front porch gesturing and arguing. They soon separated, one darting toward the barn, the other around the cabin.

"Okay, get ready. The guy behind the cabin is going to find our tracks. They will know we are near."

"How could they know that?"

"Easy: the fireplace is hot; the horses are loaded; the Jeep is packed; our tracks are fresh. They know."

They both heard a sharp whistle from behind the house.

"That's it!" Jim declared. "They will be coming."

The two men met behind the house. After animated conversation, both vanished into the forest following fresh tracks.

"All right, we've got to make a run for it. Stay with me. We have to move fast."

They bolted from cover and ran deeper into the forest where the snow went over the top of Leslie's shoes. Jim planned to make a wide circle through the woods, maneuvering up hill to an strategic position, then dash down to the cabin. He knew the two men would track them and counted on it. He also knew Leslie couldn't last long in street shoes. Their only chance for escape lay in the possibility of leading the men far enough into the forest so they could make it back to the truck before being caught.

He stopped to listen periodically, permitting Leslie to catch her breath. He tried to camouflage their intentions, heading away from the cabin for several minutes before circling back. "Okay," he said when they reached the jumping-off point. "Let's rest a moment, then run as fast as you can to the cabin. When we get there, you grab the keys from your Jeep first and then get the keys from their Jeep and meet me at the truck. Got that?" She nodded.

Leslie had collapsed to a sitting position in the snow, gasping for breath.

"Let's go Leslie It's time. You ready?"

She nodded, unable to get enough oxygen to talk. Her feet stung from the cold. "I'll try. I don't know."

He pulled her up and they began running wildly through the trees, branches tearing at their arms and faces, slipping and skidding down the mountain. They didn't have time for caution, still two-hundred yards from the cabin. Jim moderated the pace, giving her a chance to stay close. She stumbled and fell repeatedly and Jim yanked her up each time to press on, her eyes wide with fright, gasping for air. No matter how she tried, she couldn't keep up.

"Come on! Come on!" he urged. "We have to move! We have to get to the cabin well ahead of them." He grabbed her hand and literally dragged her through the brush. She fell again and again, her face scratched and bleeding.

She fell and rolled onto her back. "I can't, Jim" she gasped.

"My ankle. You go. They aren't after me."

"No, I won't leave you! Come on!"

With his help, Leslie pulled up painfully but faltered when she placed weight on the injured ankle. Jim put a shoulder under her arm and they hobbled onward.

"This is life and death! We have to hurry, Leslie. You have to run. Come on!"

They made it to a point half way across the clearing where she found him sawing wood the first day. Jim could hear the noise of their pursuers closing from the rear. He glanced over his shoulder in time to see both men slanting through the tress across the slope, attempting to cut off the escape route.

"Damn! They figured it out. They can see us now! We don't have time to get to the cabin. Let's get out of this clearing."

They stumbled and fell into a spruce thicket as the first man broke from the woods behind them and stopped at the edge of the clearing opposite.

Jim pressed her down behind a fallen tree, rolled onto his stomach and aimed the rifle. He shouted, "Hold it right there! Move another step closer and I'll shoot! Drop your guns and step back!"

Both men had advanced well into the clearing. They glanced at each other and then dove forward, firing repeated bursts toward the sound of his voice. Dirt and splinters flew, stinging his face. Jim didn't flinch. He aimed carefully and fired twice, instantly killing both men.

He got up and turned to see Leslie, hands over her mouth, eyes riveted on the two men sprawled on the snow. She then stared at Jim, shocked and confused, unable to believe what she had just witnessed.

"My God! Did you have to do that? Did you have to kill them? Oh, Jim!"

"What? Do you think I had a choice? They didn't give me a choice, Leslie." He stared at her for a moment, trying to understand her concern for the men trying to kill them. "Don't you realize what is going on here? They would have killed you, too. Now come on! We need to get out of here." He reached for her.

"Don't!" She recoiled, staring at his hand like something too horrible to touch. "Leave me alone!"

She staggered to her feet and fell. Jim fought off her resistance and carried her to the cabin. He didn't understand her reaction and didn't have time to fret about it. After depositing her on a chair in the living room he said, "I'm going back. They have to be buried. Won't be too long."

He dragged the men to the open garbage pit east of the cabin and began shoveling dirt over their bodies. The pit, four feet deep, would hide the evidence forever. No one would dig into the garbage. He worked feverishly.

Leslie recovered breath and tried to stand, but couldn't tolerate the pain. She was still dazed and shaken by the horrible scene; sick to her stomach; sick of heart; astonished, sad and desperately needing to vomit. She fell back on the chair. The wave of nausea passed leaving her trembling and cold.

She thought, I can't believe what he did. I have never seen anything so savage. Killing those men didn't bother him. He killed without thinking. Maybe it was self-defense, but where are his feelings? Those men were nothing more to him than paper targets. How many men has he killed? I could never understand a man who can kill so easily. I have nothing in common with him. I would die before taking the life of another human. Maybe he did have to shoot in self-defense this time, but he didn't have to be an assassin. Oh, Jim.

She dreaded the moment he returned and she put an end to what seemed like such a promising relationship.

*****

Jim took off the heavy winter coat and shoveled dirt over the inert forms until a deep male voice broke the wintry silence, paralyzing everything but his heartbeat.

"We meet again, Ahmed!"

Jim froze. A sinking sensation swept his body, settling in the pit of his stomach. He released the shovel and raised his hands. The possibility that there might be a third gunman in the jeep hadn't occurred to him. He slowly turned to face the voice.

"Kareem? What the hell? What are you...?" Reality struck with crushing finality. He didn't need a reply. He knew the answer. The stunning impact of being surprised diminished as he wrestled with the unavoidable truth of what would happen next.

Kareem circled, closing the distance with an Uzi automatic pistol leveled at Jim's chest. The Libyan's bitter expression contorted as he neared. "Yes, we meet again. I have waited for this moment. And now, Ahmed, it is your turn to die." His voice dripped hatred.

Jim recognized the hopelessness of his dilemma. Kareem was too near, leaving him nothing left to do but face the end. He stood straight, faced Kareem, sighed resolutely and waited.

Kareem's angry expression transformed into a sneer as he extended the gun. "My life begins when you die, American! Allah's will be done!" He screamed the oath, raised the gun and screamed, "Allahu Ak–"

The explosion was not deafening. To Jim it sounded like a dull thud and then sound ceased altogether. Time stopped. The breath rushed from his lungs, driven out by an invisible vise. His legs buckled as he stumbled and fell forward.

Kareem crumpled toward Jim at the same instant, collapsing like a rag doll into a heap on the snow.

Jim landed on hands and knees, gasping for air, staring at the scarlet stain radiating from beneath Kareem's body, now inches from his face. The bizarre interlude lasted but a moment before his ability to think engaged. He blinked, stood, spread his arms and looked down, surprised to find no evidence of a gushing wound. Nothing made sense. He turned in time to see Leslie slipping down the side of the cabin to a sitting position on the porch, staring at the rifle in her hand. She pushed it away and watched it clatter across the porch, then passed out.

Chapter Thirty-Three

DENNY BLAKEMORE

There you have it, the story Jim and Leslie related to me eighteen months after that final, fateful day on the mountain. After Leslie shot Kareem, Jim chose to leave all the vehicles at the mines and ride the horses out the back way to Silverton. Good idea, as it turned out, for a team of agents were waiting at the mine road intersection.

Their account is not the end of the story. The president did not contact me after I delivered the account of their story, so I have no idea if he called off the CIA search. Leslie and Jim failed to contact me on the first of January this year, one year after I delivered the story to the President, so I published. Repercussions from disclosures contained in this book, while staggering, certainly should not have been unforeseen. Let me review the fallout, events I'm sure most of you already know:

President Denning resigned after a week of intense political pressure and ingested a fatal dose of sleeping pills.

Senator Charlie Collins: Indicted; awaiting trial

FBI Director: indicted; awaiting trial.

CIA Director: indicted; awaiting trial.

National Security Adviser, indicted; awaiting trial.

EX CIA Operations Director: Adrian Burt, indicted; furnished vital and decisive evidence to gain immunity.

Members of the joint FBI/CIA team: involuntary retirement and loss of retirement benefits.

The executive and legislative arms of the American government suffered ruin at the polls for supporting the folly of presidential arrogance and incompetence. Respect for American foreign policy and the moral reputation of America in general will take many years to recover.

I am not sorry for the part I played. I mourn the loss of contact with Jim and Leslie and think of them every day of my life. I can only hope that they are alive and have access to this book. I don't quite know how to relate what I must say next, but do so with profound sorrow, for what I must say unveils the utter futility and senselessness of everything that happened.

During the final week of my leave of absence–time spent researching this book–I stopped overnight in Houston, Texas. Jim Colby's son, Jimmy, had worked as an engineer there before his death in the Rome crash. I went to Houston to tie up the loose ends for this book–trifling matters concerning his son's history. My records indicated that he worked for American South Laboratories, a soil and material testing company, before boarding the doomed airliner.

I threw my bags on the hotel bed and phoned American South headquarters. A pleasant feminine voice answered.

"America South. May I help you?"

"Yes, please. My name is Denny Blakemore. I would like to talk to someone about an engineer once employed by your company."

"Maybe I can help you, sir. No one has worked here longer than I have."

"The engineer I'm trying to learn something about was named James Colby."

"I'm sorry, sir. Mister Colby isn't in."

Isn't in? What the Devil? My brain locked for a moment. I recovered and said, "Yes, I know. I need to talk to someone about him, though. Someone who once knew him."

"I am very sorry, sir, but Mister Colby is away from the office inspecting a field project this afternoon. May I take a message?"

The conversation didn't make sense. "Look, miss, I think one of us is confused."

"Perhaps I don't understand what you want to know, sir. All I can tell you is what is on the check-out board. Mister Colby is in the field today. I will be happy to take a message."

The back of my neck started tingling. I collected my wits and said, "Okay. Tell me, how long has this Mister Colby worked for your company?"

"Let's see...almost five years now, I believe."

Can you imagine my confusion? "Has another engineer named Colby ever been employed by your company?"

"Not in the eighteen years I have worked here."

My heart rate accelerated. "His wife's name wouldn't be Juliet, by any chance?"

"Why, yes, it is."

Needless to say, when James Colby returned from work that afternoon he found me waiting in his office. My legs nearly folded when I saw him–an exact replica of his father. He invited me to his home where I met Juliet. We talked.

"Your father thought you died in the Rome crash of flight 8109, along with your wife and son."

"He did? We didn't board that flight. Juliet got sick. Pregnancy related. A doctor advised us against flying. We decided to vacation at a wilderness resort in the Adirondack's. Two weeks without a phone or television."

"Your father believed you were on that airplane."

"Really? That's odd. I sent a card to him explaining what happened before we left New York City, and how to contact us. He must have left town before the letter arrived. I don't know if you know this, but Dad was killed in an accident while we were on vacation. Hit by a car in New York City. I never figured out what he was doing there." He frowned and looked puzzled as my last disclosure began to register. "Wait. That is really odd. You say he thought we were on the airplane?"

I watched his expression change as pieces of the puzzle shifted but still didn't quite fit.

Before I could answer, he said, "How could you know he thought I was on that airplane? Okay, maybe we should go back and start over. You aren't here by accident, are you? Why are you here?"

"It's a long story, Jimmy, and I will answer every question. But first, I want to know what happened after you returned from vacation?"

He smiled, shook his head. "Boy, did we ever surprise everyone back home. They had a funeral service for us. Can you imagine?

The stone is still there. Our fifteen minutes of fame, I guess."

"Yes, I know. I know everything."

"Do you happen to know what my dad was doing in New York City?"

I told him the story.

ABOUT THE AUTHOR

Larry Cunningham is a retired Marine Corps Lt. Colonel, fighter squadron commander. He wrote USMC plans for the evacuation of Vietnam, Cambodia and Laos. He flew many combat missions and served as Air Officer during the siege of Khe Sanh.

He is an ex-cattle rancher, high school science teacher, college fiction writing instructor and poet. He often speaks at writer's meetings and conferences.

* * * * *

Look for Cunningham's next book coming soon!

www.ingramcontent.com/pod-product-compliance
Lightning Source LLC
Chambersburg PA
CBHW050716180626
46814CB00002B/461